MURDER
ON
BONFIRE NIGHT

by Margaret Addison

A Rose Simpson Mystery

Rose Simpson Mysteries (in order)

Murder at Ashgrove House
Murder at Dareswick Hall
Murder at Sedgwick Court
Murder at Renard's
Murder in the Servants' Hall
Murder on Bonfire Night

To Kate

Chapter One

Major Spittlehouse did not consider himself to be of a nervous disposition. Why, the Great War to end all wars had proved, if proof was needed, that if anything he veered towards the courageous type. While he did not feel compelled to follow danger, neither did he feel inclined to retreat from it. Rather, he gritted his teeth and faced it head on as best he could, just as he had been trained to do. It was, after all, merely a continuation of what he had been taught to do from a young age, like the long line of Spittlehouses before him, a distinguished group, stretching back into history, setting an example to man and beast.

The major puffed out his chest proudly as he acknowledged that, on the battlefield at least, a Spittlehouse was a man to be reckoned with, to be relied upon; he was a man who generated respect equally among his superiors and subordinates. Major Spittlehouse coughed. Of course it was his own assessment admittedly, and one did not want to be thought boastful or conceited, but there it was. And there was little harm, he thought, in acknowledging the truth, particularly when it was only to oneself. He would never have voiced such a thing aloud. All of which, of course, made it somewhat embarrassing that a mere woman could reduce him to a timorous wreck, and not any woman, one's younger sister at that.

The major frowned and felt the colour creep unbidden and unwanted to his cheeks. Inwardly he cursed himself for his weakness, though thankfully there was no one present to witness his flushed complexion. He never had dealt very well with what he termed 'unpleasant domestic situations'. Of course a woman's tears would make any decent man feel wretched, and it was inevitable that Daphne would weep profusely, intermingled with great flashes of anger. In the normal course he considered himself to be a man of action, but in this instance, which would require such careful handling, he had an overwhelming desire to prevaricate, to bury his head in the sand like the proverbial ostrich and hope that the situation would resolve itself of its own accord without his interference.

That was the effect that anticipation of a confrontation with Daphne always had upon him. It made him nervy; he could not think of a better word for it. And there would be a battle all right. There was no use deluding himself that she would be agreeable to what he had to say. You couldn't reason with women the way you could with men. They became hysterical, their voices suddenly went shrill so that the servants could hear every word they said. Especially women like his sister. Impulsive, that's what his parents had called her. And after … after that awful business, they had said that she wasn't very strong. She had to be looked after, cossetted if you will, which had always made him laugh in a bitter sort of way because, if nothing else, surely Daphne had shown herself to be strong, at least in the physical sense of the word.

He gave a deep sigh and stared around the soothing and familiar surroundings of his study. With some reluctance he rose from his captain's chair, with its shaped mahogany back and seat upholstered in brown leather, worn soft and comfortable from frequent use. It felt as much a part of him as his neat, carefully trimmed moustache and filled a similar purpose. For he was vaguely aware that to a certain extent he hid behind the moustache as he would more successfully have hidden behind a beard if it had been in fashion. The favoured chair provided him with a similar haven, located as it was behind the great pedestal desk positioned some distance from the study door, a physical barricade between himself and any unwanted visitor. And he certainly would consider his sister an unwelcome guest, even though he had asked his manservant, Masters, to pass on the message to her that he would like a word. As soon as she returned from the village, he'd instructed him. Looking at his watch, he thought that would not be long now, for Sedgwick could possess few attractions for a woman like Daphne.

He made a face and cursed his own stupidity. They should have their talk in the drawing room, not in here, the place he considered to be his personal sanctuary. His sister would taint it; she would destroy its peace and calm, that which he had so carefully cultivated. Her perfume, he knew from bitter experience, would linger annoyingly in the air for hours. It would take an age before the atmosphere was restored to the pleasing masculine smells of cigar smoke and whisky.

It was too late now to do anything about it, too late to alter his instructions to his servant. For he could already hear Daphne's footsteps in the hall, as he strained his ears to catch Masters' voice.

Major Spittlehouse waited with growing apprehension, imagining how Daphne had taken the news that she had been summoned to her brother's study, a room to which she seldom received an invitation, and rarely chose to enter of her own accord. He pictured her tutting to herself, removing her hat with slow, deliberate actions; trying to string out the task to make him impatient, jabbing her hat pin in to the brim, pretending for all the world that it was him.

To pass the time until his sister's arrival, the major turned his gaze to the French windows, which looked out on to a well-tended garden. He watched with a degree of interest as his old gardener, Bennett, bent almost double, his back deformed with age, undertook the long, laborious work of removing all the summer bedding plants, placing them in open trays to be labelled and dried out in the Autumn sun, prior to storage. The grounds seemed almost irresistibly inviting, as if they were beckoning to him to step out and leave the house and its troubles behind him. Perhaps he was even tempted for a moment to acquiesce; certainly he was aware that for a brief time at least he faltered on the threshold between house and garden.

He was brought to his senses abruptly by the sound of Daphne's footsteps as she crossed the hall, loud and purposeful, her heels clicking on the maple floor of light and dark grey squares. She was on her guard, he thought; he could almost feel the hostility in her strides. He imagined it welling up inside her, as if her fury were his own. With each step she took it would rise within her so that he knew, with an awful sense of inevitability, it would brim over and she would explode in his study, angry and defensive, as soon as her brother dared raise the disagreeable matter that was foremost in his mind.

'Well, what is it, Linus? What do you want to see me about? Couldn't it have waited until dinner?'

Daphne Spittlehouse had come into the study without knocking, and for all his waiting for the moment, her brother had been taken unawares. Certainly he was still staring out of the window with his back towards her when she opened the door, so that he was obliged to turn around too quickly, in rather an undignified fashion, to face her arrival. He was uncomfortably conscious of the look of surprise upon his face and instinctively felt himself to be at a disadvantage. His sister, in comparison, stood before him looking nonchalant and composed. And, unless he was mistaken, there was a faint look of amusement in her eyes at his obvious discomfort.

'Ah … yes. Masters gave you my message then, did he?' He said rather gruffly as he tried to gather his thoughts.

'He told me you wanted to see me,' his sister replied giving him something of a cold stare, 'which of course is why I'm here.' She might well have added that otherwise she would never have considered setting foot inside his stuffy old study, but did not, though the implication was clear by her expression.

The major cleared his throat and Daphne permitted her gaze to drift idly around the room, a contemptuous look upon her face as if she found the masculine air which hung about the place, unsoftened by a woman's touch, vaguely depressing. She didn't actually wrinkle up her nose, though she was sorely tempted to do so. And all the while her brother was staring at her, wondering how best to broach the subject on his mind.

Now that she was standing before him, he noticed that his sister had not troubled to stop in the hall to take off her hat as he had supposed. Instead, she had marched straight in with it still upon her head, and a fox fur stole about her shoulders; she was pulling off her kid gloves even while she spoke. Idly, Major Spittlehouse noticed that her hat was a close fitting affair, almost a skull cap, with a fussy satin trim, which he did not remember having seen before; it reminded him of a Roundhead soldier's helmet and he wondered whether Daphne imagined, as he did, that she was coming into battle. The wool tweed suit was new too, now that he came to think about it, unless he was mistaken, which was quite possible as he rarely noticed a woman's attire, particularly not his sister's. All the same, it was worrying and made him fear the worst.

'Is that a new outfit?' he inquired, 'I must say, it looks jolly smart. Don't tell me you bought it in the village?'

'I haven't been to the village, Linus.' Daphne said and sighed. She sounded rather bored, 'You know what a poor selection of shops Sedgwick has.' She paused to take a deliberate breath. 'If you must know, I caught the train to Bichester.'

'To go shopping?' The major inquired hopefully.

'Don't worry, Linus.' Daphne sounded irritated. 'I haven't spent all my allowance. Would you like me to check with you in future before I buy a pair of stockings?'

'Of course not. Now … you went shopping, you say?'

'Actually, you said that. But as it happens I did. I went shopping, and then I went to the public library and changed my library books. All very dull stuff. You would have hated it.'

'I daresay.' Major Spittlehouse paused before continuing. It did not come naturally to him to interrogate his sister and he glanced out of the French windows, whether for inspiration or to muster his courage, it was hard to say. 'That's all you did, is it? In Bichester, I mean?'

'Well … I … I did meet a friend for lunch.'

Did he imagine that she hesitated for a moment before divulging this piece of information?

'We went to a very quaint little place. I hadn't been there before.'

It was obvious to him now that his sister was trying to appear nonchalant. He noticed almost belatedly that her colour was raised, her cheeks crimson and her eyes bright. At first he thought it had come about by her irritation of him. After a few moments it dawned on him that she had entered the room like that; her heightened colour had been brought on by excitement, not anger, and now her high spirits were dashed. He felt a sudden stab of both dismay and guilt. How unpleasant all this was. She had come into his study cheerful and happy, so at odds with her usual dull and melancholy self, and now he had ruined it all for her.

'You met a friend for lunch, you say?' He persisted miserably, trying to match her own blasé tone with a casual one of his own; however, even to his own ears the lightness in his voice sounded forced. It was impossible to hide his apprehension. His worst fears, he felt certain, were about to be realised.

'Yes. Archie Mayhew.' The words came out of Daphne's mouth slowly and deliberately, as if she were savouring them, knowing their effect. And, much to the major's discomfort, he found that she was watching him closely, waiting for his reaction. 'He's an articled clerk or something or other at that law firm in Bichester. You know the one? You used them to draw up the papers when you bought that piece of woodland from old Mr Turner.'

'Gribble, Hebborn & Whittaker?' supplied her brother.

'Yes, that's the one. What a mouthful. It's a wonder anyone remembers its name. Archie helped Mr Whittaker prepare the documents.

You may recall him? He's a frightfully handsome man, Archie that is, not Mr Whittaker.'

'I do.' The vision of a young man with dark, slicked back hair and an insolent grin immediately came into Major Spittlehouse's mind. He decided there was nothing for it but to take the bull by the horns. 'I take it this is the young fellow you've been seen running around with, the one that's set tongues wagging in the village?'

'How quaintly you do put things, Linus.' There was a steely edge to his sister's voice now. She looked inimically into his eyes. 'If you ask me, the villagers here are too inquisitive for their own good. I suppose that is what comes from having such narrow, parochial little lives.' She wrinkled up her nose. 'Sedgwick can go to the devil for all I care.'

'Daphne!' Major Spittlehouse looked appalled.

'You needn't look at me like that, Linus. I don't care and yet, conversely, I can't stand being gossiped about,' retorted his sister, discarding her gloves on the top of a bookcase, which happened to be situated conveniently by the door. 'Whose business is it anyway whom I go about with?'

'It's the talk of the village. Really, Daphne, I would have thought that you of all people would have had more sense.' She responded to this comment with a crease of her brow and her brother hurried on valiantly, adopting what he hoped was a kindly manner. 'My dear, you know you're making quite a spectacle of yourself.'

'Why? Because a woman over thirty is not expected to have any fun and enjoy herself?' His sister's eyes flashed back at him angrily. 'Or is it perhaps because poor Archie is perceived as coming from the clerk class? Not that I see anything wrong with that myself. He works jolly hard to earn his daily bread.' She paused to give her brother a withering look, which implied he had done very little to acquire his own wealth. The major recoiled under her glare, uncomfortably conscious of his thinning hair and his slightly portly figure, a man gone to seed. 'I do wish you wouldn't be such a snob, Linus.' Daphne gave an exaggerated sigh. 'I suppose you and everyone else wants me to busy myself doing good works. You think at my grand old age I should be helping out at parish bazaars and taking my turn doing the flowers in church.'

In one sudden, impulsive movement, that made her brother take a backward step, she threw herself into a chair, her actions so animated that her hat threatened to topple from her head.

'You'd sooner have me die of boredom than live my own life. Is it really too much to ask to want something more than this?' Daphne raised her arms in a theatrical gesture that seemed to encompass more than the room. She did not wait for her brother to reply, if indeed he would have done, before rising from her chair and pacing the room in an agitated fashion. 'Oh, I don't know why you decided that we should live in this awful little backwater, I don't really.'

'There's nothing wrong with Sedgwick,' said Major Spittlehouse defensively. 'It's a perfectly pleasant place. A most delightful little village.'

However, even as the words escaped his lips, he wondered whether his sister wasn't right. Wouldn't it have been better if they had made their home in a city, where they could have lived their lives quite anonymously, without drawing attention to themselves? It was not a new thought; it had plagued him often enough. They had chosen too open a place to live. People tended to pry into each other's affairs in a village; they dug too deeply into one another's lives, became too inquisitive.

'But that's just it, Linus,' Daphne was saying, 'it's a village. There's nothing to do here. Sometimes I think I will die with the mundaneness of it all.' She rose from her seat and began to gesture at her brother wildly, throwing her arms in the air.

The major braced himself in his chair, his eyes on her, watching her every movement as intently as a cat would a mouse.

'Oh, why don't we live in a town? Say we can. We could live in Bichester. It isn't much of a place, but it's better than this.' Her voice had become shrill as she had become more passionate. She stared at her brother imploringly, but his answering look was not encouraging. A shudder passed through her body. 'Anything is better than this,' she added bitterly, turning away so that her gaze fixed now on the French windows and the view beyond. The ordered garden made no positive impression upon her. Instead, she thought only about the wretchedness of it all.

All the while, Linus Spittlehouse stared at her apprehensively. He had hardly touched on the subject uppermost on his mind, but already he was aware of his sister's growing agitation. For Daphne had at last removed the skull cap and was picking relentlessly at its satin trim with fingers that fidgeted and would not be still. There was going to be a scene, he knew with absolute certainty. His sister was going to become hysterical and as always he would be afraid of what she might say, anxious also that her voice would carry through the house so that her words would be overheard by Masters, and goodness knew what his manservant would think. The major's only hope was that the man had retired to the kitchen to be with his wife.

Major Spittlehouse took a deep breath. 'Archie Mayhew,' he began cautiously. But he had no opportunity to elaborate for his sister had swung around on his words, her face impassioned with something akin to rage.

'I won't give him up, Linus.' There was a steely determination to her voice now; it had lowered in pitch. 'I love him and ... well, he loves me.'

These latter words were spoken quietly but with such feeling that the major was taken aback even though the sentiment expressed was not unexpected. Perhaps the fact that he remained silent and did not interrupt her gave his sister courage to continue in the same calm vein. Even so, she could not look at him as she spoke, averting her gaze instead to a patch of carpet.

'And ... I might as well tell you, we ... we are to be married.'

'What!' Her brother stared at her dumbfounded. It was far worse than he had thought. Events had evidently progressed at an alarming pace. He should have spoken before now, put a stop to things before they were permitted to escalate, but it was always something he dreaded, a weakness in him to deal with the unpleasantness of it all.

Daphne did not flinch at the intensity of his gaze. With some satisfaction she noted that the shock of her words had had the effect of making her brother speechless and she took advantage of the ensuing silence.

'My mind is quite made up, Linus.' She gave him a look of such ferocity that the major felt himself draw back. 'And there is nothing you can say, or do, to stop me. I won't let you, not ... not this time.'

Major Spittlehouse realised it was too late to approach the matter cautiously and with tact, to wrap up what he had to say with pleasantries and niceties as he had intended. His best, and perhaps his only, course of action now was to go on the attack.

'Daphne, do be reasonable. Think how it'll look. Regardless of class, this Mayhew fellow must be twelve years your junior.'

Daphne gave a sharp intake of breath. 'It's not as much as that,' she said, though her cheeks had flushed crimson.

Seeing that his words had hit home, her brother pursued his advantage.

'I don't mean to appear unkind, but have you asked yourself why he wants to marry you? Why doesn't he take a wife of his own age?'

'If our roles were reversed and I was the man and he the woman, why, no one would think anything of it,' said Daphne, evading the question. 'Why is it acceptable for a man to marry a much younger wife, but not the other way around?' She did not wait for him to answer. 'Anyway, Archie says I don't look my age. He says I look younger than I am.'

'Does he indeed?' said Major Spittlehouse, giving his sister a cynical look. Privately he thought there was little truth to Archie Mayhew's assertion. Of course, it was nigh on impossible to view one's own sister objectively. However, he thought Daphne looked her age, and perhaps a little more; yes, she looked every bit her thirty-seven years. True, her figure was good, and she possessed a certain naivety that belied her years, an immaturity, if he were to be unkind, but her face was lined.

'Oh, what does it matter what you think?' cried Daphne. 'Archie doesn't need to ask your permission for my hand. You are only my brother, Linus, not my father.' She paused and added petulantly; 'Though you act as if you were.'

Major Spittlehouse flinched. He had always considered his own position to be a difficult one. He neither commanded the respect of a parent nor, being some twenty years his sister's senior, did the role of sibling sit easily upon his shoulders. Instead, he felt he occupied a grey area that resided somewhat uncomfortably on the very threshold between parent and sibling.

'Does he know about our parents' legacy?' the major asked abruptly.

'What? Well ... no, it's not something we've discussed.' The colour had gone from his sister's cheeks and some of the fight within her. 'He loves me, Linus; the money doesn't matter to him one bit.' But to her brother's ears, she sounded less certain, as if she were trying to convince herself as much as him.

'Well, that is very fortunate,' said her brother. 'Because I may as well tell you now, Daphne, that if you marry that man, you will not receive a penny of our parents' estate. Let him keep you, if he's willing.'

'Linus ... please.'

There was a pleading note in his sister's voice now. She had slumped, all but defeated into the chair that she had so recently vacated, a shadow of her former animated self. In spite of himself, her brother was moved by her obvious distress, but he did not soften. He reminded himself that it bore little resemblance to the previous occasion. The curate had been a good man; he'd had no objection to him marrying Daphne in principle. If only the situation had been simple. He'd felt wretched at the time doing what he'd done. Worse than that, he had seen himself as the orchestrator of his sister's present unhappiness.

In this instance however, he experienced no such qualms of conscience. For, in his opinion, Archie Mayhew was a thoroughly worthless young man; a wastrel, that was the word that sprung readily to mind. He'd make his sister's life a misery, given half a chance, the major was quite certain of it. Mayhew was just the sort of fellow to become bored with her, if he were not bored of her already. Without the lure of wealth to attract him, Daphne would soon lose her appeal. And Mayhew was the type to run through her inheritance. Then where would Daphne be? Mayhew wouldn't be the faithful kind. There would be other women, a whole string of them, Major Spittlehouse knew, if he was not mistaken in his judge of the man's character ... No, he would be acting in his sister's best interests by not providing her with a generous allowance, if only she knew it. He had only to say the word to Archie Mayhew, tell him there would be no money forthcoming upon the marriage. That would put a stop to all this nonsense. Yes, that's what he would do.

Having arrived in his mind at the likelihood of a satisfactory outcome to a matter that had been troubling him for a while, Major Spittlehouse was keen to put the conversation behind him and lighten the atmosphere in the study.

'I say, Daphne, have you heard the news? Lord and Lady Belvedere have returned from their honeymoon. I believe they went to Paris. We should call on them in a day or two.' Major Spittlehouse went over to his desk and picked up a sheet of paper. 'I want to discuss the arrangements for Guy Fawkes' Night. I –'

'Oh, what do I care if the earl has returned from his honeymoon? It has little to do with me.'

'Daphne, don't –' began her brother.

'He's a lucky man, the Earl of Belvedere,' said his sister. 'Fortunately for him, he could choose his bride. He didn't have an older brother determined to deny him his inheritance.' The note of bitterness in her voice was not lost on the major.

'My dear –'

'I must say I am rather surprised at your enthusiasm to see them,' continued Daphne, now with an artificial sweetness to her voice. 'I wouldn't have thought you'd have approved of the new countess. She used to be a shop girl, or hadn't you heard?' A malicious gleam came into her eye. 'And an amateur detective, I believe. If you listen to village gossip, as I'm obliged to do, she's supposed to have been involved in solving ever so many murders. Not your type of woman at all, I'd have thought, Linus.'

'Whom Lord Belvedere chooses, or does not choose, to marry is his business not mine,' Major Spittlehouse said stuffily, though in actual fact it was news to him that the new countess had something of a reputation for being a sleuth.

'But it's your business whom *I* choose to marry?' cried Daphne. 'Oh, Linus, please be reasonable.' She was leaning forward now, trying to grab his arm, her eyes bright with unshed, angry tears. 'You hate this as much as I do, all this … fighting and being at odds with one another, I know you do. Wouldn't you much rather I wasn't here, that you had Green Gables to yourself? Why, have *you* never thought about marrying? You could, you know, if I were gone and you were free of me.'

'I am perfectly happy –'

'But you're not. Neither of us is. I live in this house with you because I have nowhere else to go and you …' she hesitated a moment to gesture towards him, 'why, you feel you have a responsibility towards me because you are my brother and you promised our parents that you would look after me. Oh, if only they hadn't made that stupid will …' She faltered and stared imploringly at her brother. The face that greeted her appeared unmoved. 'Please, Linus. I want a family of my own, a husband and children. Oh, I know you think it ridiculous, but women do have children at my age and older. Why, look at Mrs –'

'Daphne, if you marry Archie Mayhew I can promise you that you will not receive a penny of our parents' money. Now, let that be an end to it. If you'll excuse me, I have other matters to attend to.' He picked up his fountain pen and removed the cap.

'I'll contest their will!' cried Daphne.

'Will you indeed?' said Major Spittlehouse, looking up sharply. 'I suppose *he* suggested that?'

'If you mean Archie, no he didn't,' Daphne cried defiantly. 'I told you, he knows nothing about our parents' legacy.'

The muscles in Major Spittlehouse's face relaxed visibly. Indeed, he almost looked composed. Daphne had made her scene and shortly it would all be over. He had weathered her bitter recriminations. His sister had alternated between being indignant and pleading with him, though thankfully this time there had been no tears. And he had remained resolutely steadfast. Really, it had not been too bad at all. Of course it was all very regrettable but ...

'I think you're hiding something, Linus.' Belatedly he realised that all the while his sister had been watching him, and now her words cut through his thoughts as effectively as any knife. He started, and the colour went from his face. His sister smiled. 'So I am right? I thought I was. Well, Linus dear, I promise you that two can play your game.' She rose and placed her hands on his desk, leaning forward as if she intended to pounce. 'I am going to find out what you're hiding, Linus.'

The fountain pen slipped from the major's hand and fell to the floor, ink staining the carpet in the process. In his new fragile state, it reminded Major Spittlehouse of blood.

Chapter Two

'They're at it again,' said Masters, coming into the basement kitchen as his wife was putting the finishing touches to an apple pie. 'I say, Mollie, I hope you're making one of those for us too. It'll go down a treat, so it will, with a nice bit of custard.'

'Will it now?' said his wife, wiping her floury hands on her apron and giving him one of her looks. 'Boiled apple dumplings is what I had in mind for the likes of you and me.' She saw the look of disappointment on her husband's face and her heart softened. 'That's not to say I won't change my mind if you don't go and get under my feet. Worse than a child you are wanting your puddings. And don't you go picking at things when my back's turned neither. Half a fruitcake there was left yesterday, and not a sign of it today.'

'I knew when I married you, Mollie Brenning, that I was marrying an angel in the kitchen. There's many a man who'd give his right arm to have a wife like you with your light touch with pastry. Fair melts in your mouth, so it does.'

With that, Masters gave her a quick peck on her cheek, pounced on a slice of apple and danced around the room in something of a mischievous fashion, almost as if he expected his wife to give chase and come charging after him, a wooden spoon raised in her hand.

'You're a cheeky one and no mistake, Jack Masters!' said his wife, a smile appearing rather grudgingly on her face. She put the back of her hand to her mouth to obscure the fact that she was doing her best not to laugh. 'Now out of my kitchen or there'll be no dinner for the major, and certainly none for you and me.'

'Did you not hear what I said, Mol?' persisted her husband, making no attempt to leave the room, though some of the frivolity had left his manner and his voice took on a more serious tone. 'At it like hammer and tongs they were just now in the study. Not that I hadn't been expecting it, because I had. What with Miss Daphne carrying on with that young man of hers that's young enough to be her son!'

'There you go, Jack, exaggerating like there's no tomorrow and making things sound much worse than they are,' reprimanded Mrs Masters. 'I'll grant you there's a little difference in their ages –'

'A little –' protested her husband, his eyebrows raised.

'As I said,' his wife said firmly, 'he's a sight younger than her, but not as much as all that.'

'He's after her money, you mark my words if he ain't.' Masters paused to tap the side of his nose in a sly fashion. 'And that's what the major thinks and all. He'll not stand for it to have his sister made a fool of, even if it is her own doing. He'll put a stop to it no matter how much she shrieks and weeps.'

'Poor lamb,' said Mrs Masters, whose sympathy lay firmly with Daphne. 'She may be approaching middle age, but her heart's as young as a girl's.'

'Aye, she's never grown up, if you ask me,' agreed her husband. 'Behaves like a silly young girl of twenty. Of course, she was the baby of the family and, from what the major's let slip, her mother fair doted on her something rotten. Indulged as anything she was as a child and that don't do any good to anyone's character. And the poor major, who didn't ask to have a sister who's more like his daughter, well, he tries to do his best by her.'

'I might have known you'd side with him,' retorted Mrs Masters. 'It's Miss Daphne who I feel sorry for. It's no life for her keeping house for her brother. She needs a husband and a home of her own instead of having to live off her brother's charity. And why their parents didn't leave the poor girl some money in her own right instead of letting her brother inherit everything, and hold the purse strings so tight that the poor girl can hardly sneeze without his permission, I'll never know. It don't seem right him having a say over who she can marry and whether she'll get a dowry or not.'

'Ah, well, there's more to it than that,' said Masters. He turned away from her slightly to add a rather mysterious aside: 'There's a reason why the major watches her every step. She's not to be trusted.'

'Eh? What's that?' inquired his wife.

She had abandoned her cooking and was staring at her husband with renewed interest. Over the years their conversations had often followed similar lines, so often in fact that many of the topics they discussed were well worn, and the views of each so well known to the other as to make it

14

almost unnecessary for them to give voice to their opinions. Never before, however, had Masters hinted that there might be a reason for why Daphne had been made so dependent upon her brother's benevolence, that there might be more to the business than first met the eye. Well, Mrs Masters was having none of it. It didn't do to have secrets between husband and wife. She was going to get to the bottom of it and no mistake. She put her hands on her ample hips and looked encouragingly at her husband, who had now turned to face her looking rather guilty for letting slip something that he had withheld from her during their years of marriage. No, he hadn't let it slip, she decided, he had just not intended her to hear the few whispered words that he had uttered to himself. Well, he should have known better. Prided herself on her hearing, she did. See looked up at him expectantly and then, when that did not work, she moved to the door to prevent his departure.

'You'll tell me what you mean by that, Jack.'

'I'll tell you no such thing,' retorted her husband. He had returned to his playful fashion, though now it seemed a trifle false and strained. 'Now, out of my way, woman. The major, he'll want a whisky after doing battle with his sister. Always does. Hallo?' He paused as his eye caught sight of an envelope on the mantelpiece propped up somewhat carelessly against a candlestick. 'Where did this come from?' He picked it up and studied it. 'Addressed to the major and hand delivered by the look of it.' He turned to look at his wife inquiringly.

'Oh. I'm glad you spotted that, Jack. I had fair forgotten it, what with all this baking. Found it in the passage, I did. Someone must have pushed it under the door that leads out into the garden, though why they used that door and not the front one, I'll never know.'

'Aye, it strikes me as a little odd,' agreed her husband. 'It's something you'd expect of a tradesman come to deliver his bill, but then it'd be addressed to you or me, Mol, not to the major.' He looked at the envelope with more interest. 'An educated hand, I'd say. Though, can't say I recognise the handwriting. Not from one of the major's acquaintances in the village. I don't suppose you saw anyone, Mol?'

'Of course I didn't. You know as well as I do that the kitchen window doesn't look out on to that bit of garden. The envelope, it just appeared. I went out into the passage to go to the scullery and there it was. It might have lain there for half an hour or so.' She paused to glare at her husband. 'If you didn't spend all your time upstairs while I'm down here slaving away up to my elbows in flour, you might have spotted it yourself.'

Masters, however, was paying little heed to what his wife was saying. Instead, he was staring at the envelope intently. It could almost be thought that he fancied his eyes might penetrate the paper and catch a glimpse of one or two of the words written on the sheet inside. With the envelope still in his hand, he crossed to the door and wandered into the passage. His wife had quite understandably supposed that he had returned upstairs to deliver the letter, but a moment or two later he returned, the envelope still clutched unopened in his hand.

'You know, Mol, it's a funny old business about this letter. I've just been out into the garden and something odd has just struck me.'

'Oh, and what was that?'

'Well, if you were minded to leave the major a letter and didn't want to be seen doing so, then it makes sense to push the letter under the door into the passage rather than push it through the letterbox on the front door. You'd be sure to be seen by someone if you did that. But the door leading off from the passage, it faces the garden gate leading out in to the lane. Anyone could run down the lane, steal through the garden gate, post the letter and slip back again without being seen. It would be the work of a few minutes.'

'More likely as not the writer happened to be out on a walk, passed the garden gate, and decided on the spur of the moment like to deliver the letter by the back door,' retorted his wife. 'You see mystery and intrigue where there's none, Jack Masters. You'll be saying next that it's an anonymous letter, one of those poison pen things that you hear about.'

She returned her attention to the pie, purposefully turning her back on her husband who shrugged and left the room. Despite her bluster, she could not rid herself of a sudden irrational feeling of foreboding as she put the pie in the oven, burning herself in the process.

Major Spittlehouse sat at the desk in his study, staring in to the middle distance, a somewhat vague expression on his face. Evening was approaching and the darkness outside was mirrored by the appearance of dark shadows under the major's eyes and in the hollows of his cheeks, so that he seemed to have aged in the space of a few hours. The envelope that had caused such intense interest and speculation downstairs in the kitchen was now clutched in his hand, and was badly creased. Had an observer to the scene been present, he would have noticed that the envelope had been opened and relieved of its contents. Indeed, the single sheet of notepaper that it had contained was laid out prominently on the desk in front of him, the page turned over so that the message scribbled on it was hidden, as if the major found what was written to be too distasteful to read. After a while, however, Linus Spittlehouse's attention was drawn back to the offending piece of paper, but with such seeming reluctance that it appeared to be contrary to his natural inclination. Indeed, it was as if it the letter held for him a morbid fascination so that it attracted him as much as it repulsed him. With a sharp intake of breath, as if preparing himself for the ordeal and against his better judgment, the major turned over the paper and reread the words that had placed him, only a few moments before, in such a quandary, dredging up the past as it had.

The hand was unknown to him and it had therefore taken a few moments to realise that a threat lurked within the paper's folds, and another few moments to digest completely the letter's contents. With a growing sickening feeling in the pit of his stomach, it became all too apparent that the correspondent was aware of the Spittlehouses' murkiest secret, the one unfortunate event that had dominated his life and which he had been at particular pains to keep hidden. And, as Linus Spittlehouse sat staring into space with that deceptively impassive expression of his, it slowly dawned on him that all his efforts had been in vain. It was as if all the sacrifices he had made, all the trouble he had been to, had been for nought. Yet he was aware also that a part of him did not feel surprised. Hadn't he always known that it would come out in the end? As each year had passed, while part of him had grown complacent, had not another part of him feared that discovery was ever nearer, that it loomed on the horizon? And now here it was, their ruination, contained in this innocuous looking little letter written on a sheet of cheap notepaper.

He had thought matters could not get much worse. The scene that afternoon with his sister had been particularly upsetting, for he had not anticipated her threat. And now this, following on its heels as it had, well … it was too much. He felt the strain of it threaten to overpower and consume him. A part of him was even tempted to let go and succumb to the inevitable …

He was brought to his senses by the sound of his manservant's footsteps in the hall. Masters, he realised with a start, had thought the letter suspicious. Now that he recollected the way that the man had entered the room and handed it to him, holding the envelope out to him by one corner rather than placing it on the silver salver reserved for the post; it had been distinctly odd behaviour. It was as if the servant had feared the packet's contents. Major Spittlehouse stared again at the envelope. The absence of a postmark particularly troubled him. It had obviously been hand delivered and yet the handwriting was unfamiliar to him. There had been a pretence at a signature though it was so illegible that it may as well have not been written. He read the letter for a third and final time before disposing of both it and the envelope in the fireplace. He watched with satisfaction as the flames curled around them, reducing them to cinders. It was a hollow victory, however, as he was in little doubt that this was not the end of the matter. This letter, which asked for nothing save that he remember the ghastly deed that had been done all those years ago and acknowledge the effect on the Spittlehouses' standing in the community should it become common knowledge, was surely merely paving the way for the letters that would follow.

Major Spittlehouse stifled something which sounded suspiciously like a sob rather than a sigh. Blackmail, it must be blackmail. The writer could have no other intention unless of course it was to humiliate him, to watch him cower and tremble as every fretful moment he feared exposure to be looming, an everlasting damage to the Spittlehouses' good name. When faced with the two alternatives, he realised that he did not know what he feared most, to be financially indebted towards some unknown person or to have his reputation balanced precariously in the hands of this entity, whom might seek to destroy it at any moment on a whim.

The letter had been hand delivered. The significance of this fact had struck him immediately and forcibly, as if he had been physically hit in the chest. The writer had been in the village; was it not likely that he was still here? Even now, might he not be loitering in the street, or passing the time of day with the shopkeepers? Perhaps at this very moment he was outside the house, staring up at the windows, wondering if he, Linus, was reading those awful words that he had scribbled and was turning pale. On an impulse, the major dashed to the window and threw aside the drapes. But of course he could see nothing, for the windows overlooked the garden and besides it was dark outside. As he turned away from the window, defeated, the door handle moved and Masters came into the room, his reassuring presence restoring some sanity to the major's thoughts.

'Masters, this letter …' Major Spittlehouse paused to pick it up from his desk before remembering that he had cast it into the fire, 'the … the one you brought me a little while ago, did you see who delivered it? I'm afraid I couldn't quite read the signature. It must be my eyesight …' He allowed his words to trail off into nothing.

'No, sir, I'm afraid I didn't. And neither did Mrs Masters.' The manservant coughed rather apologetically. 'If you don't mind my saying, sir, it was all rather odd. The letter, it wasn't pushed through the letterbox as you might have expected. No, it was pushed under the garden door, the one leading off from the passage by the scullery. Whoever delivered it must have come through the garden gate from Lovers' Lane. We don't keep it locked during the day as a rule on account of Mrs Masters using it to walk in to the village if she suddenly finds she's took short and is in need of supplies. Takes a quarter of a mile off the route by road it does, because you can cut across Blue Meadow and '

'I am sure it does,' said the major hurriedly. Now that he had learnt what he had, he had no wish to prolong the interview with Masters and fuel the man's idle curiosity. Rather, he wanted nothing more than to be left alone and for his servant to return to his duties. For he was sure Masters was curious about the letter, had been ever since he had delivered it into the major's hand. Hadn't he stood beside him expectantly, even offered to slice open the envelope with the major's own letter opener as if he were of the opinion that his master was incapable of doing such a simple task? It was surely as obvious to his servant as it had been to him that whoever had delivered the letter had gone to considerable effort not to be seen.

A silence followed and, as the two men who had witnessed so much action together in the battlefield stood opposite one another, Spittlehouse looked at Masters in a searching fashion. He wondered if the same thought had occurred to his old batman as had suddenly come in to his own head. For the major had assumed that the letter-writer must be a stranger who had made a daytrip to the village of Sedgwick with the express intention of delivering the letter. But if so, why go to such measures to conceal his identity? Would it matter so very much if he was seen if his intention was merely to disappear back from whence he had come? And how had he known about the lane and more precisely the garden gate leading off it to Green Gables, which was so obscured from view by a mountain of climbing ivy as to be almost invisible to a casual observer?

No, though the thought was abhorrent, was it not more likely that whoever had delivered the letter, and more importantly written it, was someone known to the major? A local in fact? Yes, now that he thought about it, certainly he must be a villager, and perhaps even, though he could hardly bring himself to entertain the idea, an acquaintance or even someone he considered to be a friend? Of course there was nothing to say that the writer was a man. Weren't anonymous letters more usually associated with women? Major Spittlehouse shuddered. All of a sudden the danger seemed much closer to home.

Chapter Three

Lady Belvedere put aside her breakfast tray and stretched idly in a contented fashion, luxuriating in the fact that, as a married woman, it was deemed perfectly acceptable for her to take her breakfast in bed. A part of her protested at the decadence of it all, contrasting so sharply as it did with her previous existence, before her recent elevation in society. After all, it was not so many months ago that she had been attending on others in her role of shop assistant in Madame Renard's rather unremarkable dress shop in an unfashionable part of London. Her position there had been little more than that of a servant, and the novelty of her changed position, together with its associated privileges, was yet to lose its shine and diminish.

Pushing back the bedclothes, she rose, draped a negligee about her shoulders and made her way to the windows to marvel at the view which, though familiar now, always took her breath away. Her bedroom was situated at the back of the house and overlooked the formal grounds and the parkland beyond. Hidden within the park she knew were sunken ha-ha fences, which gave the illusion that each piece of park, no matter how differently managed or stocked, was one for as far as the eye could see. Capacious lakes, cut into the ground at different levels, similarly gave the impression of one vast single body of water. If she focused her eye on the horizon, she could just make out one of the many follies that were dotted about the place, a tower bearing a resemblance to the one in the story of Rapunzel.

'M'lady; her ladyship,' she whispered to herself, leaning her head against the windowpane, and then slightly louder, as if she were making an address: 'The Countess of Belvedere.'

She was merely referring to herself and yet how grand the words sounded and how foreign to her ear. It hardly seemed possible that everyone without exception in the village and its surrounds would address her as such, would curtsy when they saw her or doff their caps and treat her with a deference she had never previously known. It was too fantastic, and also a little frightening. The same part of her that had objected to the self-indulgence also clung stubbornly to her maiden name, reluctant to relinquish it forever.

'Rose Simpson,' she said, and she heard the note of urgency in her voice. 'Rose Simpson; I'm still me. Underneath it all, I'm still me.'

She started as her door opened and a housemaid entered to collect her tray. It occurred to Rose that, unlike herself, the girl had probably been up for hours.

'Shall I run your bath, m'lady, and lay out your clothes?'

'Yes, please do,' said Rose. 'I think I'll wear my navy blue Poiret twill suit. Betty, isn't it?' The girl nodded. 'Betty, do you know when Miss Evans will be arriving?'

Rose had first encountered Edna Evans sobbing bitterly in the kitchen garden at Ashgrove House, where Edna had occupied the lowly station of scullery maid. By chance, their paths had crossed again a month or so ago in the servants' hall at Crossing Manor, Edna having risen by then to the position of kitchen maid.

'Later today, m'lady; least that's what Mrs Farrier says. I'm to do her room next, air the bed and dust like. Quite a large room she's to have; quite as big as Miss Denning's.'

Rose smiled, wondering how Edna would like having a room of her own that she was not obliged to share with another servant. Aloud she said, recalling the servants' bedrooms at Crossing Manor: 'Is it in the attic?'

The housemaid nodded. 'All the servants' bedrooms are, m'lady, save of course for the chauffeur's, which is over the garage, and Mr Manning's. His bedroom is off the butler's pantry, so he can keep an eye on the family silver and the safe. Least, that's what Mr Torridge used to say when he was butler.'

Rose thought of the mean little attic rooms at Crossing Manor with their dull, sage green walls and bare floorboards. She had occupied one of the rooms herself, for she had adopted the guise of a servant to investigate the theft of the mistress' diamond necklace. She had found the attics a dismal place and wondered how those at Sedgwick Court compared. She must find an opportunity to explore them. Though she had already been taken on a most comprehensive guide of the main house, including the far removed rooms in the wings that had been long vacated and shut up with the ornaments crated and the furniture covered in great dustsheets, what lay behind the green baize door at Sedgwick Court remained a mystery to her. It was a fact that she had not set foot inside the servants' quarters and could only imagine the kitchen and the scullery, the servants' hall and the stillroom and the various other workrooms, linked together by a number of passages and corridors, much like a rabbit warren, and populated by a multitude of servants.

Rose was interrupted from her thoughts by the noise of hurrying feet in the corridor outside. It sounded to her ears as if an individual were being pursued relentlessly along the landing. She glanced at Betty, who looked equally taken aback by the turn of events and instinctively the two women drew closer together as if for protection. They watched with a terrified fascination as the door handle was depressed and the door swung open.

'Oh, Miss Rose,' cried an eager voice. 'I'm sorry I'm late. I wanted to arrive before you'd woken, but I had to help Cook with the servants' breakfast because they're still a bit short-staffed at Crossing, what with staff leaving ... or worse. But I said as I couldn't stay any longer, that you needed me to take up my new position.'

'Quite right, Edna,' said Rose, who might well have hugged the little maid had Betty not been present. 'It was very good of you to have stayed on at Crossing Manor until they had recruited some more staff, but I am in desperate need of a lady's maid, though Betty was doing a very fine job of it in your absence.'

The housemaid, Betty, looked from one to the other of them to reassure herself that her mistress was not in any immediate danger, curtsied abruptly and left the room. With the room to themselves, Edna ran up to Rose, a look of breathless enthusiasm on her face.

'Oh, miss, I was ever so excited, I used the main stairs! You should have seen the look on Mr Manning's face. He sent one of the footmen after me, so he did. Ever so fast I had to run.'

'Well, you are here now, which is all that matters,' said Rose laughing. 'And Betty was just telling me about your room. It is being made ready for you.'

'Oh, I can't wait to see it,' Edna said, clapping her hands together.

'It's my first full day back from honeymoon,' Rose said. 'We arrived back yesterday mid-morning but, with all the travelling, I was so tired, I couldn't quite take it all in. It didn't seem to register in my mind that I had returned here to Sedgwick Court.' She laughed, 'Oh Edna, I can't quite believe I was on the Continent for the best part of a month. It seems only yesterday it was my wedding day.'

'And Miss Rose, what a day it was!' cried Edna. 'I'm ever so glad I was allowed a day off to come and see you in your dress. Lovely you looked in all that pale gold satin. Draped beautifully, it did, and all those tiny satin covered buttons on the cuffs ... And to think your own mother made your dress herself.'

Rose smiled at the girl's enthusiasm which was infectious. In her mind's eye, she saw again her wedding day as if she were reliving it, her full-length wedding dress, cut on the bias, its lines so fluid that the overall effect was that of a liquid metal. She observed her reflection in the mirror, the cowl neckline embellished with tiny glass beads that caught the light, the puffed sleeves, which tapered in at the elbow, the simple veil that hung loosely from her head. She was once again clutching in her hands her wedding bouquet of fresh orchids, grown by the head gardener in the orangery. Her mother was wiping away a tear surreptitiously with her handkerchief, while Mrs Dobson, formerly her mother's cook before the Simpsons had fallen on hard times following the death of Rose's father, but now thankfully reinstated to the position of housekeeper at her mother's residence on the estate, was weeping quite openly.

Her bridesmaids, Josephine, Vera and Mary had worn tasteful and elegant gowns designed by the House of Renard, which had complemented Rose's own wedding outfit to perfection. These had contrasted sharply with the dress worn by the groom's sister, Lady Lavinia Sedgwick, a bright crimson haute couture gown, the vibrant hue of which was matched only by the colour of Rose's mother's face when she caught sight of the dress. Rose, already in a heightened state of excitement and trepidation, had done all she could to stop herself from giggling hysterically. It was so like Lavinia not to be outdone, even by the bride.

'It isn't too much, is it, Rose?' Lavinia had enquired. 'I didn't think you'd mind terribly if I wore something a little brighter than the other bridesmaids; I am the chief bridesmaid after all. And I don't photograph at all well in light colours.'

The Simpsons had had no living male relative to give Rose away; the job had fallen instead to Sir William Withers, KCB, Rose's new husband's uncle by marriage. She and Cedric had broken with tradition and been married in the local village church instead of in one of the great English cathedrals, preferring a more intimate wedding to a great society affair. This had not, however, prevented crowds of spectators from lining the streets to catch a glimpse of the bride. Indeed, the roads leading into Sedgwick village had been blocked with traffic for two hours as the locals and press men alike had jostled and scrambled to catch sight of the wedding party. As Rose had emerged from the silver Bentley clutching Sir William's arm, she had even caught sight of one or two photographers balanced precariously on long wooden ladders, trying to get a picture for the newspapers' society pages.

Rose hardly remembered the walk down the aisle; it was as if it were a blur. She recalled only that she had spied Cedric and, in her relief, her feet had seemed to go of their own accord towards him, so that she did not recall making her way there, only that somehow she had managed to arrive at his side breathless; but her feelings of nervousness had subsided. As she stood next to the young earl, he had turned to her to give her a quick, reassuring smile and wink. In that moment any qualms or reservations she might have had towards the suitability of a marriage between two persons from such very different positions in society had disappeared. For here was her darling Cedric, impossibly dashing and handsome in his tailcoats and cravat, waiting for her, his most ordinary betrothed, erstwhile shop girl and latterly amateur sleuth, anxious for her to become his wife. Incredibly, in that most important moment of her life to date, time had seemed to stand still for a few seconds, as if to give her the opportunity to relish its significance. For some reason her thoughts had turned to the past. She was reminded of the moment she had first set eyes on Cedric at Ashgrove House, striding across the lawns towards her and Lavinia, tall and slender, his blond hair slicked back, his chiselled features rivalling those of any matinee idol.

'Oh, his lordship looked so handsome,' Edna was saying, as if she could read Rose's mind. 'We all thought so, miss.' She turned to survey the bed. 'Now, I see the housemaid's put out your clothes.'

'Yes, but she hasn't started running my bath yet,' Rose said quickly, noting the girl's look of disappointment that her duties had been undertaken by someone else. 'Will you do that, Edna? And of course I shall need you to arrange my hair.'

'Yes, m'lady,' Edna said grandly, adopting a more deferential air.

'How is everything at Crossing Manor?' enquired Rose tentatively, a little while later as Edna brushed her hair in slow, laborious strokes. 'With the servants, I mean I say, Edna, I think that will do. Your arm must ache like anything. My hair has never shone so much.'

'Lady Lavinia's lady's maid swears by one hundred brush strokes twice a day,' said Edna. 'Eliza says I'm to start a few inches from the bottom to take out the tangles one by one and then to move up the hair to take out more knots until I reach the top of your head. She says it weakens the hair to brush it down from the roots.'

'Does she, indeed? Oh dear,' said Rose, thinking how often she had brushed her hair in just such a fashion.

'There's still a bit of sadness,' said Edna quietly, reverting to Rose's original question, 'at Crossing Manor, I mean. There's bound to be isn't there, what with the deaths? Always will be. Still, they've done what they can to brush away the ghosts. The servants' hall's had a fresh lick of paint and the furniture's been moved about a bit. But you can still feel it in the air if you've a mind to. The maids won't stay in the room after dark and some won't even go in there during the day, not alone.'

'I suppose,' said Rose, 'that in time people will forget. There will be new servants. For them it will just be a story.'

'Of course, there was a murder here at Sedgwick Court, wasn't there, m'lady? Last year if I recall?' asked Edna.

Rose stared at her maid's reflection in the mirror. She could not decide whether Edna was excited or alarmed by the fact that she had vacated one residence in which there had been a violent death only to arrive at another which had experienced a similar crime. Aloud, she said: 'It didn't happen in the house. You've no need to worry on that score. It happened outside in the maze. I think that makes quite a difference, don't you?' She did not wait for Edna to respond, but carried on. 'You needn't go into the maze if you'd rather not. But Lord Belvedere and I are determined to banish any ghosts that may linger there. He and Lady Lavinia had such fun playing in the maze as children.' She regarded her own reflection in the mirror. 'Well, Edna, I think Eliza has taught you very well. I don't think my hair has ever looked so neat.'

'Very good of you to say so, miss,' Edna said beaming. 'Course I've

26

still got loads to learn. But it's a start, as my mother would say.'

Later that morning, Rose, suitably clad in a thick woollen coat, felt hat and furs to combat the chilliness that was so often associated with late October, made her way to South Lodge. The house was situated in the grounds of Sedgwick Court beside one of the many gates to the park and had latterly become her mother's residence. It was of Georgian origin and had additionally benefited from a couple of small extensions, which had increased its already spacious dimensions. Having, until recently, been occupied by a succession of estate head gardeners and their families, it possessed a particularly lovely and well-stocked garden which, even at that time of year, when few gardens looked their best, boasted a splendid sea of blue irises and delphiniums.

Rose did not have an opportunity to press the brass door bell, for the door was flung open dramatically and with such eagerness that she found herself taking a step or two back in trepidation. She had hardly a chance to recover her composure before she was scooped up in ample arms and embraced with such enthusiasm that she almost lost her hat; certainly her fur slipped from her shoulders and fell to the ground.

'Oh, Miss Rose, aren't you a sight for sore eyes,' exclaimed Mrs Dobson, disentangling herself from the visitor and holding the girl by her shoulders a little way from her so that she might take in her appearance. 'Your dear mother will be that pleased to see you. We heard as how you got back yesterday. We thought you'd most likely come and see us today. Now, let me get you a nice cup of tea. Those foreigners don't know how to make it, drink nothing but coffee and wine, so I've heard. But there's nothing better than a cup of tea and I've just made some shortbread.'

Rose was not given an opportunity to respond before she was steered inside. Here at South Lodge at least she would always remain Rose Simpson. In the eyes of the world at large she might well now be Lady Belvedere and reside in a vast stately pile, but in Mrs Dobson's eyes she would always be the little girl she had helped to raise. Her mother too was unlikely to look upon her differently. Her daughter was still the girl who, until recently, had been obliged to earn her own living. It was with this welcome knowledge that she entered the house, overcome by a feeling of relief that here at least she would not be obliged to be on ceremony, but could be herself.

Mrs Simpson was as pleased to see her daughter as her housekeeper was, though she was slightly more restrained in her display of emotion, taking Rose's hand and steering her towards the settee in her cosy sitting room, where a fire burned brightly in the grate.

'Now, my dear, you must sit down and tell me everything,' she said. 'How did you find Paris?'

'Oh, it was wonderful,' exclaimed Rose. 'I loved everything about the city; the colours, the smells, the cafés of Montparnasse and Montmartre, Notre Dame Cathedral, the *Arc de Triomphe* on *Les Champs Elysées;* did you know it was commissioned by Napoleon? And of course the museums ... the *Louvre*, why it must house one of the largest art exhibitions in the world. And the music halls and theatres and operettas. We seemed to visit them all; a different one each night. And the Eiffel Tower; how could I have forgotten the Eiffel Tower?'

'How indeed? And the boutiques and the fashion houses?' enquired Mrs Simpson, her previous occupation as a seamstress coming to the fore. 'Did you visit any?'

'Yes, of course. Madame Vionnet's fashion house on *Avenue Montaigne.*'

'Not the "Temple of Fashion"?'

'The very same and –'

Rose stopped midway in her sentence. A commotion of sorts had erupted in the hall, the noise from which brought their conversation to an abrupt halt. Both women were taken by surprise and turned their attention towards the door. Amid the sound of footsteps, they could just make out what appeared to be raised voices, and they stood there quietly trying to catch snatches of what was being said. In the case of Mrs Dobson, whose voice was loud and distinctive at the best of times, it was not very difficult. This, coupled with the fact that the woman was obviously indignant, her emotions high so that her voice seemed to resonate around the hall, bouncing off the furniture and the floor, coming as clearly to the two women's ears as if she had been standing in the room beside them.

'You can't go in there, miss.'

It surprised both Rose and her mother that there was nothing deferential about the housekeeper's tone. If anything, it was more a hissed command than a polite request. Rose stole a glance at her mother and wondered if Mrs Simpson didn't now rather regret not employing a butler following her change in circumstances. It was apparent, however, that the visitor had no intention of complying with the servant's instructions, for Mrs Dobson was obliged to repeat her words, sounding considerably more annoyed than before.

'As I've told you, miss, you can't go in there. Mrs Simpson's with her daughter that's just back from honeymoon.'

'I thought you said she was not at home,' the visitor replied indignantly.

'She's not at home to callers,' replied Mrs Dobson sharply. 'It's only natural she wants to have a few quiet words with Lady Belvedere that's just returned. You could leave your card; I'll see she gets it, or you could come back later if you've a mind to.' Her tone, however, suggested that a future journey might also prove to be a wasted excursion.

'But I live on the other side of Sedgwick,' protested the visitor. 'It's quite a walk.' To Rose and her mother's ears, the woman sounded petulant.

What would have happened next, whether a confrontation of sorts would have occurred and a stalemate ensued, two equally stubborn and determined minds, was never to be known. For the visitor, evidently becoming impatient at being kept waiting in the hall and of the opinion that the servant would not budge, took matters into her own hands and decided to literally sidestep the housekeeper. There was a short kerfuffle accompanied by Mrs Dobson's irate voice, but this time the door to the sitting room opened and a woman in a tweed suit entered. She had not ventured more than a few steps into the room before the housekeeper burst her way in front of her.

'I'm ever so sorry, ma'am. She wouldn't take no for an answer. I tried to explain how you was talking with Miss Rose.' The housekeeper turned to glare at the newcomer. 'Ever so insistent she was that she see you.'

'That's quite all right, Mrs Dobson,' said Rose's mother, eyeing the newcomer with some reservation. 'I'm afraid that I don't think I have had the pleasure of –'

'Mrs Simpson … and Lady Belvedere, I do believe,' cried the woman, bestowing on the mother and daughter a smile of elaborate proportions.

'I'm Miss Spittlehouse. I hope you don't mind my dropping in like this. I have come to see you about the church flowers.'

Chapter Four

'The church flowers?' Mrs Simpson stared at the woman in bewilderment. 'I –'

'Yes. You are in charge of the flower arrangements in the church, are you not? Whose turn it is to do them each week, that sort of thing?' said Daphne, smiling sweetly. 'Well, I should like to offer my services. I suppose I should have done so long before now …' She uttered a high little laugh, allowing her sentence to drift into nothingness.

There was an awkward silence which, while only of a few moments' duration, was, however, sufficient to cause the smile on Daphne Spittlehouse's face to disappear and to be replaced by a look of surprise. 'Oh dear. Have I made a mistake? Is it not you I have to see about it after all, Mrs Simpson? Oh, please, do accept my apologies –'

'Not at all,' said Mrs Simpson graciously. 'I think it is Miss Bright to whom you need to speak. I believe it is she who organises the parish flowers.'

'How very silly of me,' said Daphne. However, she made no attempt to leave. If anything, the error appeared to have made her more determined to stay, for she stood resolutely in the sitting room, looking for all the world as if she were there by invitation.

Rose, who had not uttered a word since Daphne's unexpected arrival, stared at the woman with interest. The manner in which she had burst into the room so unceremoniously, if nothing else, was enough to draw her attention. That the woman had gone to considerable efforts to defy the formidable Mrs Dobson, where a lesser person might have retreated, shamefaced, was sufficient to further arouse her curiosity. Standing before them as she was, it must be very obvious to the woman, even if she were not of a particularly sensitive disposition, that her presence at that moment was not desired. Patently she was trespassing on a family reunion of sorts and yet the woman's conduct was most extraordinary. For she did not act as one might have expected. She showed no signs of embarrassment or discomfort. Indeed, she gave every indication that she intended to stay and participate in what was to follow, in essence, a private conversation between mother and daughter.

It was, however, the reason that Daphne had given for the purpose of her visit that Rose had found particularly fascinating. That she had come to inquire about the arrangements for the church flowers was so patently false as to be almost laughable. Rose stole a glance at her mother and decided that even Mrs Simpson, whom one might be forgiven for supposing possessed a less suspicious nature than her daughter, was looking at their visitor rather dubiously.

A stalemate of sorts threatened to ensue. Daphne Spittlehouse smiled her too bright smile, while Mrs Simpson stood in her own sitting room quite at a loss as to what to do next. She was painfully aware that Mrs Dobson, sullen and belligerent, remained poised and obstinate in the doorway, glaring at the back of the visitor's head. Perhaps the fear came to her that her housekeeper might decide to take matters in to her own hands to rid them of their unwanted guest in a less than courteous fashion. Mrs Simpson took a hesitant step or two forward and attempted a hospitable smile. Her actions, however, were awkward and stilted, and her smile rather weak.

Rather belatedly, Rose took it upon herself to come to her mother's aid. Had she been her late mother-in-law, her predecessor to the title of the Countess of Belvedere, Rose would undoubtedly have sent the woman on her way with some cutting remark or malicious comment, tapping the floor with a cane to emphasise her point. Rose, however, bore little resemblance to the late Lady Belvedere, her character being of a more charitable and patient disposition. Besides, it had occurred to her, as she had mulled over the possible reasons for Daphne's visit, that it was she, not her mother, that Daphne Spittlehouse was intent on seeing. Indeed, the woman had gone to great lengths to achieve her wish, forsaking propriety and convention in pursuit of her goal. Rose found herself, therefore, struggling with a natural inquisitiveness to ascertain why Daphne had sought out her company so deliberately. She had a sinking feeling that the joyous mood between mother and daughter had been irretrievably spoilt, the few happy minutes of their reunion irreparably tarnished. Even if Daphne were to leave now, the harm had been done, the moment ruined.

It was with these mixed feelings uppermost in her mind that Rose was swayed to take a middle ground, neither effusively friendly to their unwanted guest, nor overly arrogant or condescending.

'I believe your brother is a friend of my husband's, Miss Spittlehouse,' said Rose, her voice level. 'I am pleased to make your acquaintance. I do hope, however, that you will excuse us, but my mother and I have some private affairs to discuss.'

'Why, yes … yes, of course.'

The woman had entered the room full of a determined vitality. Now, however, she appeared to retreat within herself, her face forsaking the falsely bright smile. There was a slackening of the mouth and worry behind her eyes; there was even the possible threat of tears. There was also a sullenness about her, a look of petulance in the face like a favoured child that has failed to get its own way, strangely at odds with the woman's age, for she was certainly not in the first blush of youth. That Miss Spittlehouse was in a highly agitated state was patently obvious, and mother and daughter exchanged surreptitious glances, unsure how best to proceed with such a troublesome visitor.

'It would give me great pleasure, Miss Spittlehouse, if you would take tea with me tomorrow at Sedgwick Court.'

The words had escaped from Rose's lips, unbidden, before she had had a chance to take them back. Her mother gave her a look of surprise, her eyebrows raised. Even Daphne Spittlehouse looked somewhat taken aback.

'Oh, I say, would it really? That's frightfully kind of you, Lady Belvedere. There is nothing I should like more. What time do you take afternoon tea, your ladyship? Half past four?'

Daphne's delight at the invitation was evident, her thanks overly effusive, her face lighting up immediately, all traces of sorrow banished. Perhaps her joy was contagious, for Rose experienced a lifting of her own spirits. A moment ago she had regretted having spoken so rashly, now she thought that it might not be so bad after all. Her actions had been impulsive, the invitation given instinctively to alleviate the woman's disappointment at being dismissed. Now the interloper was taking her leave with a spring in her step, and Rose was left thinking that tomorrow afternoon might prove interesting if nothing else.

'Whatever possessed you, Rose, to invite that woman to tea?' demanded Mrs Simpson, as soon as they heard the front door close behind their caller. 'Wouldn't it have been better to hear what she had to say now? I doubt that it would have taken very many minutes for her to come to the point of why she had chosen to call on us.'

'You were not taken in by her story of arranging the parish flowers then?' inquired Rose.

'Well, of course not,' retorted her mother. 'Everyone knows that Miss Bright is in charge of the church flowers. Mrs Dobson and I were only discussing it the other day. We have so many flowers here in the garden at South Lodge, that I was wondering about donating a few sprays to the church in the spring and summer months. It seems a pity that more people shouldn't benefit from these abundant gardens.'

Mrs Simpson walked to the window and looked out. Rose wondered whether her mother was comparing the view with that from the mean little house which, until recently, they had shared in London. It had looked out on nothing more than a miserable cobbled yard.

'Does South Lodge remind you of the house we had before … before father died?' enquired Rose tentatively.

'Before we came down in the world?' said her mother, turning around and staring at her daughter reflectively. 'Well, yes, I suppose it does, a little.' She laughed. 'Oh … there are so many adjustments to be made. How pleased I am to have Mrs Dobson here to help me. Just like old times. It does seem like that, doesn't it? And now, of course, I must get used to the idea of having a countess for a daughter and an earl for a son-in-law. How is dear Cedric?'

'Very well. He's spending the day holed up with his estate manager. We were away for almost a month and I don't think he believes the estate can manage without him.'

'The estate and village are fortunate to have such a diligent landlord,' said Mrs Simpson. 'Cedric is aware his privileged position entails various responsibilities. One hears such awful stories about absent or neglectful landlords. And married life, are you finding it agreeable, Rose?'

'Very much,' said Rose blushing.

'I am very pleased to hear it. You know, my dear, I had some reservations about your marriage. It is so difficult when one marries out of one's class.'

'I am perfectly happy, Mother. I couldn't ask for a better husband, and I don't think you could ask for a better son-in-law.'

'Indeed I could not,' agreed Mrs Simpson, with considerable feeling.

'Cedric is a dear ... which is more than can be said for that sister of his.'

'Lavinia is all right,' said Rose laughing. 'I am very fond of her. She isn't nearly as bad as she would have everyone believe.'

'Well, you know her better than I do,' said her mother, sounding far from convinced. 'I will say this for her, though, that she has had the good sense to leave the two of you to settle in to married life without her interference. She's in the house in London, I believe?' Rose nodded. Mrs Simpson gave a heartfelt sigh. 'It is always regrettable if one must start one's married life living with one's in-laws. The company of others never makes for a good marriage.'

She spoke with such feeling that Rose wondered if she was speaking from bitter experience. It occurred to her that she had enquired very little into her parents' lives before her father had returned from the Great War irreparably damaged, a shadow of his former self. It had been a most miserable time for all concerned, and she had forgotten or become blind to the idea that her parents had shared a life together before the war, before her birth even.

'Well, you need have no fear as far as Lavinia is concerned,' Rose said, attempting to lighten the mood. 'She is intending to stay in London for the next few months, at least. I think she finds life at Sedgwick a little dull.'

Mrs Simpson made a face, but refrained from comment. It was regrettable, Rose thought, that her friend had made such an unfavourable impression on her mother. It was unlikely that Mrs Simpson would ever see Lavinia as she herself saw her. As much to change the subject of their conversation than for any other purpose, she said: 'What do you make of Miss Spittlehouse?'

'She seems to me rather an odd young woman, earnest in her manner and very eager to make your acquaintance.'

'You thought so?'

'Yes, I did. She addressed her remarks to me, but all the while she was looking at you.' Mrs Simpson smiled. 'I suppose, my dear, you must get used to that. People have always been interested in the lives of the gentry. And you are out of the ordinary.'

'On account of my humble origins?'

'Any woman who has secured the hand of one of the most eligible young men in England will inevitably create some degree of interest. And that you have made your own way in society, rather than having been born to riches, will make you more fascinating still.'

'What a Cinderella creature I am,' laughed Rose. 'Alas, I don't share her beauty.'

'Nonsense!' said her mother, who understandably had rather an inflated view of her own daughter's looks.

'All the same,' said Rose, pacing the room, 'I don't think that is why Miss Spittlehouse dropped in, to satisfy her own curiosity concerning my person, I mean. She didn't particularly strike me as the inquisitive sort.'

'No,' agreed Mrs Simpson. 'I thought her an impulsive woman. Rather a selfish one too. Mrs Dobson told her I was not at home to visitors, yet she barged her way in without so much as a by your leave.'

'I had the impression she wished to speak with me about something in particular?' said Rose cautiously.

'Oh?' said her mother, looking at her daughter apprehensively.

However, before Rose could elaborate further, Mrs Dobson came huffing and puffing into the room, as forcefully as had their uninvited guest only minutes earlier. She was bearing a tray laden with cucumber sandwiches and a boiled fruit cake, and made a great show of putting out the plates and cups and saucers, tut-tutting under her breath.

'I do hope, madam, you sent that woman away with a flea in her ear?' Mrs Dobson paused in her activities to fold her arms and give her mistress a meaningful look. 'Barging in here like she owned the place.' She screwed up her face as if she had caught a sudden whiff of vinegar. 'Treating me as if I were no more than a skivvy and her who should know better. Well, I was not going to bring in tea for her, not if you'd asked me, though I know you'd never.'

'Quite right,' said Rose.

The housekeeper's remarks had been addressed to Mrs Simpson, who remained silent. Mrs Dobson, apparently unperturbed, beamed. It occurred to Rose that her mother might be wondering whether it was appropriate to employ a servant who was quite so outspoken. Rose herself found it refreshing, particularly when she compared it with the deference displayed towards her by the servants at Sedgwick Court, which could be a little intimidating. Aloud she said:

'I am so glad you are back with us, Mrs Dobson. It is just like old

36

times.'

'Indeed it is my dear,' agreed the housekeeper. 'You'll always be Miss Rose to me, a cheeky, lively young thing, though you be gentry now and ever so grand.'

'Rose,' said her mother when the housekeeper had left them to their sandwiches and cake, 'what did you mean just now when you said that you thought Miss Spittlehouse wished to talk to you about something in particular?'

Rose chewed her mouthful of sandwich slowly and deliberately, trying to bide time. She was mulling over in her mind how best to answer her mother's question. That Mrs Simpson had her own views as to the purpose of Daphne Spittlehouse's visit was obvious. In all likelihood they mirrored her own thoughts on the matter. It was one thing, however, to have one's own suspicions, but to have them shared by another was something else entirely, particularly when that other party did not normally share one's own misgivings.

'I thought it very probable that she came to consult me,' Rose said at length, deciding that honesty was the best approach.

'To consult you? What do you mean?' demanded Mrs Simpson, though the look of horror on her face betrayed the fact that she knew full well the answer to her question.

'I think Miss Spittlehouse came to consult me as one would a private enquiry agent.'

'Oh, Rose, do you think so?' Mrs Simpson looked at her daughter imploringly and spoke in earnest. 'You must tell her that you have dropped all that now you are married. Think of the standing of the family you have married into. You are a countess now, not a shop girl dabbling in dubious hobbies; you must behave as such.'

'I never chose my hobby, as you call it,' cried Rose, 'rather it chose me. I have been unfortunate enough to be in gatherings where murders have occurred, that is all. It is hardly my fault.'

'But you will insist on investigating them, instead of leaving well alone. Poking your nose into matters that don't concern you and putting yourself into heaven knows what danger. And,' continued Mrs Simpson, clearly getting into her stride, 'it's no good you telling me that you don't seek it out. Look at that business at Crossing Manor. Fancy going there dressed as a servant and prying into everyone's affairs.'

'I was asked to investigate the theft of a diamond necklace,' protested Rose. 'I have found that I have something of an aptitude for sleuthing.'

She might well have added that her servant's disguise had been at Lavinia's instigation, and that she herself had harboured various misgivings concerning the venture. However, on reflection, she thought better of it and held her tongue. There was little point in providing her mother with yet another reason to dislike her sister-in-law. And besides, she was rather taken aback by the passion of her mother's feelings on the subject. She had known, of course, that Mrs Simpson had been troubled by the frequency with which her daughter had found herself surrounded by corpses, but that she was so strongly opposed to her daughter's detecting activities came as something of a surprise.

'Oh, do let us leave this subject and not argue,' said Mrs Simpson quickly. 'I daresay I am being silly. No one will expect a member of the aristocracy to undertake the activities of an amateur sleuth. Now, you were telling me all about Paris before we were so rudely interrupted ...'

For the next half hour, Rose regaled her mother with tales of her honeymoon. It was almost as if Daphne Spittlehouse had never forced her way past Mrs Dobson and intruded upon their conversation. Almost, but not quite. For Rose was reminded of Lavinia's words as they had left Crossing Manor. She had been adamant that Rose would always be an amateur sleuth or a private enquiry agent, and that her services would still be required and be in great demand whether she was Miss Simpson or the Countess of Belvedere. Rose bit her lip; she wouldn't tell her mother that.

Chapter Five

Rose returned to Sedgwick Court with Mrs Simpson's words still echoing in her ears. She was a countess now, and must not dabble in childish or unseemly games; that was the essence of her mother's argument against her continuing with her sleuthing activities. There was a part of her that felt annoyed, another part that suppressed a smile. Her mother had assumed, perhaps naturally enough, that her daughter's husband would be of a like mind. This was in fact so far removed from the truth that Rose had to bite her lip to stop herself from laughing aloud. What would her mother say if she were told that Cedric had been fully aware of his future wife's intention to go to Crossing Manor in the guise of a servant and had laughed heartily?

On enquiry of one of the footmen, she discovered that her husband was still engaged with his estate manager, the two of them currently undertaking a tour of the estate and visiting the tenants. She was obliged, therefore, to entertain herself until dinner. To while away the time, she chose to roam the house and permit herself the luxury of studying each room at leisure, admiring its ornaments, rich furnishings and decoration.

She might have been viewing them for the first time or, at least, with fresh eyes. She felt she had tiptoed inside a giant dolls' house, for there was a sense about the place that it was not quite real, that everything was a bit too grand. She had visited Sedgwick Court before, of course, on numerous occasions but only as a guest. Then she had given each room and its possessions a cursory glance, marvelling nevertheless at the very splendour of the place. Now she entered each room as its mistress; it was a daunting prospect. Along with Cedric, she considered herself to be a custodian of Sedgwick Court and all that it housed, keeping each item safe and preserved to pass on to the next generation. The responsibility weighed heavily upon her.

Without a gathering of guests or relations to occupy and fill the space, the house seemed vast and empty, almost like a museum awaiting its visitors. She knew it was a mere illusion and that a veritable army of servants laboured behind the green baize doors ensuring the smooth running of the house. Yet still the irrational feeling persisted, that she was trespassing in a world that was both deserted and not her own.

It was rather unsettling to know that she might spend her time doing very little if she chose. There was no mundane chore that needed undertaking by her hand, no domestic task that was aching to be done by herself alone. While she willingly embraced her new life, there was a sadness in the knowledge that she would never again be required to boil her own kettle or make do with a meagre, scanty lunch put together with her own two hands. She might always, if she wished, walk aimlessly from one room to another, marvelling at her kingdom.

Rose gave herself a good talking to. She had known that there would be a period of adjustment. She could not expect to move seamlessly from one life to another without a slight feeling of disorientation, of being something of an observer looking on, particularly when the existence she had endured previously had differed so very much from the world she now inhabited.

She strolled into the dining room, which was a particularly grand affair with its high, strapwork ceiling, wood-panelled walls and lavish furnishings. Idly Rose surveyed the highly polished mahogany dining table, which ran almost the full length of the room. Against the far wall was a large, bow-fronted Georgian sideboard, on which were placed two tapered column, silver candlesticks gleaming back at her, bright and sparkling, belying a rather sinister recent history.

With something of a shudder, Rose returned her gaze to the great polished table and a smile leapt immediately, and most welcomingly, to her lips. How ridiculous it had seemed last night for her and Cedric to sit at either end of this great wooden monstrosity, staring at each other in the distance and having to raise their voices to be heard by the other, requiring a footman to pass the condiments. The absurdity of the situation had not been lost on the young earl, even though used to such a circumstance, and together they had laughed in a childish fashion. The seating arrangements had been quickly addressed. Rose had forsaken her end of the table and joined Cedric, sitting on his right, which had enabled them to speak in normal tones and, when desired, to bend their heads together in a conspiratorial and affectionate manner. Both butler and footmen had been dismissed from the room and Lord and Lady Belvedere had made do with passing each other the mustard and the pickles.

The footmen had re-entered the room only to bring in the various dishes and clear away the plates, and the butler to refill his employers' glasses. Other than that, Rose and Cedric had been left blissfully alone to stare into each other's eyes and hold hands as the mood took them, surreptitiously disentangling themselves from one another as soon as they became aware of a servant's unwanted presence. But, to all intents and purposes, the scene had been an intimate one and the table that they had occupied, small and cosy. For they had become conveniently blind to the existence of the rest of the table stretching out into the distance, innocent of white linen, bare except for the reflection thrown out by the candelabra on the polished wood.

'Cedric, what can you tell me about the Spittlehouses?' asked Rose, as the last of the dishes were cleared away that evening. Their talk during dinner had drifted from sentiment to discussion of how each had occupied their day.

'The Spittlehouses?' Cedric raised his eyebrows and looked faintly surprised. 'The major and his sister, do you mean?' Rose nodded. 'Well, not very much, I'm afraid, though, as it happens, I'm due to meet with the major in a day or so to discuss the arrangements for Guy Fawkes' Night.'

'Are you really? Tell me, have they lived here long, in the village, I mean?'

'Oh, about four or five years, I should say. The locals still view them as newcomers.'

Arm in arm, husband and wife made their way to the drawing room to drink their coffee.

'The major happened to be a great friend of my father's,' continued Cedric, 'which is rather surprising since he was such a solitary fellow. Both loved antique and rare books. I can't say I know the man very well myself.' Cedric bent his head towards his wife to whisper in a furtive fashion, though there was no servant present at that moment to overhear their chatter. 'I've always thought the major a bit of a stuffed shirt myself. I daresay it's only his manner and he doesn't mean anything by it. But he likes to involve himself in village affairs and always thinks he knows best; his way is the right way and all that. He's ruffled a few feathers; I can tell you. But I think his heart is in the right place. Must be all that military training, what. But it doesn't go down too well in the village.'

'I don't suppose it does,' said Rose, only being vaguely interested in hearing about the major. 'But what can you tell me about his sister? Talking of her brother ruffling feathers, I think she rather did that herself this afternoon. You should have seen Mrs Dobson's face. I thought she was going to hurry her out of the house with the broom!'

'I wish I'd been there,' said Cedric, a mischievous grin on his face. 'Your mother's Mrs Dobson rather frightens me. But I'm afraid I can tell you very little about Miss Spittlehouse. All I know is that she lives with her brother but, unlike him, does not concern herself much with village affairs.' He sipped his coffee. 'I daresay my sister could probably have told you more about her had she been here; Lavinia knows all the gossip!'

Chapter Six

'Miss Spittlehouse, how do you do? Won't you take a seat?'

Daphne took the proffered chair and looked about her with undisguised delight. Rose could almost read the woman's thoughts as they occurred to her, so expressive was her face. So this was Sedgwick Court, was it? The drawing room was very grand, not that one wouldn't expect it, because of course one would, it being home to an earl. But such rich furnishings! And everyone saying how we were living in troubled times and had to make economies; little making do here! Not like it was for other people.

'Daphne, my dear, do you really need to order so many dresses?' Linus' words flooded back into her mind, boringly repetitive and persistent as he studied the dressmaker's bills, and always in that pompous voice of his that he seemed to reserve just for her. Really, he spoke to her as if he were speaking to a child. Oh dear, had the recollection caused a frown to appear on her face? That would never do. The countess would take it as a slight. She would think that her guest didn't quite approve of her.

'Lady Belvedere, how very good of you to invite me to tea, and on the merest introduction ... I must apologise for barging into your mother's house like that. You must have thought me very rude.' Daphne paused a moment to survey her surroundings. 'Oh I say, what a very fine room this is.' Something caught her eye and she was out of her seat in a moment, her plate discarded. 'Is this a genuine ...?' She did not bother to complete her sentence, her hand was outstretched and in a matter of seconds a small wooden statuette was in her grasp. 'Oh, do say it is, genuine, I mean.'

'I believe so,' said Rose, inwardly wincing at the way her guest clasped the ornament to her with such passion, finding herself fighting the urge to snatch it from her and return it to a place of safety. 'How do you take your tea, Miss Spittlehouse?'

'Rather strong, I'm afraid. I think I learned that from my brother. They take their tea quite stewed in the army, did you know? Just a splash of milk, please.' Daphne abandoned the statuette, setting it down rather haphazardly on the mantelpiece so that it was positioned at an odd angle, and returned to her seat. 'Oh, Lady Belvedere, I am so very pleased to make your acquaintance.'

'And I yours,' said Rose politely, eyeing her visitor with a degree of interest in spite of herself.

It was obvious, even to the most casual observer, that Daphne Spittlehouse could not settle. Already she had forsaken her chair again to roam the room in a restive manner. From time to time she paused in her pacing of the room to pick up some object at random and study it in a cursory manner; she took a strand of her hair and twisted it between her fingers; she pulled at the finger of one glove. All in all, she fidgeted, as if the art of sitting still was quite beyond her.

'Miss Spittlehouse, won't you tell me why you wished to see me?' Rose said at length.

Daphne stopped abruptly in her pacing of the room and looked surprised.

'Why I wished to see you? But it was you, dear Lady Belvedere, who wished to see me,' protested Daphne. 'You invited me to tea.'

'Yes, I did,' admitted Rose, 'but ...'

She said no more, allowing her words to stop abruptly in mid-sentence, wondering if she had said enough to encourage the woman before her to give voice to what was on her mind. There was a possibility that she had imagined it, that the woman was only nervous to be in her presence, but she did not think so. The silence that followed was awkward and uncomfortable. Rose ostensibly busied herself with pouring tea into the fine bone china cups and with straightening the plates of sandwiches and cakes. All the time, however, out of the corner of her eye, she was distinctly aware of Daphne's distracted movements, as keenly as if they were her own, the clasping and unclasping of the woman's hands, the clearing of her throat and even the utterance of a queer, high pitched little laugh.

'You are quite right, of course. I did wish to see you,' Daphne Spittlehouse said at last, perching herself on the edge of a chair and taking the cup and saucer offered her. After pausing a moment to take a sip of tea, and perhaps affording herself an opportunity to choose her words carefully, she looked Rose directly in the eye and said: 'How silly of me to think that I could pull the wool over *your* eyes.'

'You are referring to my detecting abilities?' Rose said rather abruptly.

44

'I am,' agreed Daphne, taking another sip of tea.

'You wish to consult me?' asked Rose.

She gave what she hoped was a look of encouragement for the woman to proceed. She found herself wishing fervently that Daphne Spittlehouse would either decide to speak freely or to leave. Anything was better than this atmosphere of pent up energy and awkwardness, and words unspoken.

'Yes, though perhaps not in the way you might imagine.' Daphne gave Rose something of a penetrating look. 'I have to confess, Lady Belvedere, that I was not aware that you were intending to continue with your … hobby, not after your marriage, I mean.'

Later, Rose thought that it was probably at that very moment when she decided that she definitely would continue with her sleuthing activities. After all, Cedric was not against the idea and her sister-in-law positively enthused at the prospect. But above all it was Daphne Spittlehouse's attitude towards it that influenced her the most. The raised eyebrow, the slightly mocking smile, the trace of arrogance about her manner, even the way she said 'Lady Belvedere', as if it were not Rose's rightful title.

'Yes,' said Rose, meeting the woman's gaze.

If Daphne's attitude had not infuriated her so, she knew that she would have remained silent, would not have been prompted to give voice to one solitary word that was in her mind. All she could think as the word escaped her lips was how glad she was that her mother was not present to see her hopes dashed. Rose wondered whether Daphne was aware of the inner turmoil that she had unleashed in her breast. Surely her face must be crimson, if only as a consequence of the woman's condescending stare? But on studying her guest, Daphne appeared blissfully ignorant to the emotions she had released. Her thoughts now were on herself for, having touched on what was foremost on her mind, she appeared to require no further words of encouragement to proceed.

'As I said,' Daphne continued, as if she had not posed a question and Rose had not spoken, 'perhaps not in the way you might think, though I suppose embezzlement might fall within your field?'

'Embezzlement?'

'Yes. I think that my brother may have embezzled my inheritance. But,' Daphne said hurriedly, seeing that Rose was about to interrupt, 'that's not why I wished to see you … consult you, should I say? Oh dear, that sounds frightfully formal, doesn't it?'

'Perhaps you are merely seeking my advice?' suggested Rose, suddenly afraid that the woman might falter and dry up.

'Oh, yes. That sounds much better, doesn't it?' said Daphne enthusiastically. 'Well you see, Lady Belvedere, the predicament I find myself in is like this …'

'She asked you to do what?' cried Cedric aghast.

'Shush, darling, the servants will hear you,' said Rose, somewhat amused by her husband's reaction. It was a few minutes after the departure of her tea guest and, following her husband's arrival, she had rung for the footman to bring more hot water and sandwiches. 'You'll say it doesn't matter, but I did promise Miss Spittlehouse that I wouldn't breathe a word about it to anyone but you.'

'The cheek of the woman! Whom does she think she is? Fancy asking you to do such a thing.'

Her husband had taken umbrage on her behalf and Rose found it oddly endearing. His brow was furrowed with his annoyance, and it gave her an idea of what he would look like when he was older and his forehead lined. As she stared at him, tenderness welling up inside her, the footman entered the room with the tray of refreshments. Inwardly she sighed. She supposed that in time she would become used to their conversations being overheard by the staff, their ever presence in their lives like shadows. Cedric, who had never known anything else, had become accustomed to it so that it barely registered on his consciousness; in time, she thought, it would be the same for her. Was there not a certain inevitability to it? After all, masters and servants inhabited the house together, lived out their lives in its many rooms and corridors. And, if they did not exist exactly side by side, at least they lived in close proximity.

Rose had little doubt that in the years that followed she and Cedric would provide the food for gossip in the servants' hall. Sedgwick Court's old retainer, Torridge, would have frowned upon and admonished idle tittle-tattle among the staff. However, following his retirement as butler, the situation had changed. Manning, his successor and the previous under-butler, would adopt a more lenient approach, she felt certain. Even so, gossiping about the family outside the house would be actively discouraged and a case for certain dismissal.

'What she is asking you to do is quite unreasonable,' Cedric was saying. 'Why, you've never met her brother, have you? And she is little more than a stranger to you. How can she possibly expect you to plead to the major on her behalf?'

'I think she thought there were certain similarities to our positions.'

'Oh?'

'We have both been faced with the unfortunate obstacle of wishing to marry someone outside our class.'

'Does Daphne Spittlehouse wish to marry a duke? I wouldn't have thought Major Spittlehouse would have a problem with that.'

'No, of course not. She … well, I suppose you might say she wishes to marry beneath her. A solicitor I think she said her young man was. Archie Mayhew. He works in his uncle's firm in Bichester. Oh dear,' said Rose, suddenly deflating. She put a hand to her head and gave her husband an exasperated look. 'It was all so very difficult, you see. I found myself taking against her. I daresay it wasn't her fault, but I couldn't help it. There was nothing that I could exactly put my finger on but –'

'There was something about her manner to you? It was her fault but you still felt guilty for not liking her so you were particularly nice to her?' said Cedric laughing. 'Darling, I can quite see that happening.'

'Something like that. It does sound rather silly when you put it like that, doesn't it?'

'Not to me. But, look here, what's this chap like? Archie Mayhew, I mean. From what little I know of Spittlehouse, he's always struck me as a reasonable sort of a fellow. A bit pompous and full of himself, but a good egg all the same. I don't see why he should have any objections to the marriage. And, even if he has, his sister is of age. She doesn't need his permission.'

'Well, unfortunately she does. That's to say she told me a bit about their parents' will. Her brother was the sole heir to their estate. They didn't leave her anything, no money in her own name or a yearly allowance, or anything like that. Instead they left strict instructions that her brother was to provide for her. That was all.' Rose put aside her teacup and began to pace the room. 'Isn't that awful? Because of course you can see her difficulty, can't you? Such instructions might be construed in a manner of ways. The major might think he was fulfilling his duty to his parents by giving his sister a generous lump sum of money or by giving her a yearly allowance, or by providing her with a roof over her head …' She left her unfinished sentence hanging in the air.

'Yes. An odd sort of a will, if you ask me,' agreed her husband. 'Open to too much interpretation. If Spittlehouse were a different sort of fellow … though I don't think his sister had come of age when her parents died; within a few months of each other, I believe. I daresay they would have changed their will had they lived. 'I must say I feel rather sorry for old Spittlehouse. The poor old chap probably didn't know what to do for the best.' He sighed. 'I take it he objects to her intended? Is that why she wishes you to plead her case? She wants him to bestow a fantastic sum of money on the two of them?'

'Yes, something of the sort. She told me that Archie Mayhew did not earn enough to keep a wife, at least not in the manner to which she was accustomed.' Rose paused. 'I had the distinct impression they were his words, not hers. Having said that, Daphne Spittlehouse does not strike me as the sort of woman who'd make do, who'd abandon everything for love … Of course it's rather hard not to feel sorry for her.'

'Yes. The major obviously must have thought he was complying with his parents' wishes by giving his sister a roof over her head and probably also giving her a generous allowance. Of course he could put a stop to the allowance. Is that what she is afraid of?'

'In a manner of speaking. She spoke of embezzlement –'

'Did she really?' Cedric looked appalled. 'That doesn't sound like the major at all. A pillar of the community and all that. Even so, she cannot expect you to speak to him about it. Tell me that you didn't agree to do such a thing, darling?'

'Of course not,' said Rose, bending forward and taking her husband's hand in hers, 'I said it would be much better if you did, your being acquainted with him, and particularly as he happened to be coming to see you already about the arrangements for Bonfire Night.'

Chapter Seven

'What are you doing with yourself today, m'lady?' enquired Edna in her best lady's maid voice. Brush in one hand, she was attempting to tame her mistress' unruly locks. 'It's another fine day and not too cold considering. The second day of November, would you believe? Bonfire Night will be upon us so it will, and then it'll be Christmas ...'

'Is it really?' murmured Rose, only half listening. She opened her eyes and stared at Edna's reflection in the dressing table mirror. It had taken her a few moments to respond for she had been lulled into a soothing, daydream like state by the steady rhythm of the brushstrokes. 'Do you mean to say Guy Fawkes' Night is on Thursday?' It was only then, as the words escaped her lips, that she recalled Cedric had mentioned he would be reviewing the preparations that afternoon for the village's bonfire festivities.

'Isn't it exciting? A proper bonfire and all. Mrs Farrier's been telling me how they set great store by Bonfire Night in the village,' said the lady's maid, pausing in her brushing. 'Quite a big occasion it is here and no mistake. His lordship's ever so generous. He contributes to the fireworks and provides all the food. Something of a family tradition. Still, you don't need me to tell you that do you, m'lady?'

'No ... my husband ...' The novelty of using those two intimate words still brought a glow to Rose's cheek. 'My husband was telling me all about it last night. It'll be my first Guy Fawkes' Night at Sedgwick. Now ... what did he say? Oh, yes there's some sort of a Bonfire Night Committee, I think he called it, which is chaired by Major Spittlehouse. From what I could gather, it is the major who is really in charge of all the arrangements.' She bent her head towards her maid. 'Between you and me, Edna, Cedric ... Lord Belvedere, is feeling rather guilty. He hasn't been able to go to as many of the committee meetings this year as he would have liked. He has rather left poor Major Spittlehouse and the rest of the committee to organise everything.'

'Well, it's not every year you get married and go on your honeymoon,' retorted Edna briskly. 'And, from what I hear about the major, he's just the sort to like to be left in charge. He's full of his own importance, as my mother would say.'

'Your mother has a great many sayings, Edna,' said Rose laughing, 'and all of them very good ones. But Lord Belvedere still feels rather badly about it and is keen to make amends. As it happens, he's meeting with Major Spittlehouse this afternoon.' She leaned back in her chair. 'Now tell me what you've heard about the festivities. Will there be plenty to eat?'

'Won't there just!' exclaimed Edna. 'Potatoes cooked in their jackets, steaming tureens of hot chicken soup, sausages and of course Mrs Broughton's special black treacle toffee; very popular with the children, it is.' The hairbrush was now all but forgotten, lying discarded on the dressing table; for Edna was employing her fingers to reel off the various delicacies, rather than to deliver strokes with the brush. 'An old secret family recipe passed down from mothers to daughters across the ages, so Mrs Broughton swears,' she added rather mysteriously.

'Indeed?' Rose's thoughts turned to the various fine dishes prepared by the cook.

'Oh, and the fireworks. Major Spittlehouse, being a military man, is very particular about them. Have to be Standard fireworks, them that's based at Crosland Hill. On account of the company producing munitions for the war effort, so Mr Manning says.'

'I think I've seen some of their promotional cards,' reflected Rose. 'Don't they say something like "A terrific bang. Right up to the sky?"'

'Oh, that would be the Air Bombs,' said Edna assuming an authoritative air. 'And then of course there's the Snow Storms … showers of beautiful snowflakes, I think they say they are. You must have seen their boxes of fireworks? Ever so colourful, they are.'

'Yes, I am sure I have,' said Rose. 'Well Edna, you have quite made up my mind for me. I think I'll take a walk in to the village to see these boxes of fireworks. But first I must deal with some correspondence I've rather been putting off. I'll ring for you when I'm ready to leave.' She smiled as a thought occurred to her. 'The children should have quite finished making their guys by now. I daresay some will be out on display. I should love to take a peek at them. Lord Belvedere informs me that I am to be responsible for judging the best guy this year.'

'Oh, yes, I've heard all about that,' said Edna excitedly, clapping her hands together. 'They're all paraded in front of the bonfire and there's a prize each year for the best guy. The children take it ever so serious like. Quite realistic some of the guys are to look at, you'd swear they were real people so Mrs Farrier says. Some of the children take weeks and weeks to make them. Of course, some of the effigies are just old rags that have been stuffed with heaven knows what, but some are quite grand, I believe.' Edna bent forward and lowered her voice. 'My dad's a bit of a miser. He says it's all fuss and nonsense and just an excuse for young lads to cause trouble and to go about banging on respectable people's doors. He don't hold with them shouting at the tops of their voices and begging like. Daresay that's why it's so popular with the children, making the guys, I mean. They can get a little money. And there's a splendid prize for the best one.'

'Yes, it's a hamper of food, isn't it?'

'A huge one, m'lady, filled with such delicacies as you never did see. Some of it comes from Fortnum & Mason.' Edna giggled. 'I'm sure I wouldn't say no to winning one of those hampers myself.'

The day being bright and particularly mild for the time of year, the walk to the village of Sedgwick was a pleasant one. When Lady Belvedere and her maid came to the village itself, they found there were ample signs that Bonfire Night was soon to be upon them. Boxes of fireworks adorned shop windows and various groups of children, some of them with their faces blackened to represent Guy Fawkes and his failed gunpowder plot, congregated on street corners around an ill assortment of effigies showing varying degrees of skill and refinement. Some had been very crudely constructed from nothing much more than old rags, and only vaguely resembled the shape of a man if an observer were to use a very vivid imagination. Others were dressed splendidly and took on lifelike forms. The guys had been stuffed with whatever filling had come readily to hand, mostly straw or old newspaper. Some were half sitting, half lying, on the ground, while others had been propped up against a wall. One enterprising group of boys had even acquired an old wickerwork pram in which to prop their guy and proceeded to tear up and down the streets, dodging pedestrians, wheeling their effigy and singing at the tops of their voices: 'Remember, remember, the fifth of November, gunpowder treason and plot; I see no reason why gunpowder treason should ever be forgot.' They were being hotly pursued by one or two gallant shopkeepers who were attempting to shoo them away and make the pavements safe, lest shoppers be deterred from crossing the thresholds of their shops for fear of injury.

Edna made to cross the road to avoid a particularly large group of street urchins assembled on one street corner. The lads themselves had mucky faces and ragged trousers to rival any effigy. They were crowded around a rough, unsophisticated guy that had the air of having been hastily put together. Rose, however, called her lady's maid back and made a point of stopping to admire every effigy she encountered and to bestow on each a monetary gift. Bending down to inspect the guys, Rose noticed that each, without exception, had pinned to its chest a piece of paper on which was written in crudely scribbled words: 'A penny for the guy'. Some of the boys even chanted the words at each passerby, and thrust out a cap or tin in their eagerness to secure some loose change.

'You're too soft by half, miss, if you don't mind my saying,' admonished Edna. 'Some of them guys are no more than old tatters. They don't deserve any money, they don't. Those young scallywags won't spend it on dressing no guy.' She sniffed and appeared to relent a little. 'They'd do better spending it on something to eat; did you see how some of them were little more than skin and bones? Poor little mites.'

'Yes. Times are hard for many. It's easy to forget,' said Rose with a sense of guilt. It occurred to her that her recent elevation in society had brought with it a sense of having been removed from the plight of ordinary people struggling to make a living and feed their families. 'I will speak to Lord Belvedere and see what we can do.'

'It's common knowledge that the family does a great deal,' replied her maid. 'Rents have been lowered and in some cases done away with altogether, least that's what Mrs Farrier says.'

'What a great authority our housekeeper is,' muttered Rose, though her thoughts had been considerably lifted by the news. Really, she would have expected nothing less of Cedric. Her thoughts returned to the gunpowder plot and the resulting festivities. 'You do see, don't you Edna, that as regards the guys, I must be seen to be impartial. I can't give money to some groups of boys and not to others. That would never do. Remember, I shall be judging the effigies on Bonfire Night.'

'Rather you than me, miss,' said the young lady's maid, who was herself only a few years older than some of the boys. 'They give me the creeps, they do, those guys, least them as is lifelike.' She gave a shudder. 'It gives me ever such a fright to see them in the dark on Bonfire Night. It doesn't seem right, does it? To throw them on to the fire, like. It's almost like throwing a body on to the flames, and everyone cheering and laughing.'

'Well, I suppose how it all came about is rather awful,' said Rose. 'Guy Fawkes and his foiled gunpowder plot, I mean.'

'I'll say, m'lady!' said Edna with relish. 'Fancy them trying to blow up the Houses of Parliament.'

'Yes. In 1605, if I remember my history lessons correctly. It was a rather theatrical attempt to assassinate the Protestant king, James I, because he had gone back on his promise to show religious tolerance to the English Catholics.'

'So they decided to blow him up?' Edna's eyes had grown large. 'And of course it failed and they were all put to death, but not till they'd been horribly tortured.' She gave another shudder.

'Yes. When you put it like that, Edna, it does seem rather awful that we celebrate it,' said Rose. 'Still, it does provide an excuse for the children of the village to have some fun.'

Later, she was to remember her lady's maid's qualms and wonder how she could have dismissed them so flippantly. For she herself had felt no sense of foreboding, no premonition of wickedness. The village, with its picturesque appearance, had provided a comprehensive camouflage. But evil had still been present, she realised, looking back on the tragic events that followed, though then it might have still been in its infancy. Nevertheless, it had been there, lurking out of sight, hidden in the shadows, a half formed thing that would fester and grow. Someone would decide to follow in Guy Fawkes' footsteps, to plot and connive to disastrous ends.

Harold Whittaker of Gribble, Hebborn & Whittaker solicitors, straightened the papers on his desk and stared despondently at his inkstand. He was a tall, lean man, though he had a tendency to hunch his shoulders as he sat crouched behind his desk. This was wont to give the mistaken impression that he was something of a small and insignificant figure. Only his eyes, almost black and very bright, looked alert, betraying a mind as keen and pedantic as it had always been. His face, unusually long in profile, had an odd hungry look, as if he were in need of a decent meal. Today his complexion was prematurely lined and grey, which added to the effect of a shrivelled old man.

The reason for Harold Whittaker's current morose state was simple enough. He had the worrisome feeling that he was about to engage in verbal conflict or, at the very least, was about to dip his toe into what was likely to become a difficult situation. The temptation, of course, was to let sleeping dogs lie, but that wouldn't do at all, not with the major's business only so very recently acquired. Had he but known it, his distaste at the prospect of confrontation was not so dissimilar to that experienced by his said client, when tackling his sister on a similar matter.

He gave a heartfelt sigh. Oh, how unfortunate it was that it should all come to a head now. For he had thought that the sale of old Turner's land might lead to further business. It was common enough knowledge that Spittlehouse employed a London firm to manage the majority of his affairs, but he had hoped, perhaps foolishly, that the successful conclusion of the Tucker business would bode well for both him and the firm. And now young Archie had to go and put a cat among the pigeons!

He was brought sharply back to the present by a knock on the door. The solicitor jerked himself upright in his seat but, even before he had time to respond, Archie Mayhew had entered the room, drawn up a chair and seated himself upon it in a comfortable, lounging fashion. Harold Whittaker might well have been forgiven for looking with not too kind an eye on this lack of courtesy and assumed familiarity on the part of his employee. However, instead, he did his best to conceal a smile.

'Simmons said you wanted to see me, Uncle Harold,' said Archie, a grin upon his face.

'Miss Simmons,' corrected Harold Whittaker, biting his lip in an attempt not to laugh.

He looked upon his honorary nephew fondly. He would have frowned had any other employee or indeed young man, come to that, displayed such a disrespectful attitude. But with Archie, of course, it was different.

He knew that the manner was assumed, and that beneath that flippant exterior there lurked a well brought up young man. For had he not witnessed the boy grow up before his eyes, and assumed an almost paternal responsibility for him? That wasn't to say that Archie did not give him cause for concern from time to time. It was true that the young man was bright and had shown a genuine aptitude for the law, much to Harold Whittaker's delight. What was not quite so auspicious was the sad fact that this talent showed itself only when Archie applied himself to the task in hand, which unfortunately was not as often as it might have been. It had caused him the odd sleepless night when contemplating the young man's future, as he was wont to do. The problem was …

Harold Whittaker paused a moment to sigh inwardly, before allowing his mind to stray on to unpleasant thoughts. The issue was not the young man's ability, but his very approach to work. Not to put too fine a point on it, he very much feared that Archie was rather idle.

'I suppose you wish to talk to me about Miss Spittlehouse?' Archie said.

'Well …' For a moment Harold Whittaker found himself at a loss for words. He had spent the better part of the morning contemplating how best to broach the subject. Not for a second had it occurred to him that Archie might raise the matter of his own accord. He took a deep breath and said: 'As a matter of fact, I do.'

'I meant to tell you earlier. I knew you would be pleased, Uncle Harold.' Archie beamed at him. 'You've always wanted to see me settled.'

'Good heavens!' exclaimed Harold Whittaker. 'Are you intending to marry the woman?'

'I am,' replied Archie, a touch of coldness to his voice. His smile had not quite disappeared, but hovered rather undecidedly upon his lips. 'I thought you of all people would want to see me marry well.'

'Well, of course I do,' his honorary uncle answered quickly, suddenly finding himself rather inexplicably at a disadvantage. 'But Major Spittlehouse's sister?' He wondered whether he should raise the matter of the woman's age, but on reflection thought better of it. Instead he said: 'Any man would of course be happy to have you as a member of their family, Archie, you can't think I doubt that. But the Spittlehouses? The major's rich, and his sister too. He'll expect her to wed a wealthy man with a private income.' He stared down at his papers. 'I daresay you'll think me rather harsh and unfeeling, but there's also the matter of the firm to consider. Major Spittlehouse's business will be very good for Gribble, Hebborn & Whittaker. His sister is of age and I daresay he can't forbid your marriage, but he can decide not to do business with us.'

'I thought a London firm dealt with most of his legal affairs?'

'They do. But after that bit of business we did for the major regarding Tucker's Wood, well, it stands to reason that's just the start of things. He was testing us to see what our work was like. I don't doubt we'll get the rest of his business in time. For one thing, we're a damn sight less expensive than those London chaps.'

'I doubt if we will,' replied Archie rather dismissively. 'His sort like to use a London firm. The likes of us are all right for buying a bit of land but not much else. I expect that's how he sees old Gribble, Hebborn & Whittaker.'

Harold Whittaker made to protest. He viewed Gribble, Hebborn & Whittaker solicitors in very much the same way he would have done a favoured child. Archie, however, forestalled him. It was possible the young man had grown bored with the way the conversation was turning, or perhaps he had reached the conclusion that to upset his uncle unnecessarily was not quite the sport he had taken it for. Whatever the reason, he held up his hand. The self-assured smile had returned to his face.

'You've no need to worry, Uncle. I was just having my bit of fun. The major's as pleased as punch at the prospect of having me as a brother-in-law.' He threw his head back and laughed at the look of astonishment which had appeared on Harold Whittaker's face.

Chapter Eight

The Earl of Belvedere sat in the library at Sedgwick Court regarding the man seated opposite him with a mixture of nervousness and apprehension. Major Spittlehouse had been a particular friend of his father's, one of only a few, and in the late earl's absence he seemed to radiate a paternal air that made the young man feel like a schoolboy again. Their surroundings did nothing to allay this feeling, for from floor to ceiling rows upon rows of books were arranged in great Georgian mahogany bookcases giving something of the impression of an ornate schoolroom. The two men themselves were seated around a carved oak, octagonal library table, with a ledger book of sorts, and one or two plans spread out open before them, though it was only Cedric who was making a show of consulting them.

The major appeared to have committed the contents to memory; certainly he was giving forth most eloquently and without any recourse to notes. Not that Cedric was paying much attention to what he was saying. As far as he was concerned, the major had summarised the main preparations for Bonfire Night succinctly enough at the very beginning of their conversation a full half hour ago. He had listened diligently enough then, but now he allowed his attention to drift and wander as the major regaled him with the finer details of the arrangements in true military fashion. His attention, however, was unexpectedly drawn back to the speaker by an unexpected change of tone, which had itself been preceded by a clearing of the throat.

'Just one other thing, my lord,' Major Spittlehouse was saying. 'The Committee has received a number of complaints from local landowners. The usual problems with boys trespassing on property and causing damage, breaking branches off trees and trampling crops underfoot, that sort of thing. Looking for sticks for the bonfire, of course, but it won't do. Gives the Committee a bad name. People think we're encouraging them, you see.'

'Well, I don't see that there is very much we can do about it,' said Cedric, stifling his frustration. He had thought the major was about to say something interesting and tried to ignore the stab of disappointment he felt on being proved wrong. 'And really, it only happens once a year. I must say, though, I thought that most of the sticks were taken from my woods and my gamekeeper's used to turning a blind eye. Who has complained, do you know? Jenning for one, I'll be bound, he likes to kick up a stink about everything. Perhaps I could speak to him, try to appease him?'

'As it happens, my lord, my woodland has been trampled,' said Major Spittlehouse rather quietly. He looked a little ill at ease, as if he had been caught off guard by the other's flippancy or the directness of his question.

'Your woodland?' Cedric looked at him in surprise, before comprehension dawned. 'Ah, yes, now you come to mention it, I think I did hear something about you buying old Tucker's bit of wood.'

The major coughed. 'I've asked my gardener to erect a fence around it for next year to keep the little blighters out.'

'I say, is that really necessary?' Cedric was struck by a sudden thought and gave the major a suspicious look. 'Surely you're not telling me that *you* have lodged a complaint?' The major nodded, though to his credit he looked a trifle embarrassed by the admission. 'But you're on the Committee!' Cedric exclaimed.

'It doesn't do to be too lenient with the little rascals, my lord,' said the major, sounding a little indignant. 'Found that out to my cost in the army. Give a man an inch and he's liable to take a mile.'

'Well, we're not at war now, Major,' Cedric said a trifle coldly. 'And we're talking about boys, not grown men. But to complain to a committee of which you yourself are chairman … Good God, man, what were you thinking? Do you want to see an end to the Bonfire Night festivities in the village?'

Major Spittlehouse lowered his head and looked abashed and perhaps a little nettled. Cedric himself averted his gaze for it occurred to him that he had rather let his surprise and annoyance get the better of him; certainly he had the feeling that he had spoken out of turn, rudely even. An awkward silence ensued, which neither man seemed predisposed or able to address. Cedric's own inclination was to end the interview, thank the major for overseeing the arrangements for Guy Fawkes' Night, and bid him a hasty farewell. He was reluctant, however, to part from his father's friend with a feeling of ill will or unpleasantness between them, particularly as he felt that he had been rather tardy in fulfilling his own role on the Committee that year. Naturally of a kindly disposition, he was acutely aware of the major's own discomfort at the situation, which appeared to be increasing with every passing minute.

Cedric reminded himself that Major Spittlehouse had been used to dealing with his father. Last year, due to the tragedies that had occurred at Ashgrove House, Cedric had been too busy with estate matters to participate in the Bonfire Night arrangements. This year their paths had rarely crossed and it occurred to him that the present situation must appear odd to the older man, having to show deference to a man young enough to be his son, but in fact his social superior. It was bound to stir up sad memories too, reminding him of a friendship that had come to an abrupt end following the untimely death of the old earl. The current Earl of Belvedere wondered whether the major would consider him a fair substitute. Certainly they did not have the years of companionship to fall back upon to quell any dispute. He sighed; he had made a mess of things and it was up to him to remedy it.

If that in itself was not sufficient to spur him into action, ever present at the back of his mind loomed the promise that he had made to his wife to raise the subject of Daphne Spittlehouse's marriage. So far, he had not even touched on the matter, having intended to mention it casually, just as the major was about to take his leave. And now perhaps it was too late. Major Spittlehouse was unlikely to be in a receptive frame of mind to permit a relative stranger to intrude on what he would undoubtedly consider to be a private matter, particularly as he had endured something of a sermon from that person already. Still, Cedric was blowed if he'd let Rose down. It might not come naturally to him to pry into the personal affairs of his father's friends, but his wife was depending on him to fulfil her promise to the major's sister.

'You're quite right, my lord,' said Major Spittlehouse rather gruffly, rousing the young man from his musings. 'I daresay I'm making a bit of a mountain out of a mole hill.'

Cedric, taken by surprise said hurriedly: 'Not at all. I spoke rather hastily. You've every right to protect your property as you see fit. It's just a pity that your bit of woodland backs on to the field where the festivities are held. I daresay it's a bit too tempting, boys being boys.'

'It's not just our boys,' said the major hurriedly. 'Some of the lads from the other villages are pilfering the wood. You know what lads are like, they like to compete with each other to see who can build the biggest bonfire. More often than not Sedgwick's won. I don't need to tell you it's something we've always prided ourselves on.' He bent forward, as if to impart some privileged information. 'We've even received reports this year that some of the wood has been stolen from our pyre by a rival gang. No mean feat either, because our mound of sticks had been covered by canvas and the like to keep the rain out. The Committee has had to organise a night watch. Between you and me, my lord, we wouldn't put it past the wretched little blighters to creep in and try and set fire to our bonfire.'

'Indeed?' said Cedric, trying to appear shocked. Memories, however, flooded back to him of his younger days when he himself had been part of a Sedgwick gang of boys pilfering wood from other villages. He consoled himself with the belief that there had been little harm in it and certainly they had not gone so far as setting light to a rival village's bonfire. Feeling the air had been cleared a little, he took a deep breath before he lost his nerve and began to pace the room so that he was not required to look the major in the eye when he commenced his speech.

'Look here, Spittlehouse,' he began, without preamble. 'I daresay you'll think it none of my business and all that, and I feel dashed embarrassed raising it, but…well, your sister came to tea with my wife yesterday and –'

'Came to tea with Lady Belvedere?' Major Spittlehouse was clearly surprised by the fact.

'Yes. Didn't you know?' said Cedric, before rushing on, fearful of another interruption. 'The thing is, she mentioned her young man and how you have rather taken against him –'

'Now, look here,' began Major Spittlehouse angrily, going a deep shade of crimson. 'I don't see what business –'

'You are quite right of course, it is none of my business,' Cedric interrupted hurriedly, having anticipated that the major would make attempts to protest. 'But Miss Spittlehouse extracted a promise from my wife that I would raise the matter with you, put her case, if you will. Whatever you may think of this Archie Mayhew fellow, and I don't doubt that you have your reasons, your sister is obviously in love with him.' He stared at Major Spittlehouse's face, which was now the shade of ripe beetroot. He felt a surge of anger. 'Dash it all, Spittlehouse, your sister is of age. Why not let her make her own decision and marry the fellow?'

Major Spittlehouse visibly bristled. 'Now, look here, my lord, it's very good of you to take an interest in my sister, but the man's little more than an office clerk and –'

'I daresay he might not be quite the man you would have chosen for your sister,' Cedric conceded, 'but I, of all people, can appreciate how it is to love outside one's class. And your sister is quite old enough to know her own mind.'

'I can do nothing to prevent the marriage,' said Major Spittlehouse quietly. 'If Daphne's set on marrying this fellow, there is nothing I can do about it.'

'The terms of your parents' will mean that she is wholly dependent on your generosity regarding her inheritance,' protested Cedric.

Major Spittlehouse stared at him in surprise. 'Oh, you know about that, do you? Well if this damned fellow truly loves Daphne he'll marry her, even if she doesn't have a penny to her name.' He stared at his hands that were resting on the table. 'Happen he'll prove me wrong, and no one will be more glad than me if he does, but I tell you, my lord, he's the worthless type. I've seen plenty of his sort in the army. They want an easy life and they don't mind how they get it. They think nothing of living off a woman until they've bled her dry. It's enough to make your blood boil. Archie Mayhew doesn't care tuppence for my sister. Why, she's almost old enough to be his mother. He'll make her life a misery, mark my words if he doesn't. That sort of fellow always does.'

During the latter part of this speech the major had risen and was now all but trembling with emotion. Cedric stared at him somewhat taken aback for he had not thought the old soldier had it in him to display such feeling. The two stood facing one another. That the major was of the opinion that he had his sister's best interests at heart was clear, yet Cedric remembered that Daphne had made some reference to embezzlement. Whether there was any truth in the assertion, or whether Daphne had only said it out of a malicious bitterness, he did not know. Certainly Rose had told him that Daphne had alluded to the matter in a most casual fashion, as if it were not a thing of any great significance. A part of him was tempted to make mention of it now, for the major was glowering at him with barely concealed anger. Yet he was certain it would only make matters worse and consequently thought better of it. Also, perhaps surprisingly, he felt a sudden touch of compassion for the soldier and his predicament.

'You need to resolve the situation one way or the other, old chap,' Cedric said more kindly, coming over and laying his hand briefly on the other man's shoulder almost as if it were he who were the older of the two men. 'Your sister feels wretched and ill done by. That she spoke about so personal a matter to my wife whom she is hardly acquainted with shows how miserable she must be over it all. I'd advise you to make your peace with her.'

'Yes. Yes, my lord. That's very good advice,' mumbled Major Spittlehouse. He had resumed his seat and now stared into the middle distance, as if the answer to his problems could be found among the many books crowding the shelves. There was, however, no lightening of his mood and his face looked even more strained than before. 'It's knowing what is best, that's the problem. If only that was all ...'

'Is something else the matter, Major?' inquired Cedric gently. 'If you don't mind my saying, you don't seem quite yourself. You look a little off colour.'

'It is just this business with my sister,' sighed Major Spittlehouse. 'Lord knows I don't like making her unhappy even if it is for her own good.'

'But you said ... Never mind. But there is nothing else troubling you?'

'You are very like your father, my lord,' the major smiled sadly. 'You see things that others do not see.'

'Oh?' said Cedric, not having been paid this particular compliment before. 'Well you did say ...'

There was a slight pause and then the major said: 'I admit there is something else troubling me.' He rose again from his seat, but this time started gathering up his papers and putting them back in to a rather battered and well-worn leather briefcase. 'But I won't bore you with it. I shouldn't have mentioned ... It is of a somewhat personal nature. Nothing to do with this Mayhew fellow or my sister, mind. But a matter that I intend to deal with alone. It doesn't concern anyone else, you see.'

He bid a hasty farewell and made for the door before Cedric had a chance to ring the bell.

'If my father were here,' called out Cedric on impulse, 'would you have confided in him?'

'You know, my lord, I just might have done.' The major paused at the door in the act of turning the handle, swung around and chuckled, though there was little mirth in his laughter.

'I know I am not my father …' began Cedric, but the major had raised his hand for him to stop what he was saying and he faltered, his unfinished sentence drifting unuttered in the air.

'It's very kind of you I am sure, my lord, but as you say, you are not your father. I'm not holding that against you, mind, but you have not a few years of friendship on which to base my character and, if you don't mind my saying, you are too young. You have very little experience of life.'

'Does that matter so very much?' cried Cedric, somewhat indignant about the sweeping assumption the major was making regarding his character.

'Yes, it does. You will judge me too harshly for my sins, you see, my lord. And heaven knows I would rather do anything than burden such a young soul with the secret that I have carried around with me for years.'

'But –'

'Good day to you, my lord.'

With that, Major Spittlehouse was gone, leaving the door ajar and Cedric to do nothing but stare after him.

Chapter Nine

'The major still up with his nibs?' enquired Masters, wandering aimlessly into the basement kitchen and rubbing his eyes with the back of his hand. His clothes, his wife noticed with irritation, were creased and crumpled, giving him something of a dishevelled appearance.

'You've had a nap, I see,' said Mrs Masters with a scornful look, her hands perched on either side of her ample hips. 'You'd better give those clothes a quick press before the major sees you, and no wonder those eyes of yours are puffy for, unless I'm mistaken, there's the smell of whisky on your breath, Jack Masters.'

'Oh, don't give on so, woman,' said the manservant, though the abruptness of his words was softened somewhat by being uttered with affection and a twinkle of the eye. 'At his beck and call night and day, I am, as well you know. If I take a moment to rest my eyes when I get the chance, what of it?'

'There are them here that have to work their fingers to the bone whether the major is here or not,' grumbled Mrs Masters. 'The dinner won't cook itself.'

'Well, I'm here now, and no doubt you've got a list of things for me to do as long as your arm to keep me busy,' said her husband, straightening his clothes with the aid of a small piece of mirror attached to the wall on one side of the fireplace. 'So the major's still holed up with his lordship, is he?'

'As far as I know; least he's not returned,' said his wife, stirring a sauce vigorously in a saucepan on the stove. Satisfied that there were no lumps, and that the liquid would not burn or spoil, she turned around and stared at him. 'Well, Jack Masters, while you were busy sleeping in the land of Nod, we had a visitor.'

'Oh?' A look of anxiety passed across her husband's face. 'I didn't hear the doorbell.' A sudden thought struck him. 'Don't tell me you opened the door, not dressed in your pinny?' He stared with distaste at the garment in question, uncomfortably aware that it was liberally decorated with a smattering of flour.

'Course I didn't,' said his wife. 'Do you think I'd have left you sleeping in your bed when there was someone at the door? No, I'd have thrown a jug of water over you if need be.' She came a step or two towards him, lowering her voice as she did so. 'When I said a visitor, I meant as how it was a secret one, one who didn't want to be seen.'

'You're not saying there's been another one of those damned letters?' demanded her husband.

Mrs Masters nodded. 'Found it in the passage I did, same as last time. I've propped it there on the mantelpiece, behind the candlestick. You can take it in to the major when he gets back.'

'If it's what I think it is, I've a good mind to throw it on to the fire and be done with it,' said her husband bitterly.

Mrs Masters gave him a look and hurriedly took the envelope from the mantelpiece, clutching it to her bosom as if she feared for its fate.

'You wouldn't dare.'

'Wouldn't I?' said her husband. 'Mol, you should have seen his face. I've been thinking and thinking about that first letter and the more I think about it the more I don't like it. Something's not right and I mean to find out what it's all about.'

'You'd do better to keep your great nose out of it, Jack,' admonished his wife, though he noticed that she now held the letter slightly away from her as if she half shared his misgivings. 'It's no business of ours what this letter's about.'

She was holding the envelope by one corner when her husband decided to make his move. With one swift movement, he had torn it from her grasp. Taken unawares, his wife could only utter a surprised exclamation as he ran to the stove. The kettle was boiling merrily, for it had been Mrs Masters' intention to make a pot of tea. Thrusting a flannel over the handle, the manservant removed it from the stove and held the envelope above the spout.

'You're never going to steam that letter open?' exclaimed Mrs Masters. 'Jack, how could you? Whatever would the major say if he knew you was reading his private letters?'

'He'll never know unless you let on,' replied her husband rather dismissively. 'I've told you before, there's something not quite right about all this. And besides, I don't like the thought of people creeping about the garden, spying on us when our backs are turned.'

'Don't,' cried Mrs Masters with a shudder, as if she felt a sudden chill.

'There we are,' said Masters, a note of satisfaction in his voice. 'It's come clean away. Wasn't stuck down proper, if you ask me. Now, let's see what this letter says, shall we?'

Rather gingerly, he removed the letter from the envelope. It consisted of a single sheet of paper folded in half. He threw a quick glance at the door, as if he feared the major might appear in the doorway and catch him in the act of reading his personal correspondence. This was highly unlikely as the major seldom ventured to the basement, which he considered to be his servants' domain. Reassuring himself that the major was not standing there, Masters unfolded the paper, surprised to find that he was trembling slightly in anticipation of its contents.

Initially he felt a stab of disappointment, for the letter was very brief, one sentence at the most. He read the words and at first they made no sense at all; he could not understand their meaning. It was almost as if he were a child again, learning to read. One word above all others seemed to jump out at him. Yet he could hardly comprehend it, for it was too ludicrous for such a word to be written in a letter to the major. He stared at the letter stupidly, reading the sentence to himself again and again under his breath, his eyes growing larger with every recital until the meaning became clear.

'What is it?' cried his wife. 'What does it say?'

For all her admonishment, she had been studying her husband's face closely, trying to ascertain the contents of the letter from his reaction to reading it. With something akin to alarm, she had witnessed his mouth fall open and the colour disappear from his cheeks.

'Nothing,' said her husband abruptly, screwing up the letter in his hand so that it resembled only a scrunched up ball. 'Nothing at all.' And with that he flung it into the fire. He did not glance at his wife even briefly. Instead, he turned on his heel and left the room. Mrs Masters was left standing open mouthed, staring at her husband's retreating back. When the door slammed to behind him, she allowed her eyes to drift back to the fire and watched with fascination as the flames licked and curled around the letter, blackening its edges and shrivelling it up until it matched her husband's words and became nothing at all.

Daphne Spittlehouse stared in to the middle distance. A book lay open on the table in front of her, yet she had barely glanced at it; certainly she did not recollect having turned a page. If someone had cared to ask her, she would not have been able to say how long she had been sitting in that same position. With a start, however, she was returned sharply to the present by the sound of a rubber date stamp in use, its noise magnified in the quietness of the otherwise silent room. She looked up sharply and met the curious gaze of Miss Warren, who was at that very moment administering the date stamp, recording the date of return in a book being withdrawn by a youth.

The major's sister was sitting in a small branch library in Bichester, a purpose-built structure of fairly modest proportions, consisting of one large room, one half of which had been given over to a reading room of sorts, and the other dedicated to the main library. The latter consisted of row upon row of books on a multitude of subjects, with apparently little thought given to subject matter, for books on history rubbed shoulders quite happily with romantic novels and books on medicine, much to the chagrin of Miss Warren, the new librarian, who was trying desperately to instigate a proper system. On her arrival it had become patently clear that the previous incumbent had returned the books willy-nilly to the shelves as the mood had taken her, and she had wondered how anyone had managed to find the book they were seeking or, perhaps more surprisingly, why there had been so few complaints. Miss Warren was resolved to rectify the position, though it was a mammoth task.

Daphne put her hand up to the bridge of her nose to shield her face from the librarian's inquisitive gaze. She wished the library did not boast a central issue desk, for it enabled Miss Warren to survey every part of her kingdom and, unlike her predecessor, to enforce a rigid silence, so that every sigh or rustle of paper was amplified, and could be quashed with one reproving glare.

She had come in to the library to sit and contemplate as she so often did. She could not think at Green Gables, for she found the house stifling with her brother's presence and her thoughts there became muddled. Few of her acquaintance visited the branch library, so there was little fear of being interrupted or disturbed. It was here, hidden and obscured among predominantly the working classes, that she could surrender to her daydreams, could imagine the life she would have with Archie, stretching out long and inviting before her; a happy existence, populated by laughter and children. Linus did not, of course, feature in this fantasy. She doubted whether her brother would be anything more than a memory best forgotten.

She looked up to find that the new librarian was still staring at her. Blow the woman, why must she gaze at her so intently? Daphne put a hand instinctively to her face and wondered whether her make-up was smudged or there was a smear of ink upon her nose to justify such scrutiny. Purposefully she turned her back on Miss Warren and let her eyes drift towards the page of her book. Soon, however, she became distracted, the words becoming hazy and out of focus so that she could not read them, even had she tried. Linus was going to tell Archie about their parents' will. He had not said as much, but the way he had asked the question … It had caught her off guard and she had behaved like a silly little fool, betraying her emotions and showing her fear. Because she was afraid; there was no escaping the fact. She did not doubt for a moment that Archie loved her, but she was not so deluded as to believe that her family's wealth did not add to her attractiveness in his eyes. She stifled a sob. Why must Linus always ruin everything? Why, every time she found the possibility of happiness, when it was within her grasp, must he intervene and turn everything to dust and ashes?

She hated him; she could not escape the fact. She despised him; it really was as simple as that. That awful pompous attitude of his, the way he regarded her and spoke to her in that patronising manner, as if he were still on the battlefield and she were a man under his command. The book trembled in her hand. She could not lose Archie. There had been others but they had disappeared, frightened away by Linus and her overbearing family. Archie, she felt sure, was her last chance of happiness. As the book shook, a steely determination came into her eyes. She would not lose him. She was damned if she would stand aside and watch Linus ruin everything.

She looked up. That wretched woman was still giving her surreptitious little glances. She was tempted to act in a furtive manner herself. In fact, it had been her intention to return her book to one of the shelves unobserved. She had even considered slipping it inside another book to read, but had thought better of it, for fear of drawing too much attention to herself. Instead, she had obscured the cover by holding the book open flat. With an act of sudden temper and defiance, she slammed it shut, causing Miss Warren to glare at her and tut. Daphne, a malicious smile upon her face, dropped the book with a clatter on to the table. She fancied there was not a man, woman or child that did not turn around to look at her as she made her exit, so loud had the noise been in the otherwise silent room.

Miss Warren herself scurried over to the table and picked up the offending book, glancing at the cover as she did so. The librarian's eyes grew wide as she read the title. '*The Household Book of Everyday Poisons*'.

'You didn't?' said Rose, throwing back her head and laughing. They were sipping pre-dinner cocktails in the drawing room at Sedgwick Court. Cedric had just finished regaling her with an account of what had transpired between himself and the major that afternoon.

'Darling, please don't laugh,' he cried, his brow furrowed. His face had become flushed at the recollection, not helped by his wife's giggles. 'I feel a dashed fool, I can tell you, demanding that he tell me what was on his mind. Whatever possessed me to be so impertinent? First I scolded him for complaining to the Committee over the village lads running amok round that blessed wood of his, and then I asked him to confide his troubles to me as if I were his closest friend.'

'I am sure he appreciated it, your offer of help, I mean,' said Rose, squeezing his hand affectionately. 'And, as regards his wood ... well it does seem rather odd doesn't it, to complain. He's lived in Sedgwick for some years, hasn't he? He must know what the village boys are like leading up to Guy Fawkes' Night?'

'How they go about collecting sticks for the pyre each year and don't care too much on whose land they trample?' said Cedric. 'Well, of course.'

'Though I suppose he wasn't really affected by their activities before,' mused Rose. 'He only acquired his piece of woodland recently, didn't he?' Her husband nodded. 'Of course, it doesn't help that it backs on to the piece of wasteland on which the bonfire is built.'

'Yes,' Cedric smiled. 'I say, darling, it's all rather odd, his buying that piece of wood like he did. I don't know why he should want it. Old Tucker has let it go a bit to seed. And, if one listens to village gossip, the major paid well over the odds for it.'

'Did he?' said Rose, only a little curious.

Manning had just appeared at the door to inform them that dinner was served and her thoughts had drifted to the menu she had agreed that day with Mrs Broughton. It had seemed to her a strange affair, sitting down with the cook to discuss the meal she was to eat that evening with her husband. Similarly, it seemed rather odd now sitting down to dinner in full evening dress when they were dining alone. She supposed that it would feel different when they were hosting house parties and Sedgwick Court was filled with guests. Then it would seem appropriate to dress for dinner and spend time deliberating over elaborate menus conjured up by a diligent staff.

'Why are you laughing?' inquired Cedric, taking his seat at the table.

'I was just wondering if you had ever dined at an ABC,' replied his wife laughing, staring at her array of cutlery. 'But seriously, Cedric darling, you mustn't worry about the major. I'm certain he'll understand that we were placed in a very difficult position. If anyone is at fault it is his sister.'

'I felt dashed embarrassed, I can tell you, enquiring about his feelings for his sister's young man. If I hadn't been his host and a man of some consequence, I think he would have told me to go to the devil.'

'Well, at least we can say that we have fulfilled my promise to his sister. When I next encounter Miss Spittlehouse I can say as much if she asks. Now, let's not think any more about it,' said Rose, regarding the rather delicious looking soup that a footman had just placed before her. She was reminded that she had an appetite and, as she took her first mouthful, it occurred to her that they had both wasted too much time discussing the Spittlehouses. Her husband, however, still appeared preoccupied with them.

'I must say, I wish I knew what was worrying the old chap,' persisted Cedric. 'He was very troubled about something.' He sighed. 'If I had been my father, I think he would have told me what was wrong. I have this nagging feeling that it was something quite awful. I told you what he said, didn't I?'

'Yes, you did,' said Rose.

She experienced a sudden feeling of tenderness towards her husband. That he should care so deeply about what was ailing his father's old friend moved her. The late Earl of Belvedere had been something of a reclusive figure, whom she realised only now her husband had rather idolised. The fact that Major Spittlehouse had been one of only a small handful of his friends, meant that the man had something of a revered quality in her husband's eyes. Because of this, she could see that Cedric felt he had an obligation to help the major as best he could, if only for his father's sake.

'You also told me that Major Spittlehouse intended to deal with whatever was troubling him himself,' said Rose. 'From what you have told me of his character, he strikes me as a man of action once he has made up his mind to do something. I predict that whatever is worrying him now will be resolved in the next few days.'

Chapter Ten

It was four o'clock in the morning according to the clock beside the washstand. Masters, heavy-headed but fully awake, groaned inwardly. He had not had a wink of sleep. Or certainly that was his impression, for he was vaguely aware that he had tossed and turned uncomfortably among the sheets and blankets and that slumber, forever at the edges of his consciousness, had nevertheless evaded him. It had been the same the previous night and he had a familiar sinking feeling, knowing that he would start the day tired and irritable. At intervals during the night, he had disturbed the sleep of his wife, who had grunted and groaned in annoyance, but had not seemingly woken. Laying back on the bed, his head on the pillow, his eyes fixed staring up at the ceiling, he moved not a muscle. Only his mind remained alert, flicking from one thing to another in its current restive state.

A faint sound like a sigh or a stifled snore made him turn and regard the sleeping form of his wife. Her well-worn, familiar face greeted him, with the hair now greying at the temples and the fleshy cheeks that had lost their youthful definition. The sleep of the just, he thought with a sudden stab of tenderness. He brushed a strand of hair away from her face and resumed his former position, though now his gaze was focused on the wall in front of him rather than the ceiling above. Perhaps it was fitting that sleep escaped him, he thought bitterly to himself, for had he not behaved in a sneaky and devious fashion? If he had not opened that blasted letter and read the words that had never been intended for his eyes, would he not this very moment be sleeping in blissful ignorance? His mind would not be troubled as it was now, trying to fathom the meaning behind those hateful, scribbled words.

He had acted instinctively in destroying that wretched letter, afraid that his wife would try to snatch it from him and read its contents. For he could see in her eyes that she had been troubled by the expression on his face. He never could keep anything from her. Malicious lies, that's what they'd written in that letter. No person in his sober mind could think anything else. At least that had been his first thought. It was only after his second sleepless night that he was conscious of a nagging feeling at the back of his mind. What motivation could anyone have for making such wild and ludicrous allegations? And the furtive and secretive manner in which the letters themselves had been delivered. Surely it did not make any sense unless there was, at the very least, a grain of truth to the accusation …

What would people say if they knew the village harboured a murderer in its midst?

Barely a sentence, but the content so frightful that the words were ingrained in his memory, as if they had been written there. He thought of them each morning, and then last thing at night; it was as if the note were forever in his hand, demanding to be read. Endeavour as he might, he could arrive at no plausible explanation for why anyone should seek to accuse a man of such high standing as Major Spittlehouse of such a crime. His employer was an upright and honourable fellow if ever a man was; did he not know that better than anyone? For had he not been in his employ for nigh on thirty years? And you didn't do that without getting to know a person, all his little foibles and eccentricities. He had been there with him on the battlefield, experienced the horror and brutality of life in the trenches, had witnessed other men fall and crumble, but not the major. There he had come into his own and his character had flourished. No, in his humble opinion, you couldn't get a better man than the major, and he'd say as much to anyone who cared to inquire. Grant you, of course, the man could be a little fussy and pedantic at times but that was only fitting due to his having led a regimented life; he wanted things done just right, all ship-shape and Bristol fashion as the saying went, and happen the world would be a better place if more followed his example.

A murmur from his wife reminded him that he said as much to Mol when she was wont to complain about their employer's peculiarities and her husband's devotion to him. It was a pity there weren't more like him, that's what he always said to her, though she might roll her eyes and give him that look of hers as much as to say that she knew he thought more of that major of his than he did of her, his own wife.

He sat up with a start. The war … He always tried not to let his thoughts drift back to the battlefield. It brought back too many painful memories long buried, flashes of events that had occurred and men he had known, but were now gone. He might be laying the table for dinner and suddenly an image would appear unbidden before his eyes, the face of a fallen comrade that he had quite forgotten. Or the shriek of a seagull would take him back and he would recall the cries of the wounded. Both events, when they happened to occur, creeping up on him as they were wont to do, taking him unawares, would leave him shaken and trembling. He was reminded above all else of the seeming futility of it all; the Country had lost a whole generation of men, some little more than boys. The lucky ones, of whom he was surely one, had not come back unscathed. To make matters worse, they had not returned to a land fit for heroes to live in, whatever Lloyd George had promised. Thirteen years after the war had ended, and there was still poverty and inequality in equal measure. But the major ... he was one of the good ones. He had stood shoulder to shoulder with his men as they faced the onslaught; not for him the life of safety accorded to those of higher rank sitting far away in their ivory towers, formulating attacks that would result in multiple casualties.

However, that was not to say that someone might not hold Major Spittlehouse accountable for the loss of a loved one. For the major had led his men into battle and grief made people act in irrational ways. Didn't he, Masters, know that well enough from bitter experience? For he had witnessed many a poor blighter driven half mad with sorrow. It was this sudden thought that had made him sit up abruptly. It was, he felt sure, the explanation for the letters. Someone blamed Major Spittlehouse for the death of a loved one in the war. Someone, and more likely than not a woman he thought, for poison pen letters were oft as not a woman's sport, was seeking to blame the major for the loss of a husband, a son, a father or a brother perhaps.

He felt a sudden lifting of the spirits. Major Spittlehouse was not a murderer. He had only been following orders and done what his Country had expected of him. Masters breathed a sigh of relief. Now he knew the heart of the matter, he could do something about it. That, he realised now, was what had been worrying him. And it would be easy enough. He'd speak to this writer of the poison pen letters, if he had to lie in wait for her by the garden gate! He would tell her how it had been, how the major was a decent sort who'd done his best for his men in the most awful of circumstances. Why, he might even have known the fellow to whom the poor woman was related, perhaps he'd been a close chum and then the two of them could commiserate and reminisce a little. He could put the poor soul's mind at rest, bring her a bit of comfort like. He liked the idea of that, doing his bit. And it would put a stop to those letters. He didn't want the major to receive any more of them damned letters. He had seen only too well how the colour had drained from his face and he'd trembled when he'd read the first one. Goodness knows what it had been doing to his insides.

The manservant settled his head on his pillow and drifted off into a contented sleep. It was true that he was awoken barely two hours later by his wife shaking him in an irritable mood to tell him that he'd overslept and he'd best get cracking, that his head throbbed and his eyes ached, but at least his mood was lightened. For he now knew what he must do, and he was determined to put his plan in to action that very day.

'Linus,' Daphne sailed into Major Spittlehouse's study without pause or hesitation and launched into the subject foremost in her mind without preamble, 'Masters says you met with Lord Belvedere the day before yesterday.' She gave him a reproachful look. 'You never said.'

'You never asked,' replied her brother rather coldly, drawing himself up to receive the inevitable onslaught. Secretly he cursed, bitterly resenting his sister interrupting him in the midst of his reading of *The Times*. It was a daily ritual of his and one he enjoyed, the only time during the day when he requested not to be disturbed. He sighed. Really, was it too much to ask? And today he was particularly riled, for Daphne had very pointedly been avoiding his company since their last painful discussion. She had claimed headaches and tiredness and taken her meals in her room. Not that it had prevented her journeying to Bichester, he'd noted.

'Linus, do put your paper down. Don't bury your head in its pages and pretend I'm not here,' implored Daphne. She was tempted to make a grab for the newspaper and tear it from his hands, but thought better of it. Instead, she said: 'I wish to speak with you.'

'About my meeting with the Earl of Belvedere?' asked her brother, feigning surprise. 'I didn't think you thought very much of our local gentry. And really, my dear, we were just discussing the arrangements for the Guy Fawkes' festivities.' He lowered his newspaper to meet her gaze.

'I must say, you've never shown much interest in Bonfire Night before. Not, of course, that I'm not delighted. It will do you good to involve yourself more in village events and –'

'Oh, do shut up, Linus. I do believe you are being purposefully infuriating.' Daphne flung herself unceremoniously down on to a convenient chair.

'Daphne –' her brother began, clearly taken aback.

'Look here, Linus, I don't care a damn about your little bonfire or which child has made the best guy or the order of the fireworks or anything like that. I have much better things with which to occupy my time –'

'Archie Mayhew, for instance?' The words cut through the air like a sword, rendering both brother and sister silent. Certainly, the major noted that some of the fight had left Daphne as, with shoulders hunched, she sank back in to the fabric of the chair. He felt a pang of compassion mixed with guilt, which he quickly brushed away. It would not do to become sentimental.

'Linus, please …' said Daphne so quietly that the words were barely audible.

'It's no use, Daphne, my mind is quite made up. I have no wish to go over old ground. You know my views on the matter.'

'Lady Belvedere thought you were being awfully unfair,' Daphne said rather sulkily, her bottom lip jutting out in such a manner as to remind the major of a petulant child.

'Did she indeed?' Major Spittlehouse felt the colour rush to his face as he imagined the conversation between the two women, in particular the unsavoury picture of himself that Daphne had no doubt painted. He put aside the newspaper with obvious reluctance, rose from his chair and began to pace the room. He felt restless, yet the activity also provided him with an excuse not to look at his sister's wretched face, the eyes brimming with unshed tears nor, conversely, for her to bear witness to his crimson cheeks. After a minute or two, when he felt his anger had abated and his complexion had returned to its usual hue, he turned to face her, and when he spoke his voice was soft. 'Really, Daphne, whatever possessed you to try and get Lord and Lady Belvedere to fight your cause? What were you thinking?'

'I don't suppose I was thinking,' said Daphne dully, the significance of his words not fully registering in her consciousness until a few moments later when she leapt up from her seat in barely concealed excitement. 'So he did say something? Oh, I was afraid he wouldn't. I thought she was just pretending to be kind, saying that she would ask him, but not really meaning to.'

'Oh, he said something about it all right,' said her brother, some of the colour returning to his cheeks. 'And dashed embarrassing it was for the both of us, I can tell you. He knew full well it was none of his business. If he hadn't promised his wife … well, never mind. All water under the bridge now. But I won't have you discussing our affairs, Daphne, and certainly not with Lord and Lady Belvedere.'

'I thought she'd understand,' Daphne said, more to herself than to her brother. She had retreated again to the chair and seemed to curl up in its depths and looked as if she wished for nothing more than to go to sleep. 'Lady Lavinia was very against their marriage, you see. She didn't want her brother to marry beneath him. But now of course they are the best of friends.'

Major Spittlehouse remained quiet. In truth, he did not know quite what to say. He didn't feel anger toward his sister, only a sense of sadness tinged with pity, though his cheeks still flushed with the embarrassment he had felt when the young earl had first raised the subject of Archie Mayhew.

'First there was Bunny,' Daphne continued, and gave a malicious little smile when she saw her brother wince, 'and Father and Mother frightened him away. Did you know that he didn't even bid me farewell? Then there was Harold. At least he had the decency to call off our engagement. I don't know what you said to him, Linus, or rather I do. You may rest assured that I told Lady Belvedere all about it. And now Archie …'

Again she was up on her feet, her hands clenched. The listless, despondent pose had vanished to be replaced by a vibrant, agitated woman, who caught her brother by the lapel. 'I won't let you ruin everything, not this time. I won't give him up, Linus, I won't.'

She let go her grasp and turned away, shielding her face with her hand from her brother's gaze. She wouldn't look at him, but Major Spittlehouse looked at her. He wondered whether she was weeping or regretting her outburst. On closer examination, however, her posture now appeared composed, her manner resolute. He feared that behind her hand he would see not tears but a look of steely determination. He wondered how it was possible for one person's emotions to fluctuate at such an alarming rate. It was one of the reasons he had never known quite how to handle her; one minute his sister could be in the pit of despair, the next filled with exuberance.

He stood there watching her, all the while praying that she would not make good her promise. Fear and honour; they were such conflicting emotions he thought. They could drive a man to do different things, the coward to run away, the brave man to stand his ground. In this particular case however, he thought, they were intertwined; the way forward was all too clear.

Chapter Eleven

The fifth of November dawned bright and sunny on Sedgwick, belying the fact that in keeping with the time of year it was cold and chilly outside. Edna, who had just drawn back the curtains, observed these facts.

'But at least it's not raining,' she said, as much to herself as to anyone else.

Lady Belvedere, just returned from her morning bath, caught her words and stared out of the window, before making a show of looking at the clothes that Edna had laid out carefully on the bed for her to inspect.

'I can't abide it being wet on Bonfire Night,' Edna was saying. 'There's nothing so miserable as standing around a bonfire that won't light, your clothes all dripping wet and being cold to the bone. Something wicked it is, and no one thinks they can go home, not without seeing the bonfire blazing and the sky lit up with fireworks.'

'Yes, it is wretched,' agreed Rose with feeling, recalling many an occasion when she had experienced something similar. 'But I don't think that will trouble us this evening. It'll just be a bit cold until the bonfire's lit and then we can all huddle around it and get warm.'

'And then we'll be too hot and have the smoke blow in our faces and have to be careful of the sparks,' laughed Edna. 'I sometimes wonder why we still do it, when we're all grown up, like, and should know better. Still, the children like it well enough and I suppose it's tradition.' She glanced at the clothes laid out on the bed. 'Now then, m'lady,' she said adopting her best voice, 'I thought your blue tweed suit would do well enough worn under your wool crepe coat. That should keep you warm and cosy like; you don't want to wear one of your furs, the smoke would cling to it something rotten; it would be the devil to get rid of the smell.'

'You're quite right,' agreed Rose. 'Tweed and wool should do very well.'

'And you can wear your royal blue felt cloche, the one with the black ostrich feather,' said Edna with satisfaction. 'That will set it off something smashing.'

'Oh, Edna,' said Rose, feeling slightly giddy, 'do you realise this is my first proper, official engagement as Lord Belvedere's wife?' She took a deep breath. '"The new countess judges the competition of effigies at the Sedgwick Bonfire festivities and gives out the prizes."' She laughed. 'How very silly it all sounds, doesn't it? But I will admit to being a little nervous. I can't tell you how glad I am that you are here to help me with my wardrobe.'

'I'm pleased to be here too, miss,' said Edna shyly. 'And I can't tell you how good it is to have my arms up to the elbows in fine silks and satins instead of vegetable peelings and dirty water, to say nothing of not having to wear a mop cap. Ever so grand I feel, being what they call an upper servant and not one of those that's holed up in the kitchen and expected to wait on the other staff.'

Rose laughed at the younger girl's enthusiasm and an image came to her of the first time she had set eyes on Edna in the vegetable garden at Ashgrove House. She was reminded that Edna had then occupied the lowly position of scullery maid and had been crying her eyes out fearing the wrath of the cook.

'A lot of water has flowed under the bridge since we first met one another,' said Rose reflectively.

'That it has, m'lady,' said Edna, 'though I always said as how you'd be a countess one day. And now here's me your lady's maid. And Miss Denning has arranged for me to go on a course next week. 'The Art of Hairdressing', it's called. I'll be able to do your hair ever so grand after.'

'I am sure you will,' said Rose, passing her fingers through her curls and fervently hoping that Edna would not insist in future on arranging her hair in too elaborate a style. 'But today my hair will be mostly covered by my hat. And whatever our various misgivings about the weather and bonfires, I daresay we will enjoy this evening's festivities.'

It was only later, looking back, that she wondered if there had been a break in the sunshine, whether a cloud had covered the sun for one brief moment as if to forewarn of the impending catastrophe.

Harold Whittaker took a deep breath and let his hand hover rather indecisively above the black Bakelite telephone perched on the edge of his desk. He permitted his fingers to flutter in the air for a moment, as if caught in a breeze, before he withdrew his hand, resting it on the desk before him. He closed his eyes and sighed, patently aware that he lacked the moral courage to ascertain the truth. Of course, he could quite easily argue that his reservations were natural and might be expected from anyone suddenly finding themselves in his rather delicate position. After all, Major Spittlehouse was a wealthy client, one that he had courted. It was, therefore, hardly surprising if he found the prospect of him becoming something close to a relative slightly daunting.

But that was not it, or at least not all, the solicitor admitted rather reluctantly to himself, though he might pretend it to be otherwise. What was the point of deluding himself, asserting that the cause of his recent sleepless nights and listlessness was anything other than doubt and panic in equal measure? Since the moment Archie had first announced that he intended to marry the Spittlehouse woman, the older man had found himself restless. No good could come of it, he had felt certain. And, if that was not enough, he questioned the very truthfulness of Archie's assertion that he had the major's endorsement. Yet the boy had uttered the words with such delightful sincerity and conviction that he had felt wretched in doubting him. Archie was a dear boy; no one could dispute that. Surely he was not some consummate liar? However, the engagement had not yet been given out, and the major had made no reference to it when they had chanced to meet at the cocktail party of a common acquaintance. What could have been more natural than that one or other of them might have alluded to it? Yet both had remained resolutely silent on the matter. It was only now, on reflection, that Harold Whittaker wondered whether both had felt awkward, embarrassed even. Was the major, he wondered, expecting him to raise the subject? Perhaps it was his duty to do so, for he was as good as Archie's closest relative, if not by blood, then by the role that he had played in the boy's life following his father's death. He had almost convinced himself of the fact a few minutes ago when his fingers had reached out to grasp the telephone receiver. Yet in that final moment he had stayed his hand as doubt had again crept in.

Major Spittlehouse could not be in favour of Archie for a brother-in-law. It was not just the difference in their social positions that made the boy an unsuitable choice. In Harold Whittaker's humble opinion, Daphne Spittlehouse had little to offer a young man other than material wealth. She lacked both beauty and personality, so much so that she had made so vague an impression on him that he had had to rack his brain to remember whether he had ever been formally introduced to her or not. Archie, with his charm, youth and good looks, could surely not be satisfied with such an insipid woman. Her appeal, if indeed she had any, lay purely in her purse.

He did not blame the young man for wishing to marry well in the financial sense, but to choose Daphne Spittlehouse for a bride! Did it not betray a cold ruthlessness or a shocking indifference? To marry a woman so much older than himself for monetary purposes, with whom he could have little in common and would soon become bored … Major Spittlehouse was very likely of the same opinion. He would certainly want to ensure his sister's ongoing happiness and would dissuade an unsatisfactory suitor, whose motives for marriage were questionable. The marriage, if it went ahead, would be a failure. Both parties in time would become discontent and miserable. Goodness knows he didn't want Archie to be unhappy, any more than he did the poor woman. Naturally, that wasn't to say that the money she might bring in to the business would not be very welcome, because of course it would. And they might be able to attract a better class of clientele. The work the firm would be required to do might become more profitable and interesting. Really, he was thinking more of Archie's future than his own …

It was then that fear had raised its ugly head. It might very well be tempting to encourage the union of these two people for purely business reasons, but Harold Whittaker acknowledged that, for his own very selfish personal motive, the marriage must not proceed. Major Spittlehouse should not be given an opportunity to invest in the firm, though the other partners, old Mr Gribble and sprightly Mr Hebborn, would undoubtedly welcome the gesture with open arms. But for Harold Whittaker it would spell disaster. He knew the major well enough to know that Major Spittlehouse would not permit his sister to enter into a business transaction without first having a thorough perusal of the books. And then of course the transgression, or what he himself termed the little irregularity, would come to light. It went without saying that he had meant to put the money back before now, really he had, but then there had been that business with the motor car being damaged beyond repair and his wife's debts at bridge. He had given her quite a talking to; how could anyone owe so much playing such an innocuous little game as bridge? But of course the losses had to be repaid and promptly too because people did talk. A firm of solicitors, and one that was so much a part of the establishment of Bichester as Gribble, Hebborn & Whittaker, could not countenance any scandal; it must be perceived as being beyond reproach. No, it would not do if people thought the Whittakers could not pay their dues. It would lower their social standing and adversely affect business, because who would want to employ a firm of solicitors which had the whiff of desperation or poverty associated with one of its partners?

Harold Whittaker gave an involuntary start. He might be accused of theft, when of course he had meant to do no such thing. Old Gribble would give him the benefit of the doubt, Hebborn might be swayed either way, but Major Spittlehouse he knew to be an upright man with sober integrity. If he detected something rotten in the state of Gribble, Hebborn & Whittaker, he was certain to want to get to the bottom of it. He was likely as not to be as determinedly persistent at getting to the truth as a dog with a bone. Harold Whittaker gave a little shudder. He might be sent to prison, though surely it would not come to that. Gribble would want to keep things quiet, though Hebborn might be quite happy to sing it from the steeple tower; the man had never much liked being regarded by the others as the junior partner. At the very least, he would lose his position in the firm and in Bichester society. He would be disgraced and sneered at. And Archie … what would Archie think of him? And his wife of course. She would not want to stay and share in his humiliation. Likely as not she would go to her sister's and not come back.

Harold Whittaker sniffed. It sounded suspiciously to his own ears as if he were trying to stifle a sob. He must pull himself together, for this would not do. Miss Simmons might any moment tap on his door and walk in; young Archie would not even pause to knock. He dabbed rather ineffectually at his eyes with his handkerchief and blew his nose. The act of doing something, however common place and mundane, rather than letting his thoughts run riot, helped lift his spirits sufficiently for him to regain his equanimity. It was no use worrying and speculating over something that had not yet come to pass; indeed, it might never come to fruition. Happen as not Archie had been exaggerating about his relationship with Miss Spittlehouse. Likely as not he had been teasing his uncle and seeking a reaction. It was very wrong of the boy, but then there was a sense of mischief about him that the solicitor and his wife had always found endearing. Either way, before he considered which course of action was open to him, it would be as well to find out the true lay of the land. On no account must he surrender to fear or panic, which of course was easier said than done, or all would be lost.

He scratched the side of his head absentmindedly, an outward sign that his brain was working relentlessly. If only he knew it, it was a mannerism which often reduced Archie to a fit of the giggles. Telephoning the major, Harold Whittaker decided on reflection, would not be a good idea. It was too formal and official and might draw attention to things that were best left well alone. He required another chance meeting, where he could raise the matter tentatively in conversation. Harold Whittaker stood up and began to pace the room. Now that he had made up his mind what to do, he was impatient, wishing it to be done and over with. He could not afford the luxury of waiting for a suitable occasion to arise. It might be weeks before it did and he felt he could not wait another hour to know his fate. He must orchestrate something. Now, how to go about it, that was the thing …

He was roused abruptly from his musings by a knock on his door.

'Come in,' he croaked in a voice that bore little resemblance to his own. Miss Simmons entered rather hesitantly he thought, as if she had bad news to impart or feared that she was disturbing him.

'Mr Whittaker, I do hope you don't mind my asking,' she began rather quietly, 'and it really isn't something I'd usually do, but would you have any objection to our closing half an hour early this evening?' She saw her employer's look of surprise and hurried on. 'What with it being Guy Fawke's Night, I mean. One or two of the younger staff, and Mr Mayhew in particular, are anxious to go to the bonfire festivities at Sedgwick. I have never been myself, but I understand they are rather grand, and apparently the roads to the village are not very good. Mr Mayhew tells me that the traffic will be something awful later on, to use his words, and, well … I thought I would ask …'

Miss Simmons' sentence had faltered to an abrupt stop. She had meant to continue, to say something along the lines that she doubted very much any proper work would be lost and that she was certain that the gesture of goodwill would be appreciated by the staff. However, the expression on Mr Whittaker's face was so peculiar, that the words had frozen on her tongue. She couldn't tell whether he was annoyed at what he perceived to be her impertinence, or whether he considered the idea had merit.

The Bonfire Night festivities at Sedgwick! Harold Whittaker's heart leapt. Why hadn't he thought of that? It was the perfect opportunity. Major Spittlehouse had something to do with a committee that organised the event, didn't he? Why, the man was always going on about it. Indeed, it was hard to keep him quiet once he had started on the subject and, while Harold Whittaker had only ever listened with half an ear so that he might nod politely in the appropriate places, the fact had stuck in his memory. Sedgwick had celebrated Bonfire Night for as long as he could remember. The event would follow familiar lines and was certain to run smoothly. Now, if he could just orchestrate it such that he snatched a word with the major at the very moment the man was congratulating himself for a job well done … why, he might even go so far as to make some ingratiating remark about the wonderful festivities. In his mind's eye, he saw Major Spittlehouse beaming smugly and benevolently. And then what would be more natural than that their conversation should drift to talk of the close relations between their respective dependants? Yes, it would all be most satisfactory.

Harold Whittaker was roused from his contemplations by his secretary giving an apologetic little cough.

'Ah, Miss Simmons, do forgive me,' the solicitor said hurriedly. 'I was just thinking about the fireworks that I have seen at Sedgwick in the past, and very impressive they were too. In fact, I wouldn't mind seeing them myself this year.' He gave her an indulgent smile. 'You're suggesting we shut up shop half an hour early, are you? Just the thing, I'd say, though I don't intend to make a habit of it. But just this once I suppose it wouldn't do any harm. I will expect everyone to work especially diligently today mind, you can tell them all that from me …'

'I don't know, Jack Masters, tossing and turning in bed you were last night. I'd be surprised if I had a wink of sleep, I would really,' complained Mrs Masters, her hands on her hips, as she paused in her work for a moment. They were undertaking their mid-morning chores and, in her opinion, her husband's performance had been far from satisfactory.

What was more, she had no qualms about telling him so. 'And you as much use to me this morning as that daft girl Biddy, who you know as well as I do is not the full shilling.' She was referring to the Spittlehouses' maid-of-all-work, who came in daily to assist Mrs Masters and as often as not was on the receiving end of her tongue.

'Don't give on so, Mol, there's a dear,' said her husband tiredly, rubbing his eyes.

'It's a guilty conscience, that's what it is,' said Mrs Masters, getting in to her stride. 'Serves you right, it does, stealing the major's post like that.' Her face clouded suddenly and she turned away.

'There's been another one, hasn't there?' surmised her husband excitedly, well used to his wife's various moods and mannerisms. 'Give it here, will you?'

'And have you tear it up and throw it on to the fire?' she said. 'That I won't. What will the major say if he finds out?'

'He'll thank me,' said Masters firmly. 'Now, Mol, my dear, give me that letter.'

While he had been talking he had run around the table and taken his wife in his arms. Taken unawares and before she could think what to do, afraid that Biddy might any minute come upon them in such a compromising position, her husband had slipped his hand into the pocket of her apron and withdrawn the offending envelope.

'Give that back this instant, Jack Masters,' cried his wife.

But the manservant had leapt out of her way and was now leaning against the fireplace. Having torn the letter recklessly from its envelope, he was reading it intently, a look of concentration in his eyes. All the while his wife watched on, studying the expression on his face with anxiety, trying to interpret his raised eyebrow and furrowed brow, fearing the worst. Much to her surprise, however, his face suddenly broke out into a broad smile, and he began to chuckle.

'Don't you fret, my love,' said Masters. 'It's good news, very good news indeed.'

And with that he turned on his heel and walked out of the room with something of a spring in his step, whistling to himself as he went, as if all were right with the world. Not for the first time, his wife was left to speculate and ponder as to the contents of the mysterious letter meant for her employer.

Chapter Twelve

'Rose, darling, you've hardly eaten a thing,' observed her husband, a look of concern momentarily clouding his youthful good looks. They were seated in the majestic dining room at Sedgwick Court, attempting to partake of a particularly large luncheon.

'I'm afraid I'm really not very hungry,' said Rose, pushing her food around her plate with her fork in rather a listless fashion.

'Do eat something, darling. We will only be having a very light supper this evening before we leave for the firework display,' Cedric reminded her. 'Mrs Broughton and her kitchen staff will be up to their ears this afternoon making chicken soup and black treacle toffee. We'll be as good as left to fend for ourselves this evening. A cold supper of ham and bread is all we can expect and a cold rice pudding to follow if we're lucky.'

'All served to us by an attentive footman and accompanied by fine wines,' laughed Rose rallying. 'Really, Cedric, I can tell you've never had to make do with a scratch supper.' She leaned forward and took his hand. 'But you needn't worry, darling, I'm not sickening for something. To tell you the truth, I'm a little nervous, that's all.'

'About tonight?'

'Yes, but don't worry. Edna and I have settled on my outfit and I daresay the children will be far more interested in cramming their mouths full of black treacle toffee and their parents sampling Mrs Broughton's delicious chicken soup than to pay me much attention.'

'I'll say!' said Cedric with feeling. 'Not of course that they won't want to set eyes on the new Countess of Belvedere, because obviously they will,' he added hurriedly. 'But what I mean is, you should see the little perishers. They are like a swarm of ants when they descend on the toffee. We'll be very lucky if we're left with more than a few crumbs.' He chuckled. 'I know for a fact that Mrs Broughton doubles the amount of toffee she makes each year, but it still goes quick as anything.'

'I think I should feel less anxious if I knew the precise order of events for this evening,' said Rose.

'Oh, well, it is all rather informal,' said her husband lightly, tucking in heartily to his slice of mutton. 'I suppose the first thing to happen is the lighting of the bonfire. That always raises a cheer once its blazing. Everyone huddles around it if it's cold. And then it's the judging of the guys. That's when you come in, darling.'

'I must admit I'm rather dreading it,' admitted Rose. 'What if everyone thinks I've made the wrong decision regarding the best guy? And what if I reduce any of the children to tears? I should feel absolutely awful.'

'Oh, it isn't as bad as all that,' said Cedric. 'There's really nothing to it. For one thing, you won't know which child has made which effigy. That's to avoid accusations of bias or favouritism, because of course some of the children will be the sons and daughters of our estate staff or tenant farmers and the like.' He smiled. 'Anyway, I'll be standing beside you and we can confer if you like, though I'm sure you'll be much better at judging that sort of thing than me.' His face erupted suddenly into a broad grin as a recollection came to mind and he chuckled heartily. 'I say, you can't be any worse than Lavinia. She judged the effigies one year when my mother was in bed with a cold. She chose the guy with the prettiest face. It kicked up quite a stink, I can tell you.'

'Oh, why?' asked Rose, curious and not a little alarmed.

'Because there wasn't much more to the guy than a well painted face. You see, the children had got bored and hadn't bothered finishing the body or dressing it even, so that it was little more than a head shaped bit of rag stuffed with straw. I thought there was going to be a riot, but you'd be surprised how readily children can be placated with the promise of more chocolate and toffee.'

Rose laughed. 'That sounds just like your sister. Well, I daresay I can do better than that.'

'That's the spirit. Oh, I forgot to say, after the lighting of the bonfire and before the judging of the guys, I make a bit of a speech. Nothing fancy, you understand, just thanking everyone for coming, that sort of thing. I'll keep it very short, because of course everyone's dying to know who's won the hamper and they are absolutely pulling at the bit to demolish the food, which happens after the judging of the guys.'

'And then?'

'The firework display. I must say, it should be quite a show this year.' Cedric beamed at his wife. 'So you see, darling, there's nothing to worry about. It should all go off without a hitch.'

Archie Mayhew sat in the rickety old bus that was winding its way from Bichester to Sedgwick at, what appeared to the young man at least, something of a snail's pace. He consulted his wristwatch for the third time during the journey, willing the hands to be still. His impatience, he acknowledged in some part, was due to annoyance at himself. He should have remembered that the traffic was getting worse each year on Guy Fawkes' Night as more and more people descended on Sedgwick, the attractions of its bonfire festivities drawing them to the village like an invisible thread.

Of course, he couldn't have known that old Whittaker would have been so amenable to the suggestion that his staff leave the office half an hour early. If he'd had any inkling, he'd have asked the old man himself instead of sending in simpering Simmons to plead their cause. He'd have asked for an hour too, instead of a meagre thirty minutes. Archie looked at his watch again. Blast! Likely as not if the driver didn't put his foot on the throttle, he'd be late and Daphne was bound to create one of her scenes. With a sigh, he stopped feeling irritable for a moment and gave way to wondering instead why Uncle Harold had been so generous about the whole thing. He had half expected the old man to consult with Gribble and Hebborn before agreeing to their request, much less that he would go so far as to show any enthusiasm for the idea. Why, hadn't Simmons said that he was even minded to go to the festivities himself this year?

Archie stared out of the window which was steamed up with the heat and breath of the vehicle's many passengers and thought what a primitive and unpleasant form of transport a public bus was, particularly when it was overcrowded as it was now. He'd been jolly lucky to find a seat. The thought crossed his mind that his uncle was probably even now making his way to the festivities in the relative comfort of his motor car. He could have been seated beside him now if only he'd asked, instead of being knocked and jostled by a variety of elbows and bags. But of course he hadn't asked, just as he had not said that he was going to the festivities because Daphne had particularly requested that he do so. If truth be told, he hadn't liked how the old man had taken the news about him and

Daphne, the look of shock, the way the colour had seemed to drain from his face … He fidgeted uncomfortably in his seat causing the rather plump lady sitting beside him, a large wicker shopping basket balanced precariously on her knee, to tut loudly. No, he hadn't liked it at all. He had found it unnerving and that was before … No, he wouldn't think about that. It wouldn't do any good. He looked at his watch again and sighed. He was going to be late.

Not half a dozen seats in front of him, Miss Warren sat perched very upright on the edge of her seat. She clutched a leather bag, of indeterminate age, tightly to her, as if she feared that the sudden jolts of the bus might cause her to drop it; perhaps she was even fearful it might be snatched from her, so firm was her grasp. Yet, unlike the young man, she was quite oblivious to the slow progress being made by the bus. For her thoughts were elsewhere, on matters of greater importance than what time she would arrive in the village. She threw a rather furtive glance at her fellow passengers, uncomfortably aware that she had unintentionally made eye contact with the old man sitting across from her, who in turn was eyeing her suspiciously.

The librarian took a deep breath and loosened her hold on the bag, though she took the precaution of first balancing it more securely on her lap. She had no wish for its contents to fall out on to the floor and give her away. She stared idly first out of the window and then down again at the innocuous faded brown bag. How nondescript and innocent it looked. Yet her eyes were constantly drawn back to it almost against her will. The reason for this she readily acknowledged was that its spacious interior hid her crime. She uttered a heartfelt sigh. She had always prided herself on being a law abiding person, and yet now she was little more than a common thief. The notion was abhorrent to her. What would her parents say if they were alive now? God rest their souls.

She wondered if her guilt was apparent to those seated around her. Her flushed cheeks and restive manner, even the way she clutched her bag so tightly that her knuckles showed white, surely gave her away. Certainly the old man seated opposite suspected her of being up to no good, or was that merely her own guilty conscience asserting itself? She stifled a sob. Really, she would never have done it if she had realised how miserable she would feel. Still, it was only for a few hours, and then she could put them back and all would be well. And her intentions were honourable, she reminded herself, though a part of her had in fact been tempted to let matters resolve themselves without her interference. For really, was it any of her business? One thing, however, was certain above all else; it was too late now; she would have to see it through as best she could unless circumstances determined otherwise. Really, it was all in the fate of the gods.

It was fast approaching darkness by the time the Earl and Countess of Belvedere made their way to the piece of waste ground which had been allocated for the bonfire festivities. They picked their way between brambles, hindered somewhat by the stoniness of the path, which wound its way between the hedgerows. Rose marvelled at how their servants, who had departed some time before, had managed to negotiate the path, laden as they had been with an assortment of furniture, food and utensils.

It was not long before Rose and Cedric had emerged in a clearing, the sounds of laughter and chatter and general high spirits had warned them they were near. Excited children tore in front of them, pushing and shoving, running and stumbling in the darkness, their shrill voices echoing in the night's sky. Momentarily, the earl and countess were obliged to pause in their walk, which provided Rose with an opportunity to survey the scene. To one side of the field, she could just make out an enormous mound silhouetted against the sky, which she took to be the bonfire. Her assumption was presently confirmed as being correct, for a man approached it with a blazing torch in his hand. He held it at arm's length as he crouched beside the mound. Stretching forward, he thrust the torch expertly into the centre of the pile to light the tinder. Moments later, the fire took hold and a general cheer was taken up by the crowd as they looked on; even the children paused in their games to take in the spectacle.

As the minutes passed and the bonfire began to blaze, the throng surged forward as if by a common accord until, at a safe distance, they were huddled around the bonfire. Cedric and Rose moved forward to take their places; like the others, they stood transfixed, mesmerised by the flames that consumed and spluttered, and the smoke that entered their throats and noses rendering their voices dry. Rose glanced about her at the rather eerie spectacle of a mass of faces bathed in a mixture of jumping shadows and orange light, the effect of which was to distort the features so that the crowd now took on an almost goblin-like appearance. Her inclination was to shrink back into the darkness where she might watch the proceedings from a safe distance.

Perhaps others were becoming rather bored of staring at the flames, for she was suddenly acutely aware that for some she was becoming the focus of their attention. She patted her cloche self-consciously, rather regretting the ridiculous ostrich feather, which she hoped was not too visible in the dark.

Cedric turned and smiled at her, touching her arm, before moving away from the bonfire to be helped by a servant to mount a wooden crate which had been turned on its back. From his slightly elevated position, the young earl delivered his speech very much on the lines he had indicated to his wife earlier. With the exception of one or two of the children, the crowd appeared to listen attentively. Rose herself was overcome by a sense of pride at her husband's performance, her cheeks flushed and her eyes bright. As she listened to his words, she allowed her eyes to glance around the field so that for the first time she noticed the old trestle tables that had been erected to accommodate the various refreshments. She spotted Mrs Broughton, busy presiding over the tureens of chicken soup, and instructing her staff to lay out plates piled high with alternately sausages and black treacle toffee cut into thick slabs. Bottles of lemonade had also been produced as well as bowls of hot mulled cider. Her gaze returned to her husband, who was in the process of concluding his speech. He caught her eye and winked. Now was the moment she had been dreading, the judging of the guys.

She discovered that the effigies were located a little way from the refreshments, in something of a rough approximation of a line. Some appeared to have been discarded quite haphazardly, while others had been posed in crude approximations of humanlike postures. With Cedric beside her, holding up an oil lamp, Rose bent a little forward, in order to study each guy closely, before making her slow way along the line. The light illuminated the guys in a ghostly fashion. Some she recognised as ones she had seen in the village, their appearance little altered from when she had last seen them; others had undergone a considerable transformation, with freshly painted faces and fine clothes. One or two of the guys she was fairly certain she had not seen before, their masks and clothing quite foreign to her. A few of the poses were really very good, and both she and Cedric laughed at the inventiveness of the young creators, as they pointed and giggled at a particular effigy that had caught their fancy, stepping forward and craning their necks to get a better look.

Rose remembered afterwards only that they had taken their time to admire each effigy. Had they walked quickly along the line, hardly pausing to stop, then perhaps they would not have noticed the guy which was half sitting, half lying, at a peculiar angle, as if it had somehow stumbled into its lopsided position. As it was, it drew their attention, not only because of the strangeness of its pose, but also because the clothes that it wore appeared to be of particularly good quality. There were no obvious rips or tears in the tweed jacket, no stains that had made it unwearable by a living person. Beside her, Rose heard Cedric give a sharp intake of breath.

'Well, I'll be blowed! That looks jolly like the major's tweed jacket.' He edged closer to the guy. 'Dash it all, it is. I'd know it anywhere, the fellow never seems to wear anything else. Well, I never; I wonder what made him donate it to be worn by one of the guys? It'll end up on the fire as likely as not if he's not careful.'

'Perhaps the lining's ripped, or there's some other damage to it that we can't see,' said Rose, though she felt the hairs begin to stand up on the back of her neck. There was something about the effigy that made her suddenly feel apprehensive. The temptation was to walk on to look at the next guy, but something was all wrong. 'Darling –'

'I know,' said Cedric quickly, as if she had given voice to her fear; or perhaps he sensed it, or shared it even. For he held up the oil lamp and she was aware that his body stiffened. A moment later, and he had darted forward and was standing over the guy. The effigy's head was all but covered by a flat cap pulled down well over its face, obscuring the painted or moulded features if indeed there were any. To remove the cap was the work of a moment, and with trembling hands Cedric did so, lifting up the lamp with his other hand so that it was only a few inches from the effigy, its glow falling full upon the guy's face. The lamp wobbled precariously in his hand and Rose thought she heard him utter a noise that sounded like an exclamation. Listening out keenly as she had been, it sounded very like a stifled cry quickly checked. With a growing feeling of apprehension and dread, she found herself by her husband's side, tugging at his arm to get his attention.

'What is it? What's the matter?' And then when he didn't say anything: 'Is it a … a body?'

'Yes,' said Cedric abruptly. Even in the weak glow from the lamp she could see that his face was set in a rigid expression. With an odd sense of detachment, she watched as he proceeded to examine what, up until a few moments before, they had thought to be a guy.

'There's no pulse,' said Cedric. 'He's dead all right.'

It was perhaps only then that they remembered they were being observed. For they had all but forgotten the crowd of villagers gathered in a semicircle some way behind them, the children watching excitedly and with something akin to bated breath, eager to find out which guy would be announced the winner.

'We must get the children away from all this,' said Cedric hurriedly. He moved a little further down the line, selected a guy at random and held it up. 'This one's the winner,' he declared in a loud voice. A cheer went up from the crowd. 'Who made it? Very well done. Now if you go and see Mrs Broughton over there, she'll give you the hamper. Very well deserved; give them a round of applause.'

The excited winners, a group of three boys, whooped and shrieked and tore off to the refreshment tables, eager to get their prize. The crowd followed at a slower pace, many curious to know what delicacies were in the hamper. For others, the end of the judging of the effigies marked the beginning of the refreshments and they surged towards the trestle tables, keen to have their fill. And so it transpired that in only a few moments the earl and countess were all but alone, standing beside the discarded guys.

'Has he been –'

'Murdered?' finished Cedric. 'I'd say! Someone's done quite a good job at bashing in the poor fellow's head. It was all covered up by the cap, thank goodness, otherwise the children might have spotted something was amiss when they were lining their guys up beside him.' He made a face. 'What I'd like to know is who could have done such a thing? Someone rather sick in the mind, I'd say.' He moved to his wife and put an arm around her trembling shoulders, steering her away from the corpse. 'Don't look, darling; it is all rather horrid.'

Rose required little encouragement to move away from the body. She had encountered a number of murders and bodies in her time, but the horror of it all did not lessen; she had no wish to view the battered remains of the deceased.

As she and her husband retraced their steps, they were arrested by a lone voice in the dark. Had Rose been alone, she might very well have screamed. One thing she knew for certain was that someone was making their way towards them, a tall figure with a purposeful stride.

'I say, Lord Belvedere, is anything wrong?'

'Oh, lord,' said Cedric, 'that's all we need. I had hoped we'd be able to get through to the police first before we had to tell him about the body.'

'Who is it?' Rose asked curiously.

'Major Spittlehouse.'

'Major Spittlehouse? But I thought that was his body,' cried Rose, inclining her head in the direction of the corpse.

'No. I say, Spittlehouse,' said Cedric turning his attention towards the approaching figure, 'I'm afraid I've got some very bad news. Something rather awful has happened.' He paused until the man drew level and lowered his voice. 'Someone has murdered your manservant.'

Chapter Thirteen

In the immediate aftermath of the discovery of the murdered servant, events appeared to Rose rather fractured and disjointed. She found herself in something of a dreamlike state looking on, an observer of sorts as snatches of images caught her attention before her focus drifted elsewhere. There had been a murder; the words stuck in her brain. Amid all else, she was aware of the smell of the smoke and the noise of crackling sticks from the bonfire. The pale faces of her husband and the major, highlighted in the darkness, glowed in the weak light from the oil lamp.

Since Cedric had informed the major of his devastating find, they had spoken in hushed tones, turning every now and then to glance at the body. Major Spittlehouse, his face strained but controlled, had knelt beside the body and felt for a pulse, perhaps hoping that Cedric had been mistaken in his presumption of death. Meanwhile, Rose had shivered in her thick coat, rather wishing that, despite Edna's concerns regarding the smoke, she had worn her furs.

A hoot of laughter had suddenly filled the night air and Rose was brought sharply back to the present. She remembered vaguely that they were gathered there for a celebration, and that she was surrounded by a crowd of people who were quite oblivious to the recent turn of events. The laughter, however, still sounded unnaturally loud and inappropriate given the circumstances. She realised also that she had all but forgotten that there were children there. They were in high spirits, busy stuffing toffee into their mouths, eagerly awaiting the start of the fireworks, blissfully unaware of the tragedy that had unfolded at the other end of the field.

The laughter had also roused Cedric and Major Spittlehouse from their whispered exchange. If their conduct since discovering the body had been muted and constrained, now there was a sense of urgency to their actions, as if they had been awoken from a stupor. With surprising quickness, Cedric had summoned together some of the house servants, issuing them with instructions concerning the dispersal of the crowd. Rose watched as the food was hastily packed away in wooden crates and the trestle tables dismantled. She had expected to hear cries of protest from the children, but there were none. Instead, an air of excitement had overtaken the crowd, as if they were awaiting the next part of the festivities.

'Darling, are you all right?' Cedric appeared at her shoulder. 'You look frightfully cold. It's beastly that you had to see the body like that.' He glanced at his servants, the majority of whom were busy rounding up the villagers. 'We're moving the festivities to Sedgwick Court.'

'Are you really?' Rose found it hard to hide her surprise. It had not occurred to her that the firework display would continue in light of the death.

'It seemed to be for the best, to get everyone away from here, I mean. The children don't know what's happened and I should like it to remain like that for as long as possible.'

'But –'

'Imagine, Rose, how awful it would be if they all came galloping over to gawp at the corpse.' Cedric passed a hand through his hair so that it stood up on end.

'But to go on with the firework display –'

'The major thinks me quite mad, and I daresay you do too, and perhaps I am a little, but I don't want the whole evening to be ruined.' He looked at her earnestly. 'It means so much to the children, you see; they've been looking forward to it for months.'

'Perhaps it is for the best,' Rose admitted rather grudgingly.

'Do you really think so?' Her husband's face relaxed into something approximating a wan smile.

'I think perhaps I do.' Rose said with greater enthusiasm, putting out her hand to him; for a moment they seemed to cling to each other, oblivious to all else. 'Cedric, I'm so terribly sorry about all this.'

'Well, you are hardly to blame,' Cedric said, squeezing her hand. 'Now, as my old nurse would say, this won't put socks on the children.' His voice was artificially bright, like his smile, as he turned to survey the crowd. His following words, however, were addressed exclusively to his wife. 'Naturally we'll be taking down the names of everyone here tonight before they're permitted to leave. The fireworks will be let off down by the lake. I've asked Manning to take charge of things because of course Spittlehouse and I will stay here with the corpse until the police arrive.'

He bent his head to her and lowered his voice. 'He's pretty cut up by it all, poor fellow, though he won't let on. He's not the sort of man to lose his head and go to pieces.'

They stood together, their hands barely touching, each reluctant to break away from the other. At last Cedric said: 'I'd better get on. But I'd like you to go with them, darling. There's no need for you to stay.'

Rose made to protest but thought better of it. Instead, with weary steps she followed the long procession of servants, children and villagers as they made their way to Sedgwick Court. Before they were quite out of sight, she turned to cast a last glance at the scene. The bonfire was still burning brightly, lighting up the night sky with its flickering flames, casting alternate shadow and light on the two men standing guarding the corpse.

Turning her attention to the procession, Rose was relieved to find that the children were in fine form, though she thought some of the villagers were vaguely aware that something was afoot, for their chatter had become more muted and remained so until they arrived at Sedgwick Court. There, however, they busied themselves with various tasks, among which was helping the servants to unload the trestle tables and food, and carrying the fireworks down to the lake.

Before Rose could decide how best she might help, she was conscious that a woman had appeared at her shoulder, clearly agitated.

'What's wrong? What's happened?' The voice was breathless, as if the woman had been running. 'My brother won't tell me. He told me to come here and wait for him.'

'Miss Spittlehouse, is that you?' Rose stretched out a hand to grasp the woman's fingers, which were icy cold. It occurred to her then that the major would not be the only one distressed by the identity of the corpse. 'I am afraid I have some rather distressing news. I think we had better go into the house.'

'But I don't understand,' Daphne said for what seemed to Rose the umpteenth time. 'Why would anyone want to kill Masters of all people?'

They were seated in Rose's boudoir, drinking hot, sweet tea that scalded their mouths and brought a flush to their cheeks after the cold.

Daphne, Rose noticed, could not sit still. She held her cup at a precarious angle as she gulped down her tea, spilling some of it in to the saucer. It was something of a relief when the woman discarded her cup on a convenient occasional table and took to pacing the floor. There was a restive air about her, as if she were roaming the room looking for occupation. Certainly she picked up ornaments at random, and stared at them absentmindedly, before putting them back carelessly. Rose watched her curiously, feeling herself on edge, as if she had caught some of the woman's jittery mood. She reflected that Daphne was understandably agitated by the news, but thankfully not distraught. It had not been necessary to send for the doctor to prescribe her a sedative.

'This must all be very distressing for you,' said Rose. 'Had Masters been with you very long?'

'Oh, for simply ages,' said Daphne rather carelessly. 'Well, that's to say he had been my brother's servant for years. He was his batman in the army, or whatever they call it. They served together during the war.' She paused and added almost as an afterthought: 'I suppose Linus will be very upset by all this. I didn't really think about that.'

'Yes, I am sure he will,' said Rose, pondering at the lack of feeling displayed by his sister for the fate of their servant. It was possible that Daphne read her mind, for she added: 'I suppose you think me rather heartless? The truth is that I didn't much care for Masters. He considered himself very much my brother's servant, not mine.'

Daphne walked over to the window and looked out, seemingly attracted by the noise of the fireworks which were now in full flow, ravishing the night sky, lighting it up for a few moments with each burst. The colours reflected off the lake so that the spectacle had something of a magical, fairy-tale feel to it, so at odds with the sombre mood that filled the room. Something else caught her attention. Straining her ears, she could discern noises from within the house itself. In the distance, behind the green baize doors, was the sound of small running feet, clattering about on the wooden staircases and on the old linoleum worn smooth by usage and the passage of time. Here and there a door banged, accompanied by the sound of giggles and the raised voices of admonishing servants.

'What's that? What's that noise?' There was a note of fear in her voice, which was not lost on her companion.

'It's only some of the village children,' said Rose. 'I expect they're playing a game of hide and seek.'

'Don't you mind?' asked Daphne incredulously. 'If it were me, I should mind terribly.'

'They are in high spirits, that's all. Besides, they are tearing about the servants' quarters, not the main house. Mrs Broughton will soon bring them to heel when she lays the food out for them in the servants' hall.' She stared at the restless woman. 'Won't you sit down and have another cup of tea, Miss Spittlehouse? There is plenty left in the pot and, if there isn't, I can always ring for some more.'

'I don't seem able to sit still,' admitted Daphne, flinging herself down on to the chair she had recently vacated and tapping a beat with her fingers on its arm. 'I suppose it's all this waiting. Do you think my brother will be very long?'

'I shouldn't think so,' said Rose, though she was far from certain. For she thought it unlikely that Cedric and Major Spittlehouse would be content to forsake the scene before a policeman of appropriate rank had arrived from Bichester to take charge of the investigation. The village constable was an able enough fellow, but he was more used to dealing with incidents involving drunk and disorderly conduct than suspicious death. They might, therefore, be reluctant to leave the body under his sole charge or, at the very least, feel obliged to remain with him until reinforcements had arrived. Fleetingly, she wondered if Inspector Connor would be assigned to the case. She shuddered at the thought that he might be accompanied by the objectionable Sergeant Harris.

Rose was roused from her musings with a start by the sound of hurrying footsteps on the floor of the landing outside. Both women stared at the door expectantly, anticipating the arrival of the earl and the major. When the door opened, however, it was Mrs Simpson who entered the room.

'Rose, I came as soon as I could,' Rose's mother marched straight up to her daughter and embraced her. 'Oh, my dear, is it true?' It appeared only then that she noticed that Rose had a guest. 'How do you do, Miss Spittlehouse?' She turned her attention again to her daughter. 'Your footman was all for announcing us, but I told him I knew the way. They really have got their hands full looking after the children. They appear to be running amok in the servants' hall and causing no end of mischief.

Still, Mrs Dobson will soon have them under control. She insisted on coming with me when we heard the news. We were a little late setting off for the bonfire and ran in to one of your servants. He was carrying some more oil lamps to the field.' She paused a moment for breath. 'It is all most unfortunate. How has poor Mrs Masters taken the news? Is someone sitting with her?'

'Masters was married?' cried Rose, looking aghast.

Their eyes turned to Daphne, who began to look uncomfortable under their accusing looks.

'Oh, I'm afraid I'd quite forgotten about her.' Instead of blushing at her unpardonable oversight, Rose noticed that the woman had gone quite pale. 'I suppose she'll have to be told. How awful.'

'Surely she knows about her husband's death?' demanded Mrs Simpson.

'I really don't know,' said Daphne, sounding doubtful. 'She won't have been at the festivities because she can't abide the fireworks on account of the noise. She is always going on about it to anyone who'll listen.'

'Well, I never did! I'll go over there myself,' said Mrs Simpson, gathering up her things. 'And you needn't trouble yourself to accompany me, Miss Spittlehouse, though you might think you ought. I'll take Mrs Dobson with me. She happens to be by way of being a friend of Mrs Masters.'

With that, she threw Daphne something of a dismissive look, tinged with contempt, hugged her daughter briefly, and hurried from the room.

'Would you like to sit down?' enquired Cedric, holding up the oil lamp and looking about him for anything that would double up as a seat. 'It could be quite some time until the police arrive. You've had an awful shock, old chap. I daresay you could do with a brandy.' He glanced over to where he knew the trestle tables had been standing only a half hour earlier, but which was now in pitch darkness. 'I should have asked them to leave a bottle of that cider.'

'It's very kind of you, my lord, I'm sure,' mumbled Major Spittlehouse. But he did not lift his gaze; his eyes remained resolutely focused on the dead servant whom, even in the weak glow from Cedric's lamp, resembled now little more than a dark shape.

'I've asked some of my servants to bring some more lamps; the police will require more than the light from the bonfire and I don't know how long the oil in this lamp will hold out.'

'Thank you.'

A silence filled the space between them, heavy and uncomfortable, a mixture of sorrow and bewilderment. Cedric shuffled his feet and, without really intending to, loosened his grip on the lamp, allowing its glow to waver and drop, so that its light fell on the grass. He tightened his hold, but the lamp still hung from his hand in rather a precarious manner.

'It's a rum old business,' he said at last, quite at a loss what to say, but resenting the awkward silence that had sprung up between them, and which only emphasised the fact that they were standing alone in an abandoned field in near darkness. If he were a fanciful man, he might have imagined that the ghosts of tortured souls roamed the earth about them or, perhaps more likely and worrying, that the murderer was close at hand, observing their every move.

'It is that,' agreed the major. 'But you needn't worry that I'll go to pieces. I've seen plenty a sight on the battlefield that would make your hair curl.' He glanced away and stared instead at the bonfire which, still ablaze, was burning brightly, spitting and crackling in the night air. The major grunted; when next he spoke it was rather gruffly. 'Not that I'm not upset by all this, because of course I am. We'd been through a lot together, Masters and me. Through thick and thin, you might say. He was my batman during the war and, well …. he was more a friend to me than a servant, least that's how I thought of him. Don't know what he thought about me. If it hadn't been for him … well, I'm not sure that I'd be standing here with you today, and that's a fact.'

Traces of emotion had revealed themselves in the latter end of the major's speech and Cedric, considerably moved, stood looking on helplessly. There was a part of him that wished he had said nothing and let the silence endure. But another part of him recognised that perhaps after all it had been right to encourage the major to talk. For in public the man usually kept his emotions closely in check. Perhaps Masters had been his confidant, or at the very least, a man who had shared his experiences of the war, and all the horror associated with it, which still haunted and tainted the lives of those who had survived. And now the manservant was dead, and murdered at that, left hidden among the effigies on a piece of waste field at a time when the village had come together to rejoice and celebrate …

'We'll find out who did this, old chap,' said Cedric, patting Major Spittlehouse's shoulder. 'I give you my word.' It occurred to him then how much better his father would have been at all this, for he had been both a contemporary and a friend of the man's. Did he imagine it, or was there a look of fear in the major's eyes; true it had been fleeting, but he could have sworn it had been there. Why, Cedric wondered, should the major be frightened? It made no sense. He must want the murderer found as much as the next man, more so in fact.

It was only then that an uncomfortable thought struck him and, as it did so, he realised that it had always been there, from the moment when they had first discovered the body of the murdered man. It had been lurking there at the back of his mind, refusing to be acknowledged; only now did he give it voice. With clumsy fingers, he caught hold of the major's sleeve, pulling at the fabric so that the man was obliged to turn and look up at him, the glow from the lamp highlighting something of a surprised look upon his face.

'He was wearing your jacket,' Cedric said. 'Masters was wearing your jacket.'

Chapter Fourteen

It seemed to Rose that they had been waiting a very long time indeed for Cedric and Major Spittlehouse. It was, therefore, a surprise when she glanced at her wristwatch and found that only two and a half hours had passed since she had first arrived at the bonfire festivities. She sighed inwardly, resenting the enforced waiting game she was obliged to play. It would not have been so bad if she had not been stuck with a companion with whom she had very little in common. She gave a surreptitious glance over at Daphne, who appeared to be now in rather a listless mood, slumped in an armchair, her eyes glazed. Only her fingers remained active, as if they were not quite a part of her, tapping a monotonous beat on the arm of the chair. Rose watched the flickering fingers out of the corner of her eye, anticipating each tap before it was made. She was very tempted to ask Daphne to stop, but she had little inclination to rouse the woman from her thoughts. To do so would invite conversation, and she welcomed the silence as an opportunity to gather her own thoughts.

In stark contrast to the woman's current languid condition, Rose was reminded of the moment Daphne had burst, uninvited, into her mother's house and demanded their immediate attention. She had put her own interests paramount, with little regard for anyone else. It had not bothered her that Rose had just returned from honeymoon or that Mrs Dobson had made it perfectly clear that her presence at such a time would not be welcome. And tonight, when it would have been perfectly understandable if she had shown some emotion at the brutal death of a longstanding servant, she had displayed very little. It had slipped her mind even that the poor fellow had a wife yet to be informed of her husband's death. Rose sighed. It didn't do to dwell on such things, for she of all people knew how murder affected people in different ways. Some were overly demonstrative of their emotions, crying and screaming and tearing their hair out, while others retreated within themselves, hardly daring to breathe, much less to converse with another living being.

Rose allowed her gaze to fall on Daphne again and deemed that it would hardly matter to the woman if her hostess were there with her or not. And Rose did not want to be there, marooned in this room, awaiting the arrival of others to bring news. The amateur sleuth in her was impatient, pawing at the ground and pulling at the bit to get going.

'Miss Spittlehouse, would you mind awfully if I left you for a little while?' Rose came forward and placed a hand on Daphne's arm. The woman turned and stared at her with eyes that were initially blank and unseeing, as if she had just awoken from a dream and was still not quite all there. 'I feel I should show my face, so to speak,' continued Rose. 'Downstairs in the servants' hall and outside by the lake, I mean. It sounds as if the fireworks have stopped, doesn't it? Everyone will be going home in a minute and I feel I ought to say goodbye and thank them all for coming.'

'No ... I don't mind, not at all,' Daphne mumbled and looked away. 'It doesn't seem quite real, somehow. It's all like a bad dream. I keep thinking that I'll wake up in a moment and find this is all make believe; Masters dead and even my being here with you now, waiting for Linus.' She clasped Rose's arm, her fingernails jabbing into the girl's skin as she did so, her eyes suddenly filled with emotion. 'That's why I forgot about Mrs Masters. It wasn't because I didn't care, it was because it didn't feel real somehow, what had happened, I mean. You do believe me, don't you; please say you do?'

'Yes,' said Rose, trying to keep the doubt from her voice. What Daphne was saying now seemed to be at variance to what she had said before. Had she not expressed a particular dislike for her brother's servant? She thought it better, however, to agree with the woman. 'I shall only be gone a short while,' she said, making for the door. 'If you require anything, you have only to ring the bell.'

Outside on the landing the house seemed oddly deserted, though muffled sounds came to Rose's ears from behind the green baize doors. She heard shouts and cries of excitement accompanied by the sound of hurrying footsteps on the servants' staircases. It appeared to her that the children were making quite a game of running up and down the many stairs that descended from the attics above to the basement below. She walked into one of the rooms whose window overlooked the grounds at the back of the house encompassing the lakes. She felt that she knew Sedgwick's grounds by heart now, though it was pitch black and in reality she could make out very little, save for a few lanterns in the distance, held up and carried at shoulder height. The fireworks had come to an end and the villagers were obviously making their way back from the display, in something of a winding procession to judge by the way the lights from the lanterns waved and lurched in the inky darkness. She could judge their progress across the grounds as they wound their way along the gravel paths between the tight box hedges and well-manicured lawns. It would not be very long now before they reached the top terrace and then the house itself; she must make haste.

Rose had told Daphne that she ought to bid farewell to the villagers. It was, however, the children that she particularly wished to seek out. Being closeted in the room with her guest as she had been, with little to do but think, she had taken the opportunity to plan the first tentative steps of her inquiry into the manservant's death. Not for a moment had it crossed her mind not to probe into Masters' death. She could no more leave it to the police to do than she could forsake her new husband and Sedgwick. She felt, as she had often felt before, that she had an obligation to try and solve the crime. Murder seemed to follow her wherever she went of late; the very least she could do was to try and solve each case to the best of her ability.

And on reflection, as she had sat bored and impatient in the boudoir, eager to be gainfully employed in the investigation, it had occurred to Rose that her first task must be to consult the children, in particular those children who had brought their guys to the festivities and positioned them in line for the judging. This of course threw up the question of how best she might go about the task. The sound of running feet, muted by an encasement of wood drew her attention again to the servants' staircase, which was located at the end of the landing. The staircase itself was enclosed behind an innocuous wooden door, and consequently hidden from view. While there was nothing in theory to prevent her from opening the door and going down the steps to the basement below, she thought that her servants might take a dim view of such an action on her part. Certainly she would feel awkward, as if she were a trespasser, venturing unbidden into her staff's private domain. If nothing else, her presence would be an inconvenience, adding to their already heavy burden of having to control a host of unruly infants.

As she stood dithering, a movement in the great entrance hall below attracted her attention. Peering over the banisters, she spied one of the footmen crossing the hall to undertake some mission or other.

'Charlie, is that you?' Rose said, hurrying down the grand staircase, afraid lest the footman should disappear. 'I know you all have a great deal on your hands, but would you be so good as to gather the children together for me? I mean the ones who made the guys. I should like to have a word with them. Perhaps you could have them come out into the hall to see me?'

'As you wish, m'lady,' said the footman, at considerable pains to keep both his face and his voice void of expression. The feat, however, appeared to be beyond him, for a moment later he added rather apologetically: 'Begging your pardon, m'lady … I hope I'm not speaking out of turn if I say they're little ruffians, they are. Mrs Farrier's near tearing her hair out in the servants' hall trying to keep them in line, Mr Manning too. If it hadn't been for Mrs Dobson coming like she did … well, Mr Manning, he was all for going to get Mr Torridge, he was, threatened to do so just to put the fear of God in them, like. Mr Torridge wouldn't stand for any of their nonsense. Running around the table they were and bumped into the dresser. Five plates and two cups, that's what they've broken, china everywhere, and the racket ...' He moved a step or two towards Rose. 'I wouldn't want to bring them into the hall, m'lady. Who knows what damage the little blighters … that's to say, the children … begging your pardon, m'lady … would cause? And happen as not, some of them are light fingered. Mr Manning told Jack and me to keep a close eye on the spoons –'

'Very well, Charlie,' said Rose quickly, keen to put an end to the footman's grumbling lest the police should arrive before she had carried out her task, 'I'll see them in the housekeeper's sitting room, that's if Mrs Farrier has no objection of course.'

Rose waited in the hall while Charlie scurried off to round up the children as best he could. She knew that he would take the opportunity to warn the other servants of their mistress' imminent arrival in the servants' quarters and that they had better be on their best behaviour or else. A few minutes elapsed. She imagined that a flurry of maids had been dispatched to dust and tidy the housekeeper's sitting room and that attempts were also being made to straighten the other rooms and corridors that had suffered as a result of the children's excitement and over exuberance. She was not unduly surprised to find that it was the housekeeper herself who came to fetch her.

'Ah, Mrs Farrier, how very good of you,' Rose said, addressing the thin, pale woman, who was dressed all in black, save for white lace cuffs and a small lace collar. 'I do hope you don't mind my using your sitting room? I just wanted a word with the children. I understand from Charlie that they have kept you all very busy.'

'That they have, m'lady, and no mistake,' said the housekeeper rather grimly through pursed lips. 'Up to mischief, that's what they've been, not that we can't manage them, because we can. Give Mrs Dobson and me a few more hours with the mites and we'd have had them as meek as lambs, so we would, and so well behaved that even their own mothers wouldn't recognise them. 'Twas a pity Mrs Dobson had to leave sudden like she did. Now, this way if you will, m'lady.'

The housekeeper led Rose through the green baize door into a long and winding passage, off which were located a number of rooms. Some of the doors were open and Rose took the opportunity to glance into them briefly as she passed, trying to guess their particular function. A washroom, a housemaid's closet, a brushing room, a boot room ... the names floated through her mind. Those were the minor rooms. Some were populated with servants who bowed and curtsied to her. There were more important rooms, she knew, such as the kitchen, the scullery, the stillroom, the butler's pantry, and of course the servants' hall which lay at the very heart of the servants' quarters. It was this room that dominated the servants' lives with its bell board; the one communal area where they might gather together to eat their meals and chat and gossip in their few idle hours.

'I'll ask that you'd please excuse the mess that there is on account of the children, m'lady,' Mrs Farrier was saying. 'Spotless, it usually is, I can assure you. I pride myself on it, Mr Manning and me both and Mr Torridge before him. I always says how we keeps a neat and tidy ship, most particular we are about it, I can tell you.'

'I am sure you are.'

They stopped abruptly outside a door. Rose had been so busy looking about her that it was all she could do to stop herself from walking in to the housekeeper. She found she had a sudden, childish urge to giggle, and bit her lip. The events of the evening must be catching up with her to put her in such a strange mood. It was only to be expected. She had bent forward to take a closer look at a guy she was supposedly to judge only to discover it was a murdered corpse.

Her first impression of Mrs Farrier's sitting room was that it was very similar to the housekeeper's sitting room at Crossing Manor. There was the same genteel shabbiness about it for, while it contained a few very good pieces of furniture, they were rather worn and faded. The overall effect, however, was not unpleasing, for there was something comfortable and homely about the room which, Rose realised with a sudden stab of longing, was lacking in the grand drawing room upstairs. This sitting room reminded her of the mean little house she had shared with her mother. She remembered how they had refused to part with one or two pieces of furniture that had had particular sentimental value to them. The pieces had not been worn or faded, but they had still looked very out of place, dwarfing the small room in which they had been crammed both by their size and grandeur ...

There was a noise in the passage outside and, before Rose could quite gather her thoughts, the children shuffled into the room, their caps clutched in hands that were sticky from toffee, their faces smeared black from the smoke and habitual dirt. They were rather a motley group of children of various ages and differing heights, mostly boys, with ill-fitting clothes that they had either outgrown or would be growing into, and shoes that were quite down at heel. They blinked up at her with dark, suspicious eyes, their faces solemn.

'Hallo. I cannot tell you how very pleased I am to see you all,' began Rose kindly, smiling brightly and attempting to put them at their ease. 'I do hope you have had enough to eat?'

One or two of the children nodded, the others stared up at her, their eyes large and apprehensive; all remained resolutely silent, although one small boy with a rather runny nose sniffed audibly.

'I wanted to see you all,' Rose continued, not discouraged by their silence, fully aware that they were probably overawed by their surroundings, 'because I wanted to congratulate you on your splendid guys. I could tell that a great deal of work had gone in to making them. I can't tell you how difficult it was to decide on an eventual winner. If I could have done, I should have given a hamper to each of you.'

'Tom shouldn't have won,' mumbled one brave soul. 'My guy was much better than his.'

The child in question received a sharp jab in the ribs from the elbow of the tallest boy there, accompanied by a hissed instruction that he keep quiet or else. The smaller boy shrank back and glared at him. Judging by their appearance, they were siblings. The older boy turned and addressed Rose with an air of composure beyond his years.

'Very kind of you, I'm sure, your ladyship.'

Rose pretended not to notice his younger brother sticking out his tongue at his brother behind his back, nor that the sniffing child was now wiping his nose unceremoniously on the back of his sleeve. She heard however a soft tut of reproach from the housekeeper standing beside her.

'What is your name?' asked Rose of the older boy.

'Jude Browning, miss,' replied the boy. Mrs Farrier tut-tutted this time quite audibly. 'Your ladyship, I mean.'

'The guys were laid out in a very straight line,' Rose began carefully. 'Did you put them all out together? All at the same time, I mean?'

'Most of 'em,' replied the boy named Jude. 'One or two of the boys were late arriving, weren't you, Ben,' Jude said, half turning to address one of the other boys who nodded. 'We had to squeeze Ben's guy on to the end of the line. It meant we had to budge all the others up.'

'And the guy with the tweed jacket?' enquired Rose, desperately trying to appear nonchalant.

'Funny you mention him,' replied Jude, eyeing her with a degree of suspicion. 'He was already there, laid out on the ground, like. We didn't recognise him. That's to say, none of us put him together, like. He just appeared there out of thin air, as bold as brass.' Jude took a step forward and bent towards Rose in something of a confidential manner. 'Gave us quite a turn it did, seeing him all laid out like that. It made us wonder who had made him.'

'We thought a group of girls had done it like and didn't want to let on,' piped up Jude's younger brother, obviously not wishing to be left out. 'Ever such fancy clothes they'd put him in. There was nothing wrong with that tweed jacket he was wearing; it weren't torn or anything. A proper gent could 'ave worn it, it was that fine.' He paused to scowl at his brother. 'And you needn't look at me like that, Jude, as if I'm telling tales, 'cos you said as much –'

'No, I didn't,' hissed his brother.

110

'Don't you go pretending you didn't, or I'll tell Mum. You know how she can't abide you telling lies.'

'That'll do,' cried the housekeeper. 'If you can't keep a civil tongue in your head –'

Jude pointedly ignored both Mrs Farrier and his brother and said: 'I suppose Bert's right. We'd have got quite a bit for that jacket down at the market, and no mistake. Not that we had a mind to take it of course, because we didn't.'

'I'm sure you didn't,' said Rose, giving the boy a look of encouragement. She didn't want the boys' petty sibling squabbling, or Mrs Farrier's reproaches, to discourage the children from talking to her.

'The guy in the tweed coat was already there, you say? And you didn't see who brought him?'

'No. But, like Bert says, we thought a bunch of girls had made him.'

'Did you see anyone?' Rose said carefully. 'A man perhaps, or a woman?'

'No, nobody,' said Jude. He clutched his cap tightly in his hand and Rose was painfully aware that his clothes were rather tattered and his trousers far too short for him. 'Of course it was dark by then and we only had one torch among us. But no man or woman wouldn't have made that there guy. The competition, it's only for us children, see? They wouldn't have been able to win the prize, so there'd be no point to it.'

'I do see,' said Rose gravely, rather dreading asking her next question. She was permitted a moment or two of grace while young Bert interjected with a comment of his own.

'Tom's father helps him make his guy,' he muttered, half under his breath.

'No he don't!' cried the sniffing child. 'You take that back Albert Browning, or I'll punch yeh.'

'That will do,' cried Mrs Farrier. 'Any more of that and you'll all be out of here on your ears.'

'Bert, you keep quiet, do you hear?' said Jude, half turning to face his brother. 'Can't you see the lady wants to ask us some questions about the guy?' He turned his attention back to Rose and stared at her with serious eyes. 'There was something wrong about that guy, wasn't there? It didn't look quite right, not like a proper guy at least.'

'Did you look at its face?' asked Rose, feeling rather sick.

'No, there wasn't time. Its face was covered by its cap, and I was busy positioning my own guy, as were the others. Though I admit I was tempted to take a peek. I wanted to see if the features of its face had been moulded proper like, or just painted on like ours were.'

'Oh, thank goodness for that,' cried Rose.

She had spoken quietly to herself but apparently just loud enough for Jude to hear. For, as the other children shuffled out of the room with the promise of more toffee in the servants' hall to take home to their mothers and younger siblings, the boy bent forward so only Rose could hear.

'It weren't no guy, were it, miss?' And when she didn't reply immediately, 'I thought as much.'

Chapter Fifteen

Rose emerged from the green baize door to a commotion of sorts. The footmen were crossing the main entrance hall carrying between them a variety of hats, scarves and gloves; thick overcoats were also draped over their arms. They had evidently just relieved four gentlemen, only recently arrived, of their outdoor attire. The men in question loitered in the entrance hall. Manning, the butler, stood to attention, ready to attend to their needs. He beckoned them towards the library, where he informed them hot drinks would be served. Certainly the men appeared in need of something to ward off the chill of the November evening for they breathed in the warmth of the house and spent a moment or two rubbing their hands together in front of the fire that blazed in the hall.

'Ah, that's better,' said Cedric. 'I don't know about you chaps, but I feel chilled to the bone.' He paused to glance up at one of the other gentlemen, who was considerably older than himself; a solid, well-built man with a face which had the suggestion of a florid complexion when it was not pale with the cold. 'Though I expect you're used to this sort of thing, aren't you, Newcombe?' the earl continued. 'I daresay it comes with the territory. Ah, Rose, darling, I didn't see you there. Do let me introduce you to Detective Inspector Newcombe. We're by way of being friends. Newcombe plays on the Sedgwick cricket team, don't you know. He's something of a fast bowler, aren't you, man? We were in no end of trouble before he joined our side. Newcombe, may I introduce my wife, the Countess of Belvedere.'

'Lady Belvedere, how do you do?' The inspector gave Rose something of an appraising look, which appeared to comprise mostly of a barely concealed curiosity. She did not think it was her looks which interested him. Rather she wondered if he were familiar with her reputation for being something of an amateur sleuth. He smiled briefly at her and indicated the man standing beside him, whom he introduced as Sergeant Bell. Inwardly she breathed a sigh of relief that Inspector Connor, and particularly Sergeant Harris, had not been assigned to the case. It was only when she looked beyond them that she spotted Major Spittlehouse.

He was standing a little apart from the others and had not joined in the general discussion about the weather. He held himself upright in a military fashion and yet Rose had the odd impression that his natural desire at that moment was to droop his shoulders and slouch, or perhaps to lean against the fireplace for support, for all the world as if he carried the universe upon his shoulders. That he had been deeply affected by his servant's death was obvious from both his demeanour and the solemn expression upon his face, which was set in such rigid lines that Rose feared that any moment it might crack. Beneath his skin she glimpsed a battle raging, on one side a desire to succumb to his feelings and on the other a perceived duty to maintain a stiff upper lip. She had not yet been formally introduced to him, their first meeting having been overshadowed by the discovery of the murdered man, which had quite done away with any of the usual formalities and pleasantries. Her husband was at that moment busy conversing with the policemen. She was thus afforded the opportunity to edge forward and make her own introductions.

'Major Spittlehouse, I am very pleased to make your acquaintance. I just wish it was not under such unfortunate circumstances ...' How inadequate the words sounded, even to her own ears. 'If there is anything that I can do?'

'What?' The major gave an involuntary start. He had been so oblivious to his surroundings and so absorbed in his own thoughts that it had taken him a moment to register that he was being addressed. 'Oh, that's very kind of you, Lady Belvedere. It has been a most frightful shock and ...' He stopped abruptly, his eyes large and suddenly focused. 'My sister?'

'She is quite all right,' said Rose quickly. 'You have no need to worry. She is resting upstairs.'

'Ah ... good. Did you tell her ...?'

'About your servant's death? Yes. I thought it best to tell her the truth; that he had been murdered, I mean.'

The initial look the major shot at her suggested that he strongly disagreed with this viewpoint. However, he said nothing and, with remarkable quickness, he composed his features; it might even be presumed that he went so far as to nod his head. 'I suppose it's for the best,' he said rather wearily. 'She would have to have been told in the end.'

'Yes,' agreed Rose. 'I thought I ought to say something when I had the

114

opportunity to do so. It would have been awful if she'd heard it as a piece of gossip.'

The major lifted his head and addressed the senior detective. 'I assume you'll want to speak with me, Inspector? But first, if you have no objection, I should like to go up and see my sister. She'll be pretty shaken up by all this, I can tell you.'

'Of course,' said Inspector Newcombe. 'And it'll fit in well enough with my own plans. I'd intended to speak to Lord and Lady Belvedere first anyway, being as it was they who found the body.'

Cedric led the way to the library, the two policemen following. Rose, however, held back a little to take a moment to stare at the retreating back of Major Spittlehouse as he mounted the staircase. She noted that he did not rush up the stairs, if anything he seemed to take his time. It was if he was weighing up everything with each step that he took. She frowned and admonished herself for being fanciful. But the odd feeling that she had lingered and would not go away. For some reason, she felt a sense of apprehension at the major's progress up the staircase, though she could not put a finger on why she should be anxious. It was quite natural in the circumstances that the major should wish to see how his sister was holding up. Would it matter so very much if the two of them conversed before they were formally interviewed by the inspector?

Rose gave one last look and followed in the wake of the other gentlemen. When she entered the library, the two policemen and her husband were in the process of arranging themselves around the octagonal library table, drawing up chairs so that they might all be seated.

'Oh, there you are, darling,' said Cedric, procuring a chair for her and positioning it next to his own. Inspector Newcombe was seated opposite them, with Sergeant Bell to his right. Husband and wife watched as the inspector made a show of shuffling the few papers in front of him and the sergeant took out his notebook in preparation.

'Now, I've made a few rough notes of my own based on the bare particulars as they were told to me by your lordship, Major Spittlehouse and Constable Abbott, when I first arrived on the scene,' began the inspector. 'Very sketchy they are of course, and we'll need to put flesh on the bones so to speak, but suppose I use these as the basis for my questions to you?' It was undoubtedly a rhetorical question, but so steadfast was his gaze that both the earl and the countess felt obliged to nod. 'Good.' The inspector gave a smile which encompassed the two of them. 'Very well, without further ado, let's begin, shall we? It's likely to be a long old night for Bell and me.'

'Righto,' said Cedric, crossing his legs languidly, 'though first I would be grateful if we might get one thing straight before we start, if you're willing that is, Newcombe?'

'Oh, and what is that, my lord?' The inspector looked at him, seemingly intrigued, though a smile played about his lips and Rose wondered if he had an inkling of what was coming next.

'I should like my wife to be involved in this investigation. She's a first rate amateur detective, don't you know.' Cedric turned and winked at Rose. 'You do want to investigate this murder, don't you, darling?' She felt a flutter in her chest and returned his smile, with a murmur of assent. How different it all seemed to when she had had to fight her own corner at Crossing Manor in servants' clothes, with only poor Sergeant Perkins to plead her cause.

'I do indeed know,' Inspector Newcombe was saying, when she had torn her gaze from Cedric and returned her attention to the policeman. 'The station at Bichester is full of the Crossing Manor business and the role Lady Belvedere played in solving it.' Addressing Rose, he said: 'You are known at Scotland Yard too I believe, m'lady? As I understand it, you've helped them solve one or two of their murder cases?'

'Yes,' said Rose. 'I suppose you could say that.'

'Of course you could,' interjected Cedric with feeling. 'You should hear my sister on the subject, Newcombe. Really, my wife is far too modest.'

'And naturally enough,' continued the inspector, as if the earl had not interrupted, 'you're worried I'll come down all officious and bureaucratic like and tell you I don't want any meddlesome amateurs queering my pitch?'

'I say, Newcombe, you have it in a nutshell,' beamed Cedric, and Rose laughed. Really, she didn't think she had ever met a policeman quite like Inspector Newcombe. There was a warmth in the way he regarded them, almost like a benevolent uncle. It did not surprise her when he said:

'Well, I can tell you I'm not like that. Any help I am offered is most gratefully received, I can tell you, providing it's of the right sort that is.

Not that I'd say that to everyone, because I wouldn't. But I like to think that I'm a good judge of character and you've got something of a proven record in this field, Lady Belvedere. Besides,' he added, a twinkle in his eye, 'I don't doubt that, whatever I say, you'll go off investigating by yourself anyway and we might as well work together than apart. If nothing else, it'll mean I can keep a bit of an eye on you. It's a dangerous business. I don't want to end up investigating two murders, not if I can help it.'

'I say, that's the spirit,' exclaimed Cedric. 'It's jolly decent of you, Newcombe. I knew we'd be able to count on you; I knew it the moment you bowled that first over on the cricket field.'

'Even so,' said the inspector, a more serious note creeping into his voice, 'I'd ask that you be careful and don't take any risks. This is a nasty old business, and no mistake. It takes a certain mind to kill a man, dress him as a guy and leave his body to be burnt as part of some village festivities.' He looked sharply at Cedric. 'I take it that's the way it was, my lord? I assume the usual practice is to throw the effigies on to the bonfire at the end of the evening before the flames have quite died down?'

'It is and it isn't,' replied Cedric. 'No, Inspector, you needn't look at me like that. I am not trying to be deliberately abstruse. Some of the children do throw their guys on to the bonfire to be burnt it's true, and it raises quite a cheer, I can tell you. But just as many take their efforts home with them.'

'I suppose they become rather attached to them,' said Rose. 'From what I've seen, they put an awful lot of work in to making them. I'm not at all surprised that some don't want to discard them.'

'And of course there's nothing to stop them using the same guy next year,' said her husband. 'All they need do is stuff it with a few more rags or straw and repaint its face.'

'If what you say is true, then it seems rather a precarious and uncertain way to try and dispose of a body,' mused the inspector. He pondered for a moment and appeared struck by a sudden thought. 'I suppose if no one claims a guy, it's thrown on to the bonfire as a matter of course?'

He stared at Cedric for confirmation and the young man nodded. 'That's right.'

'But he'd be taking an awful risk, our murderer,' continued the inspector. 'Who's to say that somebody wouldn't decide to give the guy a closer look before they threw it on to the bonfire? Of course it was dark, I'll give you that, but even so, all it would take was a lamp to be shone on its face and the truth would out. And of course the weight and feel of it would be very different from the effigies.'

'There'd be a risk too that some of the village children might claim it as their own. It's the sort of thing they'd do for a bit of a lark,' said Cedric, shuddering at the thought.

'Had no attempt been made to disguise the face?' enquired Rose. 'I'm surprised the murderer didn't hide it with a mask.'

'Well, a cap had been pulled down over the face, as you know,' said the inspector, 'But all the murderer had done to the face itself was to smear it with a little bit of dirt to take away the pallor. Didn't make too good a job at it either.'

'Wouldn't that suggest that the man's death wasn't premeditated?' asked Cedric.

'It might and it might not,' said Inspector Newcombe. 'But what I can't figure out is why our murderer went to all that effort. Why didn't he just push the body into the pile before it was lit and be done with it? It would have been easy enough for him to get it a fair way in and disguise it with all the tinder and twigs that would have been there. No one would have been any the wiser and he could be pretty certain then that it'd go up in flames all right.'

'I think I can answer that for you, Newcombe,' said Cedric. 'For as long as I can remember, before the bonfire's lit, we've always checked through the pile looking for hedgehogs.'

'Hedgehogs?' Inspector Newcombe sounded incredulous.

'Yes. The little creatures like to crawl in and sleep under them, don't you know.'

'Well, I never!' exclaimed the inspector. 'I never knew that. And this practice of sweeping the bonfire is carried out every year, you say?'

'Without fail, Inspector.'

'So if a corpse happened to be lurking there in the pile it would be discovered before the bonfire was lit?'

'It certainly would,' enthused Cedric. 'The sweep's pretty thorough, I can tell you. If it can find a hedgehog, it would definitely uncover any body, no matter how carefully it was hidden.'

'Now, as I understand it,' continued the inspector, glancing at his sergeant to make sure that he had taken a note of the practice regarding the hedgehogs, 'the village children brought their guys with them to the field and positioned them in a line in preparation for the judging?' He turned his gaze on Rose. 'And that was to be undertaken by yourself, Lady Belvedere?'

'That's right, though actually my husband and I did it between us as I hadn't done it before.'

'Just so. What we need to do now is have a word with these children.' Inspector Newcombe paused and glanced at his watch. 'I suppose they've all gone back to their homes by now, it being rather late and the firework display done with? Bell, I'd like you to take a constable with you first thing in the morning and have a word with them. Happen they might have seen something. It would be too much to hope of course that they might have seen our murderer positioning the body in the line.'

'I do hope you don't mind, Inspector,' began Rose rather tentatively, 'but I have actually spoken to the children about it already.'

'Have you indeed?' The inspector raised an eyebrow. 'That was jolly quick of you, Lady Belvedere.'

'I thought it best to speak to them tonight before they were aware of what had happened. And as they were all gathered together here, why it seemed the perfect opportunity.'

'I see. Did you tell them about the murder?'

'Of course not,' replied Rose rather indignantly. 'I thought it not my place to do so and besides, I didn't want to frighten them.'

'Well, and what were the results of your investigation, Lady Belvedere?' It was hard to tell if the inspector was peeved or not.

'The body was already there before any of them arrived. The children naturally assumed it was just another guy and arranged their guys around it.'

'They didn't take a look at its face?'

'No, thank goodness. I don't think it interested them particularly. I believe they were under the impression that a group of the village girls had made it, given that it was wearing rather fine clothes.'

'It's lucky they didn't decide to strip the guy and take the jacket,' said Cedric. 'That's the sort of things boys do, to spite the girls.'

His mouth had curled up slightly at the corners, and Rose wondered whether he had done just such a thing in his youth. A vision sprung up before her eyes of a beautifully painted effigy dressed in a gown of crimson silk, that she could well imagine his sister might have made, and a group of boys, led by Cedric, ripping the dress to shreds, a hysterical Lavinia chasing them around the field and threatening to tell her mother.

'Well, it's fortunate for them they weren't so inclined. They'd have been in for a nasty shock,' said the inspector. 'I suppose you'll tell me, Lady Belvedere, that they didn't see anybody lurking about so to speak?'

'No, they didn't, not a soul.'

'Of course we'll know more tomorrow once we've ascertained the time of death,' said Inspector Newcombe. 'But it looks like the body might have lain there for hours. The pile's swept for hedgehogs just before it's lit, didn't you say? So there'd be no reason for anybody to be about before the children arrived with their guys, I suppose? What about your servants taking down the food and setting up the tables?'

'They tend to leave that until the very last minute,' said Cedric. 'It's a frightful job getting everything ready, I can tell you. Usually they have only just got everything set up in time for the lighting of the bonfire. I'll check with my butler of course and the cook, but I don't doubt the children were the first to arrive. Ah … now, wait a minute.'

'What is it?' The inspector looked up sharply. Rose felt herself on edge. Even Sergeant Bell had paused for a moment in his notetaking, his pencil suspended in the air, hovering above his notebook.

'Major Spittlehouse was telling me only the other day that the Bonfire Committee had organised a night watch of the bonfire,' Cedric said. 'Apparently there has been some trouble with gangs of children from other villages trying to pilfer the wood from our pyre.' He chuckled. 'It happens every year and I won't deny that I did a bit of it myself when I was a boy, but the major had got a bit of a bee in his bonnet about it this year. So much so that he'd organised this night watch. It's just possible that they might have seen something, or someone, should I say?'

'There's no suggestion that the man was murdered last night,' said the inspector sounding disappointed. 'He'd have been missed for one thing and our medical man's preliminary findings are that he had not been dead more than a few hours. As I've said, we'll know more tomorrow, but there it is.'

120

'I'm not suggesting that, Inspector. Knowing the major as I do,' said Cedric, 'I think it highly likely that he arranged a final watch to take place today. Late afternoon, I would imagine.'

'Very well, we'll have a word with him about it. Talking of which, let's get the major and his sister in, shall we? I should like to know the last time this Masters chap was seen alive and happen as not they can tell us.' He looked up and smiled as the door opened and one of the footmen entered. 'Ah, here's the coffee.'

Chapter Sixteen

'Linus!'

Daphne Spittlehouse sprang up from the armchair in which she had been slouched, very nearly toppling the occasional table beside her in her haste. She ran forward impulsively, her hands outstretched and then stopped abruptly. Whether this was because of the look upon the major's face or the swift recollection that she very seldom embraced her brother, was not clear. What was certain, however, was that she all of a sudden felt awkward and self-conscious. She stood there hesitant, twisting her hands together and biting her bottom lip between her teeth.

'Oh, Linus ...' The words were said in such a very pathetic way and accompanied with such a heartfelt sigh that Major Spittlehouse wondered for a moment if Daphne were about to faint and crumple to the floor. He strode forward instinctively, but his sister seemed to collect herself and with a great determination of effort and will stood straight, her shoulders back and her chin thrust forward. For a moment brother and sister stood staring at each other, neither speaking.

'It's all right,' Major Spittlehouse said at last. 'You've had an awful shock, that's all.' He found that he had half extended an arm towards her. He stared at it stupidly and let it drop down to his side.

'It is true, then? Masters is dead? Oh, a part of me hoped that Lady Belvedere had got it all wrong,' cried Daphne.

'It's true enough. He's dead all right,' said Major Spittlehouse grimly.

'And ... murdered?'

The second word was said with such revulsion by the speaker that she actually appeared to recoil. The major, watching her steadfastly, merely nodded, a slow and deliberate movement.

'But who would want to kill Masters of all people?' Daphne cried. Vaguely she was aware that she had said something very similar to Rose, and caught her breath. It seemed such a very long time ago that she had last spoken to the countess; it might almost have been a different day.

'Don't you know?' said Major Spittlehouse quietly.

'What?' Had she heard her brother correctly? At once she was on her guard. 'Well, of course not. Why ... why should I know?'

'I just thought you might, that's all.' The words were spoken softly enough and yet …

'No.' Daphne stared at her brother dumbfounded, her bottom lip trembling uncontrollably. 'Tell me what you mean by saying such a thing, Linus.'

The major stared at her for a few moments before lowering his gaze. 'Forgive me. I was not thinking straight.' He passed a hand over his brow and bent his head. 'I am not quite myself.'

'You most certainly are not.' She watched him keenly, a grim look upon her face. Vaguely conscious that she was staring at him with a mixture of hatred and disbelief, he looked up to meet her gaze. He flinched under her penetrating stare and turned away. Now neither could see each other's eyes, which had seemed to bore through the other as if each had been a piece of wood.

'It is frightful, isn't it?' Daphne said at last to break the silence, if nothing else. She pulled at her bottom lip and glanced at her brother. 'I don't want to think about it.'

'Then don't,' said Major Spittlehouse brusquely. 'There's no reason why you should. Put it out of your mind.'

'And how might I do that, Linus?' She sounded weary. 'You make it sound so very easy, but it isn't. It isn't at all.'

'It can be if you want it to be. It needn't be complicated. I'll send for the doctor and ask him to give you a sedative to help you sleep.'

'And what would be the use of that?' Daphne stared miserably down at the carpet. 'The policemen will want to speak to me. It was them I heard arriving in the hall just now, wasn't it?'

'The police be damned,' replied her brother with feeling. 'They'll have to make do with me tonight.'

'You are being quite ridiculous, Linus, but it is sweet of you.' She turned and stared at him and put out her hand. For a very awkward and brief moment, they held hands. 'I'm … I'm very frightened.'

'You needn't be. It'll be all right.'

'Will it? How can you say it will be?' She turned away again and hid her face. 'Oh, it's all so horrible. Who could have done it, Linus? Who could have done such a thing?' How many times that evening, she wondered, had she asked a variation of that question?

'I don't know,' answered her brother dully. 'If you don't know who did it, then I don't know.'

With his words, the closeness that had been there momentarily evaporated as quickly as it had formed. There was now the usual distance between them.

'They disguised him as a guy,' Daphne was saying, more to herself than to him. 'They left him there on the ground to be thrown on the fire like a piece of wood, they –'

'Stop it, do you hear me?' cried her brother. He was vaguely aware that his voice had risen. He eyed her coldly. 'Is it not enough that he's dead?' His face was ashen. 'We'd been together a long time, he and I. He may have been my servant but I thought of him as a friend.'

'I know. I am sorry, Linus.'

'Are you, are you really?' There was an earnestness in his voice that was not lost on her.

'Yes. It's funny. Sometimes I forget you feel things as I do.'

'It's not so very odd,' her brother replied rather gruffly.

It is possible that their awkward and disjointed discourse might have continued for some time more, had they not been aware of the sound of footsteps on the landing outside. A mutual silence fell upon them and moments later Lord and Lady Belvedere entered with compassionate looks upon their faces. Their manner to their guests was sympathetic. Even so, Daphne gave them something of a startled look and clenched her hands into tight fists.

'Do they want to see me, the police, I mean?' she asked anxiously.

'Not yet,' reassured Cedric, taking in the woman's agitated state. He spoke gently in much the same way as he might have spoken to a frightened child. 'They'd like to speak to your brother first.' He glanced at his wristwatch. 'I daresay they'll decide not to question you until tomorrow morning given the hour.'

'That's just what I was saying,' said the major rallying. 'Perhaps you would be so good as to arrange for someone to escort my sister back to Green Gables?'

'Of course,' Rose said. 'I am happy to accompany Miss Spittlehouse myself.'

'But, Mrs Masters,' cried Daphne. 'I shan't know what to say to her. Oh, don't look at me like that, Linus. I'm not good at that sort of thing, you know I'm not. I shall only make things worse. You know it is you she will want to see, not me.'

'You needn't worry,' said Rose, a touch of coldness in her voice. 'My mother telephoned to say that she and Mrs Dobson have taken Mrs Masters to stay with them at South Lodge. They thought it best that she not be left alone tonight or troubled with doing domestic tasks.'

'Quite right,' agreed Major Spittlehouse. 'That was very thoughtful of your mother, Lady Belvedere. I appreciate Mrs Simpson's kindness and would be grateful if you could pass on my thanks. I popped in to Green Gables myself on my way here to break the news to Mrs Masters of her husband's death. I found the house quite shut up and not a soul about. It gave me quite a turn, I can tell you, till I spotted a note your mother had left on the mantelpiece in the hall.'

'So you would have me wait there all alone until you came home?' said Daphne shrilly. She gave her brother something of an outraged look and bit her lip.

'I thought I might send for Biddy to sit with you,' answered her brother, clearly embarrassed by her tone in company.

Rose wondered if this was the usual way she spoke to her brother; assuredly there was an awkwardness between them. Had she not known better, she would have said there was a sense of hostility in the air, and something else also. It took her a while to determine what it was, this other emotion that filled the room and tainted the air. Suspicion. It was distrust that hung about the room; she had attended the aftermath of too many murders to be in any doubt.

'I don't want to go home; I want to stay here,' said Daphne obstinately.

Major Spittlehouse looked about to protest, but appeared to think better of it. Instead, he said: 'Very well. I suppose there's no harm in your staying here until I've been interviewed. After that I'll see you home myself and I daresay we can do for ourselves tonight until Biddy comes in the morning to do the chores. That is, of course, if you have no objection to my sister staying here a little while longer, Lady Belvedere? I don't want us to inconvenience you.'

'Of course not, it would be a pleasure,' Rose answered politely enough, though in truth she would have preferred that his sister not stay at Sedgwick Court for a moment longer than was absolutely necessary.

Unfair though it might be, Rose could not rid herself of the notion that there was very little about Daphne Spittlehouse that was likable. The woman was aware of the awfulness of what had happened only insomuch as it affected her. She had not considered the poor man's widow nor, it would appear, her own brother. This impression was not helped with Daphne adding as a mumbled aside, which only Rose, who happened to be standing next to her heard: 'I shan't ever want to go back to Green Gables, not ever. I want to stay here.'

'Ah, Major Spittlehouse, good of you to join us,' said Inspector Newcombe, indicating a chair that was positioned opposite his own. 'And how is your sister?'

'Dreadfully upset as you might imagine. Poor girl's quite gone to pieces. Lady Belvedere is very kindly sitting with her now; I didn't think it wise to leave her alone.' The major hesitated a moment before taking the seat offered and gave the inspector an earnest look. 'I say, I do hope you won't think it necessary to question her tonight. What she needs is a good night's sleep.'

'Well, I don't think we'll need to speak to her tonight,' said the inspector, glancing at his wristwatch, 'particularly given the time. We'll be making an early start tomorrow with the interviews. That's not to say that my sergeant and I won't be up to all hours, because we will. Reviewing the list of people who attended tonight's celebrations for one thing, and seeing if the police surgeon and our fingerprint chaps have any more to give us.' He looked up and addressed Cedric, who had followed the major into the room and gave a brief smile. 'It was good of you to arrange for those lists to be made, my lord; it's helped us no end.' He returned his attention to Major Spittlehouse. 'First light, and Bell and I will be up at the scene. I'd like to see it in the daylight and get a feel for the place. There's only so much that you can see in the dark with lamps and flash bulbs and the like. That's the trouble when something like this happens out of doors. I'm leaving a chap or two, of course, to make sure it's left as it is.' He leaned back in his chair and sighed. 'Not that we're expecting to find much when it's light. The place will have been trampled by that many feet given that it was the scene of the village's Guy Fawkes' festivities.'

Major Spittlehouse sat on the chair, with his back very straight and erect, aware that the inspector was trying to put him at his ease, but vaguely conscious that Sergeant Bell was seated a little behind him to his left. If he were to turn his head a little, he would see him. The overall impression, however, was that the man was not there. He swallowed hard. The sergeant was present, he must remember that. He would be taking down what he said in shorthand. The major gave an involuntary shudder. He must be careful. He must not be lulled in to believing that everything would be all right and lose his head. He glanced up and saw that the inspector was watching him closely, and when he tilted his head slightly, he caught sight of Lord Belvedere propped up against the mantelpiece, lounging in what the young man probably thought to be a nonchalant manner. To the major, it was anything but, for he saw the alert look in the earl's eyes, half obscured though it was by a feigned look of indifference. He must be on his guard.

'You have no objection to my being here, do you, old chap?' enquired Cedric, having promised Rose that he would attend in her enforced absence.

'Not at all, Lord Belvedere,' said Major Spittlehouse. Only the frown that creased his forehead for a moment suggested otherwise.

The inspector gathered his papers and proceeded with his preliminary questions. They appeared to the major harmless enough, focusing as they did on how long Masters had been in the major's employ, and what he knew of the man's character.

'One couldn't have asked for a better servant,' declared the major with feeling. 'Knew his job like the back of his hand, he did.'

'When you retired from the army some eight years or so ago, Masters and his wife came to work for you and Miss Spittlehouse?'

'Yes. They did for us as you might say,' agreed the major. 'My parents had died and my sister was all alone. She came and kept house for me. With the exception of a gardener and a daily maid, both of whom lived out, the Masters' saw to our needs.'

'You must have known this Masters fellow well?' said Inspector Newcombe. 'You'd been through the war together, hadn't you? I'd say you'd get to know what made a man tick?'

'I daresay I knew him as well as I knew any man,' agreed Major

Spittlehouse rather gruffly. He added with an unexpected ferocity: 'And before you ask, Inspector, I can't imagine why any soul would have wished him harm.'

'And yet someone murdered him.' said the inspector softly.

Cedric made a move as if to interrupt, but apparently thought better of it. He caught the senior policeman's eye, however, and the two exchanged a look.

'You wished to say something, Lord Belvedere?'

'Yes … no … that is to say, it probably has nothing to do with the murder.'

'We'll be the judge of that if you don't mind, Lord Belvedere.'

'Yes, of course, Inspector. I'll mention it at the end. I should hate to interfere with your line of questioning.'

'Very well. Now, Major,' said Inspector Newcombe, returning his attention to Major Spittlehouse, 'perhaps you could give me a few details about the arrangements for the Bonfire Night celebrations? You were on the committee, I believe, the one that organised the event?'

'That's right. I've been a member for four years, chairman for the last three.' The major sat back in his chair. 'I'm not sure that I can tell you very much, Inspector. Each year is very like the other. The bonfire's lit, then there's the judging of the guys of course, followed by the firework display.'

'The judging of the guys happens every year?'

'Like clockwork. The children look forward to it. Some of them make a real effort and some of them don't. That's not to say of course that it doesn't cause some problems, because it does. Thieving of clothes off washing lines and the like is very common. Some of course are content with using just rags and sheets, but there are others who like to dress their guys in something grand –'

'I see,' said the inspector hurriedly, fearing that the major might well be about to embark on a particular hobby horse of his. 'Now, tell me about this night watch, if you will, Major Spittlehouse.' Was it his imagination, or did he see the major give a small involuntary start? 'Lord Belvedere was telling me that you were having some trouble with gangs of children from the neighbouring villages trying to pilfer the wood from the bonfire for their own. You'd organised a night watch to tackle it, I understand?'

128

'It was no more of a problem than usual, Inspector, but this year we thought we'd try and do something about it.'

'And when was the final watch? Did it by any chance meet this afternoon?'

'It did indeed, Inspector. We thought it likely as not that some of the boys would make a last attempt to steal some wood a few hours before the lighting of the bonfire. Of course it would have ruined it for the village. You can't have a bonfire night without a decent bonfire.'

'Quite. Now, what time would this have been?'

'Half past four, thereabouts. I went down myself to have a look. There were three of us there from the Committee. We walked the perimeter of the field and ended up beside the bonfire.'

'Did you see anyone?' The inspector had leaned forward and was staring at the major keenly. Even the sergeant had looked up from his notes.

'Not a soul, Inspector.'

'I take it the body wasn't there?'

'Of course not. What sort of a fool do you take me for, Inspector?' cried the major indignantly. 'I think I might have noticed if there had been a corpse lying on the ground. Heaven knows I've seen enough bodies in my time.'

'All right,' said Inspector Newcombe hurriedly. 'It's just possible that you might have mistaken it for a guy, particularly if you only saw it from a distance.'

'I'm telling you there was nothing there. Neither a living soul, nor a dead one.' The major still sounded disgruntled. 'As I've said, we had a quick look at the bonfire, did our rounds of the field and left.'

'What time did you all leave?'

'I didn't look at my watch, but I'd say we left before five.'

'Take a note of that, will you, Bell? And if you could give my sergeant the names and addresses of the other two members of your watch before you go, I should be much obliged. It's possible they may have seen something.' The inspector shuffled his papers. 'Now, I'd like you to tell me what happened after five o'clock this afternoon. You went home, I assume, after your watch?'

'Yes. Though there's nothing much to tell. Mrs Masters had laid out a cold supper in the parlour.'

'Masters waited on you?'

'No, I served myself.'

'And your sister? Did she eat with you?'

'No, I ate alone. My sister popped her head around the door and told me she wasn't hungry. She seemed rather surprised to see me. I suppose she thought I'd still be out in the field.'

'And Masters, where was he?'

'I don't know. I don't recollect seeing him before I set out for the festivities.'

'It's possible then that he might already have gone out before you came back from the watch?'

'Yes. Though you'd need to ask Mrs Masters; she'd know.'

'Thank you. We shall be speaking to the deceased's wife tomorrow morning. Now, after your supper, what did you do?'

'I shut myself up in my study for an hour and a half or so. I had some letters to write. Then I set out for the field.'

'At what time did you leave your house?'

'A quarter to seven. I remember looking at the clock on the mantelpiece and thinking that I ought to leave or else I'd be late. I thought it wouldn't do for a man in my position not to be there when they lit the bonfire, what with me being chairman of the Bonfire Committee and all.'

'Did Miss Spittlehouse accompany you?'

'No. I called up to her; my sister was in her bedroom, I think. She came out on to the landing. She said she didn't want to stand around in the cold waiting for the bonfire to be lit and that she'd make her own way there a little later. Besides, she told me she had a few things to do first.'

'I see. So you set off for the bonfire alone. No sign of Masters, I suppose?'

'No, Inspector. I've told you. I didn't see him. I didn't see him again until …' The major's voice faltered with emotion.

'Quite,' said the inspector hurriedly, fearing the onset of an awkward silence. 'You live at Green Gables, don't you, Major? How long would it take you to walk to the field? Fifteen minutes at a brisk walk?

'Yes, about that. Of course the other villagers were making their way there about that time, same as me. Quite a procession we made. I was obliged to stop and talk to one or two of them. It made me late. I remember rushing in the end and I still missed seeing the bonfire being lit.'

'Indeed? We shall need their names, these friends you stopped and spoke to.'

For the first time the major hesitated, as if it had just dawned on him that he might be considered a possible suspect in his servant's death. Cedric felt a pang of sympathy for him.

'If you think it necessary, Inspector,' said Major Spittlehouse at last. He passed a hand over his military moustache and tugged at it absentmindedly.

'Pray, please continue,' prodded the detective.

'There's not much else to add,' said the major rather indignantly. 'When I arrived, the bonfire was already alight, as I've said. Lord and Lady Belvedere were just making their way over to the line of guys for the judging. I could tell something was wrong,' he said, turning to address Cedric, 'the way you and Lady Belvedere paused to take a second look at … at Masters. You leapt forward, if you remember, my lord, and went to feel for a pulse; at least that's what it looked like. Your wife had turned away.'

The words were scarcely out of the major's mouth when the door opened. As if by one accord their eyes were drawn to stare at it to glimpse the newcomer. In Major Spittlehouse's case, he was obliged to turn around in his seat.

'My sister?' cried Major Spittlehouse as Rose entered. He even went so far as to spring out of his seat.

'She is quite all right, Major,' said Rose for the second time that evening. 'She's resting and asked to be left alone, that's all. She'll ring if she requires anything.'

It was as if Rose's entrance had broken a spell of sorts, for her husband had abandoned his nonchalant air and the lounging position that he had adopted beside the fireplace. He took a step forward so that he was level with the major. The bored indifference had left his voice and was replaced with a note of urgency. 'The jacket,' said Cedric. 'You must tell them about the jacket, you really must. Your life may be in grave danger.'

Chapter Seventeen

'What jacket?' asked Inspector Newcombe sharply. He looked from Cedric to the major, and back again, with something of an annoyed look upon his face. Rose, from her position behind the major, which afforded her a very good view of the inspector's expression, thought it likely that he was not best pleased at this latest turn of events. He most probably suspected that something of significance had been withheld from him, something which ought to have been disclosed at the very beginning of the interview.

Rose stared at the major's back, which was solid and unflinching. She was hit with the sudden realisation that the man intended to say nothing at all about the jacket. It was to be left to Cedric to enlighten the inspector. Her husband, however, obviously thought it the major's duty to do so, and there ensued an uncomfortable silence, interrupted only by the ticking of the clock on the mantelpiece.

'Come now, gentlemen, out with it,' said the inspector somewhat irritably. 'There's no use holding anything back and keeping it to yourselves. In an investigation of this sort things have a habit of coming out. It's best that you tell me now. The more we know, the sooner we'll get the murderer.' The silence continued and the inspector tried again. 'Anything, no matter how trivial or irrelevant you might think it to be, may well prove to be the vital clue we're looking for.'

'It isn't in the least bit insignificant,' said Cedric at last, a little sullenly. 'Masters was wearing the major's jacket when he was killed.'

'Was he indeed? Is that true, Major?'

The inspector was looking distinctly interested by this piece of information. Rose, who had barely had an opportunity to converse with her husband since the discovery of the body, leaned forward in her chair. Even Sergeant Bell had looked up expectantly.

'Yes, Inspector,' continued Cedric, when it became patently clear that the major did not intend to speak on the matter. 'Masters was wearing the major's tweed jacket. It's quite distinctive. A brown Harris tweed with a dark green stripe running through it interlaced with a purple stripe. I've never seen another one quite like it. The major always wears it come rain or shine. I don't think I've seen him in anything else, except for tonight, of course.' He glanced over at Major Spittlehouse, as if for confirmation, which was not forthcoming. 'It was your jacket that he was wearing, wasn't it? I thought it a trifle odd at the time. I said as much to you when we were waiting for the inspector to arrive.'

Rather pushed into a corner, Major Spittlehouse said slowly, as if he were uttering the words grudgingly: 'Yes, it was my jacket.'

'Was your servant in the habit of borrowing your clothes?' demanded Inspector Newcombe.

'Of course not,' retorted the major, a trifle angrily.

'And yet he was wearing your jacket tonight,' countered the inspector. 'Why was that?'

'I don't know. I can give no explanation for why he should do such a thing.'

'He didn't ask you if he might wear the jacket tonight?'

'No.'

'You didn't by any chance suggest to your servant, Major, that he might like to wear it?' said Rose, a vague, ridiculous thought having suddenly entered her head.

It was the first time she had spoken since the matter of the jacket had been raised, and she had caught them all unawares, how silent had been her presence up to then. It was obvious that Major Spittlehouse for one had forgotten that she was there. He started in his chair and half turned in his seat, his face a livid shade of crimson.

'Certainly not, Lady Belvedere.'

'Yet, how do you explain the fact that your manservant was wearing your jacket?' demanded the inspector.

'I have already told you that I can't.'

It was Cedric who asked the question that was on everyone's lips: 'Why weren't you wearing the jacket yourself this evening, Spittlehouse?'

Perhaps he was aware that all their eyes were upon him for, when the major spoke, it was somewhat indignantly.

'If you must know,' he said, 'Masters suggested that I wear my dark grey wool overcoat this evening. He said it was supposed to be bitterly cold later and Mrs Masters didn't want me to get a chill. Those were his exact words, I believe, or something very much along those lines. I'd have been far too warm if I'd worn my tweed jacket underneath the overcoat, so I didn't. Besides, Masters said it would give him an opportunity to give the jacket a proper clean.'

'I see,' said Inspector Newcombe thoughtfully. 'It was the deceased's suggestion that you not wear your tweed jacket this evening, presumably in order that he might wear it himself?'

'That would appear to be the case, Inspector,' said Major Spittlehouse. He gave an annoyed grunt and flared his nostrils.

'Tell me, Major, why were you so reluctant to tell me about this business concerning your jacket? If Lord Belvedere hadn't mentioned it, we'd have been none the wiser.'

'I didn't want to put the man in a bad light. It was entirely out of character for him to do such a thing. I didn't want you to think badly of him.' The major stared miserably at a piece of carpet in front of him.

'Is that the only reason you didn't tell us?' asked Inspector Newcombe, looking far from convinced. 'You thought it reflected badly on the man's character?'

'Yes. For no other reason. I can assure you.' Major Spittlehouse returned the policeman's gaze. His stare was unwavering. 'And if it were up to me you'd still be in the dark about it.' He glanced over at Cedric. 'I wish you hadn't seen the need to mention it, Lord Belvedere.'

'Do you?' said Cedric, a frown creasing his forehead.

'There was no need to,' repeated Major Spittlehouse dully.

'There was every need,' Rose whispered to herself. 'And I find it hard to believe that a man of the major's intelligence cannot see that.'

'What did you make of Major Spittlehouse?' Cedric asked, leaning nonchalantly against the fireplace once more. It was some half an hour or so later, and the major and his sister had left Sedgwick Court for Green Gables. 'Why didn't you press him further about the jacket? It was obvious that he was hiding something.'

'I think it more likely that the man was in shock,' said Inspector Newcombe. 'Murder does that to a person, even to a man such as Major Spittlehouse who has witnessed violent death. People react in different ways; I've seen it often enough. Some can't stop talking, and others can't stop crying. A man like the major just becomes silent and retreats inside himself. I expect he was the same during the war. He needs time to adjust and digest things inwardly. We'd have got no more out of him tonight, not once he had set his mind to withdraw. Tomorrow morning he'll be quite a different person once he's had a good night's sleep, you mark my words.'

'If you say so,' said Cedric, sounding sceptical. 'It seems to me that he was being deliberately unhelpful and not at all like his usual self. The major I know would have had a fit if he'd discovered his servant wearing his clothes, and his favourite jacket at that. No, the man was subdued all right. Something's rattled him, even if he won't admit it.'

'Talking of which,' said Inspector Newcombe, 'I should like to know about this Masters fellow. Were he and the major anything alike in appearance? It's difficult to view a body and imagine what it looked like in life. Even the most sunburned face becomes pale and the most animated features become still. It didn't help of course that we were viewing the corpse in the dark with only the artificial light from bulbs and torches to help us.'

'I suppose they were rather similar,' answered Cedric on reflection. 'They both sported those carefully trimmed military moustaches for one thing. And they were rather similar in build, though the major was a good six inches taller than his servant, I would have said, and slightly broader across the shoulders.'

'But they might have been mistaken for each other in the dark.' said Inspector Newcombe. 'Particularly if Masters was wearing Major Spittlehouse's jacket.'

'Well, that's certainly what I thought,' said Cedric, warming to the subject. 'And I implied as much to the major when we were waiting for you to arrive. I almost mistook Masters for the major myself when we first came across the body. It was because of that damn tweed jacket, of course. And it didn't help that the cap had been pulled down over the corpse's head and his face smeared with dirt. Even then, I wouldn't have been entirely sure of his identity if I had not heard the major call out to me when he did.'

'So it's quite possible then that the servant was murdered in mistake for his master,' the inspector mused.

'Very possible I would have said, Inspector,' said Cedric. He turned his attention to his wife, who all the while had been standing at the window, looking out at the pitch darkness. He was aware that she had been following their conversation, betrayed by the slight tilt of her head. 'Darling, you have been awfully quiet. What do you think?'

Rose turned and faced the room. She found that it was not only her husband that was waiting on her reply, for both the inspector and sergeant were looking at her expectantly.

'I agree with you that it is certainly possible in theory that one was mistaken for the other,' she said slowly, choosing her words with care. 'Of course I had never met the major until this evening, and to my knowledge I don't believe I had ever laid eyes on Masters when he was alive, so I cannot comment on the similarity in their appearance. It is not that, however, that interests me.'

'Oh?' said the inspector, sounding intrigued. 'Pray tell me what does interest you, Lady Belvedere?'

'Simply that the major was at pains to hide the fact that he may have been the intended victim,' answered Rose. 'That reason he gave for not telling you about the jacket did not ring true. There is something about his servant wearing his jacket that worries him. I think he was being truthful when he said the man wore the jacket without his permission. It startled him, I think, and now he is afraid.'

'If that is the case, why not tell us?' said Inspector Newcombe. 'If the major is in danger as both you and your husband suppose, why does he not tell us so that we might protect him?'

'It is possible that he is not certain,' said Rose. 'It might be that he merely harbours a suspicion. I think he is the sort of man who would think very carefully before he acted or said anything. We must remember that he has had an awful shock. He will want to think over what has happened before he decides what to do.' She paused a moment before adding: 'There are of course two other possible reasons for his not wanting us to consider him the intended victim.'

'Oh, and what are they?' asked Inspector Newcombe, raising an enquiring eyebrow.

'Motive. Perhaps Major Spittlehouse has something he is hiding, which he does not wish us to discover.' The inspector gave a puzzled frown and Rose attempted to clarify. 'What I mean is that someone might have wanted to kill the major for a reason he would rather not disclose.'

'Because it would put him in a bad light, to use his phrase?' said

Cedric.

'Exactly.'

'And what is the other reason?' asked the inspector. 'You said there were two.'

'It just occurred to me that it is possible that he is protecting the murderer.'

There had been some more speculation concerning the major's reticence on being interviewed, and then the evening had wound up naturally enough and almost of its own accord for the Belvederes. Cedric had chanced to look at the clock on the mantelpiece and discovered that it was well past midnight. It had been a long night, and an eventful one, and everyone appeared tired and fatigued. It was not, however, the end of the evening for the policemen, who intended to return to Bichester police station to write up a report and to review the evidence that had been gathered in the few hours since the corpse's discovery.

Cedric had offered to put them up at Sedgwick Court, but they had politely declined, though the offer of the use of the library for their interviews had been gratefully accepted. The village hall might well have proven more suitable for such an office, but the former facilitated Rose's involvement in the investigation and, though this was not expressly mooted as a reason for adopting Sedgwick Court as their village headquarters, it was present in all their minds.

It was a weary earl and countess who mounted the grand staircase and made their way to bed. The servants, without exception, had retired for the night. Manning had done his rounds as soon as the policemen had made their departure. The other servants had gone to their quarters some time before, tired after an exhausting day of preparation for the bonfire festivities, coupled with the unexpected, and most probably unwanted, task of supervising the village children and adults following the removal of the firework display to Sedgwick Court.

To Rose, the house seemed eerily silent save for the sound of their own footsteps, which themselves were muffled to some extent by the thick pile of the carpet. She knew that should she speak, her voice would echo around the walls of the great hall and be unbearably loud in the quietness.

She glanced at her husband, who appeared to be struck by the same thought, for his manner was subdued. Apart from squeezing her hand he said nothing, and they proceeded up the stairs in a companionable silence, each lost in their own thoughts. Rose reminded herself that the events of the evening had been an even greater blow for Cedric than for herself, that he must still be reeling from the shock of it all. The bonfire festivities had been a long established tradition at Sedgwick, one that had been going on for centuries without major mishap. Tonight had been the exception. Never again would the villagers be able to look at the effigies without the knowledge that once one had been a murdered man. Would the children's enthusiasm to make the guys be diminished, she wondered, when they discovered that the guy they had assumed had been made by a group of girls had in fact been a body? It was quite possible of course that the judging of the guys had become so tainted and associated with death that it would no longer be held.

As she lay in bed that night, Rose thought of Major Spittlehouse's reluctance to mention the tweed jacket and what it might signify. Was it possible that the murderer had assumed that the man he had killed was the major and not his servant? Had Masters really been killed in error? And why had he been wearing his employer's jacket? All these thoughts whirled around in her mind as sleep eluded her. She thought of Mrs Masters, a woman whom she had never met, and who was even now a guest in her mother's house. How had she taken the news of her husband's violent death? Was she tossing and turning in her bedclothes as Rose was now, unable to get to sleep? And Daphne Spittlehouse, what was she really thinking and feeling? Masters had been wearing her brother's jacket. How did she feel knowing that there was a possibility that her brother had been the intended victim?

Rose sat up with a start. The Spittlehouses' will. How had she forgotten about that? She remembered Daphne's anguished visit, the way she had told her about the provisions of her parents' will. Her brother had been the sole benefactor. His sister would only receive her inheritance at his discretion. In the meantime, she had been given what she perceived to be a relatively meagre allowance, which might be withdrawn without notice on her brother's whim. Daphne Spittlehouse had been a desperate woman in fear of losing the man she loved. Surely only for that reason had she taken the unusual course of confiding her troubles to a stranger.

And Rose had been unable to help. Cedric's pleading of Daphne's cause to her brother had fallen on deaf ears. The major had been steadfast in his belief that Daphne would not receive a penny from him if she were to marry Archie Mayhew, a young man he considered rather worthless and thoroughly unsuitable as a suitor for his sister.

Tomorrow Inspector Newcombe would tell Major Spittlehouse that it was possible that he had been the intended victim rather than his servant. It was a fact of which she was certain the major was already fully aware, even if he had not yet admitted it to himself. The question was, would Major Spittlehouse advise the police of the strained relations between himself and his sister? Would he provide them with a motive for why she might wish him dead? Rose thought it unlikely. The major was the sort of man who would deal with any threat to himself in his own way. They all knew him to have been fond of his servant. He would want justice for him; he would not let his murderer go unpunished. Despite the warmth from the fire, which was still glowing in the hearth, Rose shuddered. It would feel like a betrayal of trust, but she was determined to mention the provisions of the Spittlehouses' will to the inspector, if only for Daphne's safety.

Chapter Eighteen

Daphne awoke the following morning in the certain knowledge that something terrible had occurred which had the most awful ramifications. Her recollections of the previous evening, however, were rather hazy on account of her brother having given her something to make her sleep. She had taken it without protest, and now her thoughts and memories were rather jumbled, so that she had the odd feeling of not knowing quite what was real and what she had dreamt.

The appearance of Biddy, the maid-of-all-work, with her morning cup of tea informed her that the situation regarding the Masters' was forever altered. For it should have been Mrs Masters bringing her her tea and opening her curtains to let in the day, not the maid, who was little more than a child and looked as if at any moment she might spill the tea on to the eiderdown, and then where would they be?

Daphne sat up in bed and grabbed the offending cup and saucer to prevent a catastrophe from occurring. It was only when she was satisfied there would be no spilt tea that she noticed that the little maid's eyes were swollen and red from recent crying, and that she appeared to be snivelling. Her uniform looked none too clean either. There was a reason, Daphne supposed, why Biddy rarely ventured upstairs into the bedrooms. She was, however, sufficiently moved by the girl's distressed appearance as to comment on it.

'Are you frightfully upset by all this, Biddy?' She asked tentatively. 'It must have been an awful shock.'

'Oh yes, ma'am,' cried the maid, a fresh bout of tears threatening to erupt and spill down her cheeks. 'Mr Masters was awful kind to me, he was. He used to make me laugh something rotten with all his jokes and his tricks that he'd learnt in the army. Mrs Masters was forever after him for distracting me from my work. She used to tell him that she had little enough help in the house as it was, without him keeping me from my chores. She didn't mean anything by it, of course. It was just her way.' She paused to dab at her face with a handkerchief, which to Daphne's eyes looked distinctly soiled. 'It's a crying shame what's happened to him. Who could have done such a thing? And he the kindest person you'd

140

ever be likely to meet.'

'I don't know,' said Daphne, rather alarmed by the maid's display of emotion. 'Where is Mrs Masters now? Is she still at South Lodge?'

'Yes, ma'am, as far as I know. She's taken it awful hard, she has, or so I've been told and I've no reason to doubt it. She was that fond of him, it makes you weep. They meant everything to one another, they did. Never had any children, they didn't. I don't know how she'll cope without him.' Biddy sniffed. 'It won't be the same for me either, not having him here to tease me and make me laugh.'

'Was she so very fond of him?' said Daphne, more to herself than to the maid, who had already left the room. She realised that until now she had never given much thought to her servants' feelings. She had only ever thought of them as the couple that did for her and her brother. Mrs Masters was an appendage of Masters', that was all. She had never considered that they might have emotions or personalities. She had thought that Mrs Masters would be upset by what had happened to her husband, it was only natural that she would be. But that the woman might possess great wells of emotion that resembled her own feelings for Archie had not occurred to her.

Archie! The name set a fire in her stomach and sent her pulse racing. During all of this she had not once thought of Archie. Last night, when Lady Belvedere told her of the discovery of the body and during the endless hours she had waited for Linus, she had thought of nothing very much, only that she was afraid. She should have thought of Archie, searching for her among the crowd in vain. What had he thought when he couldn't find her? Had he been rushing around tearing his hair out, sick with the worry of it all? She saw him now, running towards Sedgwick Court, stumbling on the stones on the makeshift path from field to Court, out of breath, his eyes wild, his actions clumsy. Where was he now? Had he returned to Bichester, or was he perhaps waiting outside her window for a sign that she was there?

She threw aside her bedclothes, almost upsetting the cursed cup and saucer in the process, and tore to the window. It overlooked the front garden, and beyond that she caught a glimpse of the street. Archie was nowhere to be seen. He was not leaning against the cherry tree staring up at her window. She turned, with a quite ridiculous feeling of sadness, and blindly felt for her dressing gown, which hung from a hook on her door. She wrapped it about her, as if it were a blanket, and paused to stare at the clock on her bedside table. It was quite a shock when the hands informed her it was past ten o'clock. She crept out on to the landing and peered over the banister. All was quiet. Her brother must be in his study. With deft steps, she began to descend the staircase, her eyes focused on the telephone on the table in the hall below.

The morning had brought another fine day, cold but with pale sunshine that fought its way through the gaps in the curtain. These were the days that Rose usually enjoyed. They involved brisk walks followed by afternoons in front of the fire. Today, however, everything was marred. The good weather seemed inappropriate in light of the tragedy that had occurred the previous evening. It had the effect, however, of lifting her spirits sufficiently that the thoughts that had haunted her last night, making sleep impossible, had diminished in their magnitude. They were no longer insurmountable, or at least solely her responsibility, for the realisation had struck her that she might confer with Cedric.

She glanced over at her husband, whose sleep seemed untroubled, and traced the profile of his face gently with her fingers. Since their marriage, she had enjoyed this intimacy of waking up beside him and staring at his profile unchecked. The novelty of doing such a thing had yet to wear off. She still marvelled at his handsome features, at the jawline that looked chiselled even in sleep, and the fair hair that lay ruffled and untidy on his pillow. It contrasted sharply with his daytime habit of wearing it neatly slicked back.

They should have been lying there talking about the success of the bonfire festivities, marvelling at the inventiveness of the children in compiling their guys, laughing at those that had borne a striking resemblance to people in the village. Instead, Rose felt a reluctance to waken her husband, and an inclination to lie there and watch him sleeping for as long as possible. Wakefulness would only bring him troubles and cause his forehead to frown. She knew Cedric well, knew that he would consider himself partly responsible for what had happened, though the notion was quite ridiculous. But it had been his bit of wasteland on which the festivities had been held, and Sedgwick Court had provided the refreshments and contributed heavily to the purchase of the fireworks.

Even Rose felt that she bore some responsibility, for it was she who had judged the guys. She had paused and stopped before the dead man, had leant forward and touched his face. It was ludicrous of course, but there it was, lurking at the back of her mind, refusing to be quashed.

That morning she breakfasted with her husband, instead of indulging in the married woman's privilege of taking her breakfast in bed. She had a particular reason for wishing to eat with Cedric. It was not only the enjoyment of his company that drew her, wonderful though that was, nor a wish to allude to the horrors of last night. Rather she wished to speak to him about Daphne and, in particular, the provisions of her parents' will and her brother's response to her intention to marry a young man of whom he thoroughly disapproved.

'You think it gives her a motive for wishing Major Spittlehouse dead?' said Cedric, tucking in to his kippers and kedgeree. It was a relief to Rose to note that he had lost none of his appetite. She herself nibbled on a piece of toast.

'Yes. I'm not really suggesting that she would do such a thing but, if it is determined that the major was the intended victim, it might be worth finding out what happens to their parents' money in the event of Major Spittlehouse's death. I am assuming that, as next of kin, the majority of his estate would go to her.'

'Well, I can't see the major being very forthcoming on the matter, particularly if his manner today is anything like it was yesterday,' said Cedric, through a mouthful of kipper.

'I've thought of that. Daphne might tell us. She doesn't share her brother's natural reticence,' said Rose, sipping her coffee.

'I'll say she doesn't, telling you all about her parents' will and her brother's meanness towards her regarding money. She'd never met you before and there she was spilling the beans on her family's personal matters.'

'She thought I might be able to help her,' said Rose, slightly defensively. 'I felt absolutely rotten that I was unable to do so, though really it was not my fault.'

'Of course it wasn't. And instead you had me do your dirty work,' replied her husband, not without humour. 'I don't think I have ever felt quite so awkward. Still, the major's face was quite a masterpiece; I can still picture it. I thought he was going to blow a gasket.'

'The problem is that Daphne Spittlehouse told me all about it in confidence,' said Rose, a serious note creeping in to her voice. 'I don't remember her swearing me to secrecy, but I think she would take a pretty dim view if I blurted it all out to the police. I know I would in her place. Yet I feel that I have a duty to tell them, don't you?''

'Yes, and we have already established that the major is unlikely to volunteer the information. He'll just sit there all tight lipped like he was last night and say nothing. Of course,' said Cedric, 'it would look much better for Daphne if she were to mention it herself. The police are bound to ask her if she can think of any reason why anyone might wish her brother dead.'

'And you suggest that she tells them she has the biggest motive of all?' Nevertheless Rose pondered the proposal seriously for a moment, her forehead creasing in contemplation. 'I can't quite see Daphne doing that. It would be like offering herself up as the main suspect. You saw how nervous and agitated she was last night. The major was definitely worried about her.'

'Perhaps he was anxious about what she might say. You know her habit for blurting things out.'

'I daresay you are right, about Daphne mentioning it to the police herself, I mean,' admitted Rose, at last. 'I'll have a word with her about it. I expect the police will be busy this morning viewing the scene of the crime, and then of course they'll want another word with Major Spittlehouse, so I suppose there is no great hurry. And besides, I have something else I want to do first.'

'Oh? What is that?' Cedric paused in his eating to look up, an interested look upon his face.

'As soon as I've had breakfast, I intend to walk over to South Lodge and speak with Mrs Masters.'

It was Miss Simmons who answered the telephone, adopting what Daphne thought was a particularly affected voice, not her usual tone at all. It was not the timid simpering voice with which she greeted Mr Whittaker. This voice was sharp, bordering on the rude, frightening away potential new clients rather than encouraging them. She would have to have a word with Archie about it when they were married.

Miss Simmons' voice had, however, its desired effect. Daphne took a deep breath. How easy it would be to hang up the receiver without uttering a word. She had to fight her natural inclination to do just that.

'Miss Simmons, this is Miss Spittlehouse. I should very much like to speak with Mr Mayhew, please.'

She heard Miss Simmons tut; it was a most distinctive sound. Daphne felt her blood boil and her cheeks flush. How dare she? The situation was not helped when the secretary next spoke.

'I'm afraid, Miss Spittlehouse, that is not possible. Mr Mayhew is assisting Mr Whittaker with the drafting of a particularly complicated trust deed. They have asked not to be disturbed.'

'I should like to speak to Mr Mayhew on a matter of some urgency. Please ask him to come to the telephone at once.' Daphne had spoken in her most haughty voice, the one she reserved for speaking to unhelpful shop assistants and tardy servants. It was the sort of voice that said she would accept no nonsense and that she had better be obeyed or else. For one awful moment she didn't think it was going to have the desired effect on Miss Simmons. She could feel the woman's righteous indignation rise as if it were floating along the telephone line to her.

'Very well, if you say so, Miss Spittlehouse,' Miss Simmons said at last, rather coldly, and then she was gone and Daphne was left waiting, aware of nothing but the all-consuming silence. In the quietness, she was conscious only of the beating of her heart, thumping against her ribcage. She felt ridiculously exposed standing out there in the hall. Any moment Biddy might take it in to her head to come and dust, or Linus might come out of his study and catch her. Not that there was any reason why she shouldn't be using the telephone; she had a perfect right to do so if she wished. But she didn't want them to overhear her talking to Archie, not after all the recent unpleasantness. She drummed with her fingers impatiently on the hall table. Why was it taking so long? It was only a small office. It wouldn't take a minute for Miss Simmons to tap on Mr Whittaker's door and convey her message. An awful thought suddenly occurred to her. What if Miss Simmons was only pretending to give the message? What if she had no intention of delivering it? She might only be waiting a few minutes before returning to say that she was frightfully sorry but they really could not be disturbed, and would Miss Spittlehouse be so good as to telephone later? Well, Daphne was not going to have any of that. Who did Miss Simmons think she was, giving herself such airs and graces? The Spittlehouses were undoubtedly Gribble, Hebborn & Whittaker's most affluent clients. True, most of their business was handled by a London firm, but even so …

'Daphne, is that you, darling?' Archie's youthful voice burst on to the line like a ray of bright sunshine. 'Goodness, what did you say to old Simmons? She looked as if she had swallowed a lemon. Even Uncle Harold looked worried when he saw her.'

'Archie. Oh, Archie.'

'What's the matter, old thing? You sound quite done in. I say, I'm awfully sorry about last night. Not showing up and all that.'

'Didn't you? Then you don't …? Daphne caught her breath. 'I didn't know, that you didn't come, that is.'

'But you must have known. What did you think when I didn't turn up?'

'I didn't know,' repeated Daphne dully. 'You see, I didn't go either.'

'Didn't you? Why not?' Archie sounded rather surprised and not a little annoyed. 'I might have gone to all that effort and you wouldn't have been there. At least I've got a decent excuse for not turning up. The bus was late and then one of its blasted tyres suffered a puncture. But you only had to walk a few hundred yards.'

'A little further than that,' protested Daphne. 'But really it wasn't my fault. Just as I was setting off I saw that my brother had gone out. I knew he'd be making his way over to the bonfire. I could hardly risk following him, could I? He'd have seen me and wanted to know what I was doing. I didn't want to tell him that I'd arranged to meet you. He's awfully old-fashioned about that sort of thing.' She sighed. 'We should never have agreed to meet in Tucker's Wood.'

'Well, I don't know why we did. It was your idea. I suggested that we meet in the little lane at the back of your house.'

'I wish we had now. I really wasn't thinking. I had forgotten how close to the bonfire Tucker's Wood is.' She passed a hand across her forehead. 'We've all had the most awful shock. Someone was murdered last night and their body put out with the guys to be put on to the bonfire and burnt.

146

It was awful.'

There was a shocked exclamation on the other end of the telephone line.

'I say, that's frightful! There was talk of a body in the office this morning but I didn't give it much credence. I thought it was a lot of old rot. But, now that you mention it, Uncle Harold did say something had happened last night because they were all herded off to Sedgwick Court to watch the firework display there and he had to give his name.' There was a slight pause and then he said: 'Who was killed, do you know?'

'It was Masters,' said Daphne. For the first time, talking to Archie as she was, it seemed real.

'Masters?' There was a sharp intake of breath. She could have sworn that Archie sounded surprised, as if he had expected her to say someone else. 'Who was he? The name sounds familiar, though I don't know why it should.'

'He was our servant, mine and my brother's. He and his wife did for us, you might say. It appears that someone mistook him for my brother. He was wearing Linus' jacket, you see.'

'Major Spittlehouse? Is he dead too?'

'No, of course not. I do wish you'd listen to what I'm telling you, Archie. Masters is dead and my brother is very much alive. They think someone killed Masters by mistake, thinking he was Linus.'

'Good Heavens! Did your brother tell you that?'

'No. He won't talk about it. I think he's too upset, or else thinks it will distress me. You know how protective of me he is. It was Lady Belvedere who told me.' Daphne sighed. 'She was awfully kind, she –'

'Daphne, I really must go. My uncle is calling me.' Perhaps he was aware of her disappointment for he added in a slightly lighter tone: 'I need to earn my crust if we are to be married.'

'Archie, I must see you.'

'Darling, I don't think that would be very wise. Not if your servant was murdered in mistake for your brother.'

'Why not? Why should that matter?' cried Daphne. 'What of it?'

'Oh, darling, do use your head.'

A brief silence followed; the line might as well have been dead.

'You know my brother disapproved of you, don't you?' demanded

Daphne. 'You know about our parents' will. How do you know? I never said.'

'It doesn't matter. Daphne, darling, I really must go.'

'You haven't even asked me if I'm all right. You –'

There was a click and the line was most definitely dead this time. Daphne was left speaking to no one, not even the austere Miss Simmons. She stood there in the hall, the telephone receiver still in her hand, not quite knowing what to do. It occurred to her that she had never felt quite so alone.

Chapter Nineteen

Rose made her way across the grounds to South Lodge. Despite the sombre occasion, she paused a moment to marvel at the blue irises and delphiniums in the well-stocked garden. If anyone had asked her, she would have replied most definitely that she was not consciously dragging her feet, and yet she was aware of a certain reluctance on her part to intrude on Mrs Masters' grief. She tried to reason with herself. The police would very shortly be interviewing the dead servant's wife, as soon as they had spoken again to Major Spittlehouse in fact. It therefore stood to reason that, whether Rose interviewed the woman or not, she would shortly be disturbed by the police. Still her natural inclination was to hold back, to give the woman the morning to grieve if nothing else.

She took a deep breath and pressed the brass door bell. It did not do to be too sentimental, not if you were trying to get to the bottom of a crime.

She was shown into the morning room amid much curtseying on the part of the maid. The door had barely shut when Mrs Dobson appeared, flinging the door open. It was apparent that she was vexed that she had not opened the front door herself, particularly once she ascertained the visitor's identity. She pushed the maid aside, amid loud exclamations. Rose found herself ushered into the sitting room, the same one in which she had regaled her mother and Mrs Dobson with tales of her honeymoon in Paris, only a few days before. It possessed one or two pieces of furniture from Rose's childhood which jumped out at her, reminding her of their recently changed circumstances. In her mother's lowly old house, the furniture had been too big, dwarfing the rooms. It had belonged to a life before that, when they had occupied a larger house, before her father's death had resulted in their reduced circumstances.

She saw at once that the room had a new occupant, a little round woman sitting on the settee, her head propped up on one or two cushions and pillows. A shawl was wrapped around her ample shoulders, and a blanket draped over her knees, which was large enough to cover her legs. The result was that there was very little to see of the person itself except for a pale, tear-stained face. The hair, greying at the temples, was pulled back into a severe bun, which was nevertheless coming apart, hairpins dropping out of her hair and falling over the pillows and down the woman's front. Whether this was due to a lack of skill in hairdressing or because the woman was all fingers and thumbs that morning was anyone's guess. Rose assumed it was the latter, for in all else the woman appeared tidy. It was apparent, however, that she was oblivious to the fate of the wayward hairpins. On closer inspection and to a discerning eye, she did not appear all there; that was to say her mind seemed to be in another world or was too wrapped up in its own thoughts. For she barely registered Rose's arrival. Instead, she was staring fixedly into the fire, as if she thought it might provide her with the answers to her many questions, or perhaps because she found the flickering flames soothing, sufficient to draw her attention and to dull her pain. Whatever it was, she drew the shawl even tighter around her, in a pathetic little gesture as if she were afraid of catching a chill, though to Rose the room was unpleasantly warm, to the point of being stifling.

Mrs Simpson rose from an armchair and came forward to greet her daughter. Her face looked strained, her expression anxious. It was only then that Rose realised she had barely been aware of her mother's presence in the room, so transfixed had she been by the pitiful sight of Mrs Masters, swaddled in her shawl and blanket.

The sudden movement caused by Mrs Simpson rising and taking a few steps forward seemed to awaken her guest, bringing her out of her stupor. Blinking rapidly, Mrs Masters tore the blanket hastily from her knees and made to rise. Rose ran forward to prevent her.

'No. Please don't get up on my account, Mrs Masters.' She stretched a hand out to the woman, who clasped at her fingers for a brief moment before remembering herself. She was being addressed by the Countess of Belvedere. She should be jumping to her feet and curtseying, not having her hand shaken as if she were a lady. Wasn't it enough that she was sitting in Mrs Simpson's sitting room instead of in the servants' hall? It was Mrs Dobson who was her friend, not Mrs Simpson. And hadn't Mrs Dobson been attending on her as if she were her maid and Mrs Simpson had tea with her as if she were a fond acquaintance?

'It's very good of you to come your ladyship, I'm sure,' Mrs Masters mumbled.

Rose didn't think it was good of her at all. Who was she to intrude on this woman's grief, to make Mrs Masters be deferential and show gratitude when probably all the poor woman wanted to do was to lock herself away in a room and cry her eyes out? She perched on the edge of a convenient armchair. Had she been plain Miss Rose Simpson rather than grand Lady Belvedere, how much easier the situation would have been. The gulf between them would not have been so very great. Now she must tread carefully and try to speak to the woman as an equal. Would Mrs Masters wonder why she was there? She knew she would if she had been in Mrs Masters' position. Perhaps the woman thought that she was there to represent the Bonfire Committee, or felt an obligation to visit as the bonfire had been held on land owned by the Belvedere estate. Whatever Mrs Masters thought the reason for her visit, she was certain to think it something distant and impersonal, a professional obligation rather than an act done out of genuine sympathy and kindness.

Rose took a deep breath. She was very conscious of her mother standing there, very aware that what she was about to say next would cause Mrs Simpson some displeasure; but it really couldn't be helped. Besides, it seemed to her that her best, and probably kindest, course of action was to be quite frank and transparent concerning her reason for visiting.

'Mrs Masters. I do hope you don't mind awfully my coming like this. I didn't want to intrude on you at a time like this but ... well, you may have heard something to the effect that I am by way of being an amateur sleuth? A private enquiry agent of sorts, if you like.' She purposely did not look at Mrs Simpson while she said this, imagining only too well the expression on her mother's face. Yet all of a sudden she felt flustered, as if her thoughts were confused and her words would not come out of her mouth quite in the order she wished to say them. 'What I am trying to say, and making rather a mess of it, is that I should very much like to assist the police in any way that I can to help them to find your husband's murderer.'

Mrs Masters blinked at her a couple of times and her mouth opened once or twice rather like a fish, but no sound came out. It occurred to Rose for one awful, frightful moment that she had been far too frank. She really should have introduced the subject gradually, led up to it slowly, instead of announcing it as she had done in that matter of fact way, and making quite a mess of it at that.

'I'm sorry,' she said, 'I'm so very sorry. I should never –'

'Hush, dear,' said Mrs Masters, reaching forward and tapping Rose's knee affectionately. It was obvious that she was making a tremendous effort to pull herself together. The result was that once she started talking she didn't seem able to stop. 'There now, don't distress yourself, there's no harm done and I'm sure it's very kind of you. I know if Mr Masters were here now, he'd be that pleased to think that a fine lady like you would want to be bothered with finding out what happened to him.' Mrs Masters blinked away a tear. 'He was a good man, was my Jack. As loyal as they come. I couldn't have asked for a better husband. And there was nothing Mr Masters wouldn't have done for the major. Worshipped him, he did. I used to tease him about it, tell him he was fonder of the major than he was of his own wife.' Mrs Masters took out her handkerchief and blew her nose loudly. 'It's funny. I was that worried during the war, always fearing the worse; dreading the telegram that never came. So many young lives lost. I was certain my Jack would be one of them. I kept hoping and praying. I almost got sick with the worry of it all. I couldn't believe it when he came home with hardly a scratch on him. When I think of some of the other poor... well, you heard such stories, those that came home alive that would have been much better dead ...'

Rose squeezed the older woman's hand. She was at rather a loss what to say. She had so many questions to ask, but she had no wish to hurry Mrs Masters. It seemed only right that the woman be allowed to reminisce if she wanted to. She felt a sharp stab of sympathy. How would she feel in Mrs Masters' place? If anything so vile should happen to Cedric, would she be able to speak in such an open and composed way to an inquisitive stranger? She thought it highly unlikely and a feeling of admiration joined the empathy she felt towards the woman.

'Mr Masters was that pleased when the major asked if we'd do for him and his sister. I wasn't too keen mind, because I wanted Jack to myself. But it was a good job and the pay was above average, so we couldn't say no. Not that we might have turned him down if we'd known we'd never be staying in one place for more than a couple of years.'

'Oh? Do the major and his sister travel a great deal?' asked Rose, interested.

'Not what I'd call travel exactly,' said Mrs Masters. 'We'd stay somewhere for two or three years at most, and then the major would get it in his head to pack up and leave and we'd go and live in another part of the country. Five years next Thursday we'll have been at Sedgwick. I don't think we've ever lived anywhere so long.' The thought that her husband would not be there to see in the next five years produced a fresh bout of tears. 'I thought we had nothing to fear in a village like Sedgwick. Such a pretty little place it is, and the major had always had a mind to go to towns before. I can't tell you how pleased I was when I first set eyes on this place. I said to Jack that I had a mind to stay here even if the major decided to leave after a year or two.'

Mrs Masters put her handkerchief to her eyes and began to weep silently. It had cost her a great deal to speak as she had done. It had taken everything that was in her until there was nothing left. She was now no more than a pale shadow of the woman she had been yesterday before her world had fallen apart.

Rose bit her lip and refrained from the temptation to glance over at her mother. She had a feeling her mother would give her a reproachful look, holding her responsible for Mrs Masters' current spell of tears.

'Why would anyone want to hurt my Jack?' sobbed Mrs Masters. 'He was the kindest soul on this earth.'

It was on the tip of Rose's tongue to say that it was possible that Masters had been killed in mistake for her employer. However, on reflection she thought better of it. How would Mrs Masters feel, she wondered? Surely it would only make matters worse if she learnt that the murderer had never intended to kill her husband, that Masters had been killed because of a ghastly error.

'That is what we are trying to find out,' she said. 'Did your husband have any enemies?'

'Of course not. That was what I was saying. Jack, he was kind to everyone. You should have seen how he was with little Biddy, the girl who helps me in the house, if you can call it help because she doesn't seem to know one end of a broom from the other. From an orphanage she was and timid as anything. Wouldn't say boo to a goose. But Jack, he soon had her laughing and giggling. Treated her like the daughter we never had.' Mrs Masters began to sob again, big tears that rolled down her cheeks.

'I think that will do,' said Mrs Simpson firmly, putting a comforting arm around the distressed woman's shoulders. 'Rose, can't you see that poor Mrs Masters has had enough?'

'I'm sorry,' said Rose hastily. 'You are quite right.'

She felt in that moment that she had done more harm than good. And what had she really achieved? Very little. She had learnt only that, according to his wife, Masters had been the most likeable of fellows, the least likely of all men to find himself murdered. If nothing else, it seemed to reinforce the notion that Major Spittlehouse had been the intended victim. And if that was the case, the major should be in a position to provide the police with a list of people whom might wish him harm, providing that he was willing to do so of course.

She made to go, gathering her things about her, pleased only that Mrs Dobson had not been a witness to her humiliation, to the words of reproach from her mother and the distress that she had inadvertently caused Mrs Dobson's friend. It was not the end of the matter, for she had no doubt that her mother would chastise her later on her method, but that could wait.

Rose's hand was on the door knob. She was about to turn and leave the room, when Mrs Masters' voice arrested her, thin and tearful, but perfectly clear.

'You don't think it could be anything to do with those letters?'

'Which letters?' asked Rose, rather more sharply than she had intended. She retraced her steps to the armchair. 'To which letters are you referring?'

'Those blackmail letters. Or it might have been poison pen. I don't know which they were,' said Mrs Masters, drying her eyes. 'Only, if they were poison pen, isn't it usual for them to be sent to more than one person, and I don't think anyone else has received them, least not as I've heard.'

'Are you saying that Mr Masters received some letters pertaining to blackmail?' exclaimed Rose, somewhat incredulous that Mrs Masters had not referred to the matter until now.

'No. Not Jack. Major Spittlehouse. They were addressed to the major.'

Rose felt her pulse quicken. Aloud she said: 'What had they to do with Mr Masters if they were directed to the major?'

'Jack, he was that upset about them. The thought that anyone would try and cause the major distress … well, it made his blood boil. The first letter we received, we knew something was wrong, even before we gave it to the major. It was the way it was delivered, you see. It didn't come through the letterbox as you'd expect. Someone had snuck in to the garden by the lane that runs at the back of the house and pushed it under the door, because I'd found it in the passage. We thought then as how the person who posted the letter might not have wanted to be seen.'

'Did you give the letter to Major Spittlehouse?'

'Yes, Jack did. He said the major turned as white as a sheet. Pretended he couldn't read the signature and asked him if he'd seen who'd delivered it. Of course we realised then that the letter hadn't been signed proper, that there was something fishy about it.'

Rose wondered how she might ask her next question tactfully.

'I don't suppose Mr Masters managed to catch a glimpse of the letter itself, did he?'

She had tried to infer by her voice that nothing could be more natural than for a servant to read his employer's correspondence. If her mother raised her eyebrow, she did not see it. Thankfully Mrs Masters did not appear to have taken any offence. If anything, she pulled her shawl about her and sat more upright on the settee, thankful that she had something of importance to impart.

'No, he didn't read *that* letter.'

'But he read others?' said Rose quickly. 'I think you referred to letters rather than one letter, am I right?'

'Yes. There were three in all.'

'Three!'

'Yes. Mr Masters didn't see what was in the first one. But, as I said, it worried him something rotten that someone should be sending the major threatening letters.' Mrs Masters sighed. 'Happen I should have kept quiet about the next letter, but I didn't. When it arrived I told him how it had appeared in the passage, same as the last time. He threatened to throw it on to the fire. But instead he steamed it open and read it.'

Rose could hardly contain her excitement. 'What did it say?'

'I don't know. He wouldn't tell me. But I know he was upset by what was written. All the colour went from his face. I'd never known him look so pale. And he couldn't sleep at night. Tossing and turning he was, muttering things under his breath. Kept me awake it did.'

'What happened to the letter?'

'He screwed it up and threw it on to the fire.'

'So Major Spittlehouse never saw the second letter?'

'No. He'd never have known it existed. The third one neither.' Mrs Masters' eyes suddenly became moist. 'It arrived yesterday morning. I didn't mean to let Jack have it. I meant to keep it safe. It didn't seem right withholding it from the major, it being addressed to him and all. But Jack, he got it out of my apron when I wasn't looking. I thought it was all right, that the writer had come to their senses, because Jack told me not to fret, that it was very good news.' She gave a heartfelt sigh. 'He seemed happy, joyful even. I suppose I should be pleased that his last day on this earth was …'

'Yes,' said Rose gently. She was aware that the woman was beginning to tire. 'Do you know what happened to the letter?'

'He took it with him. He didn't throw it on to the fire like the last one.'

'I have one final question for you, Mrs Masters, and then I shall leave you in peace. I can't tell you how grateful I am.' Rose smiled and pressed the older woman's hand, aware that she was about to ask the most difficult question of all. 'Can you remember when you last saw your husband?'

Mrs Masters' hand flew to her mouth. The hand, white and plump, was clenched in a fist, the nails digging into her skin. It was possible that she emitted a small cry, like a wounded animal; Rose was not quite sure.

'I don't know for certain. I shall never forgive myself. But I had no way of knowing …'

'Of course you didn't,' Rose said gently. 'No one can blame you. It would have just seemed like any other day. I expect you were used to working in the house together, hardly being conscious if the other was in the same room or not.'

'Well, that is just it,' said Mrs Masters rallying. 'I do remember him going upstairs. It must have been about half past four. I went upstairs myself just before five o'clock to lay out a cold supper for the major and Miss Spittlehouse. But I don't remember if he was there or not. He certainly wasn't in the parlour; but then he had no need to be as they were waiting on themselves last night. And he wasn't there when I cleared away the supper things and brought them down to the kitchen. I know that for a fact for, if he'd been there, he'd have insisted on carrying the tray, and I carried it down myself last night.'

Mrs Masters' eyes adopted a faraway look. It had just occurred to her that for evermore she would be carrying her own tray.

Chapter Twenty

The examination of the scene of the murder had been disappointing from Inspector Newcombe's view. It had neither thrown up any leads nor produced any particular clues. As he remarked to Sergeant Bell, the field itself, on which the body had been discovered, had been too well trampled by too many feet to leave anything of value to be uncovered. The shoes and boots of the villagers had churned up the earth to such an extent that it had been difficult to distinguish one footprint from another, let alone determine whether there were any signs which suggested the servant had not been killed there but rather dragged to the spot after death. Their expert, Mutchley, who was usually so helpful in these type of matters, swooping on clues not commonly discernible by the naked eye, said that in his opinion it was possible to put a case for either scenario, which did little to further the investigation. Of course they had all agreed that the soil on the face had probably been applied once the body was in position. A particularly nasty business that. Inwardly, Inspector Newcombe hoped that aspect of the murder had not been premeditated, that it had been done almost as an afterthought. He considered it would take a particularly warped mind to lure a man to a specific place to kill him, in order that his body might be disguised as a guy to be thrown on the bonfire. Now that he thought about it, he was sure it had been a spur of the moment decision. Any right-minded individual would have realised that a body was much heavier than a guy, even an effigy stuffed with rags instead of straw. It was, therefore, very unlikely that the corpse would ever have been tossed on to the bonfire.

It was with a degree of despondency that the two policemen retraced their footsteps to Sedgwick Court. Their spirits lifted slightly at the sight of the great stately pile. Seen in the daylight, they were afforded a proper view of the place which revealed its true grandeur. The night before, it had been little more than a dark mountain, which had loomed up at them out of the night. In the daylight, however, it was revealed as a great neo-Palladian mansion. Its smooth, plain alabaster-coloured exterior caught the late autumn sunshine. The corner towers, topped by pyramidal roofs, and the great Corinthian columns, which flanked the entrance porch, combined to give Sedgwick Court a palatial air. There was also something of an Ancient Greek temple about the building's appearance, which prompted Sergeant Bell to utter in hushed tones: 'This is a bit grand, isn't it, sir? Fancy us having our investigation headquarters in a posh place like this.'

If Inspector Newcombe was daunted by Sedgwick Court, he did not reveal the fact to his subordinate. He did not appear at all ill at ease when greeted by the butler and footmen, as if he were well accustomed to an abundance of servants and opulent surroundings.

The two policemen were directed to the library, as they had been the evening before. Sergeant Bell went immediately over to one of the windows to admire the view. He may have remained there for a while, staring out at the manicured formal gardens, framed by their neat box hedges, had the inspector not cleared his throat and started assembling his notes, staring at each page in turn.

'Well, here's how it seems to me, Bell. We've not got much to go on from the field. It didn't bring us the clues we were hoping for. It was all spoilt with that many feet walking on every bit of ground, there was nothing left for us to see except for a muddy mess. But we haven't got to let it deter us. There are more ways to skin a cat than one. It's the interviews that will help us, and finding out everything we can about the characters involved, every little secret and every little idiosyncrasy. Once we've got opportunity, we'll look at motive and narrow it down from there. Old-fashioned police work, that's what is going to get us our man.'

'Or woman,' volunteered the sergeant.

'Or woman,' acknowledged the inspector. 'Well said, Bell. It's good to keep an open mind and by that I mean remind us that it could be either. That was the findings of our medical expert, wasn't it?' He spent a few moments searching among his sheaf of papers for one in particular. 'Ah, here it is. Time of death, that's what I'm looking for. Milliner thinks it unlikely the man was murdered much before at least four o'clock yesterday afternoon. According to the Belvederes, Lady Belvedere did her bit of judging of the best guy at twenty past seven, or as good as, which meant that the body was revealed as a corpse by half past seven.'

'Well, the major was pretty definite that the body wasn't there when he and his cronies from the Bonfire Committee came to do their night watch,' said the sergeant, looking at his notes. 'Started doing their rounds at about half past four and had finished them before five.'

'Good,' said Inspector Newcombe. 'Of course it doesn't tell us when the chap was murdered, not if he was killed somewhere else and his body brought there later, but it's a jolly good start. Gives us something to work with anyway.'

'According to the children, the body was already in situ when they came to lay their guys out, sir,' said Sergeant Bell. 'That's the bit of information Lady Belvedere discovered, if you remember? I spoke with a lad named Jude Browning this morning. He is what you might call their leader. He reckons most of them got down to the field about twenty past six. Those that came separately, arrived later.'

'Good work, Bell. And that's a pretty small window for the body to have materialised where it was found. We may even be able to narrow things down further when we get the last sighting of Masters alive. What with the poor fellow having been a servant, every minute of his time was probably accounted for. It would have been difficult for him to have crept out for any length of time before his absence was noticed.'

Sergeant Bell flicked through the pages of his notebook again. 'Major Spittlehouse said that he didn't recollect seeing Masters between the time he returned from his night watch until he set off for the bonfire festivities proper at a quarter to seven. That was because he and his sister had a cold supper laid out for them and saw to themselves. Masters was not required to be present to wait at table.'

'Splendid, Bell. I say, you are doing well. That's good old-fashioned police work for you. Now, I think I can go a bit further. Didn't we reckon it took about fifteen minutes at a brisk walk for Major Spittlehouse to walk from his house to the field? Well, it stands to reason then that it took the same amount of time for Spittlehouse to walk home from his night watch. According to him, he left the field before five. On that basis, I'd say he got to his house between ten past and a quarter past five.'

'By which time Masters had already set off to wherever he went to be murdered?'

'It certainly looks like that, Bell, unless of course he was downstairs with Mrs Masters helping her with the washing up. Of course his wife will be able to tell us; she might even be able to let us know the exact time that he left the house, if she's anything like my good lady.' He got up and began to pace the room, his thumbs stuck in the pockets of his trousers. 'I wouldn't want you to think for one moment that I was being flippant, Bell, or that I didn't care about this poor fellow, because I do. From what little we've heard about the man, he was a decent, hardworking sort. He was not the type to set the world alight, he just got on with his job and did it diligently. There's nothing wrong with that. The world would be a better place if there were more like him. One thing's for certain. He doesn't deserve for his death to go unnoticed, or for his murderer not to be brought to justice. I tell you, Bell, I mean to catch whoever killed that poor man if it's the last thing I do.'

Sergeant Bell harboured no doubt as to the sincerity of his superior's words. Not only had it been evident in his voice, but he was familiar also with the man's character. The inspector would leave no stone unturned once he'd put his mind to something. He saw whatever it was to its bitter conclusion with a dogged determination. The sergeant described the inspector to his girl as being a 'solid' policeman. There was nothing very showy about the man himself and nothing very fancy about his method of police work. He was thorough and he was persistent and such an approach more often than not brought results. And the results that they brought could withstand a clever defence barrister trying to make mincemeat of them on the witness stand. Sergeant Bell knew for a fact that some of his peers found Inspector Newcombe rather dull and old-fashioned, very like the method of police work he so admired. The sergeant, however, was not one of his critics; he held the man in high esteem. He was astute enough to realise the inspector would provide him with a very thorough grounding in his chosen profession. He watched and he learnt, as he told Betty, picking up every morsel that he could. It would make him a better policeman; he was certain of it.

In this particular case, there was an added ingredient to the mix and Sergeant Bell was in two minds how he felt on the matter. On the one hand, the aristocracy had always fascinated him, but on the other he felt that they should know their place as much as the next man. That was how society worked without falling apart. He didn't think the gentry would be any good at police work, any more than he would have been suited to overseeing a house full of servants. Which of course brought him on to the question of Lady Belvedere. Admittedly she had had the foresight to question the children before the murder became common knowledge but, to his mind, Inspector Newcombe had shown an unexpected willingness for her, a mere amateur, to collaborate with them on the investigation. Sergeant Bell wondered how it would all pan out.

Rose trudged back from South Lodge deep in thought. She made her way through the grounds that had so bewitched Sergeant Bell when he had looked out through the library window to take in the view. The gardens and parkland usually had a similar effect on her, but this morning her thoughts were elsewhere. In truth, they still lay with Mrs Masters huddled on the settee in her shawl and blanket, her head propped up with cushions and a pillow. On reflection, it seemed to Rose that, despite an unpromising and faltering start, she had learnt a good deal from Mrs Masters. The murdered man had been a decent, likeable fellow, who was unlikely to have accrued many enemies during his lifetime. It was true that this assessment of the man's character had been provided by his widow, and that quite understandably Mrs Masters may have wished to paint her husband in an overly favourable light. However, the obvious affection that she had felt for her husband could not be denied. Her appearance, shrivelled and pathetic, ever on the verge of tears, had given credence to her words, and Rose had found herself genuinely moved. And it would be easy enough to corroborate, this description of the man's character. All that would be required was to have a word with the maid, Biddy. So it was not this that worried her, that absorbed her thoughts or brought a crimson flush to her cheeks. What occupied her mind as she walked was how she might tactfully convey to Inspector Newcombe that he tread gently in his questioning of Mrs Masters, not that the man didn't have far more experience in such matters than she did herself.

Rose bit her lip and slowed her pace; her mother, had she been there, would have said that she dawdled. Really, it was no good trying to convince herself that her concern focused only on Mrs Masters' wellbeing. The truth of the matter was that she was apprehensive. The policemen were probably already ensconced in the library at Sedgwick Court, and she would be obliged to inform the inspector that she had taken it upon herself to interview the murdered man's wife.

'Was that Miss Spittlehouse on the telephone?' enquired Harold Whittaker of Archie Mayhew when the young man had returned from his telephone call.

'Yes,' said Archie rather absently. He resumed his seat and took up his copy of the trust deed that the two of them had been reviewing. However, he found it difficult to tear his thoughts away from the conversation he had just had with Daphne. How he was going to be able to concentrate on something he found interminably dull at the best of times, he didn't know. Really, these trust deeds were such dreary things, the thought that he might have to draft such documents for the next thirty years or so was quite unbearable ...

'Archie, are you all right?'

Uncle Harold's words brought him up with a start. He was alarmed to discover that the older man was looking at him rather peculiarly. Even in his distracted state, Archie was painfully aware that the solicitor was regarding him rather more intently than was usual. It was a strange look; he was not mistaken. It was not his uncle's usual concerned way of looking at his nephew, a mixture of genuine anxiety and rather bitter disappointment. At least that was always what it seemed like to Archie. This was the look he gave him when he had made a mistake in naming the parties to a document, or when he had been particularly rude or insolent to a client.

Archie had intended to say nothing about the content of his telephone conversation with Daphne until he had had time to think what best to do. Far better to be quiet and thought wanting, than to open his mouth and blurt out something that he could not take back. Yet it seemed that his mouth thought otherwise, for the words came tumbling out as if of their own accord.

'No, I'm not as it happens. Miss Spittlehouse has just told me something quite extraordinary. Rather distressing in fact. I can't quite believe it to be true.'

'Archie, my dear boy, what is it? She hasn't thrown you over?'

Harold Whittaker was almost out of his seat. His voice held the expected note of pity, but also something else that Archie couldn't quite put his finger on. If he hadn't known better, he'd have said that it was relief.

'No, she hasn't done that.' Archie gave rather a bitter laugh. 'It hardly sounds believable. If I didn't know Daphne better, I'd have said she'd made it up as a bit of a joke.' Archie paused a moment to pass a hand across his forehead. 'Apparently her servant has been murdered. Masters, I think she said his name was.'

'No! Oh, how terrible for the poor girl. No wonder –'

'It happened last night, at the bonfire.'

'What?' There was a touch of fear in Harold Whittaker's voice. 'Oh, how awful.'

'There was talk of a body in the office this morning by the juniors; I didn't really think anything of it. But you said you thought something had happened last night, don't you remember, Uncle Harold? You said you were all herded off to Sedgwick Court to watch the firework display and you had to give your name.'

'But my dear boy, I didn't think it had anything to do with a murdered body,' protested the solicitor. He averted his gaze to look out of the window, which overlooked the high street. 'At the Sedgwick bonfire festivities you say?' he spoke slowly, as if he were mulling it over in his mind. 'Dear me, how frightful. And to think I was there.'

'Yes you were, weren't you?' Archie looked at Harold Whittaker rather strangely. 'I did wonder what you were doing there. I meant to ask you. I didn't think you set much stall by fireworks, you never did when I was a boy if I remember rightly.'

'Well, I suppose it was all the talk about it in the office yesterday,' said the solicitor hurriedly, though to Archie's keen eye he appeared somewhat flustered. 'What with shutting up the shop early, I thought I might as well see them for myself.'

'I wish you'd said,' Archie sounded rather riled. 'I would have asked for a lift. I suppose you did drive your car?'

'Miss Spittlehouse's servant, you say,' said Harold Whittaker, returning to the first part of their conversation. 'Well I never!'

'Yes. It appears that someone mistook him for Major Spittlehouse. He was wearing the major's jacket, you see.'

'Good Heavens! Is Major Spittlehouse all right?' Harold Whittaker looked as if he had had a very bad fright. The colour had quite drained from his face and he was now clutching the table.

'You haven't lost a client, if that's what you are worried about,' said Archie rather coldly, and had the satisfaction of seeing his uncle blush.

'Well, of course not. How can you think such a thing?' Harold Whittaker sounded indignant.

'I'm sorry, that was rude of me. It's this business. I can't tell you what a shock it was to me, when Daphne told me. Of course, I had never met the fellow but –'

'It's quite understandable old chap,' said Harold Whittaker indulgently. 'It's quite natural that you should feel upset on Miss Spittlehouse's account, very natural indeed.' He put the document that they had been perusing aside. 'I daresay this old trust deed can wait a few hours. It's not going to go wandering off, now is it?' He gave a weak laugh. 'There's a pile on my desk of other matters that require attending to, quite as urgent as this one. What say you pop in to Sedgwick and pay Miss Spittlehouse a visit? It'll put your mind at rest and Miss Spittlehouse is certain to appreciate it. I am sure the office can manage to operate without you for an hour or two.'

'No,' said Archie, rather more loudly than he had intended. 'I don't want to see her.'

Harold Whittaker looked quite taken aback. Really, he couldn't understand young people these days. If he had not been so preoccupied with his own thoughts, he might have asked Archie why he did not wish to comfort the woman to whom he was engaged, particularly if it meant leaving the office. Equally, Archie Mayhew on his part, if he had not been brooding, might have wondered why Harold Whittaker was so eager to be alone. And if he had gone so far as to study his uncle closely, he would have noticed that for some quite inexplicable reason his hand was shaking.

Chapter Twenty-one

'You went to South Lodge and spoke with the deceased's wife?' said Inspector Newcombe.

The question was a rhetorical one, for Rose had just given him a comprehensive summary of her interview with Mrs Masters. She stared at the policeman and bit her lip. It was rather difficult to tell how he had taken the news, that was to say, whether he was very annoyed or merely a little surprised. After a minute of wondering, his jaw clenched and there was the sound of a slow intake of breath gradually released. With a sinking heart she realised that inwardly he was furious, and only with considerable effort was he managing not to give any obvious outward sign. If she was left in any doubt as to the accuracy of her assessment, a quick glance at Sergeant Bell, whose face was far more expressive of feeling than his superior's, showed that he was of a similar view. For his eyes were like saucers and he was regarding the inspector with a mixture of anxiety and interest, awaiting the inevitable explosion which was yet to materialise.

'I do appreciate that it probably wasn't my place to do so and that you would much rather I hadn't,' Rose said rather quickly. 'But you see I wanted to discover from my mother how Mrs Masters had spent the night. I felt it had been rather an imposition on her, taking in the woman who was a stranger, as she had.' This explanation was not altogether a truthful one, and Rose watched the inspector's face apprehensively, wondering whether he would accept her excuse, and look more leniently upon her behaviour.

The expression on the policeman's face suggested otherwise but, if Inspector Newcombe's intention was to admonish her, he clearly thought better of it. Perhaps he was conscious that he was a guest in her house, enjoying her hospitality, or that he had given her permission to assist him with their enquiries. Or perhaps he simply had more pressing matters to attend to. For whatever reason, when he spoke next he merely asked:

'You didn't mention the jacket or the possibility that her husband may have been murdered in mistake for Major Spittlehouse?'

'No, I didn't,' replied Rose hurriedly, grasping at the olive branch.

'Mrs Masters was most dreadfully upset as you'd expect. It was obvious she had been very fond of her husband. It had been only a few hours since she had been told of his death, and that he had been murdered at that. To tell her that he might have been killed in mistake for their employer … well, I just couldn't bring myself to do it.'

'Still, it will have to be done,' said the inspector rather grimly, 'particularly if what you said about those letters is true.'

'Oh, it is, I am quite certain of it,' said Rose earnestly. 'Mrs Masters didn't strike me as the type of woman who would exaggerate or tell lies. She is not one given to talk, I'd say. She really would much rather not have mentioned it at all. But you do see, don't you, Inspector, why I couldn't say anything about the jacket? Masters really wasn't the sort of servant to wear his employer's clothes. She'll be awfully upset to learn that he was wearing the major's jacket when he died.'

'Well, I daresay there was a reason why he was, which will reveal itself in due course,' said the inspector rather grudgingly. 'If this woman is as fragile in her emotions as you say, we'd better wait a while before we question her.' He rose and began to pace the room. 'As it happens, I'd like to speak to the major first. I'd like to know if he had any enemies. If we tell him we believe he was the intended victim, he might be a bit more forthcoming than he was last night, when he was in shock and worried about his sister.' He returned to the desk and began to gather his papers together. 'And I'd like him to tell us about these poison pen letters. What was in them, that's what I'd like to know. It was a pity they were hand delivered. I'd have liked to have learnt from the post mistress if he was the only person to have been sent one.' He looked over at the sergeant. 'You go and have a word with the servants here, Bell. Happen as not one or two of them might have heard something; if anyone else had one of these letters, I mean. In my experience it's not the sort of thing that those who receive them want to broadcast, but it's the food of gossip for their servants. In a small village like this you'd expect it to be common knowledge. If it isn't, and it appears Major Spittlehouse was the only recipient of these letters, well, then it'll lead me to believe the major was probably being blackmailed.'

While Sergeant Bell went to interview the servants, realising there would be a delay of sorts before the major arrived to be interviewed, Rose made her own excuses and left the library. On enquiry, she was informed by Manning that Lord Belvedere had gone to see one or two members of the Bonfire Committee. She felt herself rather at a loss as to how she might best occupy her time until Major Spittlehouse arrived. It occurred to her that she might think of the questions she would like to put to him. Though he might still be slightly riled with her, she thought the inspector was likely to permit her to attend the interview. The gardens initially drew her, appealing to her as an ideal setting for such an activity. However, she had already been out in them that morning and she hesitated a moment feeling indecisive.

Her mind drifted to Sergeant Bell, and she imagined him in the servants' hall trying to secure information from her servants. While they might very well be tempted to gossip to him left to their own devices, she thought it likely Mrs Farrier would soon put a stop to such tendencies. Rose had learnt that, as a rule, senior servants did not like police to be in a house, and she thought it probable that Sergeant Bell had yet to learn the fine art of interrogating servants successfully. She thought fondly of Sergeant Lane, who had had such a wonderful knack of ingratiating himself with the cook and female staff of any house, and then her thoughts drifted almost inevitably and seamlessly to Inspector Deacon and the last time she had seen him in Madame Renard's flat …

Rose brought herself up short. She must have something more tangible to do than pose questions in her mind to ask Major Spittlehouse later. Her butler, Manning, was rather a good gossip, or at least he had been before he had succeeded to the role of butler, a position which had been vacated by the formidable Torridge following his retirement. Was it appropriate, she wondered, to gossip with one's butler? It had been different when she had been a guest in the house and Manning had been the under-butler. Then she had occupied a relatively lowly position in society and Manning had deemed her approachable to ask for directions, being rather nervous at the time of addressing Lady Lavinia Sedgwick.

Rose had just decided that she would ring for Manning, as her priority must surely be the investigation rather than propriety, when Edna came into vision. It seemed that fate had intervened and she requested that the girl join her in her boudoir.

'Oh, miss. Oh, m'lady. There's such a to do downstairs. Mrs Farrier's been like a bear with a sore head all morning. She's had all the maids cleaning the place top to bottom. Says the children have left marks from their sticky little paws everywhere. It's that black treacle toffee, that's what it is. It's a devil to wash off the walls and get out of the tablecloth.' She giggled. 'Some little rascal even trod a piece into the carpet in her sitting room, deliberate like. It must have been when you were talking to them because they weren't allowed in there otherwise. Mrs Broughton says they've even been into her pantry and helped themselves to sugar and pork pies. Ever so cross about it, she is.'

Edna had paused for breath and Rose realised that, had the circumstances been different, had yesterday not ended in tragedy, she might well be laughing at the children's exploits. Cedric had been right to hold the firework display at Sedgwick Court; the children had obviously enjoyed themselves immensely. She wondered whether it would be enough to wash away the taste of death when they learnt of the murder.

'Lord Belvedere and I very much appreciated all your efforts last night. I am sorry it created so much additional work for you all.'

'Oh, none of us really minded,' said Edna, 'save for Mrs Farrier and Mrs Broughton of course; rather set in their ways, they are. It's nice to see the young 'uns enjoying themselves and it makes a bit of a change for the rest of us.' She took a step or two forward and lowered her voice to a loud whisper. 'Is it true what they're saying, miss? That there was a murder last night and that's why there is police in the house?'

'I am afraid it is, Edna. Major Spittlehouse's manservant, Masters, was killed.'

'No! Someone thought it was him, only I hoped it wasn't. Ever such a nice man he was. Biddy will be that upset. Adored him, she did. Said she would have liked him to have been her father, 'cause she never knew her own, growing up in an orphanage as she did.'

'Mrs Masters said Biddy would be upset.'

All the while Rose had been pacing the room, stopping every now and then to adjust the position of ornaments, wondering how best she might approach the subject of the poison pen letters.

'You're going to find out who murdered him, aren't you, m'lady?' asked Edna anxiously. 'I know he weren't gentry but he were a good man. I'd hate to think his killer might go unpunished.'

'You know that I don't only concern myself with the deaths of the aristocracy,' said Rose. 'Of course I will do my very best to find his murderer. In fact, it seems to me he is the most deserving of justice of all the deaths I have investigated. Now,' she continued, grabbing her opening, 'if you'd like to help me catch his murderer, perhaps you could answer a question for me?'

'Oh, anything I can do to help, m'lady, you've only got to ask,' replied Edna with great sincerity.

'Well, sit down and I will.'

'Mrs Farrier won't be best pleased if she finds me sitting in your boudoir. She'll think I'm taking liberties, she will.'

'Well, I should like you to do as I ask, and if Mrs Farrier has words with you about it, you must tell her I requested it.' The little lady's maid perched on the edge of a chair, sitting very upright. 'Now, Edna, I daresay you may think this rather a strange question, but do you by any chance know if anyone in Sedgwick has received some rather unpleasant letters?'

'Bills and the like, miss?'

'No, nothing like that. Unpleasant letters,' said Rose, wondering how best to describe them. 'Letters casting aspersions about people's characters.'

'Oh! You mean poison pen letters?' exclaimed Edna excitedly. 'There was a spate of those in my nan's village. Ever so nasty they were, upsetting people and destroying their characters. Of course, Nan had nothing to hide so she weren't bothered, but some of the young lasses fair cried their eyes out that anyone could be so cruel and write such vile things. They even accused Mrs Jennings, the doctor's wife, of carrying on with Mr Smith, the butcher. One young girl, Ann, daughter of the local blacksmith, was so upset by the letter she received that she threw herself in the river. Luckily for her the grocer's boy saw her do it, and they fished her out spluttering and screaming and saying how she wanted to die. A week later, of course, and she'd thought better of it. For one thing the letters had stopped. I daresay the writer had had a bit of a fright.'

'Quite likely,' agreed Rose. 'But, yes, those are exactly the type of letters I mean. Tell me, have you heard any gossip about anyone in the village receiving them?'

'I can't say I have. Though people tend to keep it to themselves if they've had such letters. They find it shaming, 'course you know what folk say about there being no smoke without fire.' Edna made a face. 'I wouldn't like to think Sedgwick had a person like that in it, who'd write those nasty letters.'

'Neither would I. There hasn't been talk in the servants' hall about anyone receiving them?'

'I've never heard it. But that's not to say it hasn't been talked about, just not in my hearing.' Edna looked a little frightened. 'You don't think I'll receive one, do you, miss?'

'No, I don't, Edna. I don't think you have anything to worry about, really I don't. I didn't mean to frighten you.'

'You aren't going to tell me Mr Masters received one of them letters?' Edna's eyes had become as large as saucers and her mouth had dropped open.

'No,' said Rose firmly. 'No, he didn't receive any of those letters, but I think he may well have been trying to protect the person who did.'

When Rose walked out on to the landing, she discovered that Major Spittlehouse had just arrived. She kept a little back from the banisters so as not to be observed, and watched from her vantage point as the major was relieved of his hat and coat by one of the footmen, prior to being shown into the library. As soon as he had disappeared from view, she dashed down the stairs and slipped into the room before the policemen had the opportunity to close the door.

If Inspector Newcombe was surprised to see her, he did not show it. Sergeant Bell merely looked up from his notebook and gave her a brief glance. Of the three gentlemen there, it was Major Spittlehouse who appeared a little taken aback by her presence, as if he was wondering what she was doing there. Nonetheless, he greeted her politely enough and enquired after her husband. She in turn enquired politely after his sister. It occurred to Rose, however, that he was still expecting her to leave the room before the interview commenced. Instead, she seated herself without fuss in a chair behind him and waited for someone to ask her to go. Nobody did. The major, she thought, was too polite to do so and Inspector Newcombe probably thought it preferable to have her there in the room with them where he could keep his eye on her.

Rose thought that the major had lost some of his bluster of the night before. The initial shock of his servant's death and concern for his sister were behind him. He had had a night's sleep, or something approximating it, and while the tragedy was no less terrible in the daylight than it had been the evening before, the awful immediacy of it having just happened had passed. She wondered if he would be more responsive to the questions asked of him today. Looking up, she met Inspector Newcombe's eye and thought he was probably wondering the same thing. Whatever his thoughts, it was clear that he intended to take a direct approach; there was to be no beating about the bush with pleasantries.

'Major Spittlehouse, thank you for coming here today,' began the inspector. 'I daresay you are wondering why we wished to see you. You are no doubt of the view that you answered all our questions last night.'

'I think I did,' agreed the major rather gruffly, 'to the best of my ability. I think there is little more that I can add.'

'There I beg to differ.' Inspector Newcombe held up his hand as the major made to protest. 'You see new information has come to light which leads us to believe that we were looking at this murder from the wrong angle.'

'Oh?' Major Spittlehouse sounded interested in spite of himself.

'Yes. I feel it my duty to inform you that we believe you were the intended victim, rather than your servant.'

'Now look here, Inspector.' The major had jumped up from his seat so forcefully that the chair threatened to topple over. It was apparent, however, that the inspector had anticipated just such an outburst, for he continued talking very much as if the major had not spoken. He did, however, speak more loudly lest the major be tempted to interrupt him again.

'As I have just said, we strongly believe your servant was murdered in mistake for you.'

'Nonsense!'

'Is it though, Major? The man was wearing your jacket; the same jacket that you always wore. And we have it on Lord Belvedere's authority that he was of a similar build to yourself and wore his moustache in the same military style. Given the time of year, likely as not it was pitch dark when he died, or as good as. It would have been an easy mistake to make.'

Rose leapt from her seat. The inspector had broached the evidence for mistaken identity more quickly than she had expected. Hastily she crossed the room to stand beside the inspector in order that she might glimpse the major's face. All three men stared at her enquiringly, their mouths slightly open; but not one of them spoke. It occurred to her then that had she been plain Rose Simpson, such a movement would have been remarked upon. However, while Lady Belvedere choosing a rather odd moment to cross from one end of her library to the other might arouse the same level of curiosity, it did not induce comment.

'It would have been dark, Major, just as Inspector Newcombe has said,' said Rose hurriedly, fearing that the inspector would seek to interrupt her. 'In light of that fact, you must admit that it is perfectly feasible that Masters might have been mistaken for you for the reasons the inspector has given.'

'No, forgive me, Lady Belvedere, but I don't see that at all,' said the major.

'It is perfectly possible that someone who did not know you well,' continued Rose, 'or had only glimpsed you on one or two occasions might have made such a mistake.' The major looked up, and she caught his eye. She saw what she was looking for, a glimmer of hope. 'I do not think that someone who knew you well would have made such a mistake, even in the dark. According to my husband, you are a good six inches taller than Masters and slightly broader across the shoulders.'

The look of relief on the major's face was unmistakeable. He was nodding his head slowly, as if he were still digesting what she had just said. Rose was aware of the inspector beside her. She hardly dared look at his expression. She thought it likely that he would be angry. If nothing else, he would feel that she had overstepped the mark that had been drawn between amateur sleuth and official detective. She had taken over his line of questioning in a most forthright fashion. If he were annoyed, however, he made no show of it other than to firmly take back the reins.

'Now, Major Spittlehouse, I should like you to tell me about the letters.'

'The letters?' The fear in the major's voice was unmistakeable though he was making a valiant attempt to disguise the fact. It was clear, however, that he had been caught off guard and was floundering. He blinked hard and stared up at the inspector. Rose thought she could see his mind working, trying to make a stab at guessing how much they already knew.

'Yes, the letters. Tell me about the one you received that was hand delivered, pushed under the garden door. Mrs Masters found it. You asked her husband about the person who had delivered it because apparently you couldn't read the signature.'

'Did I? I can't recall. It must have been a letter from a tradesman.'

'Come, Major Spittlehouse, this really will not do. We know it was an anonymous letter and what you might call a poison pen letter, or perhaps even a blackmail letter. You only received one, but it might interest you to know that in fact two other such letters were delivered to your house.' The inspector paused for a moment before continuing; he was watching the major's face for a reaction. 'Masters read them.'

'Did he really?' The colour had drained from the major's face. 'Masters read them, you say?'

The inspector nodded and it became very apparent to everyone present that Major Spittlehouse was appalled at this news.

'His wife told Lady Belvedere that he steamed open the second letter and was so disgusted by what he read that he threw it on to the fire. He refused to disclose to her what it had said, but was so upset by its contents that he could not sleep.'

The major looked pale, but said nothing.

'Yesterday the third letter was delivered. Masters read it. He did not show it to his wife, but told her everything was all right.'

'What happened to that letter, Inspector?'

'We don't know. Masters took the letter with him but it was not found on his body. It is likely that he destroyed it.' Inspector Newcombe paused for a moment before he leaned forward and said: 'I want to know what was in that first letter, Major. What did it say?'

Major Spittlehouse swallowed hard and thought rapidly, trying to digest what he had just been told. He had thrown the first letter on the fire himself and watched it burn to a cinder. Masters had dealt with the second letter the same way. In all likelihood the third letter had suffered a similar fate. Masters had read two of the letters but had not divulged their contents. In such circumstances, his natural inclination was to say nothing. He said rather hurriedly: 'It has nothing to do with Masters' death.'

'That is for us to decide, not you,' Inspector Newcombe said curtly.

'You will tell me what was in that letter please, Major.'

Major Spittlehouse looked away. He looked first at the ceiling and then at the carpet. He fidgeted in his seat and then looked at his hands. 'Very well, Inspector, have it your own way. It was all nonsense. It said …' he paused to glance at Rose. 'Please excuse me, Lady Belvedere, I don't wish to offend you,' He leaned forward and lowered his voice slightly. 'The letter said that Miss Spittlehouse was not my sister. The writer claimed she was … my mistress. It was a load of old rot of course, but it was still rather distressing. That there was someone in the village who could suggest such a thing … and if my sister should have seen it, or received such a letter herself ….' Major Spittlehouse put a hand to his face, his cheeks crimson.

'There is no truth then to the allegation?' asked Inspector Newcombe brusquely.

'Of course not. None whatsoever.' The major's voice shook with righteous indignation. 'It was lies, all damn lies. Not worth the paper it was written on.'

Chapter Twenty-two

'So someone was sending vile letters to old Spittlehouse, were they?' Cedric said at luncheon. 'I say, that would take some nerve. I wouldn't want to be the poison penner if the major found out his identity.'

'Is penner really a word?' laughed Rose. 'I think you made it up. You can pen a letter but …' A frown creased her forehead. Sitting here with Cedric, it was so easy to forget the whole frightful business of murder for a few minutes and then, just when she did, she was pulled up short because of course it wouldn't just go away. With an awful sinking feeling she remembered. The weight returned to her shoulders as if it were a real, tangible thing, and laughter seemed dreadfully inappropriate. She looked around quickly and was pleased to see that none of the servants were present to witness her show of frivolity. She lowered her voice and said more seriously: 'They're anonymous, of course. The writer didn't write his name. Unless the major recognised his writing I suppose he'll be all right. He disguised it, I would imagine, or typed them and then just signed them "from a friend", or something frightful like that, because of course he was anything but a friend. If he were he wouldn't have sent the letters in the first place, would he, if that makes any sense?'

'It does to me,' assured her husband. 'I say, it sounds a jolly cowardly business, not to say downright horrid.'

'It is. It's frightfully unpleasant because everyone dreads getting a letter and of course everyone suspects everyone else of writing them. Still, in this instance it appears that only the major has received them.'

'Well, I suppose that's something to be thankful for. Who tends to write this sort of nonsense, do you know?' said Cedric, tucking in heartily to his plate of food; the murder had apparently done little to diminish his appetite.

By contrast, his wife picked at her food absentmindedly, pushing it around her plate. She looked down at the fish and could not rid herself of the thought that considerable time and effort had gone in to preparing the dish that sat in front of her, though she knew full well that Mrs Broughton had had a hundred and one other things to do that morning. For had she not learned from Edna that the cook and the kitchen and the scullery maids had been busy restoring the kitchen and pantry to their ordered state after the devastation caused by the children? Yet the cook had still prepared luncheon, and really she should make a stab at eating it to show her appreciation of the fact, but she had no appetite. After the guilt she had experienced for forgetting and laughing, her thoughts now dwelt on Mrs Masters. She remembered her huddled on the settee, a blanket around her, and Masters lying dead in the field, surrounded by guys and effigies.

'I think it is generally thought to be embittered old spinsters with nothing better to do,' said Rose, trying to rid herself of the unpleasant image of the dead servant. She attempted to sound flippant, but failed dismally. 'But I think it might be rather different in this case because the letters have only been sent to Major Spittlehouse. That is to say, the writer might be quite a different sort of person.'

'I wonder why the major was singled out,' pondered Cedric. 'He doesn't seem the type to receive such letters. I can't imagine the old man has ever stepped out of line. He's a pillar of the village and all that.' His eyes became large and he stopped eating, a morsel of fish suspended mid-air on his fork. 'I say, I suppose there isn't any truth to the accusation? That Daphne Spittlehouse is his mistress rather than his sister, I mean?'

'I think it highly unlikely,' said Rose, 'though the police will be checking of course; they won't just be taking the major's word for it. But it would make rather a nonsense of Daphne coming to see me about her parents' will if it were true, wouldn't it? But, as it happens, I did suggest to Inspector Newcombe that he might like to check something else.'

'Oh?' Cedric looked distinctly interested.

'Yes. I suggested that he might like to check whether Daphne Spittlehouse is in fact the major's daughter rather than his sister. It occurred to me that she just might be, even if she were not aware of the fact herself. It would fit with her age and all the facts, you see.'

'I say, I think you're right. There may be something in that,' exclaimed Cedric. 'I mean, it would make much more sense of their parents' will, wouldn't it? What could be more natural than Major Spittlehouse's parents leaving everything to their son with the expectation that he would provide for their granddaughter.' He continued, warming to the theme. 'You're suggesting, aren't you, that Daphne is the result of a relationship between Spittlehouse and a woman, whom was presumably not his wife, and that his parents took the child in and brought it up as their own?'

'Something like that. From what I've seen, the major certainly seems to treat Daphne more like a daughter than a sister. And the age difference between them means it could be possible. It might also explain his attitude towards Daphne marrying Archie Mayhew. He seems frightfully protective of her, as a father would be of his daughter.'

'Well I never! I didn't think the old major had it in him. One thing's for certain, he wouldn't want a thing like that to become common knowledge.'

'I only said it was a possibility,' stressed Rose. 'It was something that occurred to me when the police were questioning Major Spittlehouse this morning, that's all. You see, it was obvious that Inspector Newcombe had taken him rather by surprise when he asked him about the letters. The major didn't think anyone knew about them so he was rather caught unawares. He didn't want to admit what was in the letter. The inspector, however, was demanding to know what was written in that first letter. The major knew it wouldn't look good for him if he were to refuse to tell him; it would only show that he had something to hide, so he had to invent something quickly which was vaguely plausible but at the same time could easily be disproved.'

'So he came up with the notion that the writer accused Daphne of being his mistress, when in actual fact the writer claimed she was his daughter?'

'Yes, I think it's possible. Though the more I think about it the more unlikely it seems. It doesn't really explain Masters' behaviour, does it?'

'If it is proved that Daphne is the major's sister and not his daughter or his mistress,' said Cedric, 'what would that prove? Would it still mean that the major was lying about what was written in the letter he received? I mean, there is nothing to say that the writer was very concerned with facts, is there? Perhaps he just wanted to write something malicious and to hell if it was true or not.'

'Yes, I think it would matter. Though, as you say, in most cases I daresay such letters make wildly false accusations.'

'But why should this case be any different?' asked Cedric. 'Why are you so certain the major is lying, or has anything to hide, come to that?'

'Because of Masters' reaction to the second letter,' said Rose firmly. She spoke slowly, organising her thoughts in her mind as she went. 'It all goes back to that second letter. I'm referring of course to the letter that Masters read and threw on to the fire, not the one he opened and read yesterday morning.' She put down her knife and fork and looked at her husband earnestly. 'If you remember, Masters had been with the major a very long time. If Daphne was Major Spittlehouse's daughter or his mistress, come to that, I think Masters would have been well aware of the fact. Now, according to Mrs Masters what her husband read in the letter, that he threw on the fire, upset him greatly.' Rose leaned forward and laid her hand on Cedric's arm. It felt solid and comforting beneath her touch. She might have got it all wrong about Masters, but she knew in her husband she had an avid listener. 'I think what he read in that letter alarmed him. If it had merely told him something of which he was already aware or knew to be untrue, I don't think he would have been so affected by its contents. But he was clearly distressed by what he read, so much so that he couldn't sleep.'

'I wonder what could have been written in that letter,' pondered her husband. 'It must have been something dreadful. I say, you are suggesting the accusation was based on the truth, aren't you? Is that why old Spittlehouse acted the way he did? It must have been something truly awful for him to think up that nonsense he told Inspector Newcombe. If nothing else, it was dashed embarrassing for him to say what he did.'

'Yes, I think it was based on the truth. What the letter said was both awful and true. At least I think Masters thought there may have been some truth to the accusation. And that was why he was so upset and threw the letter on to the fire. Remember, he refused to let his wife read it.'

'I say, are the police going to interview Spittlehouse again? I daresay there's a chance he might crack up!'

'They're busy at the moment trying to find the third letter, the one Masters opened and read yesterday. No one knows if he destroyed it or not.' Rose gave a grim smile. 'Inspector Newcombe has taken Major Spittlehouse to the field on some pretext or other while Sergeant Bell and a constable search Masters' rooms. The major was very interested to know what had happened to that letter and I think the inspector was rather afraid that he might try and look for the letter himself and destroy it, given half the chance. The inspector certainly didn't want him to return to Green Gables unaccompanied.'

'I expect he would have done. Destroyed the letter, I mean. I think I would have done in his place. I wonder what was written in that missing third letter.'

'Oh, I have a fairly good idea,' said Rose. 'It is the first and second letters that I should have liked to have had sight of.' She smiled in spite of herself as her husband's jaw dropped in surprise. 'Yes, that's the funny part of it. You see, I thought it highly unlikely that the major would divulge the contents of the letter he had received and read, whatever it had said. He would consider it a private matter. He wouldn't involve the police. But as it happens I don't think Inspector Newcombe would have raised the matter of the letters to the major quite so suddenly and abruptly as he did if he wasn't under the impression that I had rather taken over his interview. That is to say, I had a theory that I wished to test and to do so I had to emphasise something to the major and see his face when I did so. It was a feeling I had after the major's behaviour yesterday.' She paused to give Cedric something of a smug smile. 'And it would appear I have been proved right in my assumption.'

'Oh?'

'Yes. It occurred to me that the major believed Daphne had tried to kill him, particularly given that business with Masters wearing his jacket. He was very worried about her last night, if you remember, particularly when you consider that Daphne wasn't overly fond of the Masters. There was no reason why she would be particular distressed by what had happened, no more so than anyone else, that is.' Rose paused a moment as she reflected. 'And she was not there when the body was discovered. It was not as if she had had the shock of seeing the corpse. But the major was adamant that she should not be interviewed last night. I rather think he was afraid she might say something that would incriminate her.'

'I say, do you really think so?'

'Yes I do. I think the major really believed Daphne had murdered his servant in mistake for him. You must remember that she had a very good motive for wishing her brother dead.'

'That business with their parents' will, you mean?'

'Yes. And a man like the major would still feel he had a duty to protect his sister, even if she had tried to kill him. He wouldn't want to send her to the gallows.' Rose sighed. 'You should have seen the look of relief on his face when I suggested that it was very unlikely that someone who knew him very well, like Daphne, though I didn't refer to her by name, would have made such an elementary mistake.'

The librarian stood behind the central issue desk in Bichester library. To a casual observer she appeared to be fully engrossed in her work, cataloguing the books in the library in considerable detail, for her head was bent diligently over an open book in which there was a page of writing written in a neat and meticulous hand. A keen and more perceptive onlooker, however, might have queried why she rarely glanced at the books in front of her, or why she saw the need to make frequent visits to the tables that littered the room to secure more books when she had yet to turn a page in the book in which she was writing. They might also have wondered why her pen scarcely moved over the page and why the ink was quite dry.

Fortunately for Miss Warren, the public library boasted no such observant spectators. The few people who inhabited the library on that Friday afternoon bestowed on her very little attention. They were more concerned with their own needs of finding a place where they might keep warm or while away a few hours. Therefore, she was to them no more than a part of the library landscape, an ever present figure administering the rubber date stamp and hushing those who dared to speak above a whisper in her domain. They did not notice the surreptitious glances that she cast around the room, or that today they were permitted to speak rather louder than usual without hearing the hated tut-tutting sound escape her lips. Today the library, though relatively quiet, could not be said to be silent. Instead, there was the gentle buzz of gossip in the air, snatches of which reached the librarian's straining ears.

Miss Warren gave a profound, though very quiet, little sigh. Well brought up ladies did not listen to other people's conversations. Her mother had instilled this fact in her as a child. She had been an uncommonly obedient child, taking her lessons to heart, the result being that in later life she was very much of the same view as her long dead mother. Eavesdropping was therefore to be abhorred. It was not to be tolerated on any account and certainly not a thing to be engaged in oneself. Yet, here she was, trying desperately to overhear the conversations of strangers, passing between them and stretching over tables for books she did not want merely so that she might have an excuse to listen.

She had soon discovered that the task was not an easy one and certainly could not be rushed. It became apparent that the visitors to the library had a tendency to stop speaking when she appeared beside them, looming up out of thin air, as it were. They spoke more freely when she was situated behind her central desk but, being physically removed from them, she then had difficulty catching their words. It was therefore late morning before she had heard enough to hear mention of the murder. Naturally enough, talk had focused all morning on the Sedgwick bonfire festivities of the night before, with much discussion on the quality and array of fireworks. Though reference had been made to the firework display having taken place by the lake at Sedgwick Court instead of in the usual field, which had drawn comment and speculation, it had not been until late morning that the word death had been referred to.

It was now early afternoon and Miss Warren, ostensibly cataloguing, stood transfixed on the spot behind her desk. The pen was still in her hand but she did not write and her gaze was not on the open book in front of her. If she looked anywhere it was to the middle distance, where the rows upon rows of books blurred until they became one dark shadow. She realised, even in her agitated state, that she was filled with a fear that she had never known. She had experienced sorrow and distress but nothing like this. It was a fear that seemed to engulf and shake her very body. She could not believe that she did not visibly tremble. Any moment now, someone might notice and ask her what was wrong. She stifled a sob. What could she tell them? It seemed so fanciful, ludicrous even, but it was true. A man in a tweed jacket was dead; murdered. It was not a bad dream from which she might awaken. She had not imagined it; it had actually happened and there was nothing she could do about it. For to open her mouth and say anything would only be to incriminate herself. She glanced at her bag which was now thankfully innocent of its guilty contents. The temptation to confess was great, to relieve herself of her heavy burden that she carried and must now always carry. But she could not give voice to her fears. It was too late. No good would come of it only harm. The need for self-preservation tore at her heart so that it obliterated everything else, even her guilt. She wished in that moment that she was made of sterner stuff, that she could atone for what she had done.

Chapter Twenty-three

'What I meant to say,' said Archie hurriedly, rather alarmed by the shocked expression on the solicitor's face, 'is that I thought Miss Spittlehouse might appreciate some time by herself. But of course you are quite right, Uncle Harold. I should go to her at once.'

With that, Archie Mayhew turned tail and fled. That is to say, he collected his hat and coat and walked briskly out of the solicitors' office, banging the door behind him in his haste, which made the doorframe rattle and Miss Simmons look up from her typewriter and frown. In Archie's mind, however, he was most definitely absconding, escaping the confines of the office and running to … he did not quite know where. He would have to go and see Daphne of course, if only because it was expected of him. But he did not wish to go there yet, not until he had had a chance to collect his thoughts and decide what to do.

Archie cursed himself severely. He had acted very stupidly, arousing the old man's curiosity like that by giving way to his feelings of … he hadn't been quite sure what his feelings had been. Horror, disgust, revulsion, these were the words that sprung, dark and ugly, to mind, unbidden and unwanted. He glanced down at his black gloved hand and wondered whether it was tainted, whether everything he touched now would be contaminated. He quickened his step, though he had little idea where he was going. He knew only that he wanted to put as much distance between himself and the solicitors' firm as possible. But to see Daphne after what had happened … why, he didn't feel that he would ever be able to lay eyes on her again. He wondered whether she felt the same way about him now, despite what she had said during their snatched telephone conversation that morning. He had been conscious only that old Simmons might be listening to his side of the conversation.

Was Daphne sitting there now, thinking over what he had said? He rather thought she might be and that he had likely given himself away with that business about the servant. Had he sounded too surprised to discover that the body was not that of Major Spittlehouse? The thought returned to him again and again. Was Daphne this very minute pondering their conversation, going over each sentence in her mind? Would she remember where he had paused, where he had emitted a sharp intake of breath, and most damning of all, the moment he had sounded surprised? Or would she think it only natural that he had been obviously shaken by the news, as would any reasonable person when murder crossed his path?

The beep of a car horn brought Archie abruptly to his senses. He had wandered aimlessly into the road, with no conscious thought given to where he was going. He looked about him now and discovered that his steps had taken him away from the main high street and down some side road and into another and then goodness knew where, so that now he barely recognised where he was. He had apparently walked into some squalid street or other; houses crammed together with crumbling brickwork and windows black with soot and adorned with dirty lace curtains. Had he been in any other frame of mind, he would have quickly retraced his steps to the main road, but today the filthy surroundings suited his mood. A small group of men loitering on the street corner watched him with curiosity, and two or three children playing in the gutter paused in their game to stare at him suspiciously. Archie felt in his pocket for a few coins which he gave to the eldest child who, with the other children in wild pursuit, ran laughing and shrieking with delight into one of the houses to show his mother. One of the men looked at him with a villainous expression.

Archie quickened his pace. He did not wish to pass by the men on the corner; yet to remain where he was standing in the street, or to retreat cautiously back to where he had come, would surely make him appear vulnerable. Certainly the men appeared to be looking at him now with more than idle interest, and one or two were nudging each other in the ribs. He should not have strayed into this street with his fine city clothes and showed his money in so cavalier a fashion. The street stunk of poverty and desperation, and who knew what men with nothing to lose would be driven to do?

It was then that he spotted what he considered to be his salvation, or at least a temporary sanctuary of sorts. It was a mean little tearoom squashed in between two houses, its window as grubby as the others, but with a faint glow of light penetrating the glass so that, alone in this street of sordid buildings, the shop glimmered a little brighter, a welcome beacon in a street of murkiness. Without a backward glance, he crossed the street and entered the establishment. The interior was no more pleasing than the exterior, the floor having what looked like sawdust strewn all over it, reminding him of a butcher's shop. The walls were of a dirty white colour, and the tables, innocent of tablecloths, looked as if they had not been wiped, and certainly never scrubbed.

Archie chose a table beside the window which gave him a good view of the street, and in particular of the men on the street corner. He ordered a cup of tea from a disreputable looking waitress, who looked at him with open hostility. The tea, however, when it came, though stewed and dark as treacle, was steaming hot and tasted surprisingly rather pleasant, if he could forget for a moment the chipped cup and cracked saucer. He sipped his tea cautiously and an unexpected wave of relief drifted over him. For here he would meet no friend or acquaintance who might ask him some awkward question, query why he looked so pale or was not at work. Here he could give way to his thoughts without disturbance. In this very hovel he would decide what to do. Archie sighed and discovered that his head ached with a throbbing pain. He had had little sleep the night before. The temptation now was to close his eyes and sleep. He could lean his head against the wall. He did not think that it would occasion much interest if he did. But he could not give way to his tiredness, for he must think. Foremost in his mind was the realisation that he had made a mistake. He cursed as he took a gulp of tea and scalded his tongue in the process. He had made a dreadful error for he had mistaken the servant, Masters, for Major Spittlehouse.

Rose picked up a book at random in the library at Sedgwick Court, barely bothering to glance at its pages. She lacked the concentration required for reading and discarded it almost immediately, acknowledging herself to be in a restive mood. Instead, she drummed her fingers on the polished surface of the octagonal table. Next, she began to pace the room, going from one side to the other in a makeshift circle until the rows of books blurred into one and she was forced to sit down before she became quite giddy. Her head throbbed while she herself was filled with a nagging impatience to do something. But what? She was at a loss. The afternoon stretched out long and endless before her with little to occupy her time other than to sit in solitary thought and wait for events to unfold.

Inspector Newcombe had returned briefly to Sedgwick Court with Sergeant Bell. He had been in a somewhat brusque temper, disinclined to parley. She had established, however, that the missing letter, for which the police had been searching so rigorously, had not been found among the dead servant's belongings. Rather grudgingly, the inspector had invited her to accompany him to her mother's house to interview Mrs Masters. She had declined politely, somewhat to the relief of all. For Rose was of the view that if she should choose to speak with Mrs Masters again then it would be alone. If nothing else, the poor woman could well do without a hoard of visitors descending on her, demanding that she answer intrusive questions. And, if Rose were to be completely honest, she did not wish to be present when the inspector informed Masters' widow that in all likelihood her husband had been murdered in mistake for their employer. She had no doubt that the woman would go to pieces and a distressing enough image formed itself readily in her mind, without her wishing to be there to witness the actual event.

With considerable effort, she tore the upsetting vision from her mind. It would not do to dwell on such things. It was sufficient that she knew it resided there and could be called upon to spur her on in her investigation should she find herself to be lagging or in want of motivation. With renewed determination, she was resolved not to visit Mrs Masters again until she had some definite news to impart which might provide the woman with some comfort.

Rose might well have been tempted to return to the conversation begun at luncheon with her husband, had Cedric not been required to attend an emergency meeting of the Bonfire Committee, which had been hastily convened in light of the tragic events of the night before. She knew that her husband feared what decisions the Committee might reach if he were not present. She was aware that he was very much of the opinion that the festivities should continue unaltered, representing as they did a long tradition in Sedgwick's history. In her mind's eye, she could imagine him there now, eloquent and impassioned, as he made his case, urging the members not to give way to fear.

The house without her husband and the policemen seemed unnaturally still and silent, as if it shared her own impatience. It was waiting for something to happen, or willing the hands on the clock on the mantelpiece to move forward at a tremendous rate so that the wanderers might return. Rose closed her eyes for one brief moment. Perhaps this gesture in itself was enough for a thought to come suddenly, and with unexpected force, into her head. Her eyes snapped open and the library appeared about her like the backdrop to a play. She knew the thought that had sprung so readily to mind to be quite out of the question. The books stared back at her in a mocking fashion, as if in agreement. Yet the thought proved persistent, unwilling to be put out of her mind however much she tried. It refused to go, lingering instead on the edge of her consciousness, gathering momentum until she could think of little else.

Inspector Newcombe was currently occupied with interviewing Mrs Masters, and Major Spittlehouse was presumably at the meeting of the Bonfire Committee. Indeed, hadn't Cedric told her that he was rather afraid the major would consider it his duty to tender his resignation as Committee chairman at that very meeting? Whether he did so or not was quite irrelevant for Rose's purpose. What really mattered was that he would not be at Green Gables. Daphne Spittlehouse would be quite alone. Now was the ideal opportunity to visit her and implore her to tell the police about her parents' will and her brother's reluctance to bestow on her an endowment in the light of her impending marriage. If she could only convince the woman to speak, she would not be placed in the uncomfortable position of feeling obliged to inform the police that Daphne had a motive for wishing her brother dead.

If she were to implement her plan, it was vital that she be quick, and yet Rose hesitated. The temptation was to go at once, but she rather dreaded Inspector Newcombe's reaction when he learnt that she had once again taken it upon herself to question someone about the murder before the police had had a chance to do so. She took a deep breath. She might well shudder at the recollection of how the inspector had taken the news about her conversation with Mrs Masters, but really she had no alternative but to go. She could not sit here a moment longer without purpose, waiting for the others to return. It was no use hoping that the next piece in the jigsaw puzzle would come to her of its own accord. She must progress her investigation regarding the servant's murder as best she could and if she ruffled a few feathers in the process, well, it could not be helped. If nothing else, she felt she had a responsibility towards Daphne. It would be much better if the woman could be persuaded to offer up the incriminating information against her, seemingly of her own volition.

Having made up her mind, Rose instructed Manning to summon the chauffeur to bring the Daimler around to the front door. Had time not been against her, she would have preferred to walk instead so that she might gather her thoughts. But she was conscious of nothing else but the urgency of her mission. If she could only get back to Sedgwick Court before the inspector returned, he might never know about her visit to Daphne Spittlehouse.

A quarter of an hour later saw Rose safely deposited at the front door of Green Gables, the Victorian scroll door knocker resting in her hand. She hesitated a brief second before she knocked, painfully aware that her heart was racing, whether because she was about to do something of which Inspector Newcombe would most undoubtedly disapprove or because she feared that Daphne would consider that she was interfering in matters which did not concern her, she did not know. She took a deep breath and rapped the knocker smartly against the back plate. In her agitated state the noise was monstrous; it seemed to echo inside the house as if the building were no more than a hollow shell. She waited, her ears straining for any sound of life behind the brick facade. But no one came to answer the door. It occurred to her then that perhaps the house was indeed empty. Daphne might quite reasonably have gone for a walk to clear her mind or be visiting a friend. There was no reason to suppose her to be sitting brooding and alone in the Spittlehouses' drawing room.

A wave of frustration overcame Rose. She rapped again more sharply; it was possible that the door even shook with her impatience. Yet this time, above the noise of the knocker, she heard the faint sound of footsteps coming across the hall. After some hesitation, the door was opened in a rather timorous fashion, as if whoever was behind it was rather apprehensive as to the identity of the caller. Rose found herself staring in to the face of a timid looking girl, who showed no inclination to open the door fully. Rather, she clung to her side of the handle and peeked her face around the door.

'Hallo. You must be Biddy,' Rose said kindly, taking in the little maid's red, swollen eyes.

Biddy sniffed, searched for a handkerchief in her apron pocket and blew her nose. Only then did she think to nod, clutching the handkerchief to her as she did so.

'Mrs Masters was telling me about you. She was awfully concerned that you would be very upset about her husband.'

'Oh, I am that, miss,' wailed Biddy, dabbing her eyes with the soiled handkerchief. 'I can't seem to do a thing around the house and Miss Daphne is that … oh, begging your pardon, m'lady. I don't know what came over me, not knowing it were you.' Biddy did a belated curtsey. Her curiosity overcame her shyness and she asked eagerly: 'Have you seen her, Mrs Masters, I mean? I am that sorry for her, I am. Loved him she did, though sometimes her tongue was rather sharp, but she didn't mean nothing by it.'

'She's dreadfully upset, as you can imagine, Biddy. But she's bearing up awfully well,' said Rose, not entirely truthfully. 'I'm sure she would like to see you. She said you were very fond of Mr Masters?'

'Oh, I was that, miss,' exclaimed Biddy. 'He treated me like a daughter, he did, and me who's never had a father to call me own, least not one I've ever met.'

The recollection of the dead man's virtues, coupled with a show of unexpected kindness, had the result of producing a fresh bout of weeping from the girl. Rose waited while the maid mopped ineffectually at her eyes with the sodden handkerchief, her nose running. She was appalled at her own clumsiness and instinctively put an arm around the young girl's shoulders and spoke to her in a soothing manner. They made a curious sight, the woman dressed in elegant finery comforting the girl in maid's uniform, standing on the threshold of the house, the door wide open for all the world to see. But if either wondered at the curious scene they made, it was not apparent from their expressions.

'Biddy, why is the door open? Who are you talking to?' The voice that cut through the air was sharp as a knife. There was a certain haughtiness about it that stung Rose's ears. 'I warn you, if I catch you gossiping about …'

The voice faltered, for Daphne had crossed the hall and now clearly saw the visitor's identity. Surprise and embarrassment revealed themselves on her face in equal measure and had the effect of deepening the colour in her cheeks. Her eyes opened wide and then she blinked rapidly, lowering her gaze a moment so that she stared fixedly at the tiled floor of the hall. With considerable effort, Daphne composed herself and raised her head, smiling as she did so.

'Oh, Lady Belvedere, do beg my pardon; I didn't know it was you.' Daphne Spittlehouse's voice was friendly and apologetic. Had Rose not heard the way she had just spoken to her grief-stricken servant, she might have believed the woman to be sincere. 'I thought … Biddy, don't just stand there with the door wide open and her ladyship neither in the house nor out. Really, Biddy, that is no way to answer a door. I would have thought Mrs Masters would have taught you better.' Daphne stopped abruptly. It appeared that she had just noticed that Rose's arm was about the maid's shoulders and that the maid was sobbing. 'Biddy, don't take on so. You're making a spectacle of yourself.' Despite the admonishment, Daphne's voice took on a softer note. 'Biddy, do take Lady Belvedere's coat and make us some tea.'

'Yes, Miss Spittlehouse,' mumbled Biddy, sniffing and putting away her handkerchief.

'If you will permit me, Daphne, I should like to make the tea,' said Rose. 'The poor girl has had a frightful shock. I think she could do with sitting down a while and resting.'

'But Lady Belvedere, I must protest. I couldn't possibly –'

'Please,' said Rose sweetly, 'think nothing of it. Really, I have made a great many pots of tea in my time. Biddy, perhaps you could show me the way to the kitchen. Is it through this door?'

Rose ushered Biddy through the green baize door before Daphne had an opportunity to protest further. The woman, as she had expected, made no effort to follow them into the servants' quarters. Instead Daphne lingered awkwardly in the hall, twisting her hands together and praying that her brother would not choose this moment to return home. She bit her lip and after a moment of reflection giggled in spite of herself. She could just imagine the expression on Linus' face should he find himself served tea by Lady Belvedere in his own home.

Having encouraged Biddy to sit down in one of the two comfortable old, worn armchairs placed at each side of the fireplace in the kitchen, Rose went in search of the kettle. She found a copper one, standing on three Bakelite legs, which she filled with water. While she waited for it to boil, she strolled idly over to the basement window and looked out. It appeared that the window overlooked a kitchen garden of sorts which no doubt earlier in the year was decorated with canes for broad beans and tomatoes. Though she craned her neck to take in the view, Rose could not see the garden gate. She cast a sideward glance at Biddy. The girl had all but buried her face in her handkerchief, and seemed barely conscious of her presence. Rose hastily filled the teapot with the water from the kettle, mumbled something about letting the tea brew, and with one last backward glance stole out into the passage.

She passed the door to the scullery and then arrived at the door that opened out on to the garden. It commanded a fine view of the garden gate which was situated almost directly opposite. This then was how the anonymous letter-writer had stolen into the garden and slipped the letter under the door without being seen. She noted that the person would not have been spotted by anyone in the kitchen or scullery, only by someone in the passage, if they happened to be facing the garden door at the time, or possibly by someone in the garden. Had she been at leisure, Rose would have wandered out into the grounds and examined the garden gate. She would also have walked through it to the lane that ran beyond. However, she was conscious suddenly that she had been gone a while. Daphne was undoubtedly awaiting her return with impatience and not a little annoyance. At the very least, she would be considering her visitor's conduct distinctly odd.

Chapter Twenty-four

Rose returned hurriedly to the kitchen and poured out a cup of tea, which she gave to Biddy. She did not wish to leave the girl alone and cursed the need to speak with Daphne. However, it occurred to her that when she returned to Sedgwick Court she might very well send Edna to Green Gables to keep the girl company and undertake any domestic chores the Spittlehouses might require. She could do without a lady's maid for a few days. Looking about her, Green Gables struck her as a cold and miserable place without the Masters' presence. The more she thought about sending Edna, the more the notion appealed to her, and it was with renewed spirits that she bid Biddy farewell, picked up the tray and made her way up the stairs and through the green baize door.

She had fully expected to find Daphne in the drawing room. It was something of a shock then to discover that the woman had remained waiting for her in the hall.

'So very kind of you, Lady Belvedere,' said Daphne, all but snatching the laden tray from her and carrying it into the drawing room. Rose followed in her wake, aware that there was anger in her strides. She had dared to cross the boundaries of class and was being silently punished for it.

Rose sat in a well upholstered chair with a rigid back and contemplated the best line to take. As Daphne poured out the tea, she glanced at her wristwatch and was alarmed to discover that she had already been at Green Gables for some twenty minutes. She could almost hear Inspector Newcombe and Sergeant Bell approaching. While she was now resigned to still being present when they arrived, if she was quick she might just manage to speak to Daphne before they appeared. For this purpose, she considered it fortunate that Daphne's nature was such that she did not feel the need to tread particularly carefully where the woman was concerned. There was no requirement to beat about the bush and approach the matter gently. But how best to begin?

'Daphne, I daresay you think it rather odd that I should call on you today, but –'

'Not at all. It was very kind of you Lady Belvedere,' said Daphne. 'Do you take sugar?'

She handed her visitor her tea and Rose felt the warmth of the liquid through the fine bone china. She quickly placed the cup and saucer on a convenient occasional table lest she should burn her fingers.

'I suppose you realised I would be alone,' Daphne was saying, while making a face. 'Fancy holding a meeting of that wretched Bonfire Committee, today of all days. You'd think they had better things to do, wouldn't you?'

'I wish you would call me Rose, Daphne. Lady Belvedere sounds so very formal, Anyway, as I was saying, I had a specific reason for wishing to come and see you today,' said Rose, choosing her words carefully. 'I particularly wanted to speak with you before the inspector interviewed you.'

'Oh?'

Rose was aware that she had Daphne's attention now. Fleetingly, a wary look had come into the woman's eyes. Then Daphne had lowered her gaze and stared down at her cup, her teaspoon poised in her hand.

'Would you mind awfully if I were to be quite frank?' asked Rose.

'I have often thought it is better to be,' said Daphne feigning an air of indifference. 'Of course my brother wouldn't agree with me.'

'We don't have much time, you see,' said Rose, a note of urgency creeping into her voice. 'It is very likely that the police will be here any moment and –'

'What?' cried Daphne. She looked startled, as if the sudden appearance of the police was something to be dreaded. 'Why will they be here? What do they want?' The appearance of apathy had quite disappeared. The note of panic in her voice was quite unmistakeable.

'They will want to speak with you, I should imagine. There is nothing to fear. They will want to know when you last saw Masters, I expect. To enable them to determine his movements yesterday afternoon.'

'I see,' said Daphne, relaxing a little, 'Well, I am not sure that I can be of much help.' She stirred her tea absentmindedly. 'You'll think it dreadful of me, I know, but I really can't remember the last time I saw him. You see, I was so used to seeing him about the house that I never really gave it much thought or noticed whether he was there or not. What I am trying to say is that he was something of a fixture about the place, if

194

that makes any sense?

'That is a pity,' said Rose, a touch coldly, thinking how sad it was for the manservant to have had so little presence in someone's eyes as to be almost invisible. 'But I suppose it can't be helped. Of course I should think the inspector will also want to ask you whether you are aware of your brother having any enemies.'

'That would wish him dead?' Daphne rolled her eyes. 'Well, of course I'm not aware of any. People like Linus don't make foes. That's not to say that he isn't a bit of an old windbag but …' She laughed. 'Really, I don't know why the police don't just ask my brother. Surely he knows whether or not he has any enemies.'

'Yes, of course the inspector will ask him. But I don't think the major will tell them if he has, do you?' said Rose. 'From what little I have seen of him, your brother strikes me as rather a proud man and one that would like to keep such matters to himself. Besides, I don't think he'll consider it any of the inspector's business.' She paused a few moments before continuing, watching Daphne with a degree of curiosity. For she thought the woman looked as though she was frightened but was desperately trying to conceal the fact.

'And of course,' Rose said slowly, 'there is always the possibility that he is protecting someone.'

Daphne looked at her aghast. 'Do you mean me?' Her eyes flashed with anger and her cheeks turned crimson. 'If you do, you might as well say so.'

'I do,' said Rose, rather more abruptly than she had intended. 'That is to say, I think your brother was trying to protect you last night. Were you aware that he was quite adamant that you not be interviewed?'

'That is because he thought I was upset. He has a tendency to think women are more delicate than we are.' Daphne gave a false little laugh. 'Really, Rose, what are you suggesting?'

'I think Major Spittlehouse thought there was a possibility that you had tried to kill him last night, and had murdered Masters by mistake because he was wearing your brother's tweed jacket, the one the major always wears.'

'Lady Belvedere … Rose, what you are saying is quite ridiculous.' Daphne put down her cup and saucer and began to pace the room, as if she were a caged lion who could find no means of escape. 'I wouldn't dream of doing such a thing. And it's quite preposterous for you to suggest that Linus should think I would. Really, you are being frightfully unkind.'

'I don't mean to be, but is it really ludicrous? You parents' will and your brother's opposition to your proposed marriage to Mr Mayhew gave you more than an adequate motive for wishing him dead.'

Really, the conversation was not going at all along the lines that Rose had planned. She had not meant to become riled and accuse Daphne, or encourage her to adopt a defensive stand. She felt the woman's open hostility, which seemed to dominate the room. If she were to stretch out her hand, she would feel the tension. And she could not really blame Daphne for feeling as she did. How awful to have some woman, whom she barely knew, come into her house on the pretence of kindness and accuse her of trying to murder her closest relative.

'I'm sorry, I didn't mean to upset you,' said Rose, trying to make amends. 'If it is any consolation, your brother realises now that you did not try to kill him. He knows that you would never have mistaken Masters for him, even in the dark.'

'Well, of course I wouldn't. But that doesn't change what you –'

'Daphne, listen to me,' Rose got up from her chair and clasped the woman's arm. Daphne flinched, as if she had been stung. But the gesture had served its purpose because Rose now had the woman's full attention. She saw the fear and misery in Daphne's eyes. 'Look here, one of us must tell the inspector about your parents' will and your brother's opposition to your proposed marriage. It's no use trying to keep quiet about it. It'll come out in the end, this sort of thing always does. I'd much rather it be you who tells him but, if you won't, I shall. You see, I will feel obliged to do so.' Daphne tried to pull away from her but Rose held her arm fast. 'I don't want to have to tell him but neither will I knowingly withhold information from the police.' Daphne's face was quite without expression. It was all Rose could do not to shake the woman. 'Oh, do see reason. Don't you see that you have placed me in a very difficult position? And really, it would be best if you told him; it would put you in a much better light and show you had nothing to hide.'

'But I don't have anything to hide.' Daphne almost spat out the words. 'You said it yourself that if I had intended to kill Linus I wouldn't have killed Masters by mistake.'

'No,' agreed Rose, '*you* wouldn't have made such an error. But there is nothing to say that your accomplice might not have done.'

Daphne pulled away from her now and stared at her in disbelief. The fear had returned to her eyes and Rose noticed that she was also shaking. She had clearly touched a nerve. The woman was distraught and miserable. Instinctively, Rose put out a hand to her. Daphne stepped back and glared.

'That is an interesting speculation. But you cannot prove a thing.'

'Not yet,' agreed Rose.

She might have said more, had they not both been startled by a loud knock on the front door. It cut through the tension in the room. At once they became allies instead of foes. This time it was Daphne who stepped forward and clasped Rose's arm.

'Is it the inspector, do you think? It can't be Linus; he wouldn't need to knock because he has his own key.'

'Yes. I think it is Inspector Newcombe.'

'You must help me,' cried Daphne. Her fingernails dug into the younger woman's arm making Rose wince.

'I will. But you must also help yourself. If you are innocent, you have nothing to fear.'

'And if I'm not?'

The words had escaped from Daphne's lips before she had had a chance to stop them. Instinctively she clasped a hand over her mouth and looked at Rose who stared back at her in horror. Neither woman spoke. Later Rose wondered what would have happened next had Inspector Newcombe and Sergeant Bell not chosen that very moment to enter the room, unannounced.

The inspector looked from one to the other of the two women, conscious that he had blundered into some scene or other for the atmosphere hung heavy in the room. If nothing else, he knew his presence to be unwanted but if he was embarrassed by the fact, he gave no outward sign.

'Miss Spittlehouse … and, well I never, Lady Belvedere, I must say I did not expect to find you here.' The inspector raised an eyebrow and looked pointedly at Rose.

'I came to keep Miss Spittlehouse company, Inspector,' said Rose, hoping that she sounded sincere. 'Major Spittlehouse and my husband are attending a meeting of the Bonfire Committee and I didn't think it right for Daphne to be alone at a time like this'.

'Yes. It was most frightfully good of you, Lady Belvedere,' said Daphne, rallying a little.

'I see,' said Inspector Newcombe. 'Very kind of you, I'm sure.'

Rose could not quite put her finger on it but there was something about the inspector's manner which made her feel certain that he had not been so easily deceived. However, much to her relief, he did not seem intent on pressing the matter. Rather he appeared inclined to ignore her presence entirely and focus his attention instead on Daphne. The woman in question watched him anxiously. Her eyes never left his face save to steal a glance at Rose, who wondered whether it was as obvious to the policeman as it was to herself that Daphne was afraid.

'Miss Spittlehouse, if you are feeling up to it, I should like to ask you a few questions,' said Inspector Newcombe, indicating a chair.

'Yes, of course, Inspector,' said Daphne, sitting down.

She had been standing when the policemen had entered the room and it was with something of a sense of relief that she now sunk on to the chair, taking the weight from her feet. She had not to worry now if her legs shook; they did not have to hold her up. Yet, the very moment she was seated, she felt at a distinct disadvantage. For one thing, she considered herself to be trapped for Sergeant Bell stood against the door, barring her escape.

She gave Rose a brief imploring look and clasped her hands together in her lap. It was almost as if she were afraid that they would tremble if she did not hold them tightly; Rose had the ridiculous notion that the woman might be tempted to sit on her hands to keep them still. 'And if I'm not?' Daphne's words still echoed in her head making her feel giddy. She had not had a chance to digest them before the policemen had seen fit to descend upon them, two pillars of the law to hold them to account. Inwardly she sighed. What had Daphne meant? Was Daphne …

Abruptly Rose was recalled to the present. It was obvious that Daphne had said something that concerned her for both she and Inspector Newcombe were looking at her expectantly, waiting for her to say something.

'I'm so sorry. I'm afraid I wasn't listening. What were you saying, Daphne?'

'Miss Spittlehouse has requested that you be present while she answers our questions.' Inspector Newcombe was looking at her curiously. 'I say, Lady Belvedere, are you all right? You look a little pale, if you don't mind my saying.'

'Yes. I'm quite all right, thank you, Inspector,' said Rose, attempting a smile. 'And of course I'll stay, if Miss Spittlehouse would like me to.'

'Very good. Now Miss Spittlehouse, I wonder if you could tell me when you last saw the deceased?'

'I'm afraid I can't,' said Daphne. 'You see I kept to my room for most of the afternoon. I had some letters to write. Masters waited on us at lunch, of course, but after that I don't remember seeing him. He might well have been in the basement with his wife or upstairs in the main part of the house. I really couldn't say.' She shrugged. 'I just don't remember noticing him, that's all. And it's so easy to mix one day with another, don't you find? At least it is for me.'

Inspector Newcombe stared thoughtfully at Daphne. Rose wondered whether he was of the opinion that the woman was talking too much. She worried that Daphne's tongue would run away with her and that she would say something that she later came bitterly to regret. The inspector certainly looked as if he intended to press her further on when she had last seen the murdered servant. However, on reflection he appeared to think better of it for he rather abruptly seemed to change course.

'Perhaps you would be so good as to tell me your movements yesterday afternoon, Miss Spittlehouse?'

'My movements?' Daphne said dully, as if she did not comprehend the word. It was clear she had been taken off guard and a fleeting look of alarm crossed her face.

'Yes, if you would. It is merely routine, you understand. I shall be asking the same of everyone else involved in this affair. I have already spoken with Major Spittlehouse on this very subject.' The inspector gave her what was obviously intended to be an encouraging smile. 'Shall we say from about half past four? If you could just tell me where you were.'

'Half past four … let me think. I believe I was in my bedroom,' said Daphne, casting her mind back over the previous day. 'Yes, that's right. I had some correspondence to attend to. I remember now because I looked at the clock on my bedside table and it said five o'clock and I thought to myself that I had been writing for over half an hour, and hadn't time flown and really I must stop because ...'

Daphne's voice seemed to drone on and on. Or was it only Rose who felt it did? Certainly she knew that inwardly she was willing the woman to stop. Why couldn't Daphne just answer the question simply, why must she ramble on so? Did she not know how suspicious it made her look?

'Yes? And what did you do then?' said Inspector Newcombe. He was still smiling and nodding encouragingly. The words of Mary Howitt's poem came to Rose's mind. *"'Will you walk into my parlour?' said the spider to the fly."* Rose stared down at her own knuckles; they had turned white.

'Well, I finished the letter I was writing and I wandered out on to the landing,' Daphne was saying. 'I think I had some notion about going down to the drawing room and having a cup of tea brought to me there.'

'But you decided against it?'

'Yes. Because at that moment I heard my brother opening the front door with his key.' Daphne coloured slightly. 'I daresay you'll think me awful, Inspector, but I decided to go back into my room before Linus saw me. You see, I really wasn't in the mood to hear all about the preparations for the bonfire festivities. My brother has a tendency to be rather verbose on the subject. He'd have wanted to tell me all about the different fireworks and, really, I couldn't imagine anything more dull.'

The inspector looked up sharply. 'Then you didn't actually see your brother come into the house?'

'No, I didn't. But I heard his key turn in the lock, as I've said. And when I was back in my room I heard him close the door behind him and cross the hall.'

'And you stayed in your room?'

'Well, of course I intended to, and I most certainly would have done had I not heard my brother go back out almost immediately.'

'What?' The inspector looked distinctly interested. Even Sergeant Bell looked up from taking his notes.

'Yes. I say, I thought it rather strange at the time. I suppose Linus had forgotten something to do with the festivities. But, whatever it was, he wasn't gone for very long. Because when I came downstairs a few minutes later he was in the parlour helping himself to supper.'

'Major Spittlehouse mentioned you looked rather surprised to see him,' said Rose. It was her first contribution to the interview and the inspector eyed her with not a little annoyance.

'Did he?' Daphne asked vaguely. She did not appear even a little bit interested by the fact.

'Yes, he did,' asserted Rose. 'He said you popped your head around the door and said you weren't very hungry.'

'Yes, that's right. I remember now. He was rather put out. But, as I've said, I knew he wouldn't stop talking about the arrangements for the bonfire, and besides, I knew I'd be eating heaps that evening.' She smiled over at Rose. 'Your cook's black treacle toffee is absolutely divine, Lady Belvedere. I always eat far too much of it.'

'What did you do then?' said Inspector Newcombe.

'I went back to my room, Inspector. Rather dull, I know, but there it is. I thought I might as well finish my correspondence.'

'You didn't by any chance go out?'

'No, I didn't.' Was it Rose's imagination, or did Daphne hesitate slightly in her denial? Certainly she seemed to swallow before continuing, almost as if she were playing for time. She continued, however, in the same confident, slightly bored tone. 'That is to say, not immediately. I went out later of course to go to the festivities.'

'What time would that have been?'

'Oh, about seven o'clock I should say. My brother had already left some ten minutes or so before.' Daphne made a face. 'He wanted to be there for when they lit the bonfire. I didn't. It takes an age. But I suppose he felt he had to, what with him being on that wretched committee,'

'You didn't go out earlier?'

'I've already told you I didn't.' There was a note of irritation in Daphne's voice and a flash of anger in her eyes.

'You hadn't by any chance arranged to meet Mr Mayhew?' asked Inspector Newcombe, watching her closely. 'You didn't go out to see him?'

'No.'

Daphne felt the inspector's eyes upon her. It did not stop her, however, throwing a filthy look at Rose, though Rose appeared equally surprised by the policeman's suggestion. It was not from the countess then that the inspector had heard about her relations with Archie. Another tongue had wagged. And, even as the thought came to her, she knew instinctively who it was, as if the name had been written down on a sheet of paper and placed before her. With a sinking feeling in the pit of her stomach, she knew what was to follow as if she were saying the words herself instead of the inspector. It was Mrs Masters who had betrayed her. She could hear it in Inspector Newcombe's voice, the way he phrased his questions, using the woman's very words. And, what was worse, she could imagine Mrs Masters telling him, basking in the glow of his attention while in the midst of her own sadness. The woman loved to gossip, she had always said as much to Linus, though of course he would not listen. The Masters could do no wrong as far as he was concerned and yet now that wretched woman had told the police about their business. Linus would hate that when she told him and tell him she certainly would, because goodness knew what Mrs Masters had said. Daphne felt her cheeks redden. She wouldn't have a single shred of character left. How very awful to have your character taken away by a servant.

Daphne looked up. Inspector Newcombe had paused in whatever he had been saying and was obviously waiting for her to provide him with an answer. How stupid she had been to let her mind wander, to indulge in feelings of animosity towards Mrs Masters, when all the time she should have been listening to what the inspector was saying, trying to ascertain how much Mrs Masters had told him. And here she was now, staring at the inspector stupidly, trying to fathom what question he had just asked her and wondering if she might possibly ask him if he could repeat it. And all the time she was painfully conscious that his eyes were upon her, that he was watching her every move, waiting for her to make a mistake.

Chapter Twenty-five

In the end it was Rose who came to Daphne's rescue, giving her the time she required to breathe and compose herself.

'Miss Spittlehouse was intending to tell you at the first opportunity, Inspector,' Rose was saying, as Daphne's attention was drawn back to the present. 'We were only discussing it this afternoon, weren't we, Daphne? Really, it's a great pity Mrs Masters felt the need to mention it. It would have been much better if you had heard it from Miss Spittlehouse herself.'

'I agree,' said Inspector Newcombe. 'Well, I daresay it can't be helped. Happen we should have spoken to you earlier, Miss Spittlehouse.' He still smiled, and his tone remained pleasant. Daphne recalled, when she thought about it later, that she had relaxed a little because she had thought the danger had passed. Certainly she had not seen the need to avert her gaze or clutch at the fabric of her skirt with nervous fingers. It was perhaps because of this that she was taken so unawares by what the inspector said next; she had not been ready with a mask to hide her feelings.

'No doubt Mrs Masters was a trifle upset,' said the inspector in his agreeable tone. 'It's not every day a woman is told her husband was killed by mistake for her employer. It's a rum business all right and I daresay the shock loosened her tongue and made her say more than she meant to. I'll say this for the murdered man, Major Spittlehouse must have thought a great deal of Masters, confiding in him about your parents' will as he did. Lucky for us too that the manservant was the kind of man who liked to talk to his wife about such matters, because your brother doesn't strike me as a man given to talk, Miss Spittlehouse. I don't reckon he'll breathe a word about it to us, not if we don't tell him what we know.'

The will. Mrs Masters knew about the terms of her parents' will and had told the policemen. Daphne could not help herself from uttering a faint gasp. No doubt the wretched woman had poisoned their minds against her too. How stupid she had been to think that Mrs Masters had merely made some disparaging remarks about her relationship with Archie, the differences in their ages and social positions of which Daphne knew herself to be particularly sensitive. She glanced at Rose and caught a sympathetic look for her troubles. What a fool she had been. Lady Belvedere had tried to warn her but she had paid little heed, lulled into a false sense of security by the inspector's courteous manner and dulcet tones. She cursed herself severely for being such a fool. And it was no use pretending that she had not been very shaken by the inspector's words. It was too late to compose her features into a look of vague indifference for they had already given her away. But, though she felt like crumbling, there was still a defiant look in Daphne's eye.

'It seems you do not require me to say anything, Inspector. Another has apparently already done that for me?' She looked the policeman directly in the eye; it was almost as if she were issuing a challenge. 'It would appear you know the terms of my parents' will and my brother's opposition to my marrying Mr Mayhew. I really don't think there is much more that I can add.'

'We do, as you say, know all about it, or at least Mrs Masters' version of it.'

'Ah, yes,' Daphne said, a note of bitterness creeping into her voice. 'I am sure Mrs Masters delighted in telling you; her sort always do. It must have been obvious, Inspector, to someone of your experience in questioning people, that the woman has never liked me.'

'That is as maybe,' said Inspector Newcombe rather gruffly, a vision of the grieving widow still firmly in his mind. He didn't like the way Miss Spittlehouse spoke of her servant, he didn't like it at all. He felt aggrieved for the poor woman and it made him speak more brusquely than perhaps he ought. There was little sign now of a smile upon his face as he said: 'But it seems she spoke the truth. That's to say you discussed the matter with Lady Belvedere and you gave thought as to whether you should mention it to us. And you decided to, if what Lady Belvedere says is true and I've no reason to doubt your ladyship's word.' Here he paused to give a brief nod in Rose's direction. 'Very commendable, I'm sure. But there is no getting round the fact that it gave you a motive, Miss Spittlehouse, though it sounds awful to say it out loud. It's not something that bears thinking about, a sister trying to do away with her own brother, especially one who as good as brought her up.'

'You are not suggesting I tried to murder Linus last night, Inspector?' cried Daphne, considerably taken aback by the abruptness of the

204

inspector's words and the change in his manner towards her. There was a note of anguish in her voice and she had gone very white.

To Rose's mind the woman was clearly horrified at the suggestion. Yet had not she herself made such a supposition? And hadn't Daphne as good as admitted that there was some truth in it? Was this all an act, she wondered; the pale face, the way Daphne had leapt up from her chair as if in horror and disgust? And hadn't she herself been in some way complicit? For hadn't she provided Daphne with advance notice of what the police might suspect?' She was reminded that Daphne's voice had been very clear. She had looked Inspector Newcombe directly in the eye. He in turn had given her a penetrating look. But Daphne had not flinched or looked away. Instead, she had returned his gaze, and the colour was coming back slowly to her cheeks. Was it Rose's imagination, or had the corners of the woman's mouth turned up slightly into something resembling a brief smile. Really, she didn't understand Daphne at all.

'No, I am not, Miss Spittlehouse,' said Inspector Newcombe. 'I don't doubt for a minute that you are innocent of trying to kill your brother. Lady Belvedere has already put forward a very convincing argument as to why you are unlikely to have been the culprit. No,' he paused and leaned towards her, 'I don't think that at all.'

If the inspector's words had been meant to comfort her then he had failed most miserably in his aim. For Daphne's face was now deathly pale and her lip trembled. She sank back into her recently vacated chair and Rose wondered whether she was about to give way to weeping or even about to faint. Certainly there was a desolate air about her now. Rose stared at her curiously. Why had Daphne reacted so? What could be worse than being accused of trying to murder one's own brother?

'You think I had an accomplice, don't you? You think Archie meant to kill my brother and killed Masters by mistake,' cried Daphne, as if in answer to Rose's unspoken question. 'Well, you are quite wrong, Inspector. Archie would never agree to do such a thing even if I were to ask him, which of course I wouldn't.'

'Oh, I don't think Archie Mayhew was your accomplice, Miss Spittlehouse,' said the inspector watching her closely. 'Far from it. I won't say it didn't cross my mind and that you had a perfectly good motive for wishing your brother dead. But when all is said and done, so did Mr Mayhew.' He leaned forward again and smiled. 'No, Miss Spittlehouse, I think it much more likely that Archie Mayhew tried to kill your brother of his own volition.'

'Archie wouldn't,' said Daphne, close to tears. 'It's hateful for you to say such a thing.'

'I'm afraid, in my line of work, there are a lot of things we have to do and say that seem unpleasant to those who are not thus employed,' said the inspector dryly.

'Do you have any evidence to support your theory that Mr Mayhew is the murderer, Inspector?' asked Rose.

Inspector Newcombe stared at her and frowned. Her interjection was not welcome; it was written clearly enough on his face. Daphne, however, looked up and caught her eye. There appeared a glimmer of hope in the woman's face. She had been desperate but now she looked less wretched. Rose ploughed on, spurred on by goodness knew what.

'I appreciate that Mr Mayhew may have had a motive and therefore is a suspect,' said Rose, 'but is there any particular reason to suppose that he is the actual murderer?'

'I should have thought you could have answered that question most satisfactorily yourself, Lady Belvedere,' Inspector Newcombe said, a little brusquely. 'It was you after all who drew our attention to the fact that the murderer did not know Major Spittlehouse particularly well. That is to say, he recognised a man as having vaguely the same build as the major and wearing his jacket but in the dark could not distinguish his features from that of his servant.' The inspector turned his focus to Daphne, who was watching the exchange between the two of them most avidly. 'I do not suppose, Miss Spittlehouse, that Mr Mayhew knew your brother well? My understanding is that they had only met on a couple of occasions, and only then in the course of business. Mr Mayhew is employed by Messrs Gribble, Hebborn & Whittaker in Bichester, isn't he? I believe he helped draw up some legal document or other for Major Spittlehouse.'

Daphne nodded dully but said nothing.

'Mrs Masters was most emphatic that Mr Mayhew had never been invited to Green Gables. She made a particular point of mentioning it. It stands to reason then that your young man would have had no cause to ever have set eyes on Masters. It would be easy enough therefore to mistake one for the other in the dark, two men who looked approximately alike and one wearing the other's jacket. A simple mistake to make, I'd say.' The inspector gave her something of a sympathetic look. 'We have checked and, apart from some minor legacies, you are the sole beneficiary under your brother's will, Miss Spittlehouse. In the event of your brother's death, you will inherit your family's fortune. It will make you a very wealthy woman.'

The inspector was not so heartless as to add that it would also make her a very attractive marriage proposition to any young man seeking social and financial advancement with little effort. He neither said nor inferred that it would also provide the necessary inducement for a young man of astounding good looks and charm to consider marrying a woman somewhat older than himself who possessed neither beauty nor a particularly pleasing or sparkling personality. The inspector did not say anything of the sort, but it was still in the minds of the other three people in the room. Sergeant Bell thought it as he scribbled down his notes in a neat hand; Rose thought it as she glanced over at the other woman with something akin to pity; and Daphne most definitely felt the implication, for her cheeks flushed pink and she stared down miserably at a little patch of carpet beside her feet. The room had suddenly become quiet and no one seemed inclined to speak. It was as if each were expecting the other to break the silence.

After a while, a little sound emitted from Daphne's lips. It was like the noise of the wind caught for a moment in a handful of leaves, picking them up lightly and then scattering them as they fell. Daphne Spittlehouse looked as if she had experienced the same shock as one of those discarded leaves. For a moment her eyes were wide and very clear and then she blinked and her eyelashes appeared to flutter in that same breeze. Rose watched as the woman tried desperately to compose herself. It was Daphne's mouth that betrayed her in the end, not the expression on her face, for the words came tumbling out before she could stop them.

'He didn't know about the terms of my parents' will. I didn't tell him.' She spoke in a small voice that seemed to gather momentum and with it conviction. She said more firmly: 'I kept it from him.'

'Are you quite sure of that, Miss Spittlehouse?' the inspector's voice was sceptical.

'Oh, yes, quite certain,' Daphne said, in something of a breathless voice.

She tried to put that awful telephone conversation with Archie out of her mind. She had accused him of … Yes, but he hadn't admitted anything, had he? Perhaps her thoughts had been playing tricks on her, making her believe things that were not there. She had suspected that her brother had spoken with him. While it was true that Archie hadn't denied it as such, had he actually admitted it? She couldn't remember. Daphne tried desperately to recall their conversation but it was an impossible task to perform under the watchful, suspicious eye of the inspector. She thought on balance, however, he hadn't. And, besides, she clung on frantically to the belief that Linus would not have told the policemen if he had spoken with Archie; she was sure of it. He would think of it as washing their dirty linen in public and he would be loathe to do such a thing. He would hate it like poison. For once she rejoiced in her brother's character.

But, even as she felt the wave of relief wash over her, there appeared another cloud. What about Archie? Would he say anything? He was so young, and his feelings so transparent, that they revealed themselves freely and with such vividness in his face. She felt a sudden almost maternal protectiveness towards him. He did not have the bitter experience of life that came with age. He would not realise that they were trying to trap him in to making a confession. He would answer their questions truthfully and with an earnestness that came with youth. She bit her lip. She must speak with him before they interviewed him. He had told her that it was better if they did not meet. But really there was nothing to stop her telephoning. She could telephone him at the office again but, twice in one day, wouldn't they think it suspicious? And she would have to speak to that awful Miss Simmons, who disapproved of her, and perhaps Archie would refuse to come to the telephone. There was nothing to stop him from saying he was too busy with work. Perhaps she could send him a letter. If necessary, she could pay a boy to hand deliver it to his lodgings this evening. But was it wise to put what she had to say in writing? What if the police were to discover it? Would her words come back to haunt her or, worse still, help to put a noose around poor Archie's neck? If only …

Something had made her look up. Out of the corner of her eye she glimpsed something or other that was different. The drawing room door

208

was open when before it had most definitely been closed. And Biddy was standing in the doorway, wearing an apron that looked as if it required pressing with a hot iron. Daphne bit her lip. What ridiculous things one thought about. Had she not more important matters to contemplate than her maid's uniform? It occurred to her then that none of them had heard the girl knock or open the door. It was quite possible that the girl had neglected to tap before entering. But the hinges of the drawing room door creaked a little. She had mentioned the fact more than once to Linus. Biddy must then have opened the door very gently and looked in, peeking around it and taking in the scene. And now the maid stood there on the threshold between the hall and the drawing room, wringing her apron in her hands, twisting it this way and that so that it would require now more than just a good press with an iron. The others had spotted her and, under their collective and enquiring gaze, Biddy released the door handle guiltily and put a hand out to the doorframe instead so that she might steady herself before she spoke.

'Begging your pardon, madam … sirs. A gentleman is here to see you, ma'am. It's a Mr Mayhew and he says it's ever so important.'

There was the sound of a sharp intake of breath. It took a moment for Daphne to realise it was her own. Biddy's words were going around and around in her head, the significance of what she was saying all too obvious. And, ridiculously at a time like this, when she was aware that all she should really be thinking was how ill-timed Archie's visit was, and what she could do to mitigate the damage, she could not rid herself of the thought that Biddy must be very stupid. Why else had the girl not called her aside and whispered in her mistress' ear, as a good servant would have done? There was a reason why Biddy did not answer the door to visitors, why she was kept downstairs to undertake the more menial tasks.

'Splendid,' said Inspector Newcombe, smiling affably at the little maid before Daphne had a chance to speak. 'Show the gentleman in.'

Chapter Twenty-six

If Daphne had hoped that Archie had been shown into the library while Biddy delivered her message, she was to be disappointed. It became all too apparent that the little maid had just left the visitor to stand unceremoniously in the entrance hall while she announced his arrival. For, at the inspector's words that the newcomer be invited to join them, Biddy had half turned in the doorway and beckoned to someone standing at the other end of the hall. With flaming cheeks, Daphne watched the spectacle unfold, hardly daring to breathe. To make matters worse, Archie entered the room still clutching his hat rather awkwardly in his hands. As a vent for her acute embarrassment, the mistress of the house glared furiously at her careless servant, who hastily relieved the visitor of the outdoor article. It was only when Archie had been safely divested of his hat that Daphne realised that instinctively she must have moved forward. For she was standing a few feet from the door but she did not remember either rising from her seat or advancing the necessary steps. Her arms were outstretched, as if she had been preparing to greet the visitor in an intimate fashion, and she lowered them quickly, her hands clinging to the fabric of her skirt instead. She looked down and noticed her fingers were trembling.

'Archie ...' She had spoken impulsively and the name had been uttered in a high, rather anguished voice that she hardly recognised as her own. She cursed herself furiously and bit her tongue.

'Darling ...' Archie said, in something of a hesitant fashion, a look of puzzlement on his face.

Daphne stifled a cry. For only then did she realise from the way he looked about the drawing room in rather a furtive manner, taking in the presence of the strangers, that Archie hadn't known she had company. Biddy hadn't told him! When he had entered the room he had assumed that he would find her alone. Certainly he had not expected the police to be in residence, or Lady Belvedere for that matter, and his face, unprepared for the need to conceal emotion, reflected clearly the horror that he felt at such a discovery. He stood motionless in the room while Daphne tried to assuage herself of the anger and helplessness that she felt in respect of the situation by looking contemptuously at Biddy's retreating back.

She had a sudden urge to weep, from frustration if nothing else. Everything was going wrong. Oh, if only Masters had been there to answer the door, this would never have happened. He would have shown Archie into the library and not breathed a word about his presence to the inspector. But Masters was dead and the inspector had as good as said that he suspected Archie of killing him. Had she had more time, Daphne might have persuaded him that his theory was ridiculous. But now it was too late. And they hadn't even had to send for Archie, for he had come to Green Gables of his own accord. Worse still, he had been taken completely unawares. He had not been expecting the inspector to be there. He had had no time to prepare his answers. They would not fall glibly from his tongue with his usual charm.

Daphne turned away. She could not meet Archie's gaze. She could not bring herself to see the panic in his eyes. He was young and naïve and wildly optimistic but, understandably, he would now be afraid. And they would take advantage of his fear, would take his words and twist them so that he could not remember what he had said and what he hadn't. Perhaps he would think that she had betrayed him, that her telephone call had been meant to lure him into a trap. She couldn't bear it if he should think that of her. Anything would be better than that. She took a deep breath and turned back, her cheeks flushed. She hoped that he was aware of the desperation in her eyes, that he would realise the need for caution.

'Archie, what are you doing here? You must go at once. The inspector is interviewing me.' Even to her own ears she sounded like a school mistress admonishing a naughty child. Archie did not move. He remained where he was, as if frozen to the spot. She lowered her voice so that it was barely above a whisper, though she could not hide the urgency behind her words. 'You must go.'

'On the contrary, I should be very much obliged if Mr Mayhew would stay,' said Inspector Newcombe, with an air of authority. 'Your arrival, sir, is very timely. In fact, we were just talking about you. I have one or two questions that I would be grateful if you would answer. No, Miss Spittlehouse,' he added as Daphne made to leave the room, 'there really is no need for you to go. In fact I would appreciate it if you stayed. Now,

Miss Spittlehouse was sitting here, so if you wouldn't mind sitting there, Mr Mayhew ...'

'All right,' said Archie, though the suggestion did not appear to appeal to him much.

'That's the idea. That seat, if you please.' The inspector chuckled pleasantly, as if what he had to say next was in jest. 'After all, we don't want the two of you conferring, do we?'

Daphne sat down miserably and Archie took the proffered chair. The inspector had chosen the seats well, for the two lovers were at a little distance from each other and could not easily converse without first turning around in their seats and thus making it obvious. Two solitary figures with a physical gulf between them.

Watching the spectacle, it occurred to Rose that Archie was no less unhappy about the situation than Daphne. She thought the young man looked afraid, though he was doing his best to conceal the fact. However, he had a nervous habit of rubbing the side of his nose and, when he stared across at the inspector, he passed his hand through his hair in something of a harried fashion.

It was the first time that Rose had laid eyes on Archie Mayhew and she observed the young man with considerable interest. For this was the fellow with whom Daphne was so enamoured that she had ignored etiquette and forced her acquaintance on a stranger in order to further her cause. No ordinary, common or garden acquaintance either, Rose thought, not now she was a countess, if only by marriage. But that had not stopped Daphne, in her desperation, applying to her to petition the major on her behalf.

Rose's first impression of Archie Mayhew was promising. He was undoubtedly a fine figure of a man. Though he might be rather slouched in his chair now as if he wished the back to open up and swallow him, when he had first walked into the room he had come across very differently. Unaware of the policemen's presence, he had entered the room with a confident air. He had carried himself well, helped not a little by the fine cut of his clothes and his tall, lean frame. His dark looks had accentuated his regular, even features, so that the overall effect had been most pleasing. In truth, he was far more handsome than Rose had supposed him to be from Daphne's description. But it had not been just his looks that were appealing. There had been something open and boyish about his manner, as if he greeted the world with a youthful enthusiasm, that was equally engaging. Rose did not doubt for a moment that he would be an entertaining dinner guest. She could well imagine him regaling the other diners with fascinating stories of his exploits and being one of the first to call for the carpet to be rolled up after dinner so that the guests might dance.

It was little wonder then that Daphne should be desperate to marry such a fellow. He was precisely the sort of man one could lose one's head over. Rose shuddered. Who could say what desperate lengths Daphne, impulsive by nature, might not go to to ensure that she did not lose the attentions of this man, as she had lost the love of Bunny and the curate, Harold?

'Mr Mayhew, I understand that you and Miss Spittlehouse are engaged to be married,' began Inspector Newcombe, pleasantly enough, but without preamble, phrasing what he said as a statement of fact rather than a question. 'I must congratulate you both. I am sure that you will make a very fine couple.'

Whatever Archie had expected him to say, it was obviously not this, for he looked distinctly taken aback, his cheeks crimson. 'Yes ...no... that is to say we haven't given it out yet.'

'No you haven't,' agreed the policeman. 'Now, why is that, I wonder?'

'We have only just become engaged, Inspector.' This was from Daphne, whose voice travelled hurriedly across the room, before Archie had a chance to answer. 'It is all so stupid and public this giving out. I should far rather we got married quietly somewhere before we become the subject of village tittle tattle.'

'And you are of the same view, Mr Mayhew?'

'Oh, absolutely,' said Archie, rallying a little. 'It's frightful how villages like Sedgwick tend to talk. And poor Daphne has an absolute horror of gossip, don't you, darling?' He half turned in his chair to face Daphne, smiling. She met his eye and something passed between them. Rose thought it was a warning look, a shared secret that they were debating whether to tell, or perhaps assuring each other that they would keep quiet for the sake of the other. Whatever it was, when Archie Mayhew turned back to face the inspector, his face was grave.

'And Major Spittlehouse, he must be delighted by the news of your engagement?' continued Inspector Newcombe.

'You know full well, Inspector, that he's not,' cried Daphne. 'Why must you ask Mr Mayhew such questions, when you already know the answers? One could be forgiven for supposing that you are trying to play us off against one another. If you must know, it doesn't matter. The money, I mean. It doesn't mean a thing to us. Archie would marry me if I was as poor as a church mouse, and I him.'

'Very commendable, I am sure,' said the inspector. However, some of his jovial air had left him. 'But I really wish you wouldn't answer for Mr Mayhew, Miss Spittlehouse. My questions are directed to him, not to you.'

'Then you shouldn't insist that I be present,' replied Daphne, rather petulantly. 'You are only doing it to upset me. You are waiting for Archie to give different answers to my own. You are wanting to twist our words and trip us up and make us confess to things that we didn't do.'

'Daphne!' exclaimed Archie. He looked quite appalled at her outburst and Rose thought better of him because of it. She sympathised, however, with Daphne's predicament, for the inspector certainly seemed to be playing some bizarre game of cat and mouse.

'It's true, Archie,' continued Daphne defiantly. 'They believe you killed Masters by mistake because he was wearing my brother's jacket. They think you really meant to kill Linus because of all that nonsense about his opposition to our engagement and the terms of my parents' will, which means I will inherit nothing without his consent. But I've told the inspector until I'm quite blue in the face that you didn't know about any of it, that I never breathed a word about it to you.' She paused to stifle a sob and added rather desperately: 'They don't believe me. You must make them believe you.'

Archie now sat quite rigidly on his chair. It was very apparent from his expression that Daphne's words had shocked him into silence. As if to add emphasis to the fact, the room seemed strangely quiet and deathly still after Daphne's rant. It was as if the very fixtures and fittings were waiting to hear his answer to the charge quite as much as those present in human form, who listened with attentive ears. But if he were aware that the world waited on his words Archie gave no sign of it. If anything, he rather took his time in responding, as if he were carefully deliberating his course and choosing his words with care.

'It's quite true, Inspector,' he said at last. 'Miss Spittlehouse never told me about her parents' will, or her brother's opposition to our proposed union, for that matter.' He turned in his chair so that he might face the woman to whom he referred. 'It wouldn't have mattered. It wouldn't have mattered a jot.'

'Wouldn't it?' Some normal colour had returned to Daphne's cheeks. It was obvious to all that this declaration of sorts had taken her somewhat by surprise. She stared at Archie adoringly; they might have been the only people in the room for what little notice they took of the others. It occurred to Rose that the two of them could not have played the scene any better had they rehearsed it. Archie's words had an air of sincerity about them, and it was obvious, to all those present, that Daphne had doubted whether, without the promise of her wealth, she had held much attraction for a man like Archie. It stood to reason, therefore, that she would have been at pains to keep the truth from him until they were safely married.

Rose gave a sideways glance at the inspector. If he were disappointed that his theory was disintegrating before his eyes he did not reveal it by the expression on his face. Rather he appeared like a dog searching for a bone, stubborn and obstinate, persisting in digging a hole in a certain place because he was convinced, despite the evidence, that the reward for his labours lay there.

'If Miss Spittlehouse didn't tell you, perhaps someone else did? Major Spittlehouse, for instance?'

'No,' said Daphne quickly. 'It's not the sort of thing my brother would do.'

She risked turning and giving Archie an imploring look for she had suddenly remembered his exact words when she had accused him of knowing about her parents' will and Linus' disapproval of him as her suitor. 'It doesn't matter'. That was what he had said. He hadn't tried to deny it; he had merely been anxious not to provide her with any details. She took a deep breath and tried not to meet the inspector's eye. Archie had as good as admitted that he had known about her brother's animosity towards him for the very good reason that he had obviously met with the major and discussed the matter. Linus would have left him in no doubt as to his feelings, Daphne was certain of it. And Archie, without possessing her own knowledge of her brother's character, could not be certain that

Linus would not mention the fact to the police, particularly if he considered his life to be in danger. Archie then, quite understandably, would perceive it as being in his best interests to be the first to raise the matter, so as to give the impression he had nothing to hide. But she mustn't let him speak. If she did he would tell them the whole truth and then all would be lost. Inspector Newcombe's theory regarding Archie's motive for the murder would be restored to its original position in the policeman's mind. Oh, if only Archie would keep quiet and take his lead from her!

Archie in turn had hesitated a little before replying himself to the inspector's question, as if he doubted the wisdom of giving voice to what he knew would prove damaging to himself. Another nail in the coffin in the inspector's eyes. It didn't bear thinking about and it was certainly not what he had intended to do. He had planned a different course of sorts in the dingy tearooms and it was not this. But to lie … He felt himself to be in a battle with his own conscience with each side trying to grasp the upper hand. The consequence of this inner turmoil was that the word 'Yes' was frozen on his lips and therefore not articulated as such. But to a keen observer, of which there were four in the room, it was quite obvious what he had meant to say, for his mouth had formed the word, even if his voice had not actually uttered it. Inspector Newcombe certainly was not deceived for he smiled quite openly at having his theory proved right. Surprisingly, however, in Rose's opinion, he did not press the point. Rather his questions followed another tack.

'Did you arrange to meet Miss Spittlehouse yesterday evening before the bonfire activities commenced?'

'Yes,' said Archie.

'No,' said Daphne.

'Well, I never,' said the inspector. 'A discrepancy. Now which was it? You can't both be right.'

'We are both correct in a manner of speaking,' said Daphne rather sullenly. 'We arranged to meet, but neither of us were able to keep the appointment. Really, it didn't seem worth mentioning, which is why I said we hadn't.'

'So you lied to me, Miss Spittlehouse?' said Inspector Newcombe, clearly having difficulty in keeping the anger from his voice. 'May I remind you it is for us to decide what is relevant to this case, not you.' He

216

frowned. 'I asked you most particularly whether you had arranged to meet Mr Mayhew and you said no. If you remember I pressed you on the point.'

'Well, if you must know, I didn't think it any of your business, Inspector. I knew it had no bearing on your investigation. It would only have muddied the waters. But,' Daphne continued hurriedly as the inspector made to protest, 'you are quite right. I should have told you. We did arrange to meet but Archie didn't turn up because his bus was late, and then one of its tyres got a puncture, and I … well, I decided not to go.'

'Why not?' demanded the inspector sharply. 'Did you have an argument?'

'Well, of course not,' replied Daphne indignantly. 'Archie and I don't argue about silly things. I daresay it sounds rather foolish but the truth is I didn't want to run into my brother. Rather stupidly Mr Mayhew and I had arranged to meet in Tucker's Wood which, as you may know, overlooks the bonfire site. I suppose you might say that when the time came, I took fright. If you must know, I was awfully afraid Linus would cause a scene if he spotted the two of us together without a chaperone. He's awfully old-fashioned that way, you know, and I didn't want there to be any unpleasantness. He so looks forward to that silly old bonfire. You wouldn't believe how important he thinks himself, being chairman of that wretched Bonfire Committee. I knew it would spoil the festivities for him and he'd go on about it for simply ages.' Daphne made a face. 'Really, I would never have heard the end of it, I can tell you.'

Rose did not think that Daphne could have delivered her lines any better had she been an actress on the stage. She had given a very credible performance. There was conviction behind her words. It was very possible, therefore, that Rose might have believed what she had said to be true had she not remembered the hurried exchange of looks between Daphne and Archie, when the latter had entered the room, which had suggested some shared secret. She stared at the man and woman before her. Really, it was difficult to know if they were lying completely or merely concealing some elements of the truth.

Chapter Twenty-seven

It was not until the following morning that Rose had an opportunity to reflect on the findings of the previous day and, in particular, on Inspector Newcombe's interviews with Daphne Spittlehouse and Archie Mayhew. This was simply due to Cedric having invited an old school friend and his new wife, recently returned from India, to dinner that evening. It had been a longstanding engagement and Cedric had been reluctant to break it, even if to do so would have been quite in keeping with the circumstances.

'The problem is,' he had explained to Rose when she had returned from Green Gables, 'if I do, it'll probably be years and years before I see old Chalky again. He's quite a one for travelling, you know. I can't see him remaining in England for more than a few weeks at most. He'll find it much too boring a place. He likes exploring, you see. He could never sit still, even in class. We were awfully good chums at school. Both of us hated our lessons like poison and excelled at games. We were for ever thinking up ways to try and escape. On one occasion, Chalky hauled himself out of the window of our dormitory much to the delight of the rest of us, who cheered him on no end as he climbed down the ivy that grew up the wall. Unfortunately for him, the teachers must have got wind of his escape attempt because old Metters, the deputy headmaster, was waiting for him when he reached firm ground. Poor old Chalky got an awful thrashing for his troubles but it didn't stop him concocting other plans.' Cedric chuckled at the recollection. 'Good old Chalky; it'll be awfully good to see him again.'

'Chalky?' Rose had said, feeling distinct sympathy for the small boy with the adventurous spirit. 'Is that short for something?'

'No,' laughed her husband. 'I suppose you could say it is a sort of nickname. Chalky's Christian name is the frightfully respectable Ronald, but his surname happens to be White, so we always called him Chalky; Chalky White. The same thing happened to his father during the Great War. His regiment always referred to him as Chalky on account of his surname and the name seemed to stick in the White household.' He chuckled. 'There was also a boy at school with the surname of Clark, who was always referred to as Nobby. And then of course there was old Miller, whom we called Dusty on account of the flour dust, and then –'.

Cedric was forced to stop speaking for the simple reason that his wife had suddenly, and quite without warning, collapsed into a fit of the giggles. He grinned at Rose lovingly. How nice it was to see her laugh. They had both been so serious and sombre these past two days or so. Of course it was to be expected, what with the murder and all, but it was nice to have an excuse to chuckle.

Chalky White and his new bride had lived up to expectations, proving a welcome diversion to recent events. For Cedric's old school friend had shown himself to be a very personable young man, regaling his audience with highly exaggerated, but very entertaining, stories regarding his various exploits in foreign climes, while his wife appeared the most polite and attentive of guests and an accomplished pianist, much to the delight of all. Amid the laughter and the music, murder and sudden death seemed a distant memory, even if Rose knew that they were never very far away. For they seemed to linger in the very shadows of the room, clinging to the walls and ceiling like stubborn and persistent cobwebs, waiting.

The following morning Rose was breakfasting in bed when Cedric had wandered into the bedroom from his dressing room carrying a cufflink.

'I say, darling, would you mind fastening this for me? It's damned fiddly. I've done the other one, but this one is proving to be a bit of a blighter.' He handed her the offending article and sat down on the bed beside her so that she might assist him.

'Rose, darling,' said Cedric after a moment, a sudden thought having occurred to him, 'you never did tell me what was in that third anonymous letter, the one that brought a smile to Masters' face on the day the poor fellow was murdered. He took it away with him, didn't he, the letter, I mean? The police made a thorough search of his quarters but they couldn't find it. You said you could make a guess as to the contents of the letter.'

'Yes, I did, though of course I can't be absolutely certain. However, I'm fairly sure that our letter-writer proposed a meeting between himself and the major. I think that is what brought a smile to Masters' face. You see, Masters had been looking for a chance to put an end to the letters and perhaps also to learn the details of the major's awful secret. And here was his opportunity, handed to him on a plate, so to speak. Because of course he naturally made up his mind to go to the meeting in the major's place which explains why he was wearing Major Spittlehouse's jacket. He was banking on the blackmailer not realising the deception until it was too late for him to do anything about it.'

'You're not suggesting that Masters was intending to blackmail the major himself, are you?' asked Cedric, looking appalled.

'No, of course not. I think he wanted to protect the major. But he was probably also curious as to the truth of the accusation contained in that second letter, the one that had caused him sleepless nights. If you remember, his wife told me he had been very troubled by what he had read.'

'Well it would certainly make sense of that jacket business,' said Cedric, straightening his sleeve. 'Thank you, darling. Oh, I almost forgot to ask. Has the inspector been able to determine Daphne's precise relationship to the major? Is she really his daughter?'

'Yes, he has found out, as a matter of fact,' said Rose, sipping her tea. 'He told me after he had finished his interview with Archie Mayhew. Daphne is most definitely Major Spittlehouse's sister. The inspector managed to find the old doctor who had attended Mrs Spittlehouse during her confinement. He remembered the case very well because Daphne's birth had been a particularly difficult one; her mother had almost died.'

Cedric made a face. 'I see. Then I suppose you were right, darling. The major was being blackmailed over something far more serious than having an illegitimate daughter, or a mistress come to that. I wonder what it could have been?' Absentmindedly he took a slice of the hot, buttered toast from his wife's breakfast tray and chewed it in a contemplative fashion. 'I say, I didn't tell you, did I? Old Spittlehouse tried to tender his resignation as chairman of the Bonfire Committee as we'd feared he would but the other members wouldn't accept it. Decent fellows the lot of them. They told him not to be so hasty to throw in the towel, told him to go home and think the matter over before he did anything rash.'

'That is good news.'

'I should say. I can't imagine anyone else wanting to take on the job.' Cedric returned to the bed and sat down. He put an arm around his wife and drew her to him almost upsetting the breakfast tray in the process. 'Now, do tell me, what else did you find out yesterday?'

'Well, I managed to find an excuse to go into the basement at Green

Gables,' said Rose, moving the tray to rest on the other side of the bed out of harm's way. 'I examined the door under which the anonymous letters had been pushed. I couldn't get it out of my head how awfully easy it would have been for Daphne to have gone out into the garden and posted those letters herself.'

'Daphne?' exclaimed Cedric. 'Surely you don't think she might be the author of those damned letters?'

'Well, it's certainly a possibility. Listen, darling,' said Rose, grabbing her husband's hand. 'It's not quite as ridiculous as it sounds. If Major Spittlehouse did have some awful secret then it's quite reasonable to suppose that, if anyone knew about it, it would be his sister. And remember she was absolutely desperate to marry Archie Mayhew, desperate enough to approach me, a stranger, to speak to her brother on her behalf. I think Daphne was very firmly of the belief that Archie wouldn't marry her unless she was a woman of wealth. And Major Spittlehouse had made it quite clear to her that if she married that young man he would ensure that she never received a penny.'

'So she decided instead to blackmail her brother for money in the guise of an anonymous letter-writer?' Cedric looked incredulous. 'I say, that's rather ingenious.'

'Of course, it is only a theory at this stage,' cautioned Rose, 'though it might explain why Daphne said something rather strange to me which suggested that she might not be entirely innocent. I thought at the time she was referring to the murder but she might easily have been meaning the letters. Perhaps she felt rather guilty for writing them, even if they played no part in Masters' death. I am certain of one thing though.'

'Oh? And what is that?'

'I believe she is frightfully afraid that the police think Archie was the author of those letters. As it was, the inspector as good as accused him of the murder. If it was Archie who had arranged to meet the major he might quite easily have mistaken Masters for his employer. And when Masters confronted him, and he realised his mistake, they might well have had an altercation that resulted in the servant's death.'

'I say,' said Cedric, 'I suppose it's not possible that the two of them were in it together, Daphne and Archie, I mean? Perhaps they concocted the blackmail business between them?'

'Well, I do think they share a secret of sorts,' said Rose thoughtfully. 'I had the distinct impression that they were hiding something. At first I wondered whether it was the fact that they had arranged to meet at Tucker's Wood on the night of the murder.'

'Had they really?' Cedric looked distinctly interested. 'I say, they would have had a pretty good view of the bonfire. Tucker's Wood overlooks it, you know. And of course there's nothing to say Masters wasn't killed there and his body moved to where it was later found.'

'That thought struck me too, as it did the inspector. But their secret can't have been that because Archie quite readily admitted that the two of them had arranged to meet there. Daphne lied about it but I think she only did that because she was trying to protect Archie. You see, I think the inspector is pretty certain in his own mind that Archie is the murderer. Though, according to Archie, he never went to Tucker's Wood on the night of the murder on account of the bus being late and then one of its wheels developing a puncture.'

'Well, it should be easy enough for the police to verify that,' said Cedric, rising and straightening his tie before the dressing table mirror. 'By the way, what was your impression of Archie Mayhew, you haven't said.'

'I was quite prepared to dislike him like anything,' said Rose, 'but actually I found myself rather taking to him. I do hope he doesn't turn out to be our murderer.'

'He's not marrying Daphne Spittlehouse for her money, then? enquired Cedric, looking a touch sceptical.

'I really don't know,' admitted his wife. 'He did seem genuinely fond of her, though I suppose it might have all been an act.' She sighed. 'Really, I don't feel that I have got very far in this investigation. I am positive that there is a connection between the anonymous letters and Masters' death, but I am not quite sure what it is.'

'What does the inspector think?'

'That Archie did it, like I told you. He thinks Archie meant to kill the major for the simple reason that Daphne would inherit his wealth. He simply wanted a rich wife and didn't much mind how he achieved his goal as long as he got his money. '

'Poor old Mayhew. I feel quite sorry for the chap.'

'You won't feel quite so sorry for him if he does turn out to be the murderer,' said Rose. She straightened her pillows and said: 'Inspector Newcombe seems to have quite forgotten about the letters, or else he doesn't think they have any bearing on Masters' death.' She paused before adding, 'Daphne did say something that was quite interesting.'

'Oh? What was that?' Her husband turned away from regarding his reflection in the mirror and faced her.

'On the day of the murder she said she heard the major's key in the lock of the front door, followed by him crossing the hall. It was about a quarter past five. Apparently Major Spittlehouse had just returned from inspecting the bonfire.'

'The man insists on doing that every year,' groaned Cedric. 'One final check and all that before the festivities begin. Really, I think he's half afraid that someone from a neighbouring village will creep in and set fire to the bonfire behind his back.'

'Well, apparently it was all rather strange because a minute or two later he went back out again. Daphne thought he must have forgotten something. She didn't hear him come back into the house, but he was there when she looked into the parlour later.'

'What was so very odd about that?' asked her husband. He sounded disappointed. 'It's the sort of thing I might do. Why, the fellow might have taken a sudden fancy to stroll around the garden and look at the flowers, what with the weather being fine.'

'In the dark?'

'Well, perhaps he suddenly remembered that he had meant to post a letter and went to the post box.'

'I think there is a far more likely explanation,' said Rose. 'I think Daphne heard her brother's key in the lock and him crossing the hall as she supposed, but I don't think it was him she heard leave the house. I think it was Masters done up in his guise as the major.'

'Do you really?' She had her husband's interest now. 'Wouldn't he have gone out by the servants' entrance? I wouldn't have thought it usual for him to use the front door.'

'He wouldn't have wanted to encounter Mrs Masters,' said Rose. 'He was wearing his employer's jacket, remember. I think she would have had something to say about that if she'd caught him. And he wouldn't have wanted to stop and explain that he was setting off to meet the author of the anonymous letters. She might have put a stop to it, thinking it none of his business, or else he might have been afraid that she would worry. No. I think he crept out of the front door as soon as the coast was clear.'

'And went to meet his murderer, blissfully unaware of the fate that awaited him?' said Cedric ruefully.

'It would appear so,' said Rose. 'Though of course there is another possibility. Masters might have been murdered later, after he had met with the blackmailer, or even before, on his way to meet the blackmailer.'

'You mean he might have been murdered by someone else entirely?'

'Yes.'

'But if it wasn't by Daphne or Archie then –'

'By someone who realised that Masters meant to find the writer of the anonymous letters and didn't want him to confront the blackmailer and discover the hold he had over his prey. Someone who would stop at nothing to prevent Masters from discovering his awful secret.'

Surely you're not suggesting that –' began Cedric, somewhat taken aback.

'Major Spittlehouse? But of course.' cried Rose. 'Who could possibly have had a better motive for wishing Masters dead?'

Chapter Twenty-eight

Rose was still contemplating the possibility that Major Spittlehouse might indeed be the murderer, when Manning advised her that she was wanted on the telephone. Rose glanced at her wristwatch; it was rather early in the morning for a social call. The butler appeared to read her thoughts.

'It's Mrs Simpson for you. If you'll permit my saying so, m'lady, she sounds a little anxious.'

'Hallo, Mother? Is everything all right?' asked Rose hurriedly, as soon as she had picked up the receiver. She was vaguely aware that Manning was no longer there. She was alone in the entrance hall and her voice seemed to echo in the emptiness, seeming unnaturally loud.

'Rose, is that you?' Her mother's voice cut through the silence, a little breathless. 'I know it is rather early to telephone but Mrs Masters was most insistent that I ring you at once. She's quite agitated, poor woman. Mrs Dobson told me she hardly had a wink of sleep last night, she was so restless; Mrs Masters, I mean, not Mrs Dobson, who as you know sleeps like a log.'

'It's quite all right,' Rose said hurriedly. 'I was up anyway. Is anything wrong?'

'That is what I am trying to tell you. Mrs Masters woke up this morning as white as a sheet, so Mrs Dobson told me. It appears she has remembered something which she feels might have a bearing on her husband's death. All her tossing and turning during the night brought to her mind the night before Masters died, when he couldn't sleep on account of worrying about the anonymous letters. Apparently Mrs Masters has remembered that her husband kept mumbling something to himself.'

'Oh? What did he say?' Rose clutched the telephone receiver eagerly.

'Well, it's all rather odd,' said Mrs Simpson. 'It's almost as if he foresaw his own fate. According to Mrs Masters, he kept mumbling something about a murder or murderer; she wasn't quite sure which. But she was most anxious that I tell you immediately.'

Edna sat on the edge of her seat in the bus feeling very self-conscious. Her ladyship had said she was to keep Biddy company. So it didn't seem right taking the bus by herself to Bichester, not in the middle of the morning when there was a whole list of chores still to be done at Green Gables and Biddy there on her own to do them. But Biddy had been adamant, most particular about it, she'd been.

'It's no good, Edna,' Biddy had said. 'There'll be a lot more work to do now, what with Mr Masters gone, and only me and Mrs Masters to do it. I'd better get used to it sooner than later. And I want to get the house looking nice for when Mrs Masters returns.'

'But why don't you let me help you?' Edna had protested. 'I've not always been a lady's maid, you know. I used to be a kitchen maid and before that a scullery maid. I'm used to hard work, just like you. If you'll only get me an apron, I'll roll up my sleeves and we'll soon have this place looking spick and span. Mrs Masters will be able to see her reflection in those copper pans of hers as good as if they were mirrors.'

'It's very good of you, Edna, I'm sure,' Biddy had said, looking rather doubtfully at Edna's rather fine black dress with its Honiton lace at the neck and cuffs, 'but I'd rather do it myself. It don't seem right asking you to help me, and I don't know that Miss Daphne would like it or Lady Belvedere, come to that. No,' she had added quickly as Edna had made to protest, 'if you want to help me, you can take these books back to the public library in Bichester as were took out by Mrs Masters; it'll be one less thing for her to worry about when she comes home.'

This was how Edna found herself on the rickety old bus making its slow and longwinded way to Bichester, clutching a bag of books on her lap. She hadn't had the heart to tell Biddy that she doubted very much whether Mrs Masters would ever set foot in Green Gables again, save to collect her things. The place would hold too many memories for her; she'd want to start afresh somewhere. Edna made a face. And besides, who'd want to work for someone when your husband had been murdered in mistake for them? Really, it didn't bear thinking about.

Although not very familiar with Bichester, Edna found her way easily enough to the library. Once inside, she looked around, fascinated by the shelves upon shelves of books, which reminded her not a little of the grand library at Sedgwick Court. If the woman behind the issue desk had not been regarding her so intently, she might have been tempted to stop a little and browse. As it was, she marched straight up to the desk and deposited the books she had been carrying.

'I do hope you don't mind my asking,' said the librarian in a surprisingly deferential voice given Edna's position, 'but would you by any chance be Lady Belvedere's maid?'

'Her lady's maid, yes,' replied Edna proudly, drawing herself up to her full height.

'I thought as much. You'll think it ever so strange my asking, but is it true what they say about her ladyship having been a shop girl and an amateur sleuth?'

'Yes,' replied Edna, though she spoke the word rather coldly, as if she feared what the woman might say next. If she said anything about fancy the likes of Miss Rose marrying an earl, she'd give her a piece of her mind, see if she didn't …

'Oh, thank goodness,' sighed Miss Warren, obviously relieved. 'I thought there might be very little substance to it. There often isn't, you know. One hears such a great deal of nonsense spoken in a place like this. People do like to gossip, don't they, and I suppose you can't blame them but –'

'What do you mean by thank goodness?' Edna said sharply, interested in what the woman was saying in spite of herself.

'Well, one does feel rather foolish going to the police. I mean, it might not mean anything, but one never knows, and really it is one's duty isn't it to –'

'Do you know something about the murder?' said Edna with sudden clarity. She felt the hairs on the back of her neck stand up.

'I don't know,' said Miss Warren, rather flustered. 'You see, I don't know if it has any bearing on the death, but I feel I should tell someone.'

'Well, I think Lady Belvedere would be the very person to tell,' said Edna quickly. 'She's ever so kind and she wouldn't make you feel silly or stupid.'

'Oh, do you think so?'

'Yes, I do,' said Edna firmly. 'Tell me, do you have a telephone?'

It was only minutes later that the telephone rang in the butler's pantry at Sedgwick Court.

'Lord and Lady Belvedere's residence, Manning speaking,' began the butler in formal tones, and then: 'Good heavens, is that you Miss Evans? What are you … What did you say? Miss Evans, you can hardly expect her ladyship to drive into Bichester on the whim of a *librarian* even if what she has to say is important … Very well, I'll tell her, but on your head be it. Don't be surprised if …'

The line suddenly went dead and Manning found himself staring at the apparatus in his hand, somewhat dumbfounded. He shook his head, wondering how old Torridge would have dealt with the situation. Somewhat reluctantly, he went to deliver his message.

'Oh, Lady Belvedere. Oh, your ladyship …'

Rose looked at the little woman fluttering about in front of her like a nervous butterfly unwilling to land.

'Miss Warren? How do you do?' said Rose, extending her hand. But, if she had hoped that such a gesture would put the librarian at her ease, she was to be disappointed. If anything, the woman became even more flustered than before, the colour rising in her cheeks until she positively glowed.

'I believe you have some information that you think might be helpful to my investigation?' said Rose, deciding that the best course of action was to come straight to the point. She glanced at Edna for some sign of confirmation, and the lady's maid nodded.

'Well, I don't know … when I try and put it into words it sounds rather silly … you will think me foolish –'

'There's a little room out back, m'lady,' said Edna quickly. 'A bit of a kitchen. I suggested to Miss Warren that you should go in there to talk.' The librarian made to protest. 'You needn't worry, miss. I'll stay here to make sure no one runs off with any of your books.'

Miss Warren was steered swiftly into the back room, before the woman quite knew what was happening. Rose took in her surroundings. They were standing in something that resembled a scullery of sorts, equipped with little more than an old Belfast sink and a copper kettle. The librarian stared at her, with rather a mortified expression on her face, as if embarrassed by the sparseness of the room.

'Why, this is very like the little kitchen we had in the dress shop where I worked,' said Rose cheerily. 'I feel quite at home. Now, Miss Warren, what have you to tell me?'

'Miss Spittlehouse,' stuttered the librarian. 'She often comes to the library just to pass the time, I suppose. Or else to meet her young man; he works in Bichester, you know, ever such a nice young man, awfully polite,' said Miss Warren rather breathlessly. 'When she's alone, she reads books, ever so many of them. Some of them are about … rather strange things.'

'Oh?' said Rose, only mildly curious.

'Poisons. *The Household Book of Everyday Poisons*'. That was the last book she read. Ever so furtive she was about it. She tried to keep the cover hidden. I was ever so worried.'

'Why?'

'Well, it stands to reason, doesn't it?' The librarian looked astonished that Rose was not following her train of thought. 'She meant to do mischief. Of course, one tries not to listen to gossip, but I'm afraid it's inevitable that one hears things in a library. People can't help talking when they are supposed to be quiet.' She leaned forward slightly and lowered her voice to just above a whisper. 'Apparently, Major Spittlehouse doesn't much care for her young man and she's dependent on her brother's charity because she doesn't have any money of her own.'

'I'm afraid I don't quite follow what you are saying,' said Rose. 'Are you suggesting that Miss Spittlehouse is trying to poison her brother on the basis that she has read a few books on the subject?'

'Well, I admit it sounds a little far-fetched when you put it like that,' said Miss Warren, rather apologetically. 'But when you consider what happened. Oh, I've been ever so worried. I tried to warn the major that his life might be in danger but –'

'When was this?' Rose said rather sharply.

'It was on the night of the bonfire. I took the books from the library. Ever so guilty I felt doing it, what with my position and all. But I didn't think he'd believe me unless I showed him the books. Of course, I've put them all back now but –'

'Wait a moment,' said Rose, putting up a gloved hand. 'Are you telling me that you tried to warn Major Spittlehouse before the murder? I can understand why you might have been a little concerned after you had heard of the death of his servant, but before …' She stared intently at Miss Warren, who took a step back under such scrutiny. 'Why were you so worried about the major's safety? It can't just be because of a couple of books Miss Spittlehouse was reading. Is there something else you're not telling me?'

'No, of course not,' said Miss Warren, her cheeks glowing red.

Rose was quite positive that the woman was lying. She was equally certain, however, that to press her further would be to no avail. Resigned to the fact, she decided to change tack.

'You said just now that you tried to warn Major Spittlehouse. Does that mean that you didn't actually manage to speak with him?'

'No. I thought I might have a word with him by the bonfire before the festivities began. I thought he'd be there early. I mean, I couldn't very well call on him at Green Gables, could I? His sister would have been there. Oh, it would all have been very awkward.' Miss Warren gave a wistful frown. 'But fate was against me, I'm afraid. First the bus was late and then one of the wheels developed a puncture.'

Rose had only been half listening to what Miss Warren was saying. Now, however, she gave the woman her full attention.

'Do you happen to remember seeing Miss Spittlehouse's young man on the bus?'

'Mr Mayhew? Oh, yes, I do. Such a delightful young man, and so very handsome.'

'Yes, isn't he?' Rose paused a moment before she added: 'I suppose you all waited on the bus while the wheel was changed?'

'Well, yes we did. And a very long time it took too because –'

'I suppose Mr Mayhew waited?'

'Mr Mayhew? Oh, no, he didn't stay. We were only a mile or so from Sedgwick, you see. He and some of the other young people decided to make the rest of the journey on foot.'

'Where are we going, m'lady?' asked Edna, rather breathlessly, for she was almost running in an attempt to keep up with her mistress, who was walking very fast indeed.

'I need to speak with Archie Mayhew, Edna. I need to find out why he lied to the inspector,' said Rose and then she stopped so sharply and abruptly, that her lady's maid almost collided with her. 'No ... that is not strictly true. He didn't actually lie, but neither did he tell the whole truth. He allowed Miss Spittlehouse to lie for him. He made no effort to contradict what she said, even though he knew it wasn't true.'

'But why would Miss Spittlehouse lie?' asked Edna, visibly shocked at such a suggestion. 'And to the police too. You'd think the likes of her would know better.'

'I think she was trying to protect Mr Mayhew. Or perhaps she really believed she was telling the truth. Now, if we could only find the firm of solicitors where Mr Mayhew works ... oh, look, here it is.' They had come to a glass fronted building with the words 'Gribble, Hebborn & Whittaker Solicitors' emblazoned proudly in gold letters on the glass panel of the door. 'I thought it would be located in the main street, and I was right. Oh, and I can see Mr Mayhew sitting behind the desk in the corner. Look, Edna.'

'Cor, he's awfully handsome, isn't he, miss?'

'Yes, he is rather good-looking.'

Rose took a deep breath and opened the door. She felt very much as if she were trespassing, though she reminded herself that her reception was likely to be a warm one now that she had risen in society.

On entering the establishment, she found herself in a large office occupied by a handful of gentlemen who were presumably solicitors or articled clerks. Presiding over them all was a rather formidable looking woman with iron grey hair, stationed behind the largest of the wooden desks. The woman loomed over an enormous typewriter, very much in the way she might have stood behind a lectern; certainly she appeared to be in charge and directing matters, for it was she, rather than any of the gentlemen, who came forward and greeted Rose as she hovered on the threshold.

'Lady Belvedere. May I say what a very great pleasure ...'

Miss Simmons' words drifted over Rose's head as if they had been uttered to someone else. For Rose was hardly listening to a word the woman said to her, her attention instead being directed towards Archie Mayhew. She was particularly interested to witness his reaction to her unexpected arrival at his place of work. Even as she looked on, the young man appeared to be recoiling from her, for his body was thrust against the back of his seat as far as it could go, reminding her of when he had sat before the inspector, looking for all the world as if he wished the back of the chair would open up and swallow him. She caught his eye and a look passed between them. He paled slightly but he came forward, as if she were dragging him to her via an invisible cord.

'Lady Belvedere, how very good of you to come.' Archie Mayhew gave her a very fleeting smile before turning to Mr Whittaker's secretary. 'Miss Simmons, her ladyship has come to see me on a matter of business on the recommendation of a mutual friend.'

'Oh indeed, said Rose, playing along. 'Daphne speaks of you in the most glowing of terms, Mr Mayhew.'

'Perhaps we might make use of Mr Whittaker's office, Miss Simmons? I happen to know he is out visiting a client.' Archie did not wait for an answer; already he was ushering Rose to a door just beyond Miss Simmons' desk. 'This way if you please, Lady Belvedere.'

By this means, Miss Simmons was effectively brushed aside and Rose and Edna steered into Mr Whittaker's office, the door shut firmly behind them.

'How very well done, Mr Mayhew,' said Rose, taking the chair Archie indicated. She noticed his hand was shaking.

The young man himself looked distinctly harried, his air of decisiveness having diminished now that they were no longer in the outer office. He began to pace the room in something of a restive manner, while Edna positioned herself at the door, as if she thought there might be the need for a hasty retreat.

'Please do sit down, Mr Mayhew. You are making me feel quite giddy,' began Rose. 'Now, I should like to ask you one or two questions,' she continued without preamble, 'and I would be immensely grateful if you would answer them truthfully.'

'Look here, Lady Belvedere,' said Archie abruptly, turning to face her. 'I don't want to throw a scene, and I daresay you will think I am speaking out of turn, but I don't see why I should answer any of your questions at all. Goodness knows I've already had a good grilling by the inspector. Really, I have nothing further to add to my statement.'

'You realise then that I am here to ask you questions about the murder?'

Archie glared and cursed himself silently. He passed a hand through his hair and sat down.

'I daresay you were rather surprised at my being present when the police interviewed you yesterday?'

Archie grunted and said rather irritably: 'Daphne says you are an amateur sleuth.'

'I am,' admitted Rose, a trifle self-consciously. 'And the inspector has requested that I assist him with his investigation.'

'I see.'

'Do you? I hope so. You see, Mr Mayhew, it was quite obvious to me yesterday that you were lying. No,' Rose held up a gloved hand as Archie made to protest, 'that isn't quite fair. I don't think *you* actually lied, but you certainly didn't tell the whole truth, and you permitted Daphne to lie on your behalf, without correcting what she was saying, which is perhaps a little worse.'

Archie swallowed hard. 'Daphne didn't know –'

'The truth? No, I don't believe she did.'

'I really have nothing further to say, either to you or to the inspector.' Archie got up from his chair and began to pace the room again.

'I strongly recommend that you tell me the truth, Mr Mayhew,' said Rose, watching him closely. 'If you are innocent, you have nothing to fear.'

There was a moment of unbearable silence. Even Edna waited with bated breath, wondering what the young man was going to do.

'Oh, all right,' said Archie, after a few moments' hesitation. 'Lord knows I haven't had a wink of sleep since it happened.' He flung himself down on to the chair on the other side of the desk in something of a resigned fashion. 'What would you like to know?'

'I have a theory,' said Rose. 'Perhaps you could tell me if I am correct?'

'All right,' said Archie. The colour had left his cheeks and he was clutching the edge of the desk so hard that his knuckles showed white.

'On the night of the murder you took a bus from Bichester to Sedgwick. During the course of the journey one of the wheels suffered a puncture. But, instead of waiting for the wheel to be changed, I have a witness who says she saw you set out on foot to walk the rest of the way to Sedgwick.'

'Oh.'

'You don't deny it?'

'No, why should I? I walked to Sedgwick all right and went to Tucker's Wood too. And before you ask,' Archie paused a moment to take a deep breath, 'I didn't kill anybody, and I didn't see anyone being murdered.'

'No,' agreed Rose, 'but you did discover the body. You stumbled on it in Tucker's Wood, didn't you?'

Chapter Twenty-nine

Archie nodded dully. It appeared he was unable to speak.

'It must have been a frightful shock,' Rose said gently.

'I should say!' exclaimed Archie, when he could talk. 'I was pretty shaken up about it, I can tell you. You see, I was fairly certain it was Major Spittlehouse. Of course, I didn't look at the face properly, but I recognised his jacket; it was a ghastly old tweed thing.' Archie was speaking rapidly now. 'I could see he was dead, and all I could think was …' He faltered and bit his lip.

'That Daphne had killed him?'

'Yes. I couldn't think about anything else except that I must move the body. It was very stupid of me, I know, but I was certain the police would discover that Daphne and I had arranged to meet in Tucker's Wood.' He laughed without mirth. 'Why, I even told them so myself! Anyway, I was obsessed by the notion that they shouldn't find the body there. I suppose I had worked myself up into a blue funk over the whole business.'

'So you dragged the body, or half carried it, to the nearest place you could think of, which happened to be the bonfire site?'

'Yes.' He looked at her earnestly. 'I swear I didn't intend for it to be mistaken for one of the guys. I thought I could prop it up somehow. What with all the people who would be milling around to see the fireworks, I thought it might be lost in the crowd and not found until the next morning when they were clearing up all the debris from the festivities.'

'But then you discovered that the corpse wasn't Major Spittlehouse?'

'Yes. Daphne telephoned me the next morning and told me that her servant had been murdered. I couldn't take it in at first. I thought it must mean there were two bodies.' He held his head in his hands. 'It gave me a frightful shock I can tell you, when I realised the truth. I almost went to pieces.'

'Because you knew Daphne couldn't be the murderer?'

'Yes. She wouldn't have made such a stupid mistake. The murderer had to be someone else, who didn't know the major very well, and I had aided him by moving the body.' Archie lifted his head and stared up at

Rose with a look of desperation in his eyes. 'What could I do? If I came forward and told the police what I had done, they would have thought me at best an accessory after the fact, and at worst the murderer. There was really nothing I could do except keep quiet.'

'Do you believe him, m'lady?' asked Edna, as she and her mistress made their way back to the Daimler, where the chauffeur was waiting for them.

'That he found the body as he described? Yes, I think so.'

Though it was still quite possible, thought Rose, that Archie Mayhew had killed the servant in mistake for the major, prior to moving the body. If that were the case, he was also the author of the anonymous letters, or at the very least an accomplice, for it was those that had lured Masters to Tucker's Wood. Yet, if that were the case, would Archie have admitted coming across the body as he had? And he needn't have mentioned Tucker's Wood at all to the police. And what of Miss Warren's behaviour? How very fanciful the woman seemed. Rose wondered whether her days were so deathly dull that she had to conjure up conspiracies and plots where there were none. Yet she had been right to be worried, she reminded herself, for there had been a murder.

All these thoughts were still circulating in Rose's head as they drove back to Sedgwick. She had discovered bits and pieces of the jigsaw, but they had still to come together to form a picture. Frustrated, she allowed her thoughts to drift back to the previous night and Chalky White's colourful stories that had had them all in stitches. The memory brought a smile to her face. What a pity Chalky … she uttered an exclamation. How very stupid she'd been. It was so very obvious when one thought about it. It had been staring her in the face all morning …

She leaned forward and tapped the chauffeur sharply on the shoulder. Her voice when she spoke had a note of urgency. 'Adams, please stop the car. We need to go back. We need to go back to Bichester.'

Miss Warren was just locking up her establishment. It being a Saturday, the library, like most of the other shops and businesses in Bichester, closed at lunchtime. Indeed, if she had happened to glance further down the street, she would have seen Archie Mayhew setting off for his lodgings. She did not, however, look about her, for she was too concerned with her own worries to be aware of anything else.

Much as she tried, she could not rid herself of the thought that she should never have spoken to Lady Belvedere. It had been a dreadful mistake. She thought she was … well, never mind what she had thought she was doing. The countess had been suspicious of her as soon as she had opened her mouth. But she had also been very kind. She stifled a sob. Something made her look up. It might have been the sound of hurrying footsteps, or perhaps someone had even called out her name. Whatever it was, she found herself staring into the face of the amateur sleuth. She tried to remind herself that she needn't be frightened. This was the woman who had commented favourably on her makeshift kitchen and not found it wanting. Nevertheless, the bunch of keys she had been holding slipped from her fingers and crashed on to the steps with a dull, metallic sound. Much to her chagrin, she found that tears were streaming down her face, and it occurred to her that, once started, they might never stop.

'It's you,' said Rose stepping forward. 'It was you, wasn't it?' She paused to retrieve the fallen keys. 'You wrote those anonymous letters, didn't you?' You sent them to Major Spittlehouse because you wanted to find out what had happened. You wanted to find out what had happened to Bunny Warren.'

They set off again for Sedgwick. This time Miss Warren was with them, seated beside Rose in the back of the Daimler, her bag resting on her knees. She clutched it to her, in much the same manner as she had done on the bus. Edna sat in the front with the chauffeur, finding it hard to contain her excitement. An uneasy quietness prevailed in the car. Everyone was inclined to talk, but no one wanted to be responsible for breaking the silence. Instead, they all sat waiting impatiently for something to happen.

As they approached the outskirts of the village, Rose leaned forward and requested that the chauffeur drive to Green Gables. Edna turned in her seat and gave her mistress a look of surprise, but otherwise said nothing. When they arrived at their destination Rose said: 'Edna, I should like you to drive back to Sedgwick Court with Adams. As soon as you arrive, please speak to Mr Manning and ask that he telephone to Inspector Newcombe and request that he come to Green Gables.' She paused a moment to glance at Miss Warren, who was weeping quietly. 'You had better tell him that he will be required to make an arrest.'

'To do with them letters, m'lady?' exclaimed Edna, staring at the librarian suspiciously.

'No,' said Rose firmly. 'To do with the murder of Mr Masters and ... and someone else.'

Biddy opened the door to Rose and Miss Warren. If she was surprised to see them, she did not show it. Instead she said: 'Is Miss Spittlehouse expecting you, m'lady?'

'No she isn't,' said Rose quickly. 'And it isn't her we have come to see, it's the major. Where is he? Is he in his study?'

'Yes, he is m'lady. But he won't want to be disturbed, ever so cross he'll be.'

'Well, I'm afraid that can't be helped. Don't worry Biddy, we'll make our own way. It is just across the hall, isn't it? Oh, before you go, Biddy, there is just one thing ...' Rose leaned forward and whispered something in the maid's ear, which Miss Warren didn't quite catch.

Rose tapped on the study door and waited for only the briefest of moments before she opened it and entered, the librarian close behind her. Major Spittlehouse was seated behind his desk and looked considerably annoyed to be disturbed in his lair. The frown that creased his forehead was rapidly replaced with a look of surprise, as he recognised his visitor and hastily rose from his chair and came forward.

'Lady Belvedere, what a pleasant surprise. I am –'

'Good afternoon, Major Spittlehouse. Please don't trouble yourself to stand up on my account. I'm awfully sorry to disturb you, but I was very keen that you should make the acquaintance of Miss Warren.'

'Miss Warren?' repeated the major. He looked decidedly bewildered, as if he thought Rose must have taken leave of her senses.

'Yes, Miss Warren. You were an acquaintance of her brother, I believe? You knew him by the name of Bunny; Bunny Warren.'

'Bunny ...' The colour had drained from the major's face and he sank down heavily on to his chair. He dropped his head in his hands, hiding his eyes. 'Bunny ...'

'Yes. Bunny,' said Rose slowly. 'It was Miss Warren who sent you that letter. She was desperate to find out what had happened to her brother. Of course she thought he was most probably dead, but she wasn't certain. But she was right to believe that, wasn't she? I was able to tell her where he was buried. Tucker's Wood. But of course you knew that already, didn't you?'

'Yes,' said the major very quietly. He did not lift his head, and Rose could only guess what was going through his mind.

'Miss Warren sent you two further letters, neither of which you received,' continued Rose, studying him carefully all the while she was speaking. 'Masters intercepted them and went to confront the person he considered was intent on spreading scandalous lies about you.' She paused a moment before she added: 'He was killed for his trouble, but then you know that too, don't you?'

'Yes,' repeated Major Spittlehouse in the same dull voice.

'You killed him! You killed my dear brother,' cried Miss Warren, lurching forward blindly. She would have stumbled had Rose not caught her by the arm. 'How could you?'

'I'm sorry,' said the major, 'I am so very sorry.' His voice was full of emotion now. He removed his hands from his face and got up from his seat. Rose marvelled at the man's composure. He had just confessed to murder and yet he held himself well and with a certain dignity, admitting guilt and ready to receive the ultimate punishment. 'I should be grateful, Lady Belvedere, if you would telephone for the police.'

'Inspector Newcombe should already be on his way here,' said Rose.

There was a tap on the door and Daphne entered, something of a bemused look upon her face. 'Biddy said you wished to see me, Linus,' she began, and then stopped as she took in the scene. 'I am afraid I don't understand …'

'It must be some mistake, I didn't ask to see you,' said the major hurriedly.

'No, you didn't,' agreed Rose. 'I did.'

'Daphne, go to your room at once,' said Major Spittlehouse sharply. 'This doesn't concern you.'

'Oh, but I think it does,' protested Rose. 'After all, it is not every day that one's brother confesses to murder.'

'Whose murder?' cried Daphne.

'That of Masters and Bunny Warren.' Rose turned to face Major Spittlehouse. 'You are confessing to both murders, aren't you, Major?'

'I am,' agreed Major Spittlehouse.

'No,' sobbed Daphne.

'Look here, my dear,' said her brother more gently. 'It is for the best. Now go to your room. The police will be here soon and I daresay there'll be some unpleasantness. I'd much rather keep you from it. There's a good girl. Ask Biddy to sit with you.'

His sister stared at them all for a moment, her mouth wide open as if she wished to say something, but didn't dare. With one final glance at the major, who was looking at her imploringly, she made as if to leave.

'Wait,' cried Rose. 'I'd much rather you didn't go, Daphne. It seems awfully unfair after everything your brother has done to protect you, that you should forsake him in his hour of need.' She leaned forward and grasped the woman's hand. 'You don't really want to see your brother punished for your crimes, do you?'

'Daphne, don't listen to her,' cried Major Spittlehouse. 'She doesn't know what she is saying.'

'No,' said Daphne dully. 'I want to tell the truth.' She stared at her brother with tears in her eyes. 'Oh, Linus. I didn't realise I'd done it, killed Bunny, I mean.'

'Be quiet, Daphne. Don't say another word.' Major Spittlehouse leapt forward, his hands outstretched.

His words, however, seemed to fall on deaf ears. For it appeared that, now Daphne had at last spoken, she had no intention of being silent. Indeed, the words seemed to flow from her like water from a spring.

'At least, I suppose I must always have known that I had killed Bunny. But I had forgotten, or perhaps I had deliberately put it out of my mind. I loved him, you see. I only remembered that we had argued and that he had left me without bothering to say goodbye. I thought it awfully bad of him to disappear like that. That's what Father told me had happened and I suppose I allowed myself to believe him because the alternative was too awful. It was only when Masters shouted at me on Bonfire Night that everything came back to me. We argued and it reminded me of that time with Bunny.' She stared at her hands which were trembling. 'Masters wouldn't stop shouting … He accused me of all sorts of awful things

240

including blackmail. I had to make him stop, I had to …'

Everything then seemed to happened very quickly indeed, like dominoes set in motion. Miss Warren collapsed on to a chair and sobbed bitterly; Daphne fainted; Major Spittlehouse sank back on to his chair and covered his face in his hands; and there was a knock on the door, followed swiftly with it being opened. Inspector Newcombe and Sergeant Bell came into the room and stared somewhat dumbfounded at the spectacle before them.

Chapter Thirty

'Well, Lady Belvedere, you promised to tell me how you arrived at the truth,' said Inspector Newcombe. 'We got our murderer and anonymous letter-writer in the end, but I'm blowed if I know how you worked it all out the way you did.'

'Oh yes, do tell, darling,' said Cedric. 'I've heard bits and pieces of course, but not the whole story.'

It was a few days later and they were sitting in the drawing room at Sedgwick Court. In less formal clothes, and without Sergeant Bell in tow, Inspector Newcombe looked less like a policeman than he had when he had been on duty. This impression was further heightened by his having a glass of whisky in his hand and the conversation, until then, having focused primarily on the various merits of the Sedgwick cricket team. Rose had listened to the talk idly, basking contentedly in the simplicity of village life, which seemed a far cry from the complexities of the recent murder investigation. It was thus with some reluctance that she roused herself from her pleasant reverie.

'Very well, though, in these sorts of things, it is always so difficult to know exactly where to begin.'

'How about at the very beginning?' said Cedric, grinning.

'I suppose that the very beginning occurred almost twenty years ago,' said Rose contemplatively, 'but I won't begin my story there, because I didn't find out about that until later. For me, it all began when Miss Spittlehouse came to see me to discuss her brother's opposition to her proposed marriage. Without his consent the provisions of her parents' will made it very difficult for her to marry. It struck me as very odd at the time that Daphne had been bequeathed no allowance in her own right, and was entirely dependent on her brother's generosity.'

'So that's why you suggested that Miss Spittlehouse might really be Major Spittlehouse's daughter and not his sister?' said her visitor. 'To make sense of the will?'

'Yes. But what I found even more baffling was that Major Spittlehouse had not settled an amount on his sister regardless of the terms of their parents' will. Everyone spoke of Major Spittlehouse as being a very fair and honourable man.' Rose turned to smile at her husband. 'You did too, darling, if you remember? Even Daphne admitted that she would be very surprised if her brother had ever done anything over which he might be blackmailed. And yet his behaviour towards his sister, in making her financially reliant on him and doing his utmost to prevent her from marrying, seemed most unfair.'

'And it was patently clear the fellow was hiding something,' said Cedric. 'Otherwise why would he have been sent those anonymous letters?'

'Yes,' agreed Rose. 'It was obvious the major had a secret all right which he was at pains to keep hidden. Anyway, that about sets the scene.' She got up from her chair and went and stood beside the fireplace, turning to face her audience, aware that she had the stage. 'Now, I should like to move on to the day of the murder itself. We know that the third, and final, anonymous letter was received at Green Gables on that very morning and opened by Masters. From Masters' reaction, and the fact that he was wearing Major Spittlehouse's jacket when he died, it was very obvious to me right from the start that the letter had proposed a meeting between the writer and the major, and that Masters had decided to go to that meeting disguised as his employer.'

'The meeting was to take place in Tucker's Wood?' said Cedric.

'Yes. Archie Mayhew has admitted that he moved the body from there and Miss Warren has advised me of the contents of her anonymous letters. What no one could have envisaged, however, was that more than one meeting had been arranged to take place in those woods at roughly the same time.'

'I suppose it isn't that much of a coincidence,' mused Inspector Newcombe. 'I mean, I assume they were all intending to go on to the bonfire festivities afterwards and so it stands to reason they'd choose somewhere close at hand to meet.'

'Yes,' agreed Rose, 'but it proved most unfortunate.' She sighed. 'I can't rid myself of the feeling that, if only the bus hadn't been late and one of its wheels suffered a puncture, Masters' death might have been avoided.'

'Do you know how it happened?' asked Cedric. 'The murder, I mean?'

'Yes, I think so,' said Rose. 'At least I think I can make a jolly good guess.' She cleared her throat and took a deep breath. 'Masters set off from Green Gables for his meeting with the letter-writer, whom we now know to have been Miss Warren, at about a quarter-past five. Daphne, satisfied that Major Spittlehouse was eating his supper, also set off for Tucker's Wood a few minutes later to meet Archie Mayhew before returning to the house before her brother left for the festivities. And this, of course, is when everything went wrong. For the simple reason that, because of the various problems associated with the bus, neither Miss Warren or Archie Mayhew were able to keep their respective engagements.'

'Oh, I think I have it!' exclaimed Cedric. 'Masters mistook Daphne Spittlehouse for the anonymous letter-writer, didn't he? I say, I bet the fellow kicked up a right stink if he thought Daphne was trying to blackmail her brother. I always got the impression that he didn't much care for her.'

'That is exactly what happened,' agreed Rose. 'Daphne said as much. About Masters going into a blind fury, I mean. And unfortunately for him, it made her recall something that lay buried deep in her mind. I suppose it was Masters' talk of murder and murderers, which had been mentioned in the second anonymous letter, as much as it was the man shouting at her in itself that made her remember. Almost twenty years before, she had had an argument with a man she had loved and had struck him. Only then, standing with Masters in Tuckers Wood, and hearing him talk of murder and murderers, did she realise that in so doing she must have struck Bunny, the man she had loved, a fatal blow.'

'Do you think Masters realised the significance of what he was saying?' asked Cedric rather quietly.

'No, I don't think he did. Miss Warren told me what the letter had said. "What would people say if they knew the village harboured a murderer in its midst?" Masters probably thought that Daphne was referring to the major's role during the Great War and was furious, whereas Daphne knew that in fact the letter most probably referred to the death of her lover.'

'So, in a fit of panic, she murdered Masters,' said the inspector. 'The unfortunate fellow turned his back on her for a brief second and she picked up a convenient stone and hit him on the back of the head. She told me he wouldn't stop shouting at her, that it was the only way she could make him stop. I don't think for one moment she meant to kill him.'

244

'What a waste of a life,' said Cedric sadly. 'The poor fellow was only trying to protect his employer.'

Silence filled the room as each pictured the ghastly scene in their mind. At length, Inspector Newcombe cleared his throat and said: 'That's all very well, Lady Belvedere, but you still haven't told us how you arrived at the truth. For a start, how did you know about this fellow Bunny and what had happened to him?'

'Well, I felt certain that there was a connection between the anonymous letters and Masters' death. I was also curious as to the reason behind the major's apparent determination that Daphne should not marry. Of course he couldn't actually stop her, but he could ensure that her suitors were discouraged by making them aware that, if his sister went against his wishes, she would be penniless. And Mrs Masters told me something which appeared to confirm the view I was forming. The Spittlehouses only ever stayed in one place for a few years. I thought the likely reason for this was that the major was trying to prevent Daphne from forming any romantic attachments.'

'I say, that sounds frightfully rotten,' said Cedric, 'not like Major Spittlehouse at all.'

'But that is just my point. There had to be a reason for the major's behaviour, and that of his parents before him when they composed their will. Why had they all treated Daphne so shoddily? It was certainly not in the major's nature to do so. It made me feel certain therefore that, though it might appear to the contrary, the aim of it all was to protect Daphne.'

'Or the interests of others to whom she might otherwise have done harm?' suggested Inspector Newcombe.

'You mean Major Spittlehouse and his parents wanted to ensure that Daphne didn't kill any of her other suitors as she had done this chap Bunny?' said Cedric.

'Yes,' said Rose. 'I think they felt that, if they helped her to escape justice, the least they could do was to ensure that she never had an opportunity to hurt anyone else.'

'How frightful,' said Cedric. 'What I don't understand is what possessed a man like the major to conceal the murder in the first place? It doesn't seem the sort of thing he would do.'

'I can answer that for you,' said Inspector Newcombe. 'We asked the major the very same question. It seems he wasn't there when his sister actually killed this Bunny chap. It was his father who decided to conceal the murder. As far as I can tell it went something like this. Miss Spittlehouse had an argument with her lover and struck him. It was a lucky blow, or an unlucky one depending on how you look at it, and killed him immediately. Miss Spittlehouse immediately fainted. Her father came upon the scene and realised what must have happened. Having ascertained that the fellow was indeed dead, he was faced with a dilemma, particularly when Miss Spittlehouse awoke and it became apparent that, while she remembered hitting Bunny Warren, she did not recall killing him. And that is when her father made his fateful choice not to tell her the truth and to conceal the murder.'

'And when Major Spittlehouse returned home on leave his father told him what he had done?' said Cedric. 'I say, that sounds a bit rough. What was the poor fellow supposed to do?'

'His father also told the major where the body was buried,' said Rose. 'In Tucker's Wood. It was a considerable distance from where the Spittlehouses were living at the time.'

'By Jove!' exclaimed Cedric. 'That must be why Major Spittlehouse paid over the odds for Tucker's Wood. I'd always wondered why he purchased that piece of land. I suppose he wanted to make sure no one dug up this poor Bunny fellow.' Another thought struck him. 'I say, it also explains why he made such a fuss about the village boys trespassing on his land looking for sticks for the bonfire. He was afraid they might discover the skeleton.'

'Yes,' agreed his wife. 'It also explains why the Spittlehouses have remained in Sedgwick for as long as they have, and why the major chose to live here in the first place when he usually chose to reside in towns.'

'I do hope Major Spittlehouse will feel able to stay on in Sedgwick after all this,' said Cedric thoughtfully. 'The village needs people like him. It seems to me that he's had a pretty rum deal putting his sister's needs before his own. And we need a chap like him on the Bonfire Committee to oversee everything. I say, I do hope, Newcombe, that you are not going to charge him with being an accessory after the fact or anything awful like that?'

'No. I think the poor fellow's suffered enough, don't you?' said the inspector. 'Besides, a good barrister would be certain to get him off.

Remember, Major Spittlehouse played no part in burying the body. All the barrister would need to argue was that he didn't know the body was there, that he thought it was just some fanciful story of his father's.' He turned his attention to Rose, who had resumed her seat. He thought she looked a little sad and pale. 'I know you're fretting about Miss Spittlehouse, Lady Belvedere. You needn't, you know. She'll not hang. That same clever barrister we were talking about will see to it that she's taken to some sanatorium or other. I doubt very much she'll spend the rest of her days in prison.'

'I'm glad,' said Rose. 'I can't help feeling rather sorry for poor Daphne. She never intended to kill Bunny, or poor Masters come to that. I know her father meant well, but I do wonder whether his actions only made matters worse.'

'Well, there's no use crying over spilt milk,' said Inspector Newcombe. 'What is done is done. Now, Lady Belvedere, you never did tell us how you knew Miss Warren was our anonymous letter-writer.'

'Oh, that proved to be quite simple in the end, Inspector,' said Rose, rallying a little. 'When I first made the acquaintance of Miss Warren, I couldn't understand why she had been so concerned about Daphne reading a couple of books about poisons, so worried in fact that she meant to warn Major Spittlehouse. The fact was, of course, that she was already convinced that the Spittlehouses were responsible for her brother's disappearance. Initially she thought the major was to blame, but then I think she became suspicious of Daphne. Of course, I knew none of this at the time, but I did think it very odd that she intended to approach a man she did not know to warn him that his sister might be considering murdering him.' She sighed. 'Daphne had mentioned Bunny to me. He was a young man of whom she was particularly fond. She said they had had an argument and that he had gone away without saying goodbye. I didn't think very much of it at the time until Mrs Masters mentioned that her husband had been mumbling in his sleep something about murder and murderers. But I might never have made the connection with Miss Warren had Chalky White not come to dinner and you and I talked about nicknames, darling,' she said, glancing over at her husband. 'Bunny Warren. It came to me in a flash, as you might say, when I was leaving Bichester. Miss Warren might well have some connection with Bunny, who had disappeared in mysterious circumstances. I also knew that both the letter-writer and Miss Warren had intended to meet with the major on the night Masters was killed. It was possible, therefore, that they were one and the same person.

'So they were anonymous letters rather than blackmail letters?' said Cedric.

'Oh, yes. Miss Warren only ever wanted to find out the truth regarding what had happened to her brother. She thought the letters would frighten the major in to confessing when she confronted him.'

'Which she never did because of the problems with that damned bus,' grunted Inspector Newcombe. 'Unreliable things those buses, give me a car any day.'

'Oh, you never guess what, m'lady!' cried Edna, flying into her mistress' bedroom one morning a month or so later. 'Major Spittlehouse and Miss Warren are walking out!'

'Good for them,' said Rose, sitting up in bed. 'Though I suppose when you say walking out, what you really mean is that they've been spotted having tea together in the tearooms?'

'Ever so strange is what I call it,' said the lady's maid, arranging the breakfast tray, 'what with his sister having killed her brother. It don't seem right.'

'Well, it seems to me that they have a great deal in common. They have both been far too focused on their siblings to think of themselves and their own lives. It would be wonderful for them to have some happiness.'

Rose took a bite from her slice of toast, very thankful that Edna knew nothing about Miss Warren being the author of the major's anonymous letters. The maid would certainly have had something to say about that! She wondered how to change the subject but Edna had already wandered on to another topic, that of a certain Archie Mayhew.

'Awfully cut up he is about Miss Spittlehouse,' the lady's maid was saying.

Privately Rose thought Archie should consider himself jolly lucky that Inspector Newcombe had decided not to press charges in relation to the removal of Masters' body. She had it on the good authority of the policeman himself that he and Mr Whittaker had taken Archie aside and given that young man a very stern talking to. Mr Mayhew was apparently now working very hard indeed in the offices of Messrs Gribble, Hebborn & Whittaker in an attempt to put the past behind him and restore his reputation. Indeed, word had it that he had the makings of a very fine solicitor indeed.

'Of course,' Edna was saying, 'with his looks and his charm he'll find a new sweetheart soon enough. There will be girls queuing.'

Rose smiled and said: 'Have you heard from Biddy? Is she enjoying running a guest house by the sea with Mrs Masters?'

'Oh, she is that, m'lady. She's enjoying the sea air something rotten. The major, he was ever so generous to Mrs Masters, he was. Gave her quite a sum to set up her guest house, he did. Ever so nice it is too, so Biddy says, real grand. They only get the best clientele. And Mrs Masters treats her more like a daughter than an employee; Biddy's often tempted to call her 'mother'.'

'Well, I am very glad to hear that they are getting on all right.' Rose looked quizzically at her maid. 'Edna, why are you giggling?'

'I was just thinking, m'lady. If it's as grand as Biddy says it is, this guest house, Major Spittlehouse and Miss Warren could stay there on their honeymoon after they get married.'

'Edna ...'

But the lady's maid had sailed out of the bedroom humming a wedding march and Rose was left chuckling and thinking that some good had come out of the tragic events after all.

Still laughing, she picked up a letter that she had received only that morning from the honorary secretary of the village's amateur dramatics society inquiring in to the possibility of staging a Shakespeare play in one of the many follies that were located in the grounds of Sedgwick Court. Really, it would be a very worthy event, the writer assured her, for all the proceeds were to go to a most deserving charity.

How splendid, thought Rose, as she scribbled a note to say that she was in favour of such a proposal. It did not occur to her for a moment that she was being at all rash, or that she might later regret her enthusiasm for the venture.